AMELIA'S HEARTSONG

SHENANDOAH BRIDES ~ BOOK 2

BLOSSOM TURNER

WILD HEART
BOOKS

ISBN-13: 978-1-942265-35-1

I would like to dedicate this book to four incredibly encouraging women—where sisterhood transcends blood and moves into the realm of close friendship.

Viola, Donna, and Faith, and to the sister of my heart, Suzie. Your encouragement of my writing and the fact you can see my faults and love me all the same, spurs me onward. We can laugh, cry, even challenge each other to grow in areas, all under the umbrella of unconditional love.

What a gift you are in my life.

"Seek first the kingdom of God and His righteousness, and all these things shall be added to you."

Matthew 6:33 (NKJV)

CHAPTER 1

July 1868
Shenandoah Valley

"He what?" Amelia Williams's heart battered the inside of her chest cavity with a wild thumping. She slammed her teacup into the saucer, splashing hot liquid onto her hand. The pain of the burn was nothing compared to the sting of truth. She mopped up the mess with her napkin, then lifted it to dab at the tears that fell free.

"I wanted to tell you rather than have you find out from prattling tongues like that of Hattie Mayfield. I'm so sorry, dear sister." Katherine reached across the small end table and squeezed Amelia's hand.

"But Edmund told me just the other day how much he loved me... I don't understand. Where did Josiah see this?"

"He happened upon them kissing behind the General Mercantile—"

"Who was Edmund with?" Her words came out strangled.

"The daughter of that wealthy railway builder who moved into town a few months ago. I think her name is Helen."

1

"I know the one. I've seen her strutting about town in her fancy clothes with her nose in the air and all the men buzzing around her as if she was some kind of special. But Edmund?"

"Josiah said they didn't see him. He came home directly and told me."

Amelia's heart pounded in her chest. Like an early morning mist, all her dreams of love and marriage and a happy home to raise children of her own were vanishing in the heat of one conversation. "Where is Josiah? Is there any way he could've mistakenly—"

"I asked the same thing." Katherine placed her teacup down. "Just a minute." She stood, moved across the parlor, and called down the hall. "Josiah, can you come in here for a moment?" She returned and slipped her arm around Amelia's shoulder. The warmth curbed the urge to run straight out that door to Edmund's house and confront him.

Josiah rounded the corner. The grim set to his mouth and the empathy in his eyes spoke volumes.

"I'm hoping you witnessed this from a distance and there's room for doubt."

He shook his head. "Edmund, I know, and with all the hullabaloo over the Tyson's moving into our area, and the way their daughter parades about town in her low-cut dresses—"

"Why that two-timer... How dare he—?" Amelia stood and paced, furious and heartsick.

Josiah swayed on his feet.

"Are you all right?" She hurried to his side and led him to a nearby chair.

Katherine rushed over and crouched beside him.

He lowered his head into his hands. "Whoa, I don't know what that was all about. Felt a little lightheaded for a second. It's past now." He brushed both doting women aside. "Give me room to breathe, ladies. I'm fine. Let's concentrate on the situation at hand."

Amelia walked across the room and stared out the window. "It's too late today, but I intend to take the buggy to his place first thing tomorrow and address this."

"You're not going alone," Katherine said. "I'll come with you."

"I'll take you both," Josiah offered.

Amelia held back the tears stinging behind her eyelids. "Tomorrow it is."

~

*T*he next morning came all too soon. Josiah and Katherine sat beside her in silence as the buggy rattled along. Amelia felt numb. This couldn't be her life. A thin slice of sunlight fought its way through a patch of cloud-filled sky, mirroring her heart. She must find the courage to have the hardest conversation of her life. The landscape blurred behind a sheen of tears.

All she had ever wanted was to find a love like her parents had, get married, and raise a family of her own. Nurturing came instinctively to her. She had so much love to give—the most fulfilled when encouraging the down-hearted or tending to the sick. And ever since she was a young child helping with her younger siblings, her ma had told her what a fine mama she would make someday. Was that dream about to be thwarted?

How could this be happening to her? How could her long-time friend betray her? How many times had her family and the community razzed her and Edmund about when their nuptials would be announced? After three years of courting, still she waited. Edmund kept going on about his big dreams of making it rich. He said he would not promise marriage before he could properly take care of his wife. Yet just recently he had insisted it wouldn't be long before he placed a ring on her finger.

They rumbled to a stop in front of Edmund's home.

Katherine squeezed her arm. "We'll be right here waiting, and if need be, Josiah will verify what he witnessed."

Josiah's grim nod confirmed Katherine's words.

Amelia stepped from the wagon. Her mind spun in crazy circles. Chaotic. Confused. Though she'd been here many times, this was the first when she approached the house with apprehension. Knots crowded the space between her shoulder blades.

After a light rap on the door, it swung wide, and Edmund's mother greeted her. "Amelia, dear. To what do we owe the pleasure this fine Saturday morning? Come in. Come in." She lifted her eyes and noticed Katherine and Josiah in the wagon. "I have a batch of pancakes on. Please invite your sister and her husband in. The more the merrier." She laughed and held open the screen door. The sweet offer made Amelia want to cry. She loved Edmund's mom.

"I can't stay, but can you tell Edmund I need to speak with him outside?"

Mrs. Olson's brows knit together in confusion. "I'll go get him. I do hope everything is all right, my dear." She patted Amelia's shoulder before she bustled away.

A moment later, Edmund came around the corner. He looked so tall and handsome. Her heart squeezed tight.

He took one look at her face, and his smile faded.

"I need to talk to you in private. Can we walk to the barn?"

He nodded, grabbed his hat from the rack, and flopped it on his head of curls. "I've been meaning to talk to you too."

Amelia's stomach twisted and dropped to her shoes.

He glanced up at Josiah and Katherine and touched his hat but didn't say a word. He and Amelia walked in silence across the yard. Chickens scattered in their wake, and the soft moo of the cow could be heard in the near distance. Edmund kicked a hen out of his way. His antics reminded her how much he hated the farm. They were halfway to the large red barn behind the house when he said, "I gather you know."

Tentacles of fury spread their hot fingers throughout her body. Oh, she would not make it that easy for him. "Know what?"

"By the look on your face, I thought...well I assumed you heard—"

"Heard what?" He could darn well put into words what he had done to her.

"What I've been meaning to tell you for a while. I've fallen in love with someone else."

"Love." She spat out. "Seems you use that word loosely. Not so long ago you were saying you loved me."

"I do care for you—"

"Don't bother with the platitudes, Edmund. You owe me far more than that."

"What can I say without hurting you?"

"You've already hurt me far beyond words. Imagine how it felt to hear from my brother-in-law that you were at the back of the store kissing up a storm with the new tart in town."

"She's not a tart. She's fun, intellectually engaging and—"

"And rich. Let's face it Edmund, the only thing that has kept us from marriage is your obsession with money. And how convenient you can fall in and out of love at will."

"Her father is going to give me opportunity to join his management team building the railway, and so what if I'm motivated by money? I have no desire to be a dirt-poor farmer—"

"Or marry a farm girl."

He took a deep breath. A hot blast of air pressed through his lips as if to release his frustration. All that remained in his eyes was a blank stare. "Can we remain friends?"

She almost capitulated, they had been in each other's life a long time. But how would she begin to entertain that scenario with Helen at his side. No. She spoke the words she had been thinking all night. "Friends do not do what you did to me. The least you could've done was respect me enough to break it off with me *before* starting with someone else."

"It just happened. How would I know a lady of her caliber would take a shining to a nobody like me?"

"Nothing *just happens*, Edmund. We make decisions every day of our lives, be they right or be they wrong. The fact that you think you're a nobody without the money her family totes around is sad. You were never a nobody to me."

"Ahh, Amelia." He raised his hand and slid it down her tear-stained cheek. "I'm sorry."

She slapped his hand aside. "I'm not. I'm glad I found out how weak you are *before* we were married. God has saved me from a lot of heartache." With her head held high and starch to her spine, she walked away.

Hopefully her display of strength didn't reveal her angst. After years of friendship and three years of courting, how could he cast her off like a worn-out shoe? Sure, his new Helen was prettier, slimmer, and richer than she, but did their history mean nothing? How would her sorry heart ever believe she was good enough for anyone after being so easily discarded?

She marched back to the wagon, where her stunningly beautiful sister and handsome husband only added to her pain. Had she looked more like her sister or had the money Josiah had, Edmund would still be hers.

After pulling herself up, she settled her plump frame onto the seat. What a waste of the last three years of her life. The valley wasn't exactly teeming with available men, and they sure weren't lining up at her door. All her dreams had shattered overnight.

"Are you all right?" Katherine swung an arm around her shoulder.

"Let's get out of here."

∼

"*I*'m leaving and that's that." Amelia folded her arms. A crack of thunder split the room.

Amelia jumped and Ma let out a shrill "Ahh!"

"That storm's a-coming." Pa strode to their parlor window and slammed the sash closed.

Black clouds billowed and swirled. Fat drops of rain pelted the glass in a sideways dance. The weather mirrored her stormy heart. She turned back towards her parents and placed her hands on her generous hips. Though quivering on the inside, she had to stay firm. With a lift to her chin, she narrowed her brown eyes into a deliberate squint, praying her determination spoke through.

"Looks like the storm is already here," Ma said.

Though she had always tried to please her parents, Amelia prayed for strength to hold her ground.

"Why are you so insistent on leaving the valley?" Ma's eyes held a shimmer of tears.

"Please don't cry." Amelia bit her lower lip. "Do you really want me to have to paste a smile on my face at Helen and Edmund's wedding? On my nineteenth birthday no less? I can't bear it. All of Lacey Spring is invited, and if I don't show up, it will look like sour grapes." She wrung her hands and side-stepped the hug Ma tried to pull her into. "I don't need your sympathy, I need your support." She joined Pa at the window and stared out at the rain thundering down.

"Jeb, what do you make of this?" Ma asked. "Don't just stand there in a daze, praying into the heavens. Set your daughter straight."

"We sure do need the rain."

"That's it? That's all you can think of right now?" Ma's voice rose an octave.

He wrapped Amelia in a warm hug and pulled apart facing

Ma. "Much like that dry, dusty old earth needed a good soaking, a change can bring a blessing."

"Why, I do declare, Jeb. Have you completely lost your mind?"

He walked over and pulled her into a one-sided hug. "She's an adult, Doris. We raised her well, and now it's time to let her go."

Amelia allowed the breath she'd been holding to ease out of her tense body. She closed her eyes and whispered a prayer of thanks.

"Why Richmond? For heaven's sakes, that is too far away for a mother's heart."

Amelia held firm. "I'm officially an old maid—"

"You're not an old maid," Ma said.

"I am, and you know it. Just the other day at the General Mercantile, I overheard Hattie Mayfield going on—"

"The day you believe a word that old biddie has to say is the day—"

"Doris," Pa said, "that is not the way we talk about others."

Ma flung her hands in the air. "Jeb, I love you, but ever since you got Jesus, I can't say a blasted thing about anyone without you interfering. The truth is the truth. That woman is the town gossip and you know it."

Amelia hated to cause dissention. Her stomach knotted. "Ma, the city provides distance. Change. Plus, Grandmother and Grandfather invited me to come anytime. It's not as if I'll be alone."

Ma grunted and held out her arms, and Amelia fell into her embrace. Did this mean yes?

Ma squeezed her tight, then patted her back and leaned away. She met Amelia's eyes with a warm and loving gaze. "Let your pa and I talk in private."

Pa winked over the top of Ma's head.

"And if you don't mind starting supper..." Ma suggested.

Amelia rounded the corner into the kitchen. This was her future they were discussing, and Ma had a penchant for twisting Pa's arm. Amelia couldn't let that happen. She tiptoed back to within hearing range by the doorway.

Footsteps paced the floor from rug to hardwood and back again. Her ma always paced when she was bothered.

"Jeb. Get your head out of the clouds and help me sort this."

"'Tis what I'm doing good wife. Never hurts to ask the Lord for a little wisdom, now does it?"

Amelia couldn't deny the changes in Pa since he had become a Christian. That unexplained sadness had left his eyes, and he was peaceful, not so easily irritated or riled by Ma's frustrations.

Ma harrumphed. "We did just fine without Jesus over the years, and we'll do fine going forward."

"Now, Doris."

"Don't you *now Doris*, me. I shouldn't have gone to visit my parents last year. Who knew it would lead to losing one of my daughters?"

"You still have Jeanette, Lucinda, and Gracie to fill your days, and me of course. Besides, Richmond is not the end of the earth."

"But everything about that city haunts me."

"Everything? We grew up there. We have many happy memories. Don't let the bad outweigh the good. Your parents—"

"Spoiled and favored my sister because she was the beautiful one, the belle of the ball, the witch on a broomstick—"

"That shade of green has never looked good on you." Pa's words held the perfect blend of both compassion and firmness. "Emmaline may have been beautiful on the outside, but you had the heart, the soul, the love. You have always outshone your sister, but you've never believed that truth."

"Balderdash." Ma said. "You say that now, but we both know the spell she cast over you."

That was more information than Amelia should know. A

stab of guilt pricked her conscience. She shouldn't be eaves-dropping, but she couldn't seem to make herself stop.

"Your parents apologized and treated you like gold on your last visit, did they not? And they loved Amelia. Correct?"

Ma released a long sigh. "To be honest, that's the one thing that gives me hope they've changed."

Ma's words were muffled as the rain picked up once again. A loud blow into a handkerchief followed. Was Ma crying? What in the world had happened?

"It's apparent you feel good about allowing her to go," Ma said. "Wish I felt the same, but it's clear I'm not going to change either of your minds. Off with you, old man. I need a few minutes to myself."

Amelia could not help the grin that spread across her face. A fresh start was one train ride away.

"I'm not going anywhere until I get a smile from my beautiful girl," Pa said. "Come on... just one for me."

Amelia's heart squeezed tight. She longed to have a man love her the way Pa loved her ma.

"Do you need a sweet kiss to remove the sour, because I'd be more than willing to oblige?"

Amelia smiled at Pa's teasing and scurried into the kitchen.

CHAPTER 2

*A*melia stood on the second-floor balcony drinking in the mesmerizing scene before her. From the sweeping view in the Church Hill area where her grandparents resided to the James River sparkling like a precious jewel in the far distance, Richmond thrilled her.

Edmund seemed like a fading mist under the bright sunshine of Richmond's possibilities. And her grandmother was more than eager to show Amelia off. She set up dinner parties and talked incessantly about launching her into Richmond society. Apparently, there were men aplenty, and Amelia's dream of love and marriage was once again alive and well.

How easy it had been to brush off Edmund. Had she ever loved him, or had the desire to be married been the driving force of her relationship with him? Guilt pierced her soul, but she buried it. She'd easily dismissed him because he'd lied to her and cheated on her.

How big and foreign her world had become this past week.

Though saying good-bye to her family had been tough, she didn't regret leaving the Shenandoah Valley. She was ready for a new beginning. She smiled at the view of housetop upon housetop and glanced down the quiet, well-treed street her grandparents lived on. Every house, including the one she stood in, were estate homes with large sweeping lawns, manicured gardens, and welcoming porticos or verandas. A knot of tension pinched at her shoulder blades. How would she ever fit in?

A slight rap on the balcony door startled her. She whirled around to see her grandfather as he opened it and stepped outside.

"How do you like our fair city?" he asked.

"It's so beautiful." She swept her hand over the balcony rail to the vista below.

"Not half as lovely as you. Do all five of you look alike?" He stood beside her by the rail.

"Definite similarities, all except Katherine. If you think I'm pretty, wait until you meet her. Every man gawks at her, but she doesn't seem to notice. She's so unassuming. But I've always wondered why she looks so different and where those stunning eyes came from until I met you."

"Sounds like you two are close," Grandfather said.

"We always have been. Her heart is so kind, and she proved it by the sacrifice she made for our family." Amelia's hand flew to her mouth. Goodness, Ma was going to kill her. She'd been warned not to mention anything about that situation.

"Sacrifice? What happened?" Grandfather turned to face her, his bushy brows drawing together into one line across his furrowed brow.

"I...I'm not supposed to say."

"Please, trust that we love your family. We did a lot of things in the past we're not proud of, but if your ma allowed you to come, she must trust that we mean to make up for the sorrow."

Amelia had not been privy to a lot of closed-door meetings

during their last visit, and it had been back then that ma had asked her to say nothing about Katherine's situation. So much had improved since then. Surely it would be all right to tell now.

"The Yankees burned down our house, and we were left with nothing. Katherine's arranged marriage to a very wealthy man saved our family."

Grandfather rubbed the back of his neck and hung his head. He looked up with tears glistening. "All because my dear daughter thought she couldn't come to us for help."

What had happened? If only she could ask, but Ma had shut her down every time she exhibited any curiosity. She had learned to keep quiet.

He shook his head. "But that's a story for another day. Is Katherine happy?"

"Very." Amelia said. "She just had her first son, Seth, and Josiah is a wonderful husband and father."

"Amelia." Grandmother's high-pitched voice echoed down the hall.

"We're on the balcony, Frances," Grandfather called.

The swish of petticoats and the smell of strong perfume preceded Grandmother. Her tall willowy frame and elaborate coiffure floated across the balcony, charged with sophistication and style. Amelia lifted her rounded shoulders, imitating her straight posture.

"Will you join me for an afternoon of shopping?" Grandmother asked.

"Ah, ah, ah, my dear wife. How quickly you forget our agreement. You promised I would be able to take Amelia for a tour of our city before you monopolize all her time with shopping. And I'm choosing this fine afternoon, if Amelia agrees.

Amelia's eyes darted from one to the other. She didn't want to disappoint either.

"Go ahead then, George." Grandmother waved her handkerchief. "I can barely deny you the pleasure when I intend to take up all her time thereafter." She laughed with a tinkle in her voice.

He held out his hand to Amelia. "I have much to show you. Your first history lesson of Richmond begins today."

They headed out the door to the awaiting carriage. Amelia stepped into luxury and sank into the velvety cushions. She had criticized Edmund's quest for wealth but was enjoying the comfort more than she anticipated.

The clip-clop of the horse's hooves carried a musical cadence as the skilled coachman maneuvered Amelia and her grandfather through the busy streets. Amelia couldn't keep up with all the new and exciting sights as she looked from one side of the carriage to the other. From the mules that pulled packet boats up the Kanawha Canal, to the sophistication of Capitol Square, where a statue of George Washington astride his bronzed horse faced southward, she loved it all.

"The business and industrial part of the city were hit hard during the last days of war. Over seven hundred houses were burned, as well as many of the prominent buildings. What made it worse was that our own Confederate army set fire to a good portion of the city."

Amelia gasped. "But why?"

"When they realized their defeat, they threw torches to the wind, not wanting the Union to have much to claim victory over, nor caring about the civilians, like your grandmother and me, who had refused to leave."

"That must have been terrifying." Amelia grabbed his hand. "Much like we felt hidden in that hole in the ground while our house was burned."

"War is so devastating. And to think I will never meet your brothers." Tears filled his blue eyes, now graying with age.

The memory of her older brothers teasing, laughing, and their protectiveness, flooded in. She had felt so safe walking to school with them or learning to ride her first horse with one on each side. At times the grief overwhelmed her so much she couldn't speak. She took her grandfather's wrinkled hand in hers and gave a quick squeeze. He squeezed back.

"How did they get the fire out?" she asked.

His eyes held a faraway look. "Had it not been for the incoming soldiers working relentlessly to douse the blaze, the whole city would have succumbed to the flames. As it was, the city was devastated." He patted her hand. "Richmond will never be the same."

Amelia smoothed her hand over the back of his wrinkled skin. It was as if he'd traveled back to that time.

"We watched helplessly from our balcony," he said, "shocked that our own would willingly bring this destruction upon us." He turned toward her. "I'll tell you this. Those Yankee soldiers rushing in to fight those flames didn't look like the enemy to me, and I'm not alone in my thinking. Those of us who stayed have accepted our government and been thankful for the personnel sent to rebuild this city. When Jefferson Davis abandoned Richmond with full knowledge of the orders given to destroy it, well…it left a bitter taste behind for many of us."

He rapped on the roof of the carriage and bellowed out an order through the window. "To Main Street."

He popped his head back inside and smiled. "Let me show you what has risen from the ashes, and we shall walk a bit."

"I'd love that." She squeezed his arm in excitement.

When the carriage stopped a few minutes later, Amelia stared with wonder at the bustling city around her. With one hand on her grandfather's arm, she strolled in silence. The cry of a newsboy hawking the latest edition, the scurry of maid and man about their daily business, the ladies parading in their latest fashions from shop to shop in search of a new hat, new pair of shoes, or new reticule—she loved the energy and life, so different from her country roots.

"There sure are a lot of people in the town square."

Grandfather smiled her way. "After enduring years of death and rations, people are making up for lost time. I know your Grandmother is looking forward to taking you shopping."

"I could get used to this." Amelia whirled around, throwing her arms wide. "Compared to the mundane of farm life, the city is bursting with energy."

"This will become familiar."

"I know that, but there's absolutely no way to ever know everyone, and each shopping excursion will bring new faces and conversations, not to mention the many stores to discover."

Grandfather laughed. "You mean you know everyone in your town back home?"

"There's hardly a soul I don't know, and it's a big deal when someone new moves to town." She thought of Helen but brushed it off. Helen couldn't hold a candle to the sophistication Amelia viewed all around her. She aimed to learn how to walk, talk, and dress like a true lady. And when she returned to the valley for a visit, Edmund would rue the day he'd let her go. She was glad to leave the valley behind. In a city this size, surely she would find a man who would truly love her. She looked around the square. Yes indeed, men aplenty.

"George," bellowed an older man with a white walrus mustache in a distinguished suit and top hat.

Grandfather waved him over. "Frank, come meet my granddaughter."

An aristocratic woman with an elaborate ensemble of matching dress, hat, and parasol hung on Frank's arm. As introductions were made, the woman looked down her long nose without making eye contact. "All the way from the Shenandoah Valley, you say. Is that not where your Doris landed up with her servant husband?"

Cold seeped into Amelia's bones. The woman's voice held a condescending tone.

Before Grandfather could answer, the woman laughed with

a brittle tone. "I do hope your granddaughter fairs better than your Doris or that Emmaline—"

"Edith, enough." Frank Tuttle's curt tone cut in. "George is a friend of mine, and you'd do well to remember that."

Her nose went further up in the air, and she looked away.

"Do forgive us, we have errands to run." Mr. Tuttle lifted his hat, and they bustled away.

"What was that all about?" she asked.

"Ah, my dear, something your ma and pa will have to share." He circled to the carriage. "I'd like nothing more than to continue to wander with you, but these old legs are not what they used to be. We can take it slowly on the way home so you can breathe it all in."

She smiled at him as they settled in the carriage. "I'm so glad to be here. Thank you for letting me stay with you and Grandmother."

"Our pleasure, my dear. Our pleasure indeed."

Despite Grandfather's effort to divert her attention, Amelia wondered about the woman's words. Would Mrs. Tuttle's reaction be something she was going to face again?

~

*A*melia smiled as she primped before her bedroom mirror. The last two months had been kind to her. She loved her new life, but with the leaves turning gold and energy coursing through her veins, she needed to begin her training on the finer points of becoming a lady. The demands of the social scene she had yet to taste, and she had many things to learn.

She fixed a pin into her newest hat and swiveled side to side. Her new dress hugged her ever-slimming body, and her pretty pink gloves matched the ensemble to perfection. Not having to help in the kitchen every day making meals, preserves, and pies meant she was eating far less. The results were evident.

Edmund had often made unkind comments, like asking her if she needed that second helping or telling her how beautiful she would be if she would only lose a few pounds. Try as she might, she hadn't been able to work all day in the kitchen and achieve that goal. But now, it was within her grasp, and he was out of luck. She lifted her chin. Large hazel eyes peered above newly sculptured cheeks. They were still far too rosy for her liking, but she smiled anyway. A reflection of a young lady she barely recognized smiled back at her.

The country girl thrust into a world of fast-moving trains, cobble-stoned streets, and up-town sophistication was blossoming. She didn't miss the tranquil setting of her childhood valley. Could it be she had been born for city life? But oh, how much she had to learn. She'd felt so awkward and gauche during the few tea times Grandmother had arranged.

After one last glance in the mirror, she squared her shoulders, lifted her head, and proceeded out her bedroom door. One step into the drawing room brought forth the usual flurry of Grandmother's well-laid plans.

"There you are." Her grandmother rose gracefully from the settee. "My, that color looks stunning on you. But I do declare, those shoes will never do. We'll go shopping right after breakfast and remedy that. Shall we?"

"But I—"

She ushered Amelia into the dining area without taking a breath and prattled on. Amelia waved good morning to Grandfather and he nodded to her.

"I had the cook prepare some fresh fruit and a boiled egg just the way you like. But honestly, you must be careful not to lose too much weight. Your mother will have a fit when she visits if I allow you to dwindle away." Her laughter sounded nervous.

"Grandmother—"

"You must promise you'll put aside the techniques I showed

you for losing a few pounds soon. You don't have much more to lose."

"Yes, Grandmother—"

"Now eat up. I like to frequent the shops early for the best selection."

"I can't go shopping every day," Amelia said, "but I do so want to discuss an idea with you...

"Absolutely, my dear."

"It's time to start my training on how to become a perfect lady if I'm ever to be a suitable wife—"

"It's sheer providence you bring that up today." Grand-mother slipped into her place at the table. With a gentle shake, she opened her cloth napkin before placing it on her lap in a ladylike fashion. "George, wasn't I just discussing with you a delightful idea for Amelia's future?" She lifted her eyes across the long table to her husband.

"Don't get me involved." He shook his head and his eyebrows bobbed like two dancing caterpillars. "I'm wise enough to stay out of women's business."

"Women's business?" Amelia looked from one to the other.

"It's not exactly women's business it more like...well it's—"

"Just spit it out, Frances. You're never short for words."

"Stay out of this." She waved her napkin at him.

He laughed. "That's what I said in the first place."

What was it that had her grandmother fighting for words?

"I don't want to sound pretentious. I've wanted to launch, I mean...introduce you into Richmond society, but to be honest, you—"

"Goodness," Grandfather said, "you're making this so much worse than it has to be. I'll tell her. What your grandmother is trying to say is that having been raised in the country, you have a few things to learn about the etiquette expected in our stuffy, less forgiving city. She would like you to enroll into Mrs. Feli-cia's Finishing School."

"You can quit at any time if you don't like it," Grandmother added quickly.

Heat rushed to Amelia's cheeks. She knew she was less than prepared for Richmond's finest, but she aimed to learn. She lifted her head. "I would love to go."

Grandmother relaxed against the chair, and grandfather chuckled. "See, I told you, say it plain. This girl has a heart of gold, and I do believe she likes it here. Am I right?"

Amelia couldn't hold back the grin. "I most assuredly do. I look forward to learning everything there is to know about becoming a lady fit for the social scene. I don't wish to embarrass you, Grandmother."

~

*B*ryon Preston stood at his bedroom window and, for the third time that week, spotted the same woman standing on the side of the street outside his home, staring out at the view. It seemed their schedules were similar. As he was changing out of his work suit, she paused, then passed on by. From the second floor, he could stare without worrying about propriety. He knew everyone in this neighbourhood, but she was new. Who was she? And what was it about her that drew him? The women his mother pushed his way held little appeal, and yet here he was attracted to a stranger.

His mother had only one agenda—that he would marry well. That meant uniting in a marriage of purpose, power, and privilege, but mostly money. As the eldest, it was his responsibility to ensure the Preston name lived on in all its glory. Their family titles traced back to England through a long lineage of aristocracy. Why did that rankle him so much? Were they all not just people living life, breathing the same air?

The mystery woman smiled at the vista. She must love the view from that spot on the hill. He couldn't see her eyes, but he wanted to. He'd bet they sparkled like the James River in the distance.

Her clothes bespoke a level of wealth that would please his mother. How sad he had to take that into consideration before making his introduction, but he knew his duty. Mother wouldn't accept anyone less than perfect for her son. How engrained and wrong her prejudices felt to him. Yet all of his friends talked and walked as if they were special, accepting the message that money and title somehow made them that way. A stab of guilt pierced his heart every time he went along with their banter, putting someone down for their station in life. Why did he have to have a conscience that plagued him when they obviously did not?

He would see the plight of the poor beggar or the homeless child wandering the streets, and his heart squeezed tight. Had he been born into a different family, his story could mirror theirs. He didn't know much about God other than an occasional church service at Christmas or Easter, but somehow it felt as if God expected him to do something.

He brushed the wearisome thoughts aside as the lovely woman turned and drifted out of view. He wondered if her personality would be as beautiful as she was. So often he'd been disappointed by the shallow depth of the women he had courted, who were attractive and knew they were. He decided that there was only one way to find out. Tomorrow, he would be ready and waiting when the stranger passed by. He just had to meet her.

CHAPTER 3

*D*ressed in the latest fashion, including new boots and a dress with matching gloves, hat, and parasol, Amelia sashayed up the hill toward home just the way that had been demonstrated at Mrs. Felicia's Finishing school. She worked on perfect posture as she strolled. For the past week, she'd stopped every day in the same spot, pausing long enough to turn and take in the view. She breathed in the crisp fall air and the beauty. The river sparkled in the distance, lined with trees touched in hues of red and gold. Grand homes were nestled along orderly streets. She loved the sound of the church bell ringing at the top of the hour, as it was at that moment. City life had seeped into her being as if she had always belonged.

She spun to continue on her way and ran into a solid wall. A living barrier of human flesh and bone, a man who wore the widest smile she had ever laid eyes on. Her heartbeat picked up pace.

"I was hoping to make your acquaintance," the man said, "having noticed you pause directly in front of my house almost daily. But you didn't have to knock me over to get an introduction." He stepped back and, with an exaggerated bow, he lifted her hand to kiss the back of her lacey glove. "Bryon Curtis Preston the Third, but please, just call me Bryon."

Amelia gazed into his laughing blue eyes and wished she hadn't been wearing the glove. Even with it, the sensation of his lips on her hand tingled all the way up her arm. My, but he was handsome.

"Are you going to tell me your name, or do I have to follow you home and read the sign on the gatepost?"

She giggled. Then caught herself. Decorum in every social encounter was a must, or so said Mrs. Felicia. "If you did that, Bryon Curtis Preston the Third, I would be leading you astray, for it is my grandfather's home on my mother's side. We don't share the same surname." She tried her best to sound calm, but her insides were aflutter with something she hadn't felt in a long time, if ever.

Edmund had never made her feel this way.

He cocked his head, sporting dimples on both sides of his ever-widening smile. "How about I walk you the rest of the way home and tell you all about myself? At the end of our stroll, if I've piqued your interest, you can tell me your name."

Without waiting for an answer, he held out his arm for her to grasp. She did, and he started walking.

He nodded toward a rambling three-story home on the other side of the street. It had a sweeping lawn and a welcoming portico. She'd noticed it many times during this walk because of its stately beauty and grandeur.

"That is our home," Bryon said. "Been in the family for a few generations. I'm the eldest son with one sister and one brother. I'm set to inherit that monstrosity with all its character and high-maintenance costs. Good thing God gave me some brains to work with, because keeping that old beauty in the family another generation is going to take some ingenuity. Especially since the war almost wiped us out."

They strolled along, his chatter continuing.

Her hand on his arm grew warm and cozy. She peeked up at his smiling face and caught him looking down at her. The steady rhythm of her heart quickened. There was a warmth about him that she instantly trusted.

"I'm training at Traders Bank and hope to make a good living as an investment banker."

"Investing your family money?"

"Indeed, but also learning to advise others on what would be the best option for their estates. A sometimes risky but rewarding business."

"Sounds complicated."

"It is. I have much to learn."

She liked his humility and his honesty. So unlike Edmund, who constantly had an opinion to share, even when he had no idea what he was talking about. She didn't want to think about that man, especially when she had an interesting stranger at her side. "How old are you?" she asked.

"I'm twenty-two and fortunate to have survived two grueling years at war. Seen enough sorrow and death to last a lifetime. Not my favorite subject."

"Mine either."

"Well then, my mysterious lady, we shall indeed get along just dandy."

Amelia could barely concentrate. His double-dimpled smile, strapping strength, wind-blown curly mop, and sophisticated charm had her thinking, *Edmund who?* She smiled inwardly. This Bryon had the elixir to make her forget that unfortunate name forever. Her heart sank as they reached her grandparents' home. She wanted more time with this interesting man.

"You've seen me safely home, and kept me entertained on the journey." She stopped at the gate and presented a slight curtsy, as Mrs. Felicia had demonstrated. Should she tell him of her humble roots? Yes, she would be honest up front. She knew only too well the pain Edmund's dishonesty had created.

"Amelia Florence Williams, from the Shenandoah Valley, country-girl born and raised." She spoke the words in one sweeping breath. Now, he had the choice. Run from the farm girl obviously so beneath his social standing, or…

His smile widened and both dimples danced beneath sparkling blue eyes.

One of the most difficult things she'd ever done was to move away from his engaging smile and slip through the gate. She resisted the urge to turn and smile, remembering what she had learned. Never reveal too many emotions. Remain extremely polite but somewhat aloof. Keep the mystery.

She heard his chuckle. "I will take that as an invitation to call again, Amelia Florence Williams. Until next time."

A wide smile broke free. He was still interested in her. She glided away with graceful steps just as she had been taught.

~

*H*is heart bucked as he watched her disappear into the house without a backwards glance. The view from his bedroom window had been interesting enough, but walking her home set his senses singing. She attracted him in every way. He had never believed in love at first sight, but that all changed in one beautiful walk.

If he was about to be influenced by who his parents preferred he marry, the revelation of her humble roots should give him pause. But her honesty drew him in. Most of the women he'd met played a role as if in a dramatic performance. Not this girl. In one sentence, she showed her upright character, and he was smitten.

He stood by her gate, whistling into the chilly autumn air, long after she was out of sight. As he turned to leave, the crazy thumping of his heart skipped and skidded in erratic desperation.

His smile faded when he caught the name on the gate post. Brunson.

~

"Grandmother, do you know the Preston family who live down the hill?" asked Amelia.

Grandmother almost spit out her gulp of tea. She coughed and sputtered, dabbing at her mouth with her napkin.

"Are you all right?" Amelia rose and patted her back.

She waved Amelia away. "I'm fine. I'm fine. My tea just went down the wrong pipe. It happens when you get old."

Amelia slid back into her chair. "You had me going. I thought something was wrong with the Prestons, and that would've made me ever so sad."

"Why so, my dear?" Grandmother folded her napkin and kept folding it until it was in a tight square she could hold in her hand. She didn't look up.

"I met the eldest son, Bryon, last week, and he has walked me home every day since." The smile she'd worked so hard to contain split free. "He said he'd love to meet you and Grandfather."

"He did?" Grandmother's head snapped up, and her eyebrows lifted. "Does his family know about this?"

Amelia couldn't make out what was happening, but she got the distinct notion that Grandmother didn't like the Prestons. "I never asked him. Should I? Have I made a faux pas not yet discussed in Mrs. Felicia's class?"

"No. No. It's just that Melinda Preston and I had a disagreement years ago."

"I'm sure Bryon wouldn't care about that, and he knows your last name, so whatever happened between you and his mother, is of little importance. He's so down to earth, and he knows of my humble roots and still wants to see me."

"You told him?"

"But of course. I told him the first day. He's asked many questions since then about what farm life is like."

Grandmother's guarded smile widened to touch her eyes. She clapped her hands together. "Well then, invite him for the evening meal on the weekend. We would be pleased to make his acquaintance."

~

"Amelia Williams and Elizabeth Forbes, do you know each other?" Mrs. Felicia asked.

Amelia darted a glance around the classroom. She hated being the center of attention. She shook her head and noticed that Elizabeth Forbes did the same.

"Perfect. I would like the two of you to come up to the front of the class and role play an afternoon tea. In this exercise, we'll put into practice everything we've learned about a first meeting including what is—and what is not—appropriate to ask."

Amelia walked to the front of the room, her heart hammering. Years of childhood shyness living in the shadow of her feisty and beautiful older sister, Katherine, did not prepare her for this moment. The only thing that kept her going was the thought that she would hate to embarrass her grandmother with inappropriate behavior. She slid into one of the two chairs at the front. A table had been set with tea and goodies.

"All right ladies, Amelia you will be the hostess, and Elizabeth the guest."

Amelia's mind went blank. For a moment she just sat staring. She couldn't think of one thing to say. Some giggles from the back of the room brought her out of her daze.

"Elizabeth, would you care for a cup of tea?"

"I'd love one, Amelia. Thank you."

Amelia lifted the pot to serve, and everyone laughed.

Mrs. Felicia's hand rose to silence the women. "Now, now ladies. The reason we're here is to learn and to catch the faux pas in a safe environment. There will be no laughing. Miss Williams, you may call on any of these girls to roleplay the maid you would call on in a real-life situation to pour the tea. A lady never does such menial tasks. Carry on."

Heat rushed into Amelia's face. She was sure she was fifty shades of red. She was in a room full of privileged, much younger women, who had probably never had to pick a blackberry much less make them into a pie. What would they think of her if they knew she'd milked cows for cream rather than have a maid fetch it for her?

"Maid Jacqueline, would you be so kind as to pour our tea." Amelia picked the girl who had laughed the loudest and, from the sneer on Jacqueline's face, she was none too happy about playing a maid's role. Nevertheless, she rose and tended the task.

"Why Amelia, I was delighted to receive your invitation to tea," Elizabeth said. "I've wanted to make your acquaintance for a while now." She lifted her teacup daintily to her lips. Her baby finger was held at the perfect angle in the air, giving a touch of elegance Amelia could not hope to duplicate.

"Thank...thank you." She couldn't seem to get any intelligent words to flow out of her mouth in front of this group.

"You're new in town, yes?" Elizabeth asked.

"Yes, I am."

Mrs. Felicia held up her hand. "Now would be a good time to share some particulars about your life. As if you were getting to know a new friend."

"How many siblings do you have, Amelia?"

"Four sisters and I had twin brothers but the war..." Amelia stopped. She did not care to share her grief.

Elizabeth lifted her eyebrows, and tactfully changed the subject. "What city did you come from?"

Amelia was stumped. She didn't want to reveal her humble beginnings to this group either. Was she to answer truthfully, or could she roleplay? She turned toward Mrs. Felicia. "May I ask a question?"

"Of course, Amelia."

"Are we to answer as if in real life, or are we merely roleplaying?" Again, she heard snickers at her question.

"I would suggest you answer as you would in real life, as this is a class to prepare you for your coming out into the adult world. You're doing fine. Take a deep breath and pretend we're not here." Mrs. Felicia's voice was kind and encouraging.

She turned her gaze back to Elizabeth. "I've moved here from the Shenandoah Valley."

"What city in the valley are you from?" Elizabeth looked at Mrs. Felicia to see if that was not too personal of a question to ask. Amelia had been hoping that question crossed the line of propriety, but Mrs. Felicia nodded her head.

"I'm from a town called Lacey Spring."

"And what did your family do there?"

"My sister married a wealthy rancher." She deliberately omitted what her Pa did and tried to maneuver the conversation elsewhere. "And you, Elizabeth, tell me about yourself."

Elizabeth was a far more skilled orator than she was. "Nothing nearly as exciting as you. My family has lived in this city for decades, and I've been here all my life. It's all I know. What did you say your father did?"

Amelia looked with pleading eyes to Mrs. Felicia. Surely, Elizabeth would be corrected at being so foreword, but Mrs. Felicia said nothing.

Amelia lifted her head with a jut to her chin. She'd never been embarrassed by her father's work before, and she certainly was not going to start now. "My father is a farmer."

The room went silent.

Mrs. Felicia stood and clapped her hands together. "Excellent, ladies, we shall convene tomorrow at the same time. We don't have many sessions left. Soon, you'll be ready to face the world with all the grace and decorum needed." As the women stood and gathered their things, Mrs. Felicia lowered her voice. "And Amelia, I would like to see you after class."

Amelia scurried to her seat at the back of the room. She gathered her parasol and busied herself while she waited for the others to file out.

"Imagine being raised on a farm." Jacqueline whispered to the ladies beside her as she walked by. "She's all dressed up, but there's no taking the barnyard out of her." Giggles followed the group out the door.

Mrs. Felicia waved her over and motioned to a chair, which Amelia slid into. "I'm a long-time friend of your grandmother's, and I understand what you're up against. I'm sorry I didn't intervene sooner, but I thought you had it handled when you successfully steered Elizabeth off the topic of your father. Just as I taught—you tried to get her talking about herself so she would forget the question."

Mrs. Felicia leaned forward and patted her knee. Even her touch was ladylike and soothing to Amelia. If only such culture could naturally flow from her.

"But Elizabeth learned well too, and she knew what you were doing, so I want to go through what you could say in the future if this subject comes up again. Not that there's a thing wrong with farming. Heavens, what would we eat if not for the farmer?"

Amelia blinked back the sting of tears. "Obviously the girls don't think of that when they sit down to their meal every evening."

"Most of these girls have never had to lift a finger. You're a much more rounded individual having the experience you do, but Richmond high-society is unforgiving, and I don't want you hurt. In order to survive you must hide behind a veil. Keep the mystery. Present the illusive."

"I'm not sure I understand how to skillfully do this." Amelia's stomach turned. Did she want to belong that badly? One thought of Bryon, and she knew she had to learn.

"In the future, tell people your father is an agricultural specialist with years of experience. Few people will question what they do not understand for fear of looking less intelligent, and if they do, just say, 'Oh you don't know what that is?' This snub will undoubtably stop their questions, and you'll find them tripping over their words trying to change the subject. I would also highly recommend you choose a bigger city to say you are from, where there is a bit more culture and—"

"You mean lie."

"They'll be none the wiser and less inclined to ask more questions."

"Unless they know the area and start asking what street I lived on."

"Study up. You're a smart girl. Have your answers prepared."

"But I kinda let it out today."

"You *kind of* let it out today," Mrs. Felicia corrected. "And don't you worry about those immature girls. I'll use it as a lesson tomorrow and ask them how that changed their perception of you. Then I'll tell them we were merely roleplaying to test their compassion for others not quite as privileged as they are. It will be a perfect opportunity to teach them a lesson on common decency. Enough doubt will be shed on the incident that they won't know what the truth is. From there, it will be up to you to either follow my suggestions or not."

Amelia forced back the tears. The whole experience had made her feel inferior.

"If you have more questions or think you need extra help in any area, I would be more than delighted to assist you."

"Thank you." Amelia could barely speak. Her throat was choked with a fist-sized knot.

On her walk home, she reminded herself of what really mattered. She had a very prominent man in her life who didn't care a whit that she was a farmer's daughter. And she was falling more in love every time she saw him. Based on his caring attention, her lifelong dreams of love and marriage were not so far out of reach. At least she didn't have to lie to him.

The positive thoughts buoyed her spirits until reality set in. Would she have to lie to his parents?

CHAPTER 4

*A*melia pushed one more pin into her hair, then twirled before the mirror. Those last pounds were melting away, and the new ensemble she wore cinched in her waist to the point she looked slim.

She moved from side to side and regarded her reflection. Goodness, she was almost beautiful. But maybe it was the way Bryon made her feel—complimenting her and laughing at everything she said as if she were the most delightful woman he had ever met.

She lifted her chin and pulled her shoulders back for perfect posture as she had been taught, all the while practicing her half smile. The one that didn't give too much away yet revealed just enough welcome. She had learned at finishing school that life was all about perception. It mattered not what was, but what others believed it to be. This flew in the face of how she was raised, but country life was different, and she needed to fit in. She must fit in.

She was glad that finishing school was wrapping up and she would soon be away from those shallow young women. All she cared about was gaining the skills to make her grandmother proud in any social gathering, and hopefully soon, she would meet Bryon's family with enough grace to overshadow her humble beginnings. Knowing now what she did, she would never have shared her background with Bryon on the first meeting, but it was the one thing she was really happy he knew because around him she could be her true self. Yes, for others, she could and would perform, but with Bryon, she was Amelia. Somehow that felt right.

They had been meeting for weeks now, but always at her grandparents' place. That had been a welcome reprieve while she learned the finer art of etiquette, but now she was ready.

"Amelia." Her grandmother's high-pitched voice rang out with a tinkle of laughter. "Guess who's here?"

She smiled into the mirror. Who else would be calling? She didn't have friends. Hopefully, after she entered the social scene, that would change. Or maybe Bryon's sister would become a good friend.

With a pat to her coiffed hair and a smile on her lips, she turned from the mirror and hurried out. One look at Bryon sitting in the parlor chatting with her grandparents made her heart skitter, far more than it ever had at the sight of Edmund.

"Sorry to keep you waiting," she said.

Bryon looked up with a warm smile. "Not a problem. I love talking to your grandparents, and I'd wait any amount of time to have the pleasure of your company."

Grandmother tittered, waving her handkerchief. "Now this fine gentleman is worth hanging on to. He has impeccable taste. He not only enjoys our company"—she threw her hands up to include the both of them—"but he knows a gem when he sees one."

Heat crawled into Amelia's cheeks. "Grandmother."

Bryon's eyes lit up. "You're so right, Mrs. Brunson, your

granddaughter is indeed lovely." His look made her feel every bit a beautiful woman. What was it about this man that caused such startling emotions to surge inside her?

"Off you two go." Grandfather waved his corncob pipe in the air. "The last thing you young people need is a couple of old ones to put a damper on your fun."

"How about we all have a game of checkers after we return from our walk?" Bryon suggested. "I aim to beat you one of these days, and today just might be my lucky day."

Grandfather smiled. "That sounds like an excellent idea, young man. You can surely try." The jowls on his cheeks jiggled as he laughed. He settled back in his chair and inhaled his pipe. Slow, lazy tendrils of smoke drifted up and dissipated as he exhaled.

"Must you smoke in here, George?" Grandmother said. "You know how I can't abide the smell."

"One would think that after fifty years of marriage you'd be used to it."

"As long as I live, I shall never—"

"Now, now you two." Amelia smiled and crossed the room. She kissed Grandfather on the top of his bald head and Grandmother on the cheek. "We'll be back, but not too soon. I have no intention of rushing the best part of my day." She gave Bryon a sassy grin that would not be acceptable by Mrs. Felicia's standards and slipped her hand in the crook of his arm.

"Shall we?"

"We shall, my lady."

Just the way the deep timber of his voice said *my lady* with such tenderness and depth sent Amelia's heart tripping and skipping.

As was their routine, they walked the neighborhood and talked about everything from their growing years to their daily happenings. But today Amelia had to know. She paused at the end of the block and squeezed his arm. He turned her way. "Bryon, when will I meet your family? You've been visiting me almost daily and you know my grandparents well, but I've yet to meet the ones you love."

"I thought you wanted time." They continued the stroll.

"I did at first. I was honest with you about my upbringing and how different city life is. But Mrs. Felicia's Finishing School has trained me well, and I do believe I'm ready."

His nod was slight, but he said nothing. His smile vanished and he avoided eye contact. Finally, when she thought her heart might actually stop, he said, "I have something to confess."

Amelia took a deep breath. Why did a foreboding crawl up her spine?

"My parents, particularly my mother, has a certain type of woman in mind for me to marry."

"And I'm not it?" Amelia grabbed his arm and pulled him to a stop. "Do they even know we've been seeing each other?"

"No, but—"

"No?" Her stomach lurched and fell.

"Let me explain." His words spilled out like water from an overturned glass. "The war almost wiped us out, which is why I'm working as an investment banker, investing not only what's left of our family money, but helping others as well. Truthfully, money plays a big part in my mother's choice, but power and prestige are close seconds."

"I have no money." Her head dropped, and she felt like her body was wilting in front of him. He was as far beyond her reach as that first evening star that twinkled in the heavens.

He placed a finger under her chin and raised it up. "Do you trust me, Amelia?"

She nodded. But she had trusted another man, and it had gone very wrong. Just the thought of home twisted in her gut with a myriad of emotions. She was glad to be away from the Edmund-and-Helen saga, yet she fought a tinge of homesickness, not seeing any of her family. She had so wanted to be part of Bryon's family.

"There's hope for us. I have a plan." He dropped a light kiss on her cheek. "Please, walk with me, and I'll explain."

Despite the sadness welling in her chest, she walked beside him. How many more opportunities would she have to enjoy his company before he realized he could find a wife who had so much more to offer than she?

"I still have much to learn," he said, "but I've been blessed with good instincts when it comes to investing. I'm told I have a gift. I believe I can earn more than enough to take care of a wife and family."

Her heart leapt at that. He was speaking to her of a wife. A family. Maybe all was not lost.

"As far as our huge rambling house and estate lands. I know I don't need that, and I'm sure you don't either."

She smiled up at him. He was including her in his plans. "You know I don't." The relief at not having to learn how to be a mistress to that huge estate flooded over her.

"The way I see it, I only have to convince my parents to give my inheritance to my younger brother. Surely, he can marry someone who would love the family name, the prestige, the headache." He laughed, but it sounded hollow and worried.

"How will you convince them?" Amelia squeezed his arm. "You're the eldest. That won't be easy."

"Howard is only three years younger than me. He often laments at the unfairness of being the second son. He can have the monstrosity. I don't want it. I never have. I often wished I'd been born into a regular working-class family and not into privilege. For some reason, it never felt right to think of myself as better than someone else because of birthright. Does that sound odd?"

"No, Bryon. That sounds like a man after my own heart."

He put an arm around her as they walked, and she leaned

her head briefly on his shoulder. She felt a faint kiss brush against her hair.

"Can you give me a little more time to ease my parents into the idea of grooming my brother instead of me? I want to do it in a loving and respectful way, but I have to make them understand I want to choose my wife and my life."

He stopped and turned her toward him, placing his hands on her shoulders. "I know we have a lot to learn about each other, but I hope it's not too soon to say that I believe my choice is standing right in front of me."

Amelia took in a deep breath. It was far too soon to allow a man the privilege of a kiss, and certainly not in the open air for the world to see, but the way he was looking down at her tempted her to throw propriety out the window. Piece by piece, Bryon was stealing her heart.

∾

*A*melia looked up from her perch on the window seat in the library to find little Bethany peek around the corner. She laid her book in her lap and waved her in with a welcoming smile. "Hello, Bethany."

Bethany's curly hair, twice the size of her tiny face, was irresistible. Amelia had been working on getting Bethany to trust her, but the five-year-old's timidity was a challenge.

Her mother, Lydia, was Grandmother's maid. She'd confided to Amelia that she worried about her child's shyness. The delightful child moved throughout the home almost invisibly. She peeked around corners and would run off if she saw anyone. Amelia had shared how Bethany reminded her of her childhood days hiding in the background.

"Come. I'll read you a story."

The little girl took one step forward, then turned on her

heels and raced out. The front door slammed behind her. A blood curdling cry followed.

Amelia lit out after her.

Sprawled on the ground at the bottom of the veranda steps, Bethany lay in a heap, sobbing. Blood poured from a split on her forehead. She cried harder when she touched the wound and her hand came back red.

Amelia lifted her in her arms, not caring if the blood stained her new dress, and hurried inside toward the kitchen.

"You're all right, darling. The blood is scary, but we'll get you all fixed up."

Grandmother rounded the corner. "Land sakes, what has happened here?"

"Can you find Lydia? Bethany's taken a fall. I'll get her cleaned up."

"Oh my, oh my. I can't abide the sight of blood. Makes me want to faint right here, right now."

"Go then. I can't look after you both."

In the kitchen, Amelia applied pressure to the child's wound with a cloth while she held her tight, rocking her sobs away.

"Mama's coming."

The weeping subsided, and the child stopped shaking.

"Do you think I can look at it now?"

Bethany would not speak, but her head moved slowly up and down. Amelia lifted the cloth with care. "Well look at that. The bleeding has stopped. We're going to wash this up and wrap a strip of cloth around. Do you think you could be brave and let me do that?"

Bethany nodded, her dark brown eyes shimmering with tears.

"By the time your mama gets here, we'll have you as good as new, I promise." Amelia bandaged the child and then settled herself in the rocking chair. "How about a story?" She held out her arms, and the child climbed on her lap. They were halfway through when Grandmother burst in.

"So sorry, but Lydia had gone to the market, and I had to get help tracking her down."

Lydia followed on her heels and rushed forward. "Bethany, what happened?" She fell to her knees beside the child.

"I'm fine, Mama. All fixed up." Bethany pointed to her head. "And I'm hearing a story of a red riding hood. I would like a red riding hood."

A faint smile tugged at the corner of Lydia's mouth, though the concern never left her expression. She turned to Amelia. "When your grandmother said Bethany's face was covered in blood, I almost couldn't breathe."

"Grandmother." Amelia looked up. "Not the best thing to tell a mother."

"Well, it was."

"It was just a bump and a little cut. Bethany is fine." She regarded the child. "Aren't you, pumpkin?"

Bethany nodded. "Can I listen to the rest of the story now, Mama?"

"If Amelia has the time."

Amelia smiled above Bethany's head. "I told Bethany she's helping me."

"She misses her sisters, 'cause she used to read to them and now she's far, far away."

"That's right. You're helping my homesickness, aren't you Bethany?"

Bethany's head bobbed up and down, and she sank back into Amelia's lap.

"She hardly goes to anyone," Lydia said.

"I used to be the same way," Amelia said.

"And where did you get so good at looking after blood and wounds?" Grandmother asked.

"Blood does not bother me at all."

Grandmother shuddered. "Wish I could say the same."

Amelia waved them away. "Lydia, I'll bring Bethany to you when we're done with our story." She looked down at the child. "Now, where were we?"

"The little girl with the beautiful red riding hood was about to enter the forest."

"Ahh, yes …"

CHAPTER 5

*B*ryon couldn't stay away from her, but neither did he want to start a war with his parents—particularly his mother. He lived life caught between the two worlds. He'd have to find a way to tell his parents about Amelia soon. He couldn't imagine his life without his beautiful hazel-eyed girl. Every moment in her presence made the bond grow stronger. Amelia had somehow stolen his heart in an instant, and there was no retrieving it, nor a will to even try.

He knocked on her grandparents' door, and she answered. "Bryon, do come in."

"I have a better idea. Grab your coat, I have somewhere special I want to take you." Her smile tunneled into him, warming the chill of the crisp autumn air.

"Will it be worth my while?" She gave him a saucy grin.

"I want to share one of my favorite childhood haunts with you before old man winter blows in for good. It may be one of the last warm evenings left."

"I'll be right there." She left the door ajar as she grabbed her cloak off a nearby peg and joined him.

"I've never shown this spot to anyone, so I hope you feel as special as I want you to feel." He helped her wrap her cloak around her shoulders and held out his hand. She laced her fingers into his.

"I feel honored." She gazed up at him with wide innocent eyes, making his heart gallop.

"Can we walk?"

"Yes, I found this place long before I had footmen or carriages at my disposal. It's where I go when I need to clear my head, make big decisions, or just want to be alone."

"If you take me, you won't be alone," she teased.

"With you around, I feel like I never want to be alone again." His words of honesty spilled out without thought.

"Bryon." She grabbed his arm and squeezed. "You know how to get a girl right here." She placed a gloved hand over her heart.

Oh, how he longed to kiss her right there on the doorstep. "Come on. We've just enough time to get up there for the best part of the day."

She took his arm, and they walked in silence. Bryon loved how the quiet with Amelia felt so natural. There wasn't the nervous tension he had always felt with other women, moments when he agonized over what to say next.

At the top of the hill, he led her through a copse of trees to an outcropping, where there was a large rock to sit upon. The city and river spread before them. The timing was perfect. With the fall colors at their peak, the distant river sparkling in the setting sun, there could not be a more romantic spot.

"What a view." She squeezed his hand tight. "Thank you for sharing this with me. It's so beautiful."

"Yes, beautiful." While she studied the view, he reveled in her breathtaking loveliness. Her gaze flicked to him and lingered. The way she gazed up at him, her eyes dancing with life, her hair with silky copper highlights in the light of the setting sun, those lips that begged to be kissed... He swallowed against the lump forming in his throat. It took all his strength not to take her in his arms and kiss her soundly, but a gentleman he was, first and foremost. "Shall we sit?"

The sun rested on the western horizon touching the edge of the earth. Their shoulders brushed against one another. At each subtle touch, his insides lurched. He fisted his hands.

"May I put my arm around you?" he asked.

She looked up at him, and her smile widened. "I thought you'd never ask."

The sensation of her melting against his shoulder sent his pulse racing. She fit perfectly in the curve of his body as his arm enfolded her. They sat in silence, in peaceful surrender to the ending of a perfect day. She didn't fill the air with incessant chatter or the batting of her eyelashes. She became one with him in what this place had always meant—a solace from the cares of the world.

Ribbons of vibrant red and orange splashed across the sky as the sun dipped below the horizon. An ever-deepening purple-gray became the background to a display of vivid colors. The shadows thickened, and still they sat.

"Bryon?"

"Hmm."

"Would I be too forward in admitting that I've never felt this way before?"

Tiny pins of awareness rippled over every nerve ending. How could simple words evoke such a longing to spill the truth. He was in love with her. But he must hold his tongue until he was free to say those words and act upon them.

"He crushed her shoulder into to his. "I feel the same way."

"You don't understand. I was set to marry a man who courted me for almost three years. I was happy to accept so much less than what I feel for you."

He looked down and locked his eyes with hers.

"I'm so thankful that God didn't let me marry Edmund now

that I know what real lo…I mean…well you know what I mean."
Her cheeks flamed red.

"I know *exactly* what you mean. My mother has tried to thrust so many women on me, some lovely women, but I would've been settling had I chosen any of them. I'm glad I didn't." He flashed her a smile. "But I have a question. You talk about God as if you believe He cares about the details of our individual lives."

Amelia pulled out of his embrace and turned toward him. "You don't?"

"Well, it's not like I wouldn't like to, but in our family God and church are relegated to Easter and Christmas and the occasional Sunday when it's beneficial for my parents on a social level."

"But you've been meeting me there regularly."

"To be honest, mostly to see you."

"Bryon." She slapped his shoulder playfully. "I do appreciate your honestly, but we'll have to work on that."

He threw his arm back around her shoulders and drew her close, pulling in the sweet smell of lavender, making it difficult for him to concentrate on his words. "I have no problem with learning. I'd love to have your faith."

She lay her head on his shoulder and sighed. "Bryon Curtis Preston the Third, you're just too good to be true."

What would she think if she knew he had still not talked to his parents? A barb of guilt pierced his heart. "I guess I'd better get you back before it gets dark or your grandparents will worry." He couldn't keep the longing out of his voice. It was the last thing he wanted to do.

"I wish we never had to leave," she whispered. "This is the most beautiful place anyone has ever shared with me."

He kissed the top of her head and snapped to his feet before he succumbed to far more. "We'll come again. I promise." He held out his hand and relished the feel of her fingers interlacing with his. Who knew such a simple touch could make the heart buck in craziness?

She rose with grace and walked with him in a comfortable mixture of conversation and silence.

How would he ever manage to find the words to convince his mother that she would have to shift her hopes and dreams onto another child. She had always favored him, made him out to be something special. She was in for a real disappointment, especially when she found out that he didn't want the so-called privilege of being the heir nor any girl she suggested. A lovely farm girl was the woman of his dreams.

But maybe he could start with one shock and then ease into the other.

❧

NOVEMBER 1868
SHENANDOAH VALLEY

*K*atherine rose at dawn and ambled to the kitchen. Josiah already had the wood stove burning hot. The smell of fresh coffee permeated the air.

"Good morning, my love." He kissed the top of her head.

She plunked her body down on the chair and ran a hand through her heavy curls. "Did you hear how many times Seth woke in the night? He must be going through a growing spurt. I can't seem to keep him happy."

Josiah leaned over and planted a kiss on her mouth. "You make me happy, but between the two of us keeping you awake at night, I understand why you're tired."

Katherine could feel the heat splash from her neck to her hairline. "Josiah Richardson, you should be ashamed of yourself for being so brazen." She slapped his wandering hands from her body.

A hearty laugh filled the room. "I forget you're a tad grumpy until you get your coffee." He lifted the metal pot from the stove and poured a brew.

"I forget you're a tad annoying, waking up fully alert and far too chatty. Even the sun takes half the day to reach full strength."

He slid a hot cup of coffee her way. "This should help."

Katherine took a deep breath, enjoying the aroma before lifting the cup to her lips. "I forgot to tell you last night. I received a letter from Amelia yesterday, and she sounds like she has fallen hard for a city boy. I'm predicting wedding bells in the next year."

"Hmm, that won't please your mother if she gets married and never returns to the valley."

"Won't please me either, but to be happy in love is the best."

"Like us?" He swooped down to kiss her lips.

"Like us." She smiled.

He made his way back to the stove and cracked a few eggs into a cast iron pan. With one hand he flipped the eggs and with the other he took a swig of coffee. "I insist you take a nap today, and I'm not joking about that. You work too hard, and we have the money to hire all the help we need inside and out. There's no reason to slave the day away."

"I don't slave the day away," she said, "I happily contribute. I'll never be a lady of leisure."

"I know, I know. But you have to take care of yourself, too." He slid the cooked eggs onto a plate and cut himself a thick piece of bread. "You have to learn to delegate like I have."

She rolled her eyes and took another sip of coffee. "You delegate. Since when?"

"Since this morning."

His eyes twinkled, and she laughed.

But his expression turned serious. "I want more time with

my beautiful wife and son, and we both need to change things up a bit to make sure that happens."

She lifted her brows.

"Your Pa's more than ready to be left in charge of all the growing, from the orchard to planting, harvesting, and managing all the staff needed to accomplish that task."

"And you'll stay out of it?"

"Yes, my love. I'll stay out of it. Hank is doing great as the lead hand. He's already in charge of the cattle. That leaves me to concentrate on what I love the most—horse flesh. The pure-bred Arabians Colby brought in when he was here have turned out to be golden. Best decision ever. The ranch is getting a reputation for raising the finest horses in the valley, just as we'd dreamed."

"They sure are beautiful."

"Beauty, strength, and endurance. Coming from that hot desert terrain, they make a fine addition to any working man's farm.

"Or woman."

He chuckled. "Or women. If they can ride like you, they deserve no less than one of our fine horses."

She smiled overtop the rim of her cup. "I like the way you say *ours*."

"But of course. Who is this all for, if not for you and our children?"

She lifted a brow. "Children?"

"Let's agree, I won't rest until our horse ranch is known from the mighty Allegheny on one side of this valley to the Blue Ridge on the other and beyond. Heck, how about the finest in Virginia?"

"You're wisely avoiding the question." Katherine tried to hold back a yawn, but her mouth opened wide.

His laugh split the morning air. "I dare say that talking about more children when you're sleep deprived is not a wise choice."

She giggled behind her hand that stifled another yawn.

"Go back to bed, and don't get up until at least noon. I'm going to tell Delilah to arrange for your sleep in." He rose from his breakfast, plunked a hat on his head, and kissed her lips. "See you at noon. We'll work on the books this afternoon. I'll need your sharp mind to get that nasty job done."

The back door squeaked on its hinges and slammed shut. Katherine stood, yawned, and stretched. Bed did feel like a wonderful option. She climbed the circular stairway to their bedroom and snuggled back beneath the covers. Warmth spread over her chilled limbs. She couldn't believe her wonderful life. Was it too good to be true?

A dark niggle of fear pricked at her mind. When and what would go wrong? Her life had moved from one sadness to another. She burrowed deeper under the covers and pressed her lids shut and prayed for strength to squelch the foreboding. She wouldn't entertain trouble when joy was singing on her doorstep.

Sweet peace entered as she gave her worry away to the keeper of her soul.

~

*W*ith their charities and full social calendar, it had been a feat for Bryon to get both parents in the same room long enough to have the serious discussion he needed to have.

"Out with it, Bryon." His mother waved her hand. "I know when you pace the floor you have more than pleasantries to discuss."

"Is it our investments? Are they not doing well?" A frown knit his father's brow.

"No, no. The investments are doing fine."

"Is it—?"

"Let the boy speak, Alex. Stop trying to guess."

"I've made a decision." Bryon took a steadying breath. "I don't want to be heir of this estate. I want to live a modest life—"

"Modest life. But...but..." His mother sputtered on her words. "What do you mean by a modest life? And who, pray tell, do you think is going to carry on the Preston legacy?"

"Howard could learn. He cares far more about—"

"Howard." His mother's voice rose a couple of octaves. "Howard has never had a penchant for work. All he cares about is having a good time. I love him, but he is soft. This home needs a strong leader, and that's you."

Bryon turned toward his father, who sat in his favorite chair. "Don't you think that's my decision to make?" Hopefully, his father would be the calming force.

Mother rose from the settee in one swift graceful motion. "Being the first born, I would say God made that decision."

"Since when do we bring God into our conversations?"

"Now son, listen to what your mother is saying. Howard hasn't been groomed for this role. If anything, we've spoiled him, expecting so little—"

"And your decision could bankrupt this family." Mother stood over him with her dark eyes boring into his. "Are you telling me you're truly that selfish?"

"Ahh, now we are to the crux of the matter. Money."

"Don't be insolent with your mother." His father's voice was kind, but firm. "Money is not the crux of the matter, but it is important in order to keep up this home and carry on the legacy left to us by our forefathers. It's what we do as the eldest son."

What could he say to his father, who had done everything expected of him his entire life? "I'm not trying to be disrespect-ful, and I do intend to help out with the family investments in any way I can."

Mother threw up her hands. "We don't need your help as much as we need your loyalty to the family name."

"I agree with your mother," Father said. "You could make all the money in the world, but, if it's left in the hands of your brother, it will go out as fast as it comes in. With Howard's weakness for spending, it would be a disaster. I'm continually having to rein him in."

"How was I to know that?"

"It's not something we're proud of and go on spouting about," Mother said. "Surely you have noticed his continual need for the newest fashions and his lack of ambition to work?" His mother shook her head. "What has gotten into you, Bryon?"

"I want to live my own life and Howard wants the estate. Sounds like a reasonable plan to let him take over. I'll even donate my time teaching him everything you've taught me, Father."

"We don't get to live our own lives," Mother said. "We all have responsibilities and—"

Father held up his hand, and Mother snapped her jaw closed. "We need to tell him the rest."

"No!" Mother's voice came out strained, yet firm.

"Yes," Father insisted. "Bryon needs to understand why Howard will never be trusted with the family home."

Bryon's spirits dropped. "What?"

"First tell me why this is so important to you?"

This was not going well. Mother wouldn't listen to reason, and Bryon didn't know if he could answer his father's question without alienating them both. All the arguments he had prepared so eloquently in his head fell flat, and he couldn't think straight. "I...I don't know how to explain it, but this is far more Howard's dream than it has ever been mine. I've always longed for a simpler life. I've longed to earn my own keep."

"Simple. Do you hear that, Alex? Our son wants to live like a commoner." Her hands were planted on both sides of her slim hips. "Where have we gone wrong? One son doesn't want to work at all, and the other wants out..." Her voice warbled. "What about family heritage, loyalty, and respecting your parents?" She slipped back into a chair, tears glistening in her eyes.

Bryon had never witnessed such vulnerability. His father stood and patted her shoulder. He looked at Bryon with pleading in his eyes. "Truth is, there's more to Howard's spending than we've wanted to let on. Your brother has a gambling problem."

"Gambling. Howard?" Bryon's forehead broke into a sweat. This was far worse than he'd thought.

"Picked up the bad habit at one of those exclusive men's groups, and we've had to dig him out of trouble a time or two now. Just a few weeks ago, he came to us begging for money, as he was under the threat of a duel, and you know your brother has no skill with a pistol whatsoever."

Bryon took in a breath to quiet the worry churning inside him. "But gambling is not a problem we can keep supporting. We're barely scraping by."

"We don't support it, son, but neither are we going to let someone take a gun to Howard in a duel."

"But how do you expect to prevent this from happening again? Gambling can be a bottomless pit."

"He's promised to stay away from the group, and I happen to know the proprietor of the establishment. He's going to let me know if he sees Howard anywhere around the premises. Howard has promised to focus on finding a good wife and settling down, but with all his demons to fight, he is in no position to take over the running of this estate."

Bryon couldn't argue with that point, but he felt pulled like a wishbone in two directions. He had never been one to cause his parents angst, and it didn't feel good. They clearly needed his help, but Amelia was the love of his life. Maybe if he could get his mother to agree to him picking his own wife, then he could talk Amelia into joining him in looking after this monstrosity of a home. But his parents had to accept Amelia. They just had to.

"If I agree to remain the heir, then, I have two requests. One, Howard needs responsibility and work if he's going to kick this habit. I want to him to learn and share in the responsibility of running this estate."

Both parents nodded. "That's a solid plan and something I was going to talk to you about anyway," his father said. "Howard does need some purpose to his life."

Good so far. Maybe over time, his brother would shine and Bryon would get his freedom. "And two, I want to choose my own wife."

His mother's gaze shot up. "But I've only tried to suggest the very best for you."

He sat in the chair opposite his mother and rested his forearms on his knees, leaning toward her. He took her hands in his. "Mother, I know you love me and want the best for me, but your choices are not mine. If you and Father trust me to inherit and protect your legacy, can you trust me to choose my own wife?"

"But Bryon, what's wrong with the women I suggest?"

He pulled back and sat straight in his chair. "You mean the *wealthy* women you suggest?"

"Why ever would it matter that they are wealthy? Surely, that will make your life easier." Her brows rose in indignation.

"But are they the only women with merit?"

Her fingers rose to her temples and she massaged briefly before lifting her eyes to his. "I just want the best for you. I know how difficult it is to maintain this house, and I don't want you to have to slave your life away to keep it up. I'm only thinking of your future."

"I'd rather work hard and be loved, than marry for convenience," Bryon said.

Father cleared his throat. "That sounds like a reasonable compromise, Melinda. Let the boy be happy and truly in love like we are." He smiled at his wife and rubbed his aging hand over her bony shoulders. "We're rebuilding our assets, thanks to his expertise. The boy is rather good at investing the family money. I don't believe he must marry into more."

Mother sat back against the chair, her shoulders falling. "It just looks so *needy* for Bryon to be working every day. If he agreed to any of my suggestions for a wife, his working days would be over."

"I like my job," Bryon said, "and I have no problem working hard." He stood and spoke to his father. "Thank you for understanding and for trusting my choice. I would like you"—he gazed at his mother—"both of you, to meet the girl of my dreams."

"You're courting someone?"

"Her name is Amelia Williams. I haven't said anything because you were so intent on me marrying a woman of your choosing."

"Williams?" His mother pressed two fingers to her temples. "Williams? I'm not sure which family that is." Her brow knit together.

"You don't know every family in this city, do you?" Bryon's father slid down to sit on the edge of her chair.

"I know everyone with standing—"

"See what I mean, Mother. You validate people by their so-called standing."

"Come on, Melinda," Father said. "Extend him an olive branch. You don't have to control everything."

She nudged him in the rib with her elbow. "I don't want to control *everything*."

When he laughed, she scowled at him, but a hint of amusement touched the corners of her lips.

"I'd like to invite Amelia for tea over the holidays so you can see how lovely she is."

"Sounds like the boy is smitten," Father said.

"I am." Bryon was thankful his father had interrupted the inquisition his mother was about launch. If he could just get them to meet Amelia and spend a bit of time with her, they would love her.

"All right. Invite the girl for tea." His mother stood and approached him. He stood and stepped into the warm hug she offered. "Just promise me, no more talk of Howard taking over this family. You hear?"

One great battle overcome. Now all he needed was a little time before they found out her humble beginnings and her grandparents' last name.

∽

"*I* have the best news ever to tell you later," Bryon whispered into Amelia's ear as she lowered a cup of water beside him.

"Checkmate." A grin split across Grandfather's wrinkled face. "You were a tad distracted this afternoon. Made the winning too easy."

Bryon laughed. "Your granddaughter is to blame. I swear the two of you cook up these distractions. Every time I go to move my pawn, she waltzes in or out, or says something and I can't think straight."

The pitter patter of Amelia's heartrate quickened. Who could resist such courtly charm? How opposite Edmund had been, with his condescending tones. My, was she thankful God had put an end to that relationship and saved her from a life-time of put-downs.

"I'll give you two some time alone." Grandfather struggled to get out of his chair. "I'm not too old to remember the way of a man with his maiden." He winked at Amelia with one bushy brow and shuffled across the library. "But I'll most certainly leave the door open." They heard his chuckle recede down the hall.

Bryon patted the seat beside him on the settee.

"What's your good news?" She sat as close as propriety would allow.

"I've talked to my parents and they want to meet you. With their busy social calendar this time of year, mother suggested an afternoon tea on Christmas day. Do you think that will work for you?"

A spark of anxiety flared. "I do so hope they like me."

"I'm sure they will. And I have their blessing to court the woman of my dreams and you dear Amelia are the only woman in my dreams." He reached out and laced his fingers into hers.

His touch sent a jolt up her arm. She sank back into the cushions beside him, their shoulders touching. This was too good to be true. "I'd be thrilled."

His thumb slid to the inside of her wrist, caressing a slow circular path on her palm. How could such a simple movement evoke such aliveness? She had never been so aware of a man, his nearness so palpable, his strength so inviting and tempting. She turned in his direction and lifted her head up to his.

He stared at her lips and bent his head lower.

Her breath intermingled with his as she leaned in closer. With only an inch separating their mouths, the sensitivity of her lips tingled with the impulse to close the gap and meet his. She wanted nothing more than to feel the sweet connection only a kiss could give. One hand unconsciously found a way to his chest, and the feel of his strong beating heart pulsed beneath her fingertips. His arms came around her and pulled her in.

"Amelia. Bryon. Come into the parlor. Tea is served." The click, click of her grandmother's heels on the hardwood floor was quickly approaching. They sprang apart and stood as she swept into the room.

"Grandmother. Bryon has invited me to his parent's place for an afternoon tea on Christmas day. Would that interfere with any of your plans?"

"Goodness, no. Life is meant to be spontaneous and flexible. We'll have a wonderful Christmas morning, then you can visit the Prestons and we'll schedule the evening meal thereafter." A smile creased Grandmother's cheeks. "How wonderful the two of you are progressing...I mean..." She clapped her hands together and waved them forward. "Our tea is getting cold."

Bryon held out his arm and Amelia placed her hand in the crook. Grandmother squeezed her other arm tight and nodded with the most delighted smile as they walked down the hall. It seemed she was as excited as Amelia.

CHAPTER 6

*A*melia slumped in a parlor chair gazing listlessly out the window. She loved the city, but Christmas was around the corner, and her stomach gnawed at the thought of not being with her family.

"What is it, my dear?"

"I'm all right, Grandmother." Amelia turned to her, determined to keep the doldrums out of her voice.

"I have to tell you how much I love having you here. To think of all the years I've missed." She waved her hand. "No, I cannot look back, only forward. Now, tell me the truth. What is bothering you?"

"Christmas has me missing my family more than I anticipated."

"That makes perfect sense."

"And I'm nervous about meeting Bryon's family," Amelia admitted.

"You're more than ready." Grandmother's voice registered assurance but worried lines furrowed her brow. "You've come, so far. There is no need to fret."

A flutter of excitement, and then a drop of dread, leapfrogged in her stomach.

"You have every right to be very excited, my dear. A young man doesn't invite a woman to meet his family unless he is serious about his choice."

Amelia couldn't hold back a smile. "Do you think so? In the past few months I've given more of my heart to him than I care to admit."

"I know so. The Preston family is well-respected in the upper echelon of society. Their name and prestige carry a lot of weight in the community. Every move they make is carefully planned. That's why the invite has been slow to come."

"I don't understand. You and Grandfather have opened your home and your heart to Bryon, being a willing chaperone every time he visited. You've fussed over him as if the king had come to town. Why would they behave any differently?"

Grandmother's head dropped, and she picked at an imaginary piece of lint on her dress sleeve. "How do I begin to explain?"

"Are there rules about this I missed in Mrs. Felicia's Finishing School?"

"Not rules per say. This is how Richmond's unforgiving high society works. Our family's reputation has gone under a fair amount of unpleasant scrutiny. When your mother married a mere servant—" She cut off her words with a wave of her hands. "No offense to your father, but that is not done. We were very frowned upon for not raising our daughter right. The distancing began."

"Who needs friends like that?" A flare of anger sparked inside Amelia.

"I agree. It is all so pretentious and wrong, but the last thing the aristocratic class wants is for anyone to cross the barrier and intermingle with the lower class."

"But why?"

"Those born into privilege tend to think themselves more intellectual and deserving. This is taught from birth and feeds the obvious lie. They quite like the separation of classes. It gives them power they don't want watered down. I know. Because I was one of them."

"So, I'm considered lower class?" Like an unwelcome cloud burst, unkind thoughts pummeled her insides.

"Not you. We do come from a long line of prominent lineage, and you're my granddaughter. It may be more our failure as parents..." She took a deep breath in and slowly let it out. "There were some other things concerning your Aunt Emmaline as well. Judgement came down hard. Grandfather and I were considered failures. Though we were still of the upper class, we were shunned by many."

"Things have improved, though, haven't they?" Amelia asked.

"Somewhat. And you being invited into the Preston home can only mean one thing—acceptance—for everyone follows Melinda Preston's lead." Grandmother's eyes sparkled with delight. "You have no idea how happy this has made me. Maybe now I will no longer live on the fringe. No matter how much money I give to their charities or how much volunteer work I do, it is never enough to redeem myself. But enough said. Come." She stood and waved her toward the door. "Let's go shopping for the perfect gift to give Mrs. Preston."

"Ahh yes." Amelia rose from her chair. "I remember that rule. Mrs. Felica said that one should always bring a gift when invited to dinner for the first time."

~

"Merry Christmas, dear Amelia." Bryon bent forward and dropped a light kiss on her cheek. Butterflies fluttered in Amelia's stomach as she slipped her fingers into Bryon's hand. He looked so different in a top hat, longtail coat, and shining new boots. He was dressed to perfection, and so was she, but why did he suddenly feel a class above her in his more formal wear? Her confidence plummeted into the souls of her new black boots peeking from beneath her pink gown trimmed in black braiding.

"How was your day so far?"

He looked different, but the casual way he made conversation put her at ease as she slipped on her thick winter cloak. "I had a wonderful breakfast feast with my grandparents, and they are trying so hard, but I'm missing my family something fierce today. I keep thinking about what they would be doing and long to join in."

He squeezed her hand. "I can only imagine how difficult this is for you."

She looked up at his compassionate face and leaned in to his side as he accompanied her out the door. "I'm hoping to make friends and fit in with your family. Your sister sounds lovely, and she's my age too."

"Yes, she is wonderful. You'll love her." He escorted her from her grandparents' home to the ornately decorated carriage. The matching team of horses pranced restlessly beneath the harness of silver bells. The coachman stepped down to open the door, and Bryon guided her in. They settled in the warmth of blankets and heated rocks on which to place their feet.

"I know it's a tad overdone for such a short distance," Bryon said, "but I didn't want you to walk in the sleet."

He smiled that silly grin she had so come to love, and his banter and nearness brought awareness alive. She smiled back at him with wide abandon. The touch of his hands, his woodsy scent, his body brushing against her as they jostled along—did he feel the same wonderful feeling she had each time she was in his presence?

He swung his arm around her shoulders and drew her close

intently holding her gaze. The air between them crackled and prickled with tension.

In his arms, everything else faded. Missing her family, even the nervousness of meeting his parents, disappeared in that short ride as their eyes locked and his hand warmed hers. The presence of his simple touch seared awareness into her being.

"You look stunning."

A slow curl of heat warmed its way from tip to toe. "And you look dapper. Though I must confess, this"—she gestured to his formal attire—"scares me a little."

"Why?"

"Just speaks of a world I know so little about."

"You'll do fine. They won't be able to help loving you."

"You think so?"

"I know so." His smile sent a surge of confidence her way. "Everything about you is beautiful, from your winsome personality and kind heart to your beautiful smile." His hands lifted to the sides of her face, and he bent his head until their lips nearly touched. "I'm going to do something I have been longing to do since the first day we met."

His mouth touched hers, and their lips molded together. Intoxicating sensations flowed like liquid honey throughout her body. Slow. Sweet. Sensual. The touch of his hands on the sides of her face. His manly scent. His body crushed against hers. Over and over he pulled back only to instantly return. She had never been so aware of a man. His nearness so intense, his strength so comforting, his arms so warm. When Edmund had kissed her, it had been pleasant, but this was earth-shattering.

He finally drew back with a sigh. She leaned into his embrace with her head against his chest. The rapid beat of his heart thumped in her ear.

Suddenly, the carriage lurched to a stop.

Bryon pulled back and voiced what she had been thinking.

"That jaunt was too short." His voice broke. "I wish we could keep on riding."

She agreed wholeheartedly.

The coachman swung the carriage door open, and Bryon stepped out, then turned to help her. Amelia looked up at the rambling mansion, and her breath got caught in her throat. Bryon's soft touch to the small of her back propelled her forward. She gathered her dress in both hands and her courage as she mounted the stairs into Bryon's world. Her hand tucked safely in the crook of his arm gave her strength to fight against the shyness that tugged at her insides. Oh, how she would've liked to have met them one by one on a less formal occasion.

The house reminded her of her sister Katherine's home, with its old-world charm and splendor. With one sweeping view of the grand entrance, she was glad she'd had the opportunity to get used to more than the humble farmhouse they grew up in.

"Why, Bryon, she is charming. Do bring her in." The regal woman coming toward them bore the confidence possessed only by those of certain breeding and background. Amelia's skin prickled with apprehension. How would she ever fit in? She dug deep for the sake of Bryon and extended her hand.

"Mother, this is Amelia Williams." He turned to her. "Amelia, my mother, Melinda Preston."

They shook hands politely. Mrs. Preston's gaze traveled over her from head to toe in a quick but thorough inspection. She looked down her nose, but her head did not move.

Amelia prayed the new gown her grandmother had insisted upon would meet with her approval. She didn't care much about the latest fashion trends, but she did want to make Bryon proud.

"Come and meet the family." Warmth radiated from Melinda Preston's voice, and Amelia's heartrate quieted to a steady rhythm. Had she passed that first crucial inspection?

Bryon grinned and winked at her, leaning toward her ear. "You're doing fine."

What if she didn't meet their expectations? How much had Bryon shared about her humble up-bringing? Her stomach twisted into a knot. She squared her shoulders and lifted her head like Mrs. Felicia had taught and projected a confidence she did not feel. Smiling up at Bryon, she took his arm and glided into the next room. She could do this.

Opulent decorations hung from wreaths and garland. Crimson velvet floor-to-ceiling curtains broke up the wall of windows. The fire crackled in an oversize hearth, with a mantle draped in greenery and lit bayberry candles. The room held a spicy-sweet fragrance which added to the magical feeling. Her feet sank into the plush carpet laid over spit-polished oak. Katherine's house was lovely, but this was something else entirely.

The background faded as Bryon took her elbow and propelled her further in toward the chair in the center of the room. "My father, Alex Preston."

Mr. Preston instantly stood. He was not tall but carried a commanding presence. Amelia was tempted to turn and fly out the door until a smile split across Mr. Preston's face. Warmth curled from his dimpled cheeks all the way up to the laugh lines around his vibrant blue eyes. He wrapped her hand in both of his. The smile was genuine, the handshake hearty. "Pleasure to meet you, Miss Williams."

"You look so much like Bryon."

He laughed. "I do believe I started the trend and he looks like me."

Amelia's cheeks burned hotter as she joined in the laughter. "Of course. Very true."

"We're so glad to finally meet the girl Bryon has been slipping away to visit," Mr. Preston said. "Here we thought he was so dedicated to his work that he was working long hours." He chuckled.

Melinda Preston called out. "Rose, Howard, Bryon's guest has arrived." From two different directions, a young man and a young woman appeared. All eyes were upon her. She had to remind herself to breathe.

Bryon launched into more introductions. "My sister Rose, and my brother Howard."

She curtsied and was met with friendly hellos. A flow of heat stole into her cheeks. She hated that about herself, but there was little she could do to control the blush.

Rose moved forward and curtsied, and Howard stepped out of the shadows. "Tell me, however did I miss such a beautiful woman and not snatch you up before my brother?" He lifted her hand and kissed the back, then stood back and winked.

Amelia felt awkward not sure how to respond.

"Howard." Melinda's stern voice cut his all-too candid appraisal of her short. "Surely you have enough women falling over you day in and day out that you don't have to flirt with your brother's choice."

His mother's words didn't seem to embarrass him at all. "I'm not used to missing the pretty ones. I'd love to know where Bryon's been hiding her." He flashed her another smile before stepping away to a respectable distance.

Rose moved forward. Her easy smile so resembled Bryon and instantly put Amelia at ease. "I'm so looking forward to getting to know you. Bryon has told me so much about you."

Amelia returned the friendly smile. "That would be lovely." Bryon had not been wrong when he said his sister was a warm, caring person and the one he was the closest to. It would be most interesting to know what he said to Rose about her.

She breathed much easier when the room returned to open chatter and she was no longer the center of attention. Conversation remained light and flitted from gifts they had opened to the smells wafting in from the kitchen and the anticipation of a wonderful evening meal. She and Bryon settled into the settee nearest the fire. She leaned in close and caught a calming whiff of sandalwood soap.

"How are you doing?" he whispered.

She nodded and leaned against this shoulder.

"We'll have afternoon tea and then be on our way." He squeezed her hand gently and held on. "I can imagine this is a tad overwhelming."

Overwhelming was an understatement. It took every bit of strength she had to remain calm and engaging.

One look from his mother directed at their touching hands and Bryon removed his hand from hers. But he remained close.

Mrs. Preston glided across the floor and perched herself on a nearby chair. With her back held perfectly straight, she stared at both of them.

Amelia straightened her spine and took in a deep breath. With deliberate concentration, she expelled the air slowly as she had been taught by Mrs. Felicia when in an uncomfortable situation. She looked around the room and back again in hopes of gathering a poise she did not feel.

Mrs. Preston relaxed against the back of her chair. Her eyes shifted from cool dismissal to a decided warmth.

Was Amelia imagining the change?

"Bryon tells me you're new in town? Where are you from?" Her voice held a kind-hearted invitation.

She was not imagining the shift. Could it mean genuine interest?

"I knew it." Howard declared. "I would not have missed a woman as beautiful—"

"Howard, please," Mr. Preston said. "Remember your manners. Your mother is talking."

Amelia said, "I am new to Richmond." For a moment, she thought about stretching the truth as Mrs. Felicia had suggested, but she couldn't do it. "I'm from the Shenandoah Valley."

Bryon squeezed her hand. She didn't know what that meant.

"The Shenandoah Valley? Is that not a farming community?" One of Mrs. Preston's eyebrows arched.

Amelia had thought for sure Bryon would've braced his parents with the truth before they met her, but it seemed he had not. What was she supposed to say?

"There are many farms and ranches in the area," she said.

"And you?" Mrs. Preston asked. "Were you raised on a farm?"

Amelia looked at Bryon, who shifted uncomfortably beside her. Why had he not prepared them? She whispered a prayer for strength, and a surge of courage took over. If she was ever to be accepted, telling the truth was better than having it slowly leak out. "My grandparents are from a prominent Richmond family. But I was raised on a farm. Farming puts food all our tables, does it not?" She forced a laugh and hoped that mimicking what Mrs. Felicia had said would give credibility. Heat rushed to her cheeks.

Rose gasped and Howard laughed. "She's right about that, and I do like my food. And I quite like the spunk of this girl."

Mrs. Preston did not flinch. "Do go on, my dear. What was it like in the country?"

"We always had enough to eat until Sheridan's Yankee troops took to burning our valley. We lost everything—our crops, our home, our animals."

Mrs. Preston's eyes widened. "We heard about that. Whatever did you do?"

"We crowded in with my aunt and uncle for a bit. Thankfully, my sister Katherine agreed to an arranged marriage to a very wealthy horse breeder. He gave us a home and gave my father some work. Otherwise, I'm not sure what would've become of us."

Bryon stiffened and gave her hand a quick squeeze.

She glanced his way. Had she said too much?

"Mother, should we serve the tea now?" Bryon asked, shifting in his seat. His face had turned ashen white.

"Since when do you concern yourself with the kitchen?" Mrs. Preston settled back in the chair. "There'll be plenty of time for tea. Besides, it's rude to interrupt your friend." Her eyes fell on Amelia. "What brings you to our fair city?"

Amelia's gaze shifted between mother and son. There was a lot more going on than words conveyed. Bryon's anxiety grew palpable. The carefree young man she had grown to love had worry etched across his furrowed brow. But surely this was a safe question to answer. "I visited Richmond last year and loved the city. When my grandparents invited me to come live with them, I couldn't resist."

"You live with your grandparents?"

"Yes, just up the street. That's how Bryon and I met. I was walking by—"

"Bryon, you didn't tell me she lived so close. Why, I know every family for miles. Who are your grandparents?"

"George and Frances Brunson."

Mrs. Preston sat up abruptly and blinked her eyes rapidly. "Who did you say?"

Finally, Bryon found his voice. "You heard right, Mother."

Mrs. Preston's demeaner instantly changed. Her mouth twisted then settled into a tight line.

Amelia's shoulders wilted and sagged. It was all making sense now. Bryon hadn't revealed her grandparents' names. No wonder she had received an invitation. She lifted her head with determination. "My grandparents are amazing people," she said with as much confidence as she could muster.

Mrs. Preston's eyes bulged and her face grew red. Coldness seeped back into her gaze. With a jerk of her head to the next room, she rose. "Bryon, follow me please."

Bryon squeezed Amelia's hand before following the click, click, click of retreating feet.

"Alex," Mrs. Preston said as she left the room. Bryon's father followed them, flashing Amelia a look that conveyed sadness before he disappeared.

Howard rose from his chair. "This is about the time I make my great escape. Hate family drama." He was nearly out the door when he turned back to her. "Best of luck to you, Amelia."

She longed to run but instead sat with her eyes cast down. Her hands twisted and untwisted the folds of her lovely new gown. The tick-tock of the grandfather clock on the wall sounded loud within the walls of silence.

"It's not your fault," Rose said.

Amelia looked up into the warm chocolate brown eyes of Bryon's sister with whom she had so hoped for friendship.

"I guess I'm not what your mother wants for Bryon."

Rose slipped onto the settee beside her.

"Bryon confided to me how much he likes you."

"Rose." Mrs. Preston's sharp voice cut across the room. "Teatime is over. Bryon needs to take Amelia home."

Amelia almost laughed, for tea had never been served. She held her head high as she stood, squared her shoulders, just as she'd learned. Inside, she was dying. Mrs. Felicia had been right. There was no amount of schooling that could erase the stain of her humble beginning. She would never be good enough for this world.

With the decorum of complete grace and courage, she said good-bye to each of them directly, smiling politely, repeating their names with warmth and sincerity. The coldness in Mrs. Preston's eyes and the pity in the others' twisted her heart.

She reached into her reticule and pulled out the small box with the bracelet Grandmother had helped her pick out and held it out to Mrs. Preston, who turned away without accepting the gift.

"Mother." Bryon said, a cut in his voice.

Amelia slipped the gift back in her reticule. "Thank you for your hospitality," she said, as if she had thoroughly enjoyed her afternoon.

Bryon stepped forward to accompany her.

"I think it best I make my own way home."

"It's snowing." He moved close to her ear. "And we need to talk."

"A little snow has never hurt anyone. I can walk." She squared her shoulders and swept out the door already held open by the doorman.

She waited until she was around the corner before she gave way to the sting burning behind her lids and let the tears slip free. Her hands balled into tight fists. An equal blend of sadness and fury wrestled for dominance. She'd been worried she would never be enough for the Preston name, and she'd been right. How could Bryon have let her walk into that ambush?

CHAPTER 7

*A*melia snuck into the house and reached her bedroom without anyone knowing she was back. She spent the remainder of the afternoon vacillating between tears and anger. Bryon should've known his mother would not approve of a farm girl. That had to be the reason he'd not told his parents the truth about her. Had he expected her to lie about her heritage? And the prominent Richmond family she had ties to were apparently more of a hinderance than a help.

Oh, Father God, how could things have gone so wrong? I had such high hopes. How could You let me step into rejection again? What's wrong with me and the men I choose?

A silent voice pressed into her spirit. *You never asked Me into your decision.*

Amelia wanted to brush the words aside, but He was right. She'd not asked Him about Bryon. She'd gone full steam ahead with her plan to find a husband in the big city.

A sick feeling that she would never be good enough slithered through her. The thought curled around her heart and wound its way tighter with each thread of evidence. Even with the slimmer figure, even with her new etiquette, even if she wore all the latest fashions, she was still a farm girl from a poor family, not good enough for the men at home, not good enough for the men in Richmond.

But it was Christmas day, and she had to find the strength to pretend nothing was wrong for her grandparents' sake. The fingers of cruelty had stretched out to grip her, and it wouldn't take long before her grandparents started asking why Bryon was no longer coming to call. But not today.

She splashed water on her face and went downstairs for dinner. Tears bit behind her lashes as she slid into her chair at the table with her grandparents. Evergreens graced the center of the table, a single candle flickering in the dim light. Lydia set a glazed ham on one side of the centerpiece while the succulent smell of roasted turkey wafted from a plate on the opposite side. Mashed potatoes, winter squash, and turnips steamed from bowls, while pickles, coleslaw, cranberries, and applesauce, brought color to the feast. A steaming oyster pie sat in front of her. Normally, she would be salivating, but her stomach lurched in protest. She took a tiny portion of each dish and worked hard to choke down a few bites.

"After years of war and scrimping and scrounging this feast is most delightful, is it not, George? We best appreciate every bite."

Grandfather nodded but kept his eyes pinned on Amelia. "You might remind your granddaughter. She's pushing her food around her plate more than getting it into her mouth."

Grandmother whipped her gaze to Amelia. "Don't tell me you're still worried about your weight. You look fabulous, and it's Christmas."

Amelia let out a heavy sigh, thankful for the gift of a perfect excuse. "You're the one who told me every meal counts."

"Oh, pshaw." Her hand waved in protest. "Every meal but Christmas. Do enjoy, my dear. Why, we don't want this going to waste."

Grandmother prattled on. Her chatter was a welcome reprieve to the agony that dominated Amelia's mind. She forced the food down, smiled politely, and interjected enough to keep the conversation going.

If only Grandfather wouldn't keep looking straight through her with his piercing blue eyes.

"Frances dear, can we chatter about Irwins' lovely dish set some other time. I'd really like to hear how Amelia's afternoon went."

Grandmother dabbed at her mouth. "I was merely saving the best for last. You know me. I like to savor the good stuff over a hot cup of coffee and some plum pudding, but if you can't wait…" She gestured in Amelia's direction. "Do tell. Seems your grandfather is most impatient."

A heated flush rushed to her cheeks.

"Look, she wears that charming tone. This must be good." Grandmother placed her cloth napkin on her lap and rubbed her hands together. "Young love is ever so delightful."

"It…was interesting. Bryon has a wonderful family. I especially liked his sister, Rose."

Grandmother beamed. "Tell me everything." She clapped softly. "Don't leave out a single detail. I do remember their lovely home, but I'm sure updates have been done, so fill me in on what the parlor looks like now. And what did they wear? What did they serve? Did Melinda Preston ask about us—"

"Give the girl a chance to speak, Frances." Grandfather shook his head and turned toward Amelia.

She shifted in her chair and picked at an imaginary piece of lint on her lap, keeping her eyes downcast. Her grandparents had been nothing but kind to her, and she didn't have the heart to hurt them with the truth.

"The house was grand." Her eyes darted between the two of them and back down again. "Why, the parlor was absolutely beautiful. A crystal chandelier stretched from one end of the room to the other."

Grandmother leaned closer. "I do remember that parlor. I was invited for tea once, but that was years ago." Her smile faded. "Go on."

"The far wall is all windows, with these beautiful velvet crimson drapes that hang between each of the five window panels. I bet they need those for the summer months, because the wall was facing the afternoon sun."

Grandfather's eyebrows knit together, and deep lines furrowed his brow. "Bryon's mother and father...were they friendly?"

She averted her gaze and struggled for words. A strange look passed between her grandparents.

Amelia chose the truth. "They were friendly for about the first twenty minutes."

The joy on Grandmother's face faded like the sun covered by a storm cloud.

Grandfather pushed back his chair and rose from the dinner table. He ambled his way over without taking his eyes from Amelia. A canyon of pain crossed his kind face, and he took Amelia's hand. "I understand why you've lost your appetite. Let's retire to the parlor."

The bustle of Grandmother's skirt followed as they made their way into the next room. Amelia sank into the cushions of the settee, with Grandmother close beside her. Grandfather slid into a chair across the room.

"I thought you looked like you'd been crying when you sat down to the meal," Grandfather said, shaking his head.

"Oh honey, what did they say?" Grandmother's voice wavered as she clutched Amelia's hand. "What happened? By the way Bryon was over here all the time, I thought they didn't have a problem...with the past."

"It seems Bryon never revealed that we're related. They

knew my surname, but not Brunson." Amelia lifted the handkerchief and dabbed at the corner of her eyes. "He must've known his mother would react in the way she did, or he would've told her. I can't tell you how disappointed I am in him."

"I know from experience that Melinda Preston is a force to be reckoned with. There may be some reasoning to Bryon's decision," said Grandmother.

"His mother's disapproval became obvious as I discussed my country roots, but when she found out I was related to..." Amelia didn't have the heart to finish what Mrs. Preston's attitude was toward their family. "She stormed out, taking Bryon and his father with her."

Grandmother clucked and shook her head. "Those highfalutin biddies have no idea the great people they never meet because of their haughtiness. Sad to say, I was once one of them." Sorrow and shame filled her eyes as she drew Amelia into a warm hug.

Amelia soaked in the warmth and pulled gently back. "I'm sorry, Grandmother."

"There's no need for you to be sorry. This is water long under our bridge. I'm just sorry it has now touched your life. What happened then?"

"They came back in, and Bryon's mother dismissed me as if I were a nuisance, not an invited guest, declaring it was time for Bryon to take me home. I chose to walk."

"You walked home?"

"I needed to be alone. I was honest with Bryon about my upbringing right from the beginning. At the very least he should've told me his parents didn't know. I was so humiliated with the condescending tone Mrs. Preston used when I told her I came from the Shenandoah Valley. But her anger at the mention of your name... What happened that she would be so angry, all these years later?"

Grandmother and Grandfather exchanged looks.

Grandfather's bushy brows knit together like one gigantic caterpillar. "Last year when your mother visited, we discussed the past. When you wanted to move here, she gave me permission to tell you the rest of the story if need be. Katherine already knows the details, and since you're caught in the web of our demise, you have every right to understand."

"We were hoping enough time had gone by, and people would be kinder," Grandmother said. "But no, they judge and keep their cruel judgements. Your mother is a salt-of-the-earth kind of woman. Her only fault was to love and marry your father, a poor servant boy. Their love, I might add, has lasted a lot longer than the affection in many high-society marriages around here." She sniffed pulling a lace-fringed handkerchief from her pocket to her nose. "Oh George, this is all my fault. I spoiled Emmaline beyond reason."

"No point in casting blame, Frances. You may have spoiled her, but I sat back and let it happen. We failed both girls, one with too much praise and indulgence and the other with not enough." He pulled himself up and tottered across the room to his wife. "There, there, my dear." He patted her sagging shoulders. "We cannot unwind the clock."

He turned toward Amelia. "There have been too many lies for far too many years, covering up for our wayward daughter, Emmaline. We spoiled and coddled her from day one."

Grandmother nodded and dabbed at her eyes. "'Tis true."

"From a beautiful child she grew into a stunning young woman. The whole community was drawn to her outward beauty, the men especially. From the time she was twelve, they were knocking down the door. She had the power to have them eating out of her hand in a matter of seconds. If only the inside of her had been half as lovely. All the attention went to her head, and the downward spiral began."

Grandfather stopped, and Grandmother blew her nose into

her handkerchief. "This next part is the hardest to tell, but you need to know."

Amelia looked at the two of them. She wanted to know, and yet she didn't.

"Emmaline started her dark descent by seducing a young servant, your father. She pretended to love him only because her sister truly did, and she got pregnant.

"Pregnant?" That meant Pa had another child somewhere. No, that couldn't be.

"Your mother married your father, having always loved him, and took her sister's baby in. This allowed your father to keep his daughter and Emmaline to breeze back onto the social scene with a fresh start."

If they kept the baby, then... Amelia gasped. "Katherine? Katherine is my half-sister?"

"Yes."

"And Ma is her aunt?"

They both nodded.

"That makes so much sense now."

"What do you mean?" Grandmother's head lifted.

"Ma has always been...different with Katherine. And there's been this tension between Ma and Pa concerning her."

"We should've been honest in the beginning, George, and insisted Emmaline take responsibility. Then maybe—"

"Frances, stop. We can't go back. We wanted to save face as much as Emmaline did. And truth is, Katherine was obviously better off."

But how did this involve the here and now? Amelia's head was swimming. "I don't understand. Surely Mrs. Preston is still not carrying a grudge about my mother marrying a servant after all these years, and she wouldn't know what Emmaline did, would she?

"It gets worse. Emmaline kept on with her wicked ways, and we turned a blind eye. Over the years we covered up for many things she did, but it all culminated into public disgrace when she ran off with a married man, a man who'd been married to Mrs. Preston's best friend."

Amelia's hand went to her mouth. "Oh my." No wonder Mrs. Preston wanted nothing to do with the family. She would assume the whole family was the same.

"I'm so sorry this is touching your life," said Grandmother. Her hand reached out.

Amelia placed her arm around her grandmother, who was softly weeping. How disappointing it must be to raise a child who caused such shame.

"You're such a sweet one." Grandmother patted Amelia's hand that was settled on her shoulder. "You remind me of your mother so much." She brushed a wayward lock of hair from Amelia's face. "I'm supposed to be consoling you, and here you are consoling me."

"It's sad for all of us, Grandmother."

"What will you and Bryon do?" Grandmother dabbed at her red nose with her lacy handkerchief.

The tears stinging behind Amelia's lashes broke free. "I hope you understand." She gulped back a sob. "But I can't talk about this right now." How could she begin to answer that question when, whichever way she looked at it, she felt less than? Even Bryon was too ashamed of her heritage to tell his parents. With a quick kiss to each of her grandparents' cheeks, she scurried from the room, her skirt billowing around her ankles. She stumbled down the hall and into her bedroom, blinded by the hot tears.

She dropped onto the feather quilt, and great heaving sobs racked her body. To muffle the sound, she turned her head into the fluffy pillows. The day had started out as the best Christmas of her life, only to turn into the worst.

CHAPTER 8

The parlor was quiet. Only Rose and Bryon remained. Afternoon tea had been served, but no one had partaken. Bryon stared blankly into the crackling fire. The sparks danced in a frolic of fire and flame, devouring the logs, much like his life had just been engulfed and consumed.

Rose stood and marched across the room. "I can't believe you." She pointed her finger in his face.

He lifted his eyes to her. "What?"

"How could you have done such a thing? And then you let her walk out into the snow instead of running after her."

"I had no idea Mother would launch into an inquisition at the first meeting."

"Of course she was going to prod for information, you dummy." She slid down beside him on the settee.

"She's never done that with anyone else I've courted."

"Because she knew the families and their history going back to before you were born. She didn't know Miss Williams at all. What were you thinking?"

"I thought I'd have a little time for everyone to get to know her and love her—"

"Come on, Bryon. For such a smart guy, you can be the thickest sometimes. Even if Mother could get over Amelia's lack of social standing, what did you think would happen when she found out she was a Brunson?"

"She's not a Brunson. She's a Williams."

"You're splitting hairs. You know how mother and Mrs. Brunson have thrown daggers at each other in public for years. That was her best friend's husband that their daughter ran off with. What did you expect with Amelia caught in the middle?"

"I didn't think it through."

"I doubt she'll ever talk to you again, but at the very least, you need to get over there and apologize. And the sooner the better."

"Rose." Their mother's voice had his sister spinning toward the door. "What are you encouraging your brother to do?"

"I...I..."

"You can take your advice and leave. If Bryon wants what is best for that girl, he will leave her alone as I have instructed. In return, I'll allow her to enter the social scene with the blessing of my silence. She can find any husband she likes, and my lips will be sealed. But if Bryon insists on fraternizing with that family, I'll make it hell for everyone concerned."

"Mother," Rose gasped.

"Don't you mother me."

"You have no idea the pain that family caused my dearest friend Loribeth. It would be of utmost insult to have my son courting anyone from that family."

Bryon heard the spiel for the second time that day. It was what had stopped him from running after Amelia. To what end? To cause her more hurt? He knew what a force his mother could be and the influence she wielded in the community. Any chance of Amelia finding her way in Richmond would be hampered by the wagging tongues of cruel and unusual gossip. No, he could not do that to her. At least this way she would have a chance to find a suitable husband. The thought took his breath away and squeezed his heart as if in a vice.

But he would take his sister's advice without his mother knowing, because at the very least Amelia deserved an explanation and his apology. As soon as he could slip away undetected, he would go to her.

～

A light tap at her bedroom door interrupted Amelia's maudlin thoughts. The last few days had been sorrow filled. She lifted her head from the pillow, where she had been taking an afternoon nap. All she wanted was to close her eyes and forget how cruel the world had turned in a matter of days.

"Amelia." Grandmother poked her head in the room. "Bryon is at the door. He's insisting that he must see you."

Amelia sat up and ran her hands through her tangled hair and looked down at her rumpled dress. The last thing she was prepared for was a visitor, and especially not Bryon.

"I don't want to see him—"

"Give him a moment of your time, dear. What would it hurt to hear him out?"

"My heart. That's what hurts."

Her grandmother nodded but still stood waiting.

How could she explain how the whole incident had rocked her world and taken far more emotional toll than anyone would know? Every bit of confidence she had built up in taking Mrs. Felicia's course had been dashed. And her trust in Bryon had been shaken, especially after what she had gone through with Edmund.

"Do you want me to tell him to go?" Her grandmother's voice was hesitant and soft.

"I'll talk to him, though I don't see the point. Clearly his mother doesn't like me." She stood and peeked into the mirror. "Give me a few minutes to freshen up."

"All right, dear. I'll invite him in." She lifted one shoulder. "Truthfully, I already did. It's snowing again out there." The door clicked behind her.

Amelia took her time. She both dreaded and longed to see him. Her sorry heart didn't understand it shouldn't beat faster at the thought of him. She fashioned her unruly hair into a knot at the nape of her neck and changed out of her rumpled day dress.

As she made her way from her room, their voices came from the parlor. Her grandparents were chatting as if the man hadn't just broken her heart. She entered with her chin up, despite her low spirits.

Bryon rose. His eyes held such warmth and sadness, she had to turn away. "I have the carriage waiting if you're up to a ride? Warm rocks and blankets supplied." His voice held a plea.

The last thing she wanted was to be reminded of the hope and that kiss they'd shared the last time they were in the carriage together.

She hesitated just long enough for her Grandmother to chime in. "You've been cooped up for days. Some fresh air and change of scenery would do you good."

Amelia raised her eyebrows at her grandmother.

"Please?" Bryon practically begged.

She'd best have the conversation she needed to have with him privately. "All right."

A smile split his dimples free.

She didn't want to encourage him. "Let's get this over with," she said, as he grabbed her winter cloak.

The smile and dimples vanished.

She walked ahead of him to the waiting carriage and accepted the coachman's hand as she stepped up, ignoring

Bryon's offer to help. She didn't want to feel his touch for fear she would forget her anger.

They rode in silence for a short distance. His hand caught hers as the carriage lurched to a stop. She pulled it away, as they carried on across the intersecting road. She looked out the window, where snow swirled around them.

"Please, Amelia, will you look at me?"

She turned his way. His eyes glimmered like wet pebbles from a brook, melting the ice in her heart.

"I'm so sorry." His words drenched in longing and sorrow crashed into her soul. "I hope you can forgive me for what happened. I should've expected that my mother would launch into a hundred questions. What a fool I've been—"

"Tell me. Did you know about the bad blood between our families?"

He swallowed, his Adam's apple bobbing. "I remembered there had been something between the name Brunson and my mother, but I didn't know what. I did know my mother carries a grudge for a long time and had an inkling that, whatever it was, it could still be a sticking point. That was why I never mentioned your grandparents or their surname. I was hoping they would get to know you and love you before facing that."

"And what about my childhood? Were you too ashamed of me to tell them the truth?"

"I'm not at all ashamed of you." He reached out his hand, but she didn't take it. It fell down beside her. "I did have that discussion with my parents about not wanting to be the heir. They were so hurt and devasted. They confided why they felt Howard was not capable of taking on the responsibility of the family. He seeks only a good time, doesn't want to work, and is a spendthrift." He stopped short of revealing the worst. "I couldn't go through with it. But I did receive what I wanted the most, their blessing to choose my own wife. I truly thought that choice could include whomever, from whatever background I wanted."

"Why didn't you discuss any of this with me? The history between the families or your mother's prejudice regarding background and breeding."

"I didn't want to hurt you. You'd worked so hard at the finishing school, which I didn't even think you needed in the first place. And I believed that if my family could just get to know you, they'd love you. Then the complications would be smoothed over."

"Instead, I was left humiliated, trying to find the words—"

He grimaced. "I know. Rose gave me a tongue-lashing. My approach was flawed. Keeping the details about who you were from my parents was wrong. I beg your forgiveness." His rich blue eyes glimmered.

"I've already forgiven you, Bryon, but that doesn't mean I understand. If you knew the potential problems from the moment you saw my grandparents' names on the gatepost, why did you keep visiting? Why did you let me...?" She dare not reveal how deeply she had fallen for this man.

"I was drawn to everything about you. Your unpretentious ways. Your beautiful spirit. Your laughing eyes I get lost in each time you look at me the way you are right now. It took no more than that first walk for me to fall completely in love with you."

She gasped, lifting a gloved hand to her mouth. She had not been prepared for those words, though her heart danced in delight.

"Yes. I love you, but I have no right to." His knuckles brushed down the side of her cheek before he lowered his hand. "Out of selfishness, I pursued you. Your engaging conversation and gentle personality were so different from any other woman I've ever known. You drew me, even though I tried to stay away. What a selfish fool to put you through this. I'll never stop loving you, but out of fairness to you I have to let you go."

Her heart clutched. "Why?"

"Do you like it in Richmond better than in the country?"

"Yes." But mostly because he was there and had made the transition so wonderful. What would city life be without him?

"I thought so."

"Why do you ask?" She dug her fingers into her palms. This couldn't be happening.

"You witnessed my mother in action. She's promised to either make your life wonderful as you enter the social scene, or miserable, depending on what we decide. She has threatened to stir things up for your grandparents, too, if we continue seeing each other. And trust me when I say, she has her ways. You don't deserve a hostile environment every time you walk down the street. And I'll never subject you to another display of what you witnessed the other day in my home. To be fair to you, I need to step away. I'm so angered and disappointed in my mother. She is wonderful until she turns against a person. At that point, her nasty side comes out."

Amelia could no longer hold back the watery flow. Her chin quivered, and Bryon thumbed a tear from her cheek before dragging her close. He rocked her in his arms.

"My mother would destroy your beautiful spirit, and I can't ask that of you." He smoothed his hands up and down her back until she quieted.

The soft clip-clop of the horse's hoofs stopped, and she realized they were back in front of her house. There was no hope. She couldn't make her grandparents lives miserable at their age. And it meant everything to her grandmother that she make a grand entrance into society. But what would be the point when she could not have Bryon?

She lifted her gaze to his sad blue eyes. "I guess this is good-bye."

"Good bye, sweet one." His lips lowered to within an inch of hers. She could feel his breath fan her cheeks.

She meant only to kiss his cheek, but the moment she lifted her lips, his mouth crushed hers. A desperate, frantic play of pleasure and pain ensued. She shouldn't allow him to kiss her with such passion, but she couldn't squelch the desire to touch, feel, love him in return. They belonged together.

Amelia pulled away from his embrace and practically fell out of the carriage in her haste. She ran toward the house without looking back.

As she stepped into the foyer, an option came to mind, one she hadn't wanted to consider before. She could go back to the valley. To face the newly married couple, Edmund and Helen, would be child's play compared to meeting Bryon at social functions or on the street. Her heart was far more invested than it had ever been with Edmund. She needed to sort out her feelings, where she wanted to live and what she would do with her future. Maybe it would be best she find a farmer husband after all. Surely, back in the valley, she'd be accepted for who she was. She had certainly failed in high society Richmond.

Maybe you should stay right where you are and let Me direct your path.

She pushed the inconvenient whisper of the Spirit aside. She wanted to run, and she would run.

CHAPTER 9

*A*melia had barely stepped off the train when she heard Ma's voice. "Land sakes, girl. You're thin. What in the world has happened to you?"

Ma wrapped her fleshy arms around Amelia in a tight hug and wouldn't let go. Amelia pressed back the urge to cry in the comfort of her mama's arms. "I've missed you so much."

With her hands on Amelia's shoulders, Ma pulled back. Her eyes traveled from head to toe. She clucked with her tongue. "I leave you in the care of my mother, and you come back thinner than a blade of grass."

"I'm fine. I'm healthy."

Ma's hand flew out, batting the air. "Balderdash. Let's get you home and feed you a decent meal." She nodded at a wiry thin man with a thick mustache that covered far too much of his narrow visage. "William, can you grab Amelia's luggage?"

The young man hopped to the task but not before he threw a winsome smile Amelia's way.

Amelia ignored his attention, rather annoyed that, since she'd lost the weight, far too many men were looking her way. She only had eyes for one, and he was as far removed as this valley was from Richmond. Her heart squeezed tightly, and a hollow feeling tunneled through. She worked hard to shake the melancholy that haunted her.

"Where are the girls? I thought for sure they'd be here."

"I decided to be selfish. Pa is out in the field working, and the girls are preparing a special meal for your return. I wanted to have you to myself for a few moments. I've missed you more than I can say." She squeezed Amelia's arm and propelled her from the train station.

"Amelia. Is that you?"

Amelia swiveled to look into the shocked face of Edmund. Her chin went up, and she gave him a quick nod.

"You look amazing. City life sure agrees with you."

Somehow, the satisfaction she thought she would get from Edmund's attention had the opposite effect. Her hands fisted into tight balls. She wanted to bob him in the nose. She had no desire to engage in small talk with someone so shallow. She dismissed him with a turn of her head. "Mother, where did you say the carriage was?" She swept out of the building.

Ma came running. "Well, that was—"

"Riding in style, I see." Amelia had no desire to discuss Edmund.

After a quick look behind her, Ma said, "It looked like rain, and Katherine insisted we take their rig. Not that she had to twist my arm." Ma sank into the cushioned seats. "I must admit, at my age, I rather like the comfort. Now my dear, I want to hear every detail about your time in Richmond, but most on my mind is the reason for your sudden return."

Amelia was thankful for the clunk and bang of her luggage being loaded. She had expected this question, just not so soon.

Good thing the train ride had given her ample time to drum up a reasonable scenario.

"I got more homesick than I imagined." Amelia's stomach flip-flopped. It was not an out-and-out lie, for homesickness had materialized at Christmas.

"But your letters said how much you loved the city."

The carriage lurched forward, and she had to raise her voice over the crunch of the wheels on gravel.

"I did...I do. But I left the valley so quickly when I should've taken a bit more time to ease myself into a change. Christmas turned out to be very difficult. It's all right that I'm home, isn't it?"

Ma patted her knee. "Of course. You never have to question that. Jeanette wanted your bedroom, and I'm sure glad I told her that no one was moving into your room yet."

"Thanks, Ma."

Ma lifted a gloved hand and trailed it down Amelia's cheek. "So glad to have you home."

Amelia forced a smile she did not feel. She had fooled one. Now for the others. She needed time to sort out her future. Maybe God would make it clear in the tranquility of the valley.

Maybe you should ask.

She hated these troublesome thoughts that kept plaguing her, as if God were not pleased with her decision. Surely He understood that her heart had just been broken for the second time.

~

"Why are you back, Amelia?"

Amelia's eyes shifted from her sister to the lavish room Katherine called her parlor.

"What have you done to this room? For a tomboy-gone-lady,

your talent amazes me. Why, it would rival even the snobby Melinda Preston's taste in décor."

"I don't know who Melinda Preston is, and Josiah doesn't have the word *no* in his vocabulary when it comes to anything I want. More importantly, I can see right through you." She shook her finger in Amelia's direction. "Quit trying to avoid my question."

Her sister's perceptiveness rankled. Amelia squared her shoulders and removed her gloves with care. "I came for tea, not an inquisition."

"Too bad." Katherine's large blue eyes sparkled as she flung her long black hair behind her back. "Josiah loves my hair down, but I'll have to get this out of my eyes, preferably before it lands in my tea. You have a short reprieve while I attend to this mess." She sauntered toward the door and turned back waving her finger. "Be prepared to spill the beans when I return."

Delilah bustled in. "Land sakes, girl. Don't just sit there. Come give old Delilah a hug." Her smile widened to include a row of pearly white teeth against dark glistening skin. She held out her fleshy arms and smothered Amelia in one of her famous hugs. "Your ma is right when she said you been losing too much weight. We're so glad to have you back."

Amelia could picture Delilah and her Ma going on about her well-being. They had a penchant for sharing recipes and gossip.

"I best get supper underway, but I just had to say hello and tell you how much we've been missing you. Make sure you stop by the shop and say hello to Abe. He'd be right put out if you didn't." She bustled away, her wide hips swaying beneath the folds of her sensible dress and apron.

Amelia slid back into her chair. Could she tell her sister the truth? She had fought the urge to discuss anything with Ma, knowing the way she'd been treated by Richmond society in the past. It would only bring back painful memories. Katherine was probably the only person in the world who Amelia could confide in.

Katherine strolled into the parlor with a long thick braid hanging down her back and baby Seth in her arms. "Sit." She commanded in her usual bossy tone.

Amelia slid to the chair in defeat.

"I have to feed Seth. Perfect opportunity to chat." She settled into the rocker to breastfeed. "And don't give me this nonsense about missing the valley. Remember all the letters you wrote? You said you were born for city life. And what about this wonderful man you told me you met? Now, out with it."

"Motherhood looks good on you, Sis."

"It's amazing." Katherine's smile blossomed like an unfolding rose. "Just you wait. You'll love it."

"I'm sure I'll be waiting a long time. I seem to pick the wrong men."

Katherine's eyes lifted from her child. "What happened to Mr. Blue eyes Bryon."

Amelia's gaze dropped to her lap. "History."

"What history, exactly."

"Your mother and my mother are the problem."

Katherine knit her brows together, took a moment, and nodded. "So, you know?"

"Yes." Amelia swallowed hard against the knot in her throat. "And the man I fell for, Bryon Preston, just happens to have a mother who abhors Emmaline. Needless to say, between my humble beginnings and Emmaline running off with Mrs. Preston's best friend's husband, I'll never be suitable for her eldest son."

"Oh my."

"I haven't said a word to Ma and Pa. Why hurt them with the truth?"

Katherine moved the blanket from one shoulder to the other and shifted the baby. Soft suckling sounds filled the silent room.

"I'm back here to sort out my future, mostly because Bryon lives near our grandparents, and I don't want to run into him." She bit down on her bottom lip to still the quiver and slapped both hands on her knees. "Enough about that. It looks like you and Josiah are doing well."

Katherine's smile was wide and natural. "I have to pinch myself most days to be sure this is real. I truly am happy. I never knew that loving and being loved could be so amazing."

Amelia's eyes filled with tears.

"I know. It's cruel of me to go on about love the way I am, but that's because I'm not going to let you give up so easily. You can take a few weeks to sort out your feelings, during which time you should concentrate on learning how to run a big household as Mrs. Preston. I'd be happy to run through some things you'll need to know, and then Grandmother can take over when you return."

Amelia's cheeks burnt hot. "Mrs. who?"

Katherine laughed. "Yup, you and me, we've always worn the truth on our cheeks. That tell-tale red says it all. You've been dreaming of that last name and don't you deny it. I'm going to buy you a train ticket back to Richmond, and I'll get Josiah to throw you on if I have to."

"You have no say. I live with Ma and Pa." Panic bit at her mind.

"Watch me, Amelia. Just you watch me."

"I'll never be good enough." She squeezed her simple dress in her fists. "You don't understand."

"Look at me," Katherine commanded.

Amelia lifted her eyes.

"Remember the girl who used to ride about the countryside with a rifle, wearing our brothers' dungarees? That was me. And if I can marry a rich man born into privilege and learn how to be his wife, then anyone can—especially my genteel sister who has impeccable manners and an innate sense of class. Most of what I had to learn, you already know."

"But—"

"No buts. I'll let you lick your wounds, but the whole time I'll be sharing with you all the joys of love in hopes you'll find the gumption to fight for it."

"You're bossy."

Katherine laughed. "And you're going back to Richmond."

CHAPTER 10

*A*melia stood behind a basin full of breakfast dishes lost in her thoughts. Though her head told her to leave Bryon in the past, her heart kept taking her down memory lane. Did he think of her? What was he doing at that moment? Probably at the bank, dressed in a suit looking professional and handsome. She brushed the thought of how attractive he was out of her mind. Why had it been so easy to say good-bye to Edmund, but not Bryon? He was just another bad decision, wasn't he?

"Amelia," Ma said, "we're taking the morning off and going for a walk in the orchard."

Amelia kept her voice as lighthearted as she could manage. "I'm headed to Katherine's as soon as these dishes are done. She's going to teach me—"

"Then I'll walk you there. I want to talk to you, alone." She waved her hands at the girls still seated around the table. "Jeanette, you take over washing, and Lucinda and Gracie, you dry."

Jeanette turned around as if to argue, took one look at Ma's expression, and bit her lip.

Amelia dried her soapy hands on her apron and headed to the porch to bundle up. She slipped on her hooded winter shawl and a pair of thick gloves. "Ma, you don't have to go out in the cold. Why don't we talk later?"

Ma nodded her head toward the kitchen. "I want some privacy."

Amelia turned away quickly, her stomach knotting. The last thing she needed was an inquisition from her mother.

The crunch of old snow crackled beneath their boots as they traveled the well-worn path to Katherine's. The stark nakedness of the trees allowed the sun's watery rays to shimmer against the whitewash of winter.

Ma placed a hand on Amelia's arm and pulled her to a stop. "We've always been able to talk. Can't you share why one day you were sending letters about how much you love the city and the next day you came home?"

Heat rushed to Amelia's face. She'd never made a good liar. "I'm fine. I told you—"

"Mercy sake. You're about as fine as paper in the rain. And don't give me that homesick story again. I want the truth."

Amelia gulped back her ready lie. "I didn't want to hurt you."

Ma's eyes squinted. "Hurt me how?"

"The man I fell in love with is Bryon Preston. Melinda and Alex Preston's son.

"Oh, no." Ma's hand flew to her mouth.

"And with the past—"

"You don't need to explain. I know the family, and I understand that city and their prejudices all too well." Her eyes dropped to the snow. "I'd love nothing more than for you to marry a humble farmer like I did. But you've fallen in love with a very rich man's heir. With Richmond's snobbery, you'll never be accepted."

Amelia lifted her hand. "I know, and I'm fine."

"No, you're not. That city has lulled and drawn you in, only to spit you out like it did me." Her gloved hand smoothed a trail down the side of Amelia's face.

"I can't talk about it right now." She blinked back a rush of stinging tears. "I'll carry on to Katherine's alone if you don't mind. I need to collect my composure."

Ma nodded. "I understand." She drew her into a warm hug. "I'm so sorry, my dear."

"So am I." She pulled out of the hug and turned toward Katherine's home. The mud-stained snow mirrored the gray of her heart.

~

The past few days she had tried her hardest to erase all sadness from her expression. It was exhausting. Now she gazed into her bedroom mirror. "You could not look more miserable," Amelia whispered to her reflection. "Get that grump off your face." She ran a finger under the dark shadows circling her eyes. A smile and a quick pat of the white powder Katherine had given her would do the trick. At the very least she hoped the forced happiness would stop Ma from insisting that food cured every woe.

Moving back to the valley had not been the antidote for her broken heart that she had hoped. Nor was she able to dismiss Bryon with a bit of distance as she had Edmund.

She missed the sound of the church bells ringing out the top of the hour, the cry of the newsboy hawking the latest edition, the sparkle of the James River in the distance. She missed city life and her grandparents more than she'd anticipated. But if she were honest, she missed Bryon and his lopsided grin and flashing dimples the most. With a deep sigh, she turned from the mirror.

Should she take Katherine's advice and get back to the city

sooner rather than later. How miserable would Melinda Preston make her life and her grandparents if she pursued Bryon? The only way to find out would be to go back and have an honest conversation with her grandparents. If they were up to taking Melinda Preston on, then why shouldn't Amelia fight for Bryon. One thought of Melinda Preston sent a shudder from tip to toe. But had his parents not made the promise to Bryon that he could choose his wife? Why shouldn't she be his choice? She could fake it enough to get by in public, and Bryon loved her just the way she was. Didn't he?

That constant niggling thought of not being good enough surfaced each time she gained an ounce of courage. But she couldn't get Bryon out of her mind. Maybe that was God's sign she should fight for him.

Why don't you ask Me?

She lifted her skirt in both hands and headed down the stairs. Deep down, she didn't want to hear a no. Besides, there was breakfast to make. With a sweep of her hand, she swung the apron off the hook in the kitchen. She wrapped it around her slim body and faced her mother. "What do you want done first, the bacon or the biscuit batter?"

Ma's eagle eyes bore into her, and she turned away.

"I love your biscuits," Lucinda said, as she set the breakfast table.

"Me too," Gracie piped in. Her small hands were full with a handful of forks that clanged as she dropped them on the table in a heap.

"Biscuits it is." Her sisters had saved her from another lecture from Ma on the importance of eating enough.

Jeanette stepped into the room holding her head. "I'm going to pass on breakfast today. My stomach feels really off." She swayed on her feet, and Amelia hurried to her sister's side. Before her legs folded beneath her, Amelia caught the fall.

"Get the smelling salts, Ma. Lucinda, grab a pillow."

"She's coming to." Ma raised the back of Jeanette's head to slide a pillow underneath. "Land sakes girl, you had us scared. You just missed the stove on your way down. If not for Amelia here..."

Everyone had crowded around. "Give her some room and a chance to breathe." Amelia waved them back.

Jeanette struggled to sit up. Amelia kept a hand tucked behind her head. "Take a deep breath, Jeanette. As soon as the dizziness has passed, we're going to get you into bed. There's been a nasty flu running through Katherine's house. I guess it's found its way here."

"I...I don't know what happened." Jeanette massaged her temples. "I have a splitting headache."

"I'll help you to your feet." Ma took one arm and Amelia took the other. They lifted as she stood. Her legs wobbled but managed to get her up the stairs and to her bed.

"I'll sit with her a bit and make sure she's all right," Amelia offered. "She'll need some liquids. Please bring a glass of water, and we best put on some chicken broth."

Ma nodded. "Amelia, you're a natural at this. You've always been so good when someone gets sick."

In that moment it became clear to Amelia what her backup plan would be. If she couldn't have Bryon, then she would become a nurse.

The thought dropped in as if from heaven. Funny thing how that felt like more of a word from God than chasing after Bryon did. Both options meant returning to Richmond. At least that much was clear.

～

LATE JANUARY 1869
RICHMOND

*B*ryon stared out the library window. Winter could not be longer nor grayer. His work at the bank was the only bit of sanity he had. His mother kept insisting on his attendance at dinner parties, thrusting woman after woman in his direction. Their dull conversation, incessant chatter, and exaggerated flutter of eyelashes had him coming undone.

Amelia had never been versed in such silliness. He longed for her heartfelt discussions and unpretentious ways. His heart squeezed tight. Had he made the right decision? He shouldn't have pushed her away. He should've taken on his parents and demanded they stick to their side of the bargain and let him choose his wife. But to invite her into a family with such hostility…? How could that be right?

"There you are, son." His mother swept into the room with a swish of petticoats and a waft of expensive perfume. "I've been looking for you." He didn't bother to turn from the window. "All the guests have arrived and are seated. Are you coming?"

He rolled his eyes to the back of his head before he turned her way.

"Do you remember Shelby?"

"I vaguely recall someone by that name, but it's Amelia I remember well."

"Amelia. Amelia. Will you quit going on about that girl? I heard she returned to the country where she belongs and has probably married a farmer by now."

"It's only been a month." But his stomach twisted at the thought. Had she forgotten him so quickly?

"Shelby is absolutely lovely, and she remembers you." His mother held out her arm. "Do escort me to the table, and wipe that scowl off your face. One of your best features are your dancing dimples, and we've seen far too little of them of late."

Bryon had to work on being respectful. He loved his parents but struggled with his mother and the things he was learning about her as an adult. He walked her to the dining room, all done up in its finery as if they were royalty, and slipped into his designated spot. He blew out a sigh. Life without Amelia felt bland and pointless.

"I can see you want to be here as much as I do."

Bryon turned toward the lovely blonde. He stifled back a yawn. "You got that right."

She leaned toward him and said under her breath, "Seems our parents are bent on pushing us together."

"You're very perceptive." He sat back in his chair and gave her a sideways glance. Maybe she was as irritated by the whole thing as he was. If they worked together, they could possibly keep their parent's at bay and buy a little freedom from the tedious courting game.

She whispered, "Obviously, you're as thrilled as I am at the prospect. How about we use this to our advantage?"

He smiled a genuine smile for the first time since he had said good-bye to Amelia. "You read my mind."

She laughed and managed to do so without batting her lashes. That took the edge off.

"Shelby, is it?

"I hate the name Shelby. It sounds so prissy. My friends call my Shelly."

"As long as friendship is all you want, we'll get on just fine. And when we get to friend status, I'll be sure to call you Shelly."

She laughed so loud the whole table turned in her direction, but she appeared not to care. She had a spunk that could help him stay removed from all women and give his sorry heart time to heal.

He'd been thinking on a plan. He would write Amelia and see if she would consider returning to the city. If she were brave enough, they could stand together and fight for what was theirs to choose. Love.

But...the mocking, the scorn, the ridicule Amelia would encounter, not to mention the damage his mother's wagging tongue would do to her aging grandparents.

He and Shelby chatted during dinner, earning pleased expressions from both sets of parents. When dessert was being served, his mother caught his eye and smiled.

Her pleasure only irritated him. He removed his smile, threw down his napkin, and waved off the dessert. Though he had set out to play the game, he had used up his quota of patience for one evening. He wanted that 'I told you so,' look off his mother's face.

He leaned toward the blond, keeping eye contact with his mother. "Thanks for an interesting evening, Shelby. But I'm heading out."

"I understand," she said. "Wish I could too."

He rose with a nod to the table and walked away. Surprisingly, he had liked a number of things about the petite blonde, but *like* was a world apart from love. There was a hazel-eyed beauty in a valley far away who'd stolen his heart. He doubted he would ever find it again. And to make his mother happy—the very woman who'd ripped them apart, turned the food in his gut sour.

He would do what he did most evenings, fill the loneliness with work. The door to the library swung wide. He settled into a chair behind the desk and pulled out a ledger to check Howard's entries. Surprisingly, his brother was showing a real aptitude for numbers. A smidgeon of good news, but what did it matter now? He had wanted Howard to succeed not only for Howard's well-being, but so he and Amelia could have the freedom to leave the estate and live wherever her little heart desired.

All so pointless now. He slapped the ledger shut.

CHAPTER 11

A leaden anchor dropped to the pit of Amelia's stomach as her eyes furtively skirted the kitchen. She wanted to look anywhere but at the scowl on her mother's face. She had asked Katherine to be present for backup, and backup she would need. The conversation was not going well.

"Can't you see that she must follow her heart, Ma?" Katherine insisted. "You can't protect her from getting hurt. She's hurting already."

Ma turned from vigorously stirring her pot of stew and waved the spoon in the air. "Katherine, you have no idea the world I came from, and I'm not prepared to send Amelia back to a city that so cruelly discards people."

"I don't know Richmond," Katherine said, "but I do know what it's like to have my parents control my destiny."

Ma's face crumbled, and she dropped into a nearby chair. Her head fell into her hands.

"Ma, I'm sorry." Katherine's voice gentled. "Things are

wonderful between Josiah and me now, but it was hard. Really hard. All I want for Amelia is the opportunity to choose, like you and Pa did all those years ago when you left Richmond together." Katherine crouched and placed an arm around Ma's shoulder.

Amelia had said all she could. Now she stood back praying.

Please God, let Ma see that I have to make my own way in life.

She had to return to the city and fight for what she wanted most—first Bryon, but at the very least, a career as a nurse. The idea of it had taken root and blossomed in the weeks since her sister's illness. Either way, she knew she no longer belonged in the valley. She didn't want to leave without her parents' blessing, but she had tried to get through to them to no avail. Katherine had an angle Amelia did not.

Ma brushed Katherine's arm free as she rose. Her chin jutted out, and her dark brown eyes flashed. She stomped to the pot-bellied stove and yanked the lid from the stew, slamming it on the counter. Her spoon dug in and went around and around. The only sound was the crack and pop of the fire burning hot.

Amelia stepped forward, but Katherine's hand came up to halt movement. She mouthed. "Wait." They both stared at the back of Ma's salt-and-pepper hair twisted into a tight bun, her arms stirring feverishly.

"All right, Katherine, you've made your point. I've often regretted thrusting you into an arranged marriage. I will not try to control a life that is not mine to control again." Her eyes shifted to Amelia. "And your Pa is already on your side anyway. Seems like I'm the odd one out. All I ask is that you find happiness."

Amelia sucked in a sharp breath of joy and flew into Ma's open arms. "Thank you. Thank you."

"Don't thank me. Thank your sister."

randmother beamed. "I'm beyond delighted to have you back. Sit down and fill me in on all that happened back home."

Amelia slid into the parlor chair, keeping her posture in mind. Strange that her heart felt so at home in the city. She held a sense of hope and renewed purpose burning inside her soul.

"The time back home was good to help me sort out what I really want. Two things really."

"Do tell." Grandmother lifted her teacup to her mouth and took a sip.

"Firstly, I want to start volunteering at the Bellevue Hospital."

"A worthwhile endeavor. It would not be my cup of tea." She held up her tea and laughed. "You know how I am at the sight of blood."

Amelia was not yet ready to voice her backup plan of becoming a nurse, but volunteering would give her a good idea of what the occupation entailed.

"And the second thing, my dear?"

"I know I can't keep running from my problems. I need to face Bryon and my broken heart.

"A broken heart I understand."

"What do you know about a broken heart?" Amelia asked.

"More than you would think. Your grandfather and I didn't have an easy road to married bliss." She laughed at her own humor, knowing Amelia had witnessed much bickering.

"Truly?"

"Our parents didn't like each other, and, though from the same social class, they made it all too clear we were not suitable for each other. Our hearts felt otherwise. A year passed while we were separated by these circumstances until we stole off to the next county one day and got married."

"You what?"

"There's nothing wrong with your ears."

"But...but how did your parents take that?"

"His parents, not so good. Being the only child, my parents capitulated. When we showed up on their doorstep two days later, their primary response was thankfulness to see I was all right. I announced they had two choices. One, send us packing and never see their daughter again, or two, take us in, give George a job at the bank and a chance to prove himself. Thankfully, the latter happened, and George excelled at everything he put his mind to. They grew to love him, more than me, I do believe." She smiled from behind her tea cup.

"We fought for what we wanted, and you have to do the same. Are you going to accept Melinda Preston's demands, or are you going to stand up for love? You do love him, don't you?"

"With all my heart. That's one of the reasons I returned. I have to at least try. I have to know I've done all I can."

"And Bryon?"

"He told me he loves me. But that was then. Who knows if his feelings have changed?"

"Well then, let's do all we can to help love find its way."

"Before you make plans, I have to tell you something. Bryon told me the reason he was breaking off with me was because his mother threatened to make life miserable for me...and for you and Grandfather if we carry on in the relationship."

Grandmother laughed.

That was not the response Amelia expected. Hadn't her grandmother shared how much influence Melinda Preston wielded?

"At our age, we care less and less about what others think."

"But you told me you were excited that she may once again embrace you into her circle," Amelia said.

"Pshaw." Her hand batted at the air. "It may have been nice to lay down the sword, but if she wants to pick it up, she'll find a worthy opponent in me. Besides, I have some wonderful friends. You've met the ladies who come for tea and those at my charity meetings."

She had met them and liked them.

"You'll find that not all the ladies paint everyone with the same brush." She patted Amelia's shoulder. "You, on the other hand, may suffer her gossiping tongue. Are you prepared for everyone to know you are a farmer's daughter and your grandparents are the Brunson's—the abysmal failures at parenting?"

Amelia gulped back a knot that formed in her throat. Would Bryon still want her if such knowledge were made public? Surely if he truly loved her...

"Bryon said that he was not ashamed of me. I have to try."

"That's the spirit." Grandmother clapped her hands in delight. "We'll start by launching you into Richmond society with our heads held high. Teas. Balls. And a spring Gala. In the end, parties speak far more to the masses than gossip."

"More than one?" The pulse in Amelia's throat fluttered, and her insides rolled. Would she be ready? Could she possibly remember all the rules and engage in light, meaningless conversation?

"Indeed. So much so that Rose will beg to attend and feel like she's left out of the best of the spring social scene when her snobby mother won't allow her to. Then, she'll put pressure on her mother to join, and Bryon will follow.

"But—"

"No buts. We'll combat Melinda's wagging tongue by giving them fun, fun, and more fun. Your grandfather's money will be put to wonderful use. And when they hear you're a farmer's daughter, we shall wow them with a beautiful princess. I'll get my own friends wagging their tongues at the fact that you come from a long line of aristocrats. Which is indeed true. Both my father and your grandfather's father were prominent members of society. Many will remember them."

"I'll need dance lessons." Amelia felt about as comfortable on the ballroom floor as she did posing as a socialite.

"Don't worry about that. We'll start with the teas, giving you ample time to learn the latest on the dance floor."

Amelia's stomach flip-flopped. She had confidence she would remember the steps, but it was her two left feet that were slow to follow. Could she really pull this off? Did she want to pull this off? Yes, she would master anything to make Bryon proud of her.

"We'll invite the Prestons for tea, but of course they won't come. However, we'll stir up quite the interest—create a splash around the beautiful new girl in town. Bryon will know you're back, and, by the time the Spring gala is thrown, the Preston children will beg to attend.

"And one more thing. You must walk slowly by Bryon's home daily. I want him to catch sight of you."

"I can't believe you're such a masterful schemer"—Amelia kissed her grandmother's cheek—"in such an endearing way."

Her laugher filled the room as she popped up as if she were years younger. Her hands rubbed together, and her eyes danced with mischief. "Watch and learn, Amelia. Watch and learn."

⁓

An apparition appeared outside his bedroom window. Someone with the perfect likeness to his beautiful Amelia. He shook his head and pulled his shirt on in haste. His hands trembled, struggling with the buttons as he moved closer to the window but out of view. There, in all her loveliness, Amelia stood with a parasol in hand. His heart squeezed tight and his skin tingled with awareness. Was it truly her? Or were his dreams coming alive, eating their way from his subconscious into reality. Had she returned?

She stared at the house, directly up to the second floor and his window.

It *was* her.

With a tilt of her lovely head, she smiled.

Riveted to the floor, he breathed in her loveliness. When she didn't move, he stepped out of the shadows with his hand lifted in a wave.

At the same instant she swiveled gracefully on her heels and disappeared behind the neighbor's hedge.

He flew down the steps and out the door. His legs couldn't move fast enough. Rubber limbs and lead feet slowed his pace. He slammed into the gate and struggled with the latch long enough to get a hold of himself.

What was he doing? He could run after her. He could catch up with her and look into those expressive hazel eyes. He could breathe in her loveliness and kiss her lips like he had dreamed of. But then what?

Nothing had changed. His mother and her unkind ways came to mind. The kindest thing he could do for Amelia was to rein in the desire to act upon impulse. He turned from the gate and walked back to the house with slow steps.

But why did she walk by his house and stop long enough to look up at his window? Was there an invitation in that exercise?

From that day forward, he kept his eyes peeled to the window when he got home from work each evening, in hopes of catching yet another glance. Each time he saw her, an ache gripped his heart. He couldn't stop himself from drinking in the sight of her loveliness, though he knew he could never have her. He loved her too much to subject her to a life of hostility. She returned day after day. He savored the moment like the sugar of life.

CHAPTER 12

*A*melia twirled in front of a large wall of mirrors. Her instructor, Pierre, counted out the steps to the galop, which she had mastered. Next came the polka, which she had practiced tirelessly. She'd learned every step by heart. Her feet, however, still sometimes decided not to cooperate, as they were doing at the moment.

"Keep moving, *mademoiselle*. Your feet will catch up to your quick brain. Most gentlemen will have the skill to cover a small faux pas, but if you stop, the entire room will be privy to your stumble." He whirled her around the floor.

She was thankful her grandparents had paid for private lessons and she could relax enough to make a mistake but carry on.

He clapped his hands in the air, and the small group of men playing their instruments stopped immediately.

"You've mastered everything but the Viennese waltz. It is wildly popular and much faster than the more sedate dances you have learned. Are you up to the challenge?"

Amelia wanted to scream no, but one thought of Bryon kept her going. She nodded, not sure her words would come out convincingly.

They started slowly, without music, as he explained the formation until she felt confident. When the musicians started the music, the real work began. Faster and faster she and her instructor whirled in wild abandonment, Pierre careening her around the dance floor in what she felt was a dangerous speed. She couldn't imagine doing this on a shared ballroom floor, much less with a room full of people watching.

"Whoa." She gasped for air as they finished. "That is craziness."

Pierre laughed. "You are a fast learner, mademoiselle. *Tu feras bien.*"

"I did not do fine. If you hadn't been my partner, I'd be sprawled on the floor right now." She shook her head. "This is popular?"

"*Oui, oui.*"

"I shall make sure I'm otherwise engaged when the music begins."

His laughter echoed through the room. "Come now"—he held out his right arm—"Enough conversation. Shall we let our feet do the talking?"

"Again?" That dance scared her.

"Again," he said. "And then again."

She rolled her eyes, and he rewarded her with his crooked charming smile. "You shall pay for that, mademoiselle."

❧

"But, Mother." Rose's complaint carried across the breakfast table, and Bryon set down his morning paper to listen. "It's a public charity ball. All the proceeds are going to the orphanage. You're surely not going to restrict me going, are you?"

"Not if that woman is the patroness."

Before Rose could speak, Bryon said, "Are you talking about the Spring Charity Ball?" He knew very well what Rose wanted —and why Mother refused. The ball was being hosted by the Brunsons.

Rose turned to him with a plea in her eyes. "Yes."

"I'm going," Bryon said. "Shelby has already procured the tickets." He smiled at his sister. "And she picked up four to include both you and Howard."

"Why ever would she do that?" Mother asked.

"Mother, how would Shelby know about an ancient rift you have with Mrs. Brunson?" He sipped his coffee as if this conversation meant no more to him than any other they'd have at the breakfast table. "Besides, it's more than time to get over that."

"Don't you tell me what to get over."

He shifted to better face her. "Mrs. Brunson has done you no harm. How can she be responsible for what her grown daughter chose to do to your friend?" Bryon was glad for the opportunity to say what he had been thinking for a long time.

"Well, I never."

Forgive? Forget a grudge? Both were quite true, though he was wise enough not to voice the thought. "It would be of utmost rudeness to decline Shelby's generosity. There is a great demand for those tickets, and she wants to support the worthy cause." Bryon knew exactly which things to say to pressure his mother into capitulating. She loved the orphanage and had a real heart for the children.

Mother sat back against her chair. "That does make things awkward. I see I have little choice but to recant. You may attend, Rose."

Rose's back was to her mother, so she was able to wink and

mouth a thank-you in Bryon's direction before turning demurely. "Thank you, Mother."

Bryon couldn't resist. "Shelby is saying that everyone who is anyone will be in attendance. Apparently, it's the talk of the season."

His mother turned away, shaking her head. "Not in my books." The click of her heels receding down the hall brought a giggle from Rose.

Bryon went back to his paper as if he hadn't just won a battle, but his heart was racing. The thought of being in the same room and even possibly securing a dance with his beautiful Amelia sent his sorry heart to singing. He was no more over her than he could jump over the moon.

～

*J*osiah swiped the sweat from his brow, but dizziness came over him. He wavered from side to side, almost sliding from the saddle before grabbing the horn with both hands. "Home boy," he whispered into the stallion's black mane. His body slumped forward. The horse turned in the right direction and trudged ahead. Josiah didn't have the strength to kick his flanks.

What was happening? He took in a gulp of fresh air, but it didn't clear his head or reach his lungs. What he'd thought was flu had turned out to be a continual ebb in his energy for far too long. The fatigue and his labored breathing were more pronounced. He'd have to take that much-procrastinated trip to Lacey Spring and visit Doc Phillips after all.

He was thankful the ranch had adequate help these days and he could slip away without Katherine's knowledge. She'd been voicing her concern about his weight loss and fatigue. Best not fuel that fire.

He plodded toward the house in jarring discomfort and

shifted in his saddle to ease the squeezing pain in his chest. He sucked in a deep breath. Why didn't the air hit his lungs?

~

*D*oc Phillips placed his pen upon his desk. "How long did you say you've been feeling this way?"

"A while now, but more noticeable since February."

"It's April. You're only bringing it to my attention now?"

"Men don't go running to the doctor for every hangnail. I thought whatever was happening would disappear—"

"And when it didn't?" Doc's bushy eyebrows rose and knit together.

"Can you blame a man? With Seth, Katherine, and the ranch, heck, who has time to be sick?"

"I've seen this before, Josiah, and I won't lie to you. You should've been conserving your energy, not going on as if nothing were wrong." He shook his head. "This is not good news. You must get your affairs in order."

"What?" Josiah jumped up and paced the room. "What are you saying?"

Doc Phillips's eyes held his gaze, but the look of compassion sent a chill of concern spreading through his bones. "You can't mean that I'm dying?"

"That diphtheria you had during the war damaged your heart. It's beating like an old man and accounts for your shortness of breath and dizziness. Without adequate oxygen—"

"Come on, Doc, I'm forty-one. I have a baby and a young wife I need to support."

"I'm so sorry, Josiah. Truly, I am." He moved forward and placed a hand on his arm. "But I have to be honest. Your strength will continue to diminish. And your heart could stop at any time. You need to let your family know."

Josiah stumbled from the room with his hands ripping

through his hair. He swung on his stallion and kicked the spurs hard. Fireball bolted and carried him in a whirl of dust to the outskirts of town before he allowed the tears to fall. He lowered his body to pat the neck of his horse as he slowed to a walk and swiped the wet from his cheeks.

How would he begin to tell Katherine? And Seth... *Dear God, every boy needs a father.*

His fists clenched the reins, and Fireball's head bobbed. He snorted but kept a steady gait. This couldn't be happening. Anger surged. He had only himself to blame. If he hadn't been so dang selfish and insisted on their arranged marriage.

He lifted his face to the heavens. "Why God?"

Silence filled the cerulean blue. Sunbeams danced across the silver-lined clouds, and everything was as it should be on a fine spring morning, everything but his broken and dying heart.

CHAPTER 13

"But, Grandmother. He has a girlfriend. Her name is Shelby, I'm told. A cute little blonde."

"Trust me when I say that there's nothing better than jealousy to flame the fire of burning embers. You will take my advice and follow it explicitly. Tonight is all about your ability to stir up that which has never died."

"How do you know—?"

"If he said he loved you and that he was calling things off to protect you from his mother, there'll be plenty of sparks left to work with. One does not turn on and off the taps of love at will. Remain aloof and mysterious when talking to Bryon. Make him feel what he has lost."

"Are you sure?"

"I was not born yesterday. You must trust me. You'll look every bit the princess. You'll dance and flirt with as many men as you can. When one or more takes a fancy to you, chose the most attractive one and allow him to have more than two dances. This is on the boundaries of propriety, but it sends a message that he is someone you are very interested in."

"But I'm not—"

"Of course, you're not." She waved her fan in the air. "But no one else knows that."

"And what will I do when this other gentleman comes calling?"

"You'll let him down swiftly and unequivocally. Trust me, he's not going to have fallen in love in one night. He'll be fine."

"It seems so cruel." A twinge of guilt pierced through. Should she be listening to her grandmother?

"Balderdash. Do you want Bryon or not?"

"Of course, I want him."

"Then go and get ready, my dear. This whole charity ball is for your benefit." She chuckled. "Of course, no one else knows that, and it will raise money for the poor orphan children. Think of all the good you're doing."

Amelia walked toward her bedroom.

The still small voice of the spirit whispered, *Ask Me what you should be doing.* The same message kept filtering in, though less often and a lot less clear. She was afraid to ask God, for fear the answer would not be what she wanted. So, she prayed the same prayer she had been praying for weeks. *Dear God, please make Bryon want me.*

~

*B*ryon took one last look in the mirror. His curly hair was tamed into submission, and he straightened the folds of his bowtie. His new navy jacket, tan pants, and matching paisley vest with a blend of both colors were the latest in fashion. A row of gleaming gold buttons ran down the front. He had to admit, he looked sharp. With a sweep of his hand, he put his top hat on his head. He was ready.

He would be escorting Shelby to the ball, but thoughts of his hazel-eyed beauty caused his heart to bolt. Powerful emotions he had tried to bury surged through.

Everything about the little arrangement Shelby and he had agreed upon worked. They enjoyed each other's company and the freedom it brought. Both sets of parents assumed their relationship was maturing toward the end goal of marriage. The only ones who knew otherwise were the two of them.

He did worry, though. Why would a young, attractive woman like Shelby be content with friendship? But when he had asked her, she said she wanted the freedom and time to make her own choice, and as long as they were courting, her parents left her alone.

What wasn't working was the thought that time would heal his broken heart. He had given Amelia up for a good reason, but his heart couldn't catch up to his head. Tonight, he intended to enjoy being in the same room as her. He had a notion that it wouldn't be easy, but he couldn't resist.

He ran down the steps and called out. "Rose, Howard, are you ready?"

Howard entered the hall. "A party with beautiful women? I was born ready."

Rose followed. "I hope you fall good and hard one of these days, and some woman breaks your heart the way you dally with so many of theirs."

Howard laughed. "Why settle for one when the world has so much beauty."

Rose cuffed him on the back of the neck.

"Come on you two," Bryon said. "Let's go."

Halfway to the carriage, Howard spoke to Rose. "Seems our brother is awfully eager." Howard had a tease in his voice, which he directed toward Bryon then. "And I don't think it has anything to do with the lovely Shelby. I'll take her off your hands for the evening if you so desire."

Bryon ignored him and entered the carriage. He had fifteen more minutes to prepare, and the last thing he wanted was to get in some nonsensical argument with his brother.

They picked up Shelby, and she slid in beside him. He said hello, but not much else. She chatted with the others, which suited him fine. He preferred his own thoughts. What would he say to Amelia? Would she even notice him? Would she read the love in his eyes?

"You look lovely, Shelby," Howard said. "That shade of lavender looks stunning on you."

"Thank you, Howard. Nice of your brother here to notice." She bunted Bryon with her elbow.

"Yes. Yes. You do look...enchanting."

She laughed. "You had to work hard to come up with that word. Didn't you? What's with you lately? You seem so preoccupied."

Bryon wanted to crawl in a hole. The last thing he needed was for them to hone in on that little detail. Thankfully, the carriage stopped, and they climbed out. The stately town hall with pillared columns twinkled with the welcoming light of many lanterns. Soft music and chattering voices drifted through the open doors.

He offered Shelby his arm. "Shall we?"

She slid her hand in. "I've been looking forward to this evening from the moment the ball was announced."

A faint grin twitched his lips. "Maybe you'll find your prince charming tonight."

"Maybe I already have." She smiled up at him.

A sick feeling dropped into his stomach. She wasn't falling for him, was she?

He had little time to think as the doorman took his hat and overcoat and they both headed to their respective dressing rooms. After adjusting his tie and smoothing back a wayward curl, he waited outside for Shelby, and they entered the ball-room together.

There she was. The rest of the room faded as he took in Amelia. Dazzling was an understatement. Her silver-blue gown hugged her trim figure in all the right places. As patroness of the evening, her grandmother moved around the room, making introductions and small talk. Amelia moved with graceful steps beside her. A tier of lace draped from her off-the-shoulder dress around to the front of the bodice. Short sleeves peeked through underneath. Long gloves covered her arms to her elbows. He couldn't resist staring at the creamy white flesh adorned with pearls that dropped to a hint of cleavage.

He caught sight of his brother—and other men—staring. He wanted to poke their eyes out. All he wanted to do was whisk her away to a private garden and not share her beauty with anyone.

He leaned into Shelby, with his eyes still on Amelia. "Feel free to fill up your dance card and enjoy the evening, but save one for me."

"Only one?" Again, she looked at him as if there was something more he should understand.

"You know etiquette dictates no more than two dances," he said, "or people begin to talk."

"Let them talk."

Worry pinched in. "I don't want to ruin your chances of finding your true love." He didn't like the flicker of sadness that entered her eyes. "Will you excuse me for a moment? I have someone I need to talk to." His eyes found Amelia once more. He wanted to secure a couple of dances before her card was full.

Shelby clutched his arm. "I'll come with you. Let's make the rounds together before going our separate ways. We have to keep face you know, or we'll have our parents—"

"All right." He couldn't keep the disappointment from his voice.

It took a good hour to circle the room and respectfully engage in conversation, but he had his eye on one person most of the time. Their circles were closing in, and he longed for a moment alone with Amelia, but Shelby and her grandmother made that impossible.

When they finally crossed paths with Mrs. Brunson and Amelia, the older woman took the lead. "Bryon. So lovely to see you again."

Bryon took her hand and kissed it. He then turned to Amelia, and their eyes spoke a thousand words. She presented her hand, and he kissed the back of her lace-trimmed glove, when what he really wanted was to kiss those beautiful lips pursed into a forced smile.

"And who is this?" Shelby asked.

Bryon shook his head from the spell Amelia's close proximity had cast upon him. "How rude of me." He directed his words to Mrs. Brunson. "This is my friend Shelby Terrance." He glanced at the woman at his elbow. "Shelby, meet my good friend Amelia Williams and her grandmother, Frances Brunson."

Shelby slapped his arm playfully. "We're next thing to engaged and you call me friend."

Bryon's stomach lurched. Why had Shelby said that? And why was she hanging on to him so possessively?

Amelia chatted before making an excuse to leave. But he'd noticed her eyes cloud over. He knew every nuance about her and could tell she was not taking the news Shelby had just given well.

Mrs. Brunson made a quick escape, and he watched as she ran after Amelia and stopped her from leaving the room. Amelia's head was shaking, and her grandmother's head was bobbing. He breathed a sigh of relief when Amelia turned back into the room. He'd get a chance to request a dance with Amelia and set things straight. He would deal with Shelby later in privacy. Now was not the time or the place. He didn't like the turn of events. They had an understanding, did they not?

Etiquette demanded he dance with a few ladies standing on

the outskirts who clearly did not have partners. He was not too happy with Shelby at the moment, so he made the excuse he must fill his dance card and suggested she do the same. Before leaving, he placed his name twice on her card.

"Only two?" Her lip stuck out in an exaggerated pout.

He didn't bother to answer before turning away. As he approached a few plain, ill-dressed women clinging to the wall, he empathized with their lot in life and sought to bring them a little pleasure. Rose said his soft heart would make him a fine husband someday, but he knew what it was like to be born into situations that could not be changed. He filled his card with the women standing on the sidelines, leaving room for two more, hoping Amelia would have him. He didn't want to give cause for his mother's tongue to wag, but truth be told, he wished he could dance every song with her.

Introductions were over, and the music began. People were eager to get onto the dance floor, and he was anxious to find Amelia. There she was, whirling about in the arms of his brother. Howard was looking down at her, joking about something, and she was laughing up at him.

Bryon's stomach tightened. His dance card crumpled in his hand. He flattened it out and stuck it in his pocket.

From one partner to another, he and Amelia only met as they whirled by each other with their respective partners. He tried to concentrate on the woman in front of him and not be rude, but, as the evening wore on, his patience grew thin. Amelia's breaks to the food table or the seating area were not coinciding with his. The last thing he wanted to do was hurt a young woman's feelings by not showing up for a dance. And the worst thing about it was that Amelia had no shortage of handsome men buzzing around her. In particular, Thomas Ratcliffe met her almost every time she stepped off the ballroom floor, and he had already claimed two dances.

Finally, she headed to the ladies dressing room the same

time as he had a break. If he hovered nearby, he could catch her as she came out. He caught Shelby beelining his way as he made his way out of the ballroom and ducked into the men's dressing room. Hopefully, she'd be gone before he came out, and he wouldn't miss Amelia.

But what would he say to Amelia? What was the point of torturing himself? Nothing had changed. Loneliness pressed in, sucking the air out of the room. He would do anything for her, even leave her be so she could find love—with someone else. Why bother seeking her out? Clearly, she didn't miss him like he missed her. He took a quick look in the mirror and straightened his bow tie. He would get back to the dance and somehow make it through the evening. Best to leave things at a distance.

He entered the hall from the men's dressing room as she stepped out from the women's dressing room on the other end. They moved in sync toward each other, stopping just outside the ballroom door, only an arm's length apart. Their eyes locked. His heart pumped wildly, hammering on the walls of his chest. They gazed into each other's eyes. Frozen in the weightiness of indecision, no words found him.

Amelia's mouth parted to speak, and his eyes dropped to her lips. "She's lovely, Bryon."

"Who?" His mind couldn't think with her so close.

"Your fiancée. Shelby is it?"

His heart hammered. "She's not my fiancée. We have an agreement to pretend we're more. It keeps our parents from thrusting others our way." He was shocked at the way words of truth spilled out.

Amelia's eyebrows raised. "Does she know that? Either she's extremely good at acting, or she's fallen for you."

His head ached at the thought. That would be a complication he didn't need. Better redirect the conversation. "Seems you've made quite the stir. I see Thomas Ratcliffe hanging onto your every move."

"He is a nice man." She glanced at her dance card. "I'd best be getting back." She turned to go.

"May I have the pleasure of a dance?" Why had those words slipped from his lips when he had just decided to leave her be? He could not help himself.

"Sorry, but my every available time slot has been spoken for. Had you wanted to dance with me, you should've asked me long before now." Her voice sounded sad and dejected.

"I would have, but you were—"

"There you are, darling." Shelby's voice echoed in the hall as she swept forward and clung to his arm. "I've an extra opening on my card, and there's no one I want more than you to fill it."

Amelia turned and disappeared into the ballroom. He forced a smile. He would not ruin Shelby's evening, but he would have a talk with her soon. What was going on with her?

The rest of the evening was torture. Shelby hung close, too close. And Amelia danced a third time with Thomas, signifying to the community that there was something special afoot. That truth ripped his heart open. The taste of disappointment filled his mouth with bitterness. What did he expect? That she would remain single and pine her life away thinking of him? He didn't want her to be miserable. Love wanted the best for the other person, no matter how much pain it would bring him to watch her live happily with another man.

A wall of sorrow washed in, breaking over him, dragging him down, under, pummeling his heart.

CHAPTER 14

*A*melia tossed on her bed. The comfortable down blanket and soft mattress usually had her sleeping in a matter of minutes, but not tonight. She should be exhausted from her full dance card and all the concentrating she had to do in order to keep her two left feet in their lane.

Seeing Bryon had shaken her more deeply than she'd expected. She still felt dizzy when she closed her eyes and recalled the look on his face. If she went by that alone, she would be encouraged, but if she went by the attractive blonde at his side, she would feel hopeless.

It had been a long time since she'd asked God for wisdom. Instead, she had flitted like a butterfly from one city to another. However, this she knew after receiving all the attention she'd had that evening—if she couldn't have Bryon, she didn't want anyone.

Her grandmother's plan to make Bryon jealous had only succeeding in hurting her own soul. There was only so much she could fake. She needed to take charge of her own life and stop relying on others to tell her what to do. She knew where to find wisdom, and it had been too long since she had genuinely sought it.

"Dear Jesus. Help me. You know how much I love Bryon, but a relationship with him doesn't seem a possibility. He is with a woman his mother would be pleased to welcome into the family. If I pursue him, I will only complicate his life, and that's not what love does.

What should I do with my life?"

One word came through. One thought. Crisp. Clear. Concise.

Nursing.

~

"Come." Amelia offered her hand and squeezed tight as she pulled her grandmother from the kitchen into the parlor. "And where is Grandfather? You must hear this news together."

"He's in the library, smoking that blasted pipe. Where else?"

Amelia led her grandmother to the settee. "Sit, and don't move. I'll go get him." She raced down the hall to the library and burst through the door.

Grandfather jumped in his chair. His pipe jarred in his mouth, and his shaky hand caught it as it wobbled on his lower lip. "By Jupiter girl, you gave me a fright."

She rushed over and crouched beside his chair. "Sorry, Grandfather, I have some exciting news to share, and I guess I forgot myself. Can you join me in the parlor when you're done with your pipe?"

He smoothed a weathered knuckle down her cheek. "With an apology like that, who could stay upset?" A grin split across his face, and his bushy eyebrows danced. He set his pipe on a nearby stand and lifted his hands. "Help an old man up, and I'll come straight away."

Arm in arm they entered the parlor, where grandmother sat on the edge of her seat with excitement dancing in her eyes. The look erased years from her age.

"Do tell, Amelia. Don't keep an old lady waiting. You never know when my last breath may be." Her smile radiated through the laughter.

"Can you give me a moment to sit down?" Grandfather smiled at his wife as he took a seat beside her and patted her knee. "Go ahead now." He waved his hand at Amelia.

"You know how I've been volunteering at the Bellevue Hospital."

They nodded.

"That time has helped me decide what I want to do with the rest of my life."

Grandfather snorted. "A lifetime can be a very long time."

Grandmother gave him a look. "Now is not the time to tease."

"The more I volunteer, the clearer the decision becomes. I love everything about that place. The clean white-washed walls, the regiment of doctors and nurses buzzing about their day in orderly fashion. The thought of schedules and structure actually excite me."

Grandfather's brows raised in amusement. "Not the kind of thing that would excite most young women."

"Shush, George, the girl is in the middle of talking."

"But most of all, I love working with the patients. They hit me right here." She lifted her hand to her heart. "If I can make what they have to go through easier, my life will have purpose. I want to become a nurse."

Grandmother sat back. "But what about Bryon? Are you giving up on the hope—"

"I don't think there's anything left there. You heard how his girlfriend Shelby said they're next thing to engaged."

"I'm not sure about that," Grandmother said. "Did you notice

Bryon's expression when she said that? He seemed genuinely shocked."

Amelia did remember his face, and the disappointment when Shelby showed up later when they were talking.

"Besides, there's nothing permanent about a girlfriend when the love of your life returns," Grandmother added.

"I'm not about to waste my time waiting for what may or may not happen. He had ample time to ask me for a dance at the ball, but he didn't until long into the evening when he knew my card would be full."

"Could it be—?"

"Grandmother, you're a hopeless romantic, and I hope you're right, but in the meantime, I want to take charge of my life."

"Sensible girl," Grandfather said with a gleam of pride in his eyes.

"Well then," Grandmother said, "we shall stand beside you all the way."

Grandfather made two attempts at standing from the soft cushions before ambling across the room to envelop her in a warm hug. "We'd feel honored to help you financially through school. The hospital has a wonderful academy for young women to attend. We'll check into enrollment immediately."

She smiled widely. "When I was volunteering, everyone kept telling me I was a natural. Then the head nurse told me about the spring session. She said if I act fast, I can join in, even though it's already started."

"Well, I'll be jiggered. I knew you were a smart one." Grandfather kissed her cheek. "If it's what you want—"

"It is." Amelia had never been so sure of anything in her life. Ever since that prayer the other night, she had more peace than she'd had in months.

"We're so proud of you," Grandmother said, joining in the three-way hug. A mingle of rosewater and tobacco wafted up as they embraced her. "And after witnessing how you handled all that blood with little Bethany—"

Amelia laughed. "All that blood. You should see what goes on at the hospital."

"Goodness, never." She shuddered.

Amelia pulled apart laughing.

~

"*I* wish I had the courage to knock on the Preston door and ask Bryon straight up if he'd be willing to fight for what we once had." Amelia threw down her napkin and pushed her tea aside. "Grandmother, I'm tired of the constant tea parties and social engagements. They're really not my thing, and I don't see the point. And now that I'm in school, I need every moment to read and study. There is much to learn."

Her grandmother patted her hand. "There, there. Our plan is working splendidly. You've had many a boy vying for your attention."

"That's never what I wanted."

"Be patient, my dear. I know it's been a number of months since you've been back, but look how far we've come. All the Preston children were at our spring gala." She winked. "This means Melinda Preston has had to bend to their demands. Everything is coming along exactly as planned. And believe me when I say, Bryon was made duly jealous. I watched him watching you as you whirled on the dance floor, and how wretched he looked when all the men were buzzing around you like bees to honey. Oh yes." She clapped her wrinkled hands together. "All is progressing splendidly."

Amelia dropped her head. In her heart, she was just a girl who loved a boy.

A finger lifted her chin up. "You listen to me, and you listen well." Grandmother held out her hand until Amelia stood. She gently pushed Amelia's sagging shoulders back. "Hold that head up high. Mark my word, one day your worlds will collide again, and now, after making him good and jealous, you must be ready to seize the moment. Do you understand what I'm suggesting?"

"I'm not sure."

"You take that man and kiss him soundly. Do you hear me?"

Amelia gasped. "Grandmother—"

"Don't you *Grandmother* me. I'm not too old to remember the way of young love. You need to let him know in that one kiss how much you feel. I don't care where you are—find a park, find an alcove, find an empty room, but get the job done."

Amelia giggled. "You're making me blush at the mere thought of being so forward."

"Goodness gracious." She batted at the air. "If we waited around for men to figure out everything, we'd be waiting forever. That boy needs to be reminded of what you two had." An arm went around her shoulders. "Now, off we go to the shops. You must look dazzling at every turn. And with all these classes you've been taking, we must make the most of our precious little time together. What better way than to shop?"

Her laugh was infectious. Amelia found herself joining in. But a voice deep within her soul winked into consciousness. A caution. A question. A warning.

How well have things been going following your grandmother's advice?

CHAPTER 15

June 1869

*B*ryon hopped into the carriage. The wheels lurched forward in the direction of Shelby's home. He struggled to care about anything beyond his work. He was thankful Shelby was leaving for the summer with her parents on a European trip. He was looking forward to a reprieve from her. Though he had talked to her after the ball, she had denied any shift in her thinking regarding their arrangement, insisting that she'd only been playing the part. Yet, since then, she'd cuddled too close, looked at him with fluttering eyelids, things she hadn't done before. She laughed at everything he said, even when he wasn't funny.

All too soon the carriage stopped. He hopped out as Shelby floated down the walk with parasol and fan in hand.

"Darling."

He cringed at the endearment at the best of times, but especially when no one else was around and she had no need to use it. "Our last time together before your big trip. Are you excited?" He helped her into the carriage. "Bellevue Hotel, please."

The coachman nodded.

She moved in close and placed a quick kiss on his cheek. "I shall miss you, my friend. Wish you were coming with us. You know Daddy and Mother would be tickled pink."

She'd been relentlessly begging him to come ever since her parents announced the trip.

"You know I have responsibilities."

"Well then, just marry me and all your responsibilities will be over." Her cheeks flushed red, and a grin kicked up the edges of her mouth. "Other than to invest my vast inheritance, of course."

He laughed, not knowing what to say. Was she serious? He let out the air he had been holding when she joined in.

The bellman at the Bellevue threw open the doors as they walked up the steps into the plush lobby. A massive crystal chandelier dominated the spacious room and sparkled in the dim evening light. His feet sank into deep red Persian rugs laid over gleaming hardwood. Colorful vases from the Orient graced every low table, and some stood on the floor stretching his height. The opulence rankled him. He felt uncomfortable, but the location for dinner had been her choice, and she was oohing and ahhing about the architecture and decor.

"I just love this place. The thing I'm looking forward to the most on my trip is the thought of experiencing the many beautiful hotels all over Europe."

He nodded, but his heart was thinking that Amelia would hate this as much as he did.

They were escorted to their table by the French speaking maître d, who gave them one of the best tables in the dining room.

"I stopped by earlier this week to request this special spot." She reached across the table and grabbed his hand, giving it a squeeze of excitement before letting go.

"I know exactly what I've been craving ever since we made this date. Chateaubriand for two. Are you okay with that?"

"Sounds good." But a stab of guilt jolted through. There was nothing wrong with having a nice meal out, but the excess nagged at him.

"That's what I love about you. You're so accommodating and easy to be with." She gave him a look that made his gut clench. Some distance would be good.

They chatted aimlessly, darting from one topic to another as they typically did. She'd take the lead, and he'd fill in the odd tidbit with rarely a moment of silence. It was exhausting.

"Chateaubriand for two." The waiter carried a huge platter above his head. With flair he set it in the middle of the table. "Chateaubriand cooked rare from the finest cut of tenderloin. Duchesse potatoes and wild mushrooms." His hands did most of the talking as they flew from one item to the other. "And of course, our famous sauce prepared with white wine, shallots, and moistened demi-glace and mixed with the perfect blend of freshly churned butter, tarragon, and lemon juice. *Trex delicieux!*" He kissed his fingertips and threw his hand wide. "If there is anything else I can bring for you, please just wave me over." He bowed slightly and walked away.

Shelby unfolded her napkin and placed it on her lap. Her eyes were rapt with excitement. "A perfect meal for a perfect evening."

Why did he think she meant more than she was saying? "Tell me your itinerary for your trip." That was all he had to say, and she was off and running. They finished the meal in pleasant conversation.

"I'm beyond full." Bryon waved the dessert tray away and was shocked when Shelby ordered a crème brulee.

"Where are you going to put that?" He laughed. "I've never known you to have dessert after a heavy meal like that."

"See how well you know me, Bryon. We're like an old

married couple already. I'm thinking when I get back, we should just make it official."

Bryon's amusement faded. He set the cup down none to gently. "Are you serious?"

She busied herself straightening her napkin. "I've given this a lot of thought. I really enjoy your companionship, and I think you appreciate mine." Finally, she met his eyes, and he saw the tentative hope there.

"I enjoy your friendship, but that's a long way from falling in love and pledging marriage."

Her chin tipped up. "Why is it so far? Many great marriages have been built on a lot less than what we share."

"They can be built on a whole lot more as well."

"Why are you resisting? You know your parents are going to hound you relentlessly. You could do a lot worse than me."

He didn't want to hurt her, but he needed her to understand. "I know that, but don't you want to be deeply loved? I can't promise that. My heart was broken—"

"That girl at the ball? The only woman in the room you had eyes for? Amelia, I think it was."

"Yes, Amelia." His heart plummeted at the mention of her name.

"Didn't look like she was interested in you."

"It's more complicated than that. My parents don't approve."

"They approve of me." She slid her hand across the table and held onto his. "We could be happy together. I just know it. Think about it, Bryon. Just let yourself consider it."

He had thought about it. Marrying Shelby would mean an end to his family's financial hurdles. His parents would be thrilled. He enjoyed her company and was always proud to have her by his side.

But marriage?

"I don't think—"

"How about you wait and give me your decision when I

return." She patted his arm. "That way you'll have the summer to think about it, and I'll have my last chance to see if I find someone to sweep me off my feet."

"I'm not sure that is a good idea."

"Look, do you want your parents thrusting different women at you all summer?"

That was the last thing he wanted. His answer must have shown on his face because her smile was triumphant.

"Take this time," she said. "I'll do the same. As far as the world is concerned, nothing will have changed between you and me."

"All right. Just...just don't count on me."

She patted his hand. "I know where you stand. Now, you know where I stand." She stood. "Shall we go?"

"What about your dessert?"

"I couldn't eat another bite. I was just stalling."

He laughed. "I knew it."

"See how well you know me."

"I have to pay the bill."

"Daddy gave strict instructions that this would go on his tab. He comes here often."

Bryon breathed a sigh of relief. That one meal would've taken a week's wages.

The silent ride back to her home was eerily uncomfortable. He slid across the seat to jump out and help her down, but she pulled him close and pressed her lips to his.

He was so surprised by the action, he hardly had time to respond. Felt no desire to respond. He felt... nothing.

He had his answer. Come what may, he had to tell her. He pulled back. "Shelby, I can't—"

"Ah. Ah. Ah. Not one word. You promised to think it over." She slid from the other side of the carriage and disappeared into the darkness.

Everything about the decision felt wrong. But she was gone.

～

*B*ryon pulled out his pocket watch. "Blast it." He was late for lunch with his brother. His morning meeting had gone way longer than he anticipated. He would have to hurry. He burst out the bank door and charged down the street toward the hotel, taking the corner a little too sharply. He collided with someone and reached out to steady the woman he had almost trampled. One look into her face and he couldn't let go. His mouth opened and closed, but only one word came out. "Amelia."

The immediate warmth of her hazel brown eyes drew him in. Her smile swallowed any resolve he possessed. He couldn't move.

"Bryon." The breathy way she said his name sent heat racing through his veins. "I haven't seen you since the charity ball," she whispered, turning a lovely shade of red. "How about a short walk for old times' sake."

"That would be nice." The words were out of his mouth before he could think. "There's a park nearby." He pointed down the street.

"You looked in a hurry. Are you sure you have time?"

"I was heading to lunch with my brother, but I'm so late now, I'm sure he's eaten without me. Knowing him, he's found himself a pretty girl to sit with and hasn't been missing me at all."

To be walking beside her... His heart raced in his chest. But his circumstances had not changed. In fact, they were more complicated. He should put as much distance as he could between them, but the thought of a few moments alone with her sounded like heaven.

"And you?" he asked.

"I'm on a lunch break from school. I'm studying to be a nurse."

"That makes perfect sense. With your intelligence and compassion, you'll make a great nurse. But what are you going to do if some handsome man comes along and wants to marry you? Aren't nurses unmarried women?"

"Since the only man I want to marry is unavailable, I like the idea of taking care of myself." She smiled widely, and his heart bucked madly against his chest. Did she mean him?

She continued before he could form a response. "Let's make the most of this hour, shall we?"

"Indeed."

She glanced down at his hands that held her tight. "You'll have to let me go." Her laughter sounded like the tinkling of chimes blown in the wind.

He dropped his hands and offered his arm. The smile she flashed him could've warmed a winter's day as she placed her hand in the crook of his arm as in days gone by. He pushed away the dart of reason that pierced his soul. Why was he doing this? To what end?

Their easy conversation filled the air. A perfect blend of talking, listening, and quiet. Oh, how he'd missed her.

"Tell me about Shelby."

His answer came out instantly. "She's as I told you at the charity ball, a decoy so our parents will leave us both alone."

"So just a friend?"

"She'll never be more than a friend." As he said the words, true as they were, a leaden anchor of guilt settled in his gut.

She squeezed his arm. "I'm so glad."

He should tell Amelia the rest of the story immediately... including Shelby's pending request to consider marriage. It had bothered him to no end that Shelby had let it slip to her parents, who let it out to his parents that they were considering marriage. As far as his mother was concerned, it was a done deal throwing out suggested dates and talking about guests she would just have to invite. Bryon had tried to make her understand that nothing had been decided, to no avail.

They strolled until Amelia pointed between the trees. "Can we walk a little off the path? I want to get a better peek of the James River."

Her hand slid naturally into his as he led the way. The feel of her fingers curled around his made his senses run sharp. He leaned closer. Her hair smelled of rain-washed roses. He must put a stop to this madness.

They both paused, at the same place, in sync with each other. The wide trunk of a sugar maple obscured their view from the path. He turned toward her, determined to end the agony of being so close and yet worlds apart. She looked at him in a way he had never seen anyone look at him. Love poured from her eyes. A torturous desire took over.

Suddenly, she was kissing him. Her warm lips moved softly on his. He moaned in sweet agony as he gave in to the temptation. She melted in his arms. The moments stretched, lost in a world of delight.

She pulled away, breathless.

He could hardly believe what she'd done. What *he'd* done.

"Please don't think me too forward." She looked up at him with raw vulnerability in her expression. "I've never done anything like that before. But I had to know if you still feel the same about me as I do about you. I think..."

"I do."

"I've missed you so desperately. I want to fight for us." Dainty fingers reached out to touch his face, and his concerns about Shelby were lost.

"I want that, too. I'm sorry I ever let you go. If only I could go back—"

"We can only go forward." She stood on her tiptoes and kissed his brow. "That frown has got to go."

He laughed. "How I've missed you. I feel more comfortable

with you than with any other person in the world. Not to mention how beautiful you are—" He placed his hands on the sides of her blushing cheeks and drank in her loveliness. "There's so much I want to tell you, but my brain is muddled. I can't believe you're still available and standing right here in front of me with so much grace and beauty—"

"You had better stop, or it'll go to my head."

"As if. With your unassuming ways and kindness, that would be an impossibility."

"I'd love to stay beneath the canopy of this sugar maple with you by my side for much longer, but I must get back." Amelia eased away.

"Can we meet here at the same time tomorrow and strategize how we'll make our togetherness happen?"

Amelia's hazel eyes sparkled with joy. Her smile tunneled into his soul. She hugged him good-bye. "Tomorrow it is," she whispered into his ear before slipping away.

He watched her until she was out of view before he came back down to earth and realized he had told her everything... except what he should have.

He pushed down the gnawing in his gut. If she knew the truth, she would keep her distance until things were sorted with Shelby. He couldn't fathom not seeing her for the whole summer.

One walk. One talk. One kiss, and he was a goner.

CHAPTER 16

Shenandoah Valley

"Josiah, tell me. I need to know." Katherine's vibrant blue eyes darkened. The click of her heels snapped across the wooden floor of the tack shop as she moved toward him.

Heat crawled up his neckline. He'd been caught sleeping in the middle of the day by the one person he most wanted to impress.

"I know something's wrong. You've lost weight, you're sleeping all the time, and you barely have energy to work."

"Come here." He patted the small cot beside him as he pushed his weary body into a seated position.

Over the past couple of months, he'd denied the obvious. He'd railed. He'd screamed. He'd rued the day he'd met her. He'd begged. He'd cried. He'd prayed. Finally, he was at peace. He could tell her.

Worried eyes gazed into his as she sank onto the cot beside him. He closed his eyes to the featherlight touch of her soft hand smoothing his brow and brushing a wayward curl of hair from his forehead.

"Tell me."

He breathed in the smell of spring lilacs and pulled her close. He couldn't delay the truth any longer. Time did not stand still, and his condition was worsening.

He pulled back with both hands planted firmly on her shoulders. "Doc Phillips told me that I'm dying."

She pulled in a sharp intake of breath. Her eyes flew wide open, instantly filled with fear. "No. No." Tears filled her iridescent blue eyes and spilled down her face.

He dragged her stiff body against his and rocked her gently. His work-roughened hands smoothed over her long black hair. She quieted but shuddered against him.

"But what? Why?" She pulled back.

He dusted his thumb beneath one eye to catch a falling tear.

He tried to explain, but the minute he mentioned the war and diphtheria she unraveled.

"That blasted war. First my brothers, then Charles, and now you. I can't take anymore." Her words cracked, and she gave in to sobs.

He held her tight. "I know, I know. Let it out." Her body sagged against him, and then in the next instant pushed away. With a jump, she was on her feet. "Well He can't have you. God cannot take you from me." She stomped back and forth on the wooden planks. "He brought us together. He made me fall in love with you. And now He can't have you."

Josiah stood, unsure what to say or do.

"No. I need you. Seth needs his father. You have to fight this." She shook her fist into the heavens. "Do you hear me, God? I said no." Her body collapsed to her knees, her dress billowing around her. She dropped her head to the barn floor and folded her arms.

He sank down beside her. "Katherine, I will fight with all I have, but if I leave you, God will never leave nor forsake you. We both know this truth. We need to cling to Him, not push Him away."

She lifted her face. Deep behind her tear-drenched eyes, confusion and terror lurked.

"I've been right where you are. I railed. I begged. I've been angry and afraid. It's all right. God understands our emotions." He rose and held out his hand. She placed her delicate fingers into his and stood. "Let's walk a bit."

Flowers grew in riotous abandon along the walkway. Birds dipped and swooped with one song mingling into another. The air was full of summertime scents as they walked silently, hand in hand, from the barn to the solarium.

Copious blooms hung heavy from the hanging baskets and perfumed the air with sweetness as they entered, but one look at the plaque Josiah made her all those months earlier, and she turned into his shirt and wept. He read the words afresh. *The Lord giveth, and the Lord taketh away, blessed be the name of the Lord.*

Can I really accept those words? He looked down at his weeping wife. *Can I, Lord? Can I really say, blessed be your name?*

"I have a better idea, my love." He took her hand and led her into the house, up the winding staircase, and into their personal sanctuary. He pulled her toward him and lowered his head toward her lips. The kiss was slow and deep. He savored the touch, the taste, the tenderness. Her lips pressed hard against his. What began as a gentle kiss blazed into need.

Her lips ripped from his. "Will I hurt you?"

"You'll hurt me if you stop now. I need you." His lips crushed against hers.

～

Late August 1869

*B*ryon sat at his desk, unable to concentrate on his work. It was almost lunchtime and thoughts of Amelia stirred his blood. Tortured by his behavior, guilt wedged its way in. All summer long he'd continued to meet Amelia in their favorite spot by the river. She agreed to keep their relationship a secret while Bryon promised to work on attaining the promise his parents had made to him, that he would be able to choose his own wife.

With Shelby gone, he freely enjoyed Amelia's company without having to deal with a situation that was far more complicated than he'd agreed to. A bolt of fire ripped through his heart at the thought of Amelia. When he thought of Shelby, he felt nothing. He had not missed her, and she rarely came to mind.

That last dinner when Shelby had proposed marriage haunted him. Her words came back to him. "I'm taking one last trip before we hopefully get married, darling. Thereafter, you'll be taking me everywhere my little heart desires." There was no question as to her expectations or that of their parents. Shelby was due back shortly and they counted on a ring on her finger by month's end. He would have written to her to set her straight, but with her travel plans, she wouldn't be in one place long enough to exchange correspondence.

Amelia was the only woman for him, and the instant Shelby got home, he would tell her the truth and face his parents. Then, regardless of what his parents said, he would get down on his knee and propose marriage to his only true love.

He flung his pen down on the desk and raked his hands through his hair. He soothed the jagged edges with the same excuses he told himself every day. He would set this right before anyone was the wiser. He hadn't offered Shelby a ring. He'd tried to break it off with her before she presented her idea of thinking it over. Had he not been selfish in wanting his parents to leave him alone, he would never have agreed. Now, no amount of money, lifestyle ease, or friendship could hold a candle to the way he felt about Amelia.

One more week and Shelby would be home. He'd make it clear he was not marrying her, and he would stand up to his parents. He had worked long and hard to take care of the family inheritance. Now, it was their turn to stand true to their word and let him choose his own bride.

His gut twisted. He was so sick of things as they were. He should never have let it go on this long.

~

*A*melia loved the hum of busyness at the hospital. With her practicum in full swing, she was given more responsibilities every day. From the easy, like cleaning bedding and linens and writing letters for the sick, to the more difficult jobs of supervising supplies, dressing wounds, and administering medication, she put her head down and applied herself. Hard work was no shock to a farm girl.

"Amelia." Head nurse Bridgett waved her over.

"Yes."

The stern gray-haired lady with her hair in a tight bun looked over her horn-rimmed glasses. "I'd like you to stay late tonight. Doctor Meade has requested your assistance on a surgery this evening. You know the patient who came in a few days ago after falling from his horse?"

"Yes, ma'am."

"It's not looking good, and he may lose his arm. Dr. Meade is going in for a closer look."

Amelia's heart raced, and she gulped back a fist-sized knot in her throat. "Do you think I'm ready?"

"I'll be assisting as well, so you won't be on your own, but you're more than ready for this challenge. Scrub up. Remember, hygiene is of utmost importance to fight infection."

Amelia changed from her white apron to a sparkling clean one and bent over the large basin to scrub her hands and arms. No other student had been singled out to assist with surgery. Nurse Bridgett had told the class that the privilege of assisting surgeons did not happen in the first year, and thereafter, only if one showed exemplary aptitude and talent. Could this mean what she thought it meant?

"Dear God, help me." She whispered a prayer, as she did many times during the day. So often, she felt inadequate, but nothing made her feel more alive than tending the sick and injured. Somehow, nursing felt like it was something she had been born to do.

The promises of a future with Bryon confused her deeply, for she loved him, and she loved nursing. Like a wishbone pulled in two directions, warring loves tugged at her heart. If the world knew she was planning to be the wife of a highborn gentleman, they would tell her nursing was unnecessary training, certainly beneath her station, but something deep within held her to the course. As she helped others, God's presence felt so near, as if He were pleased. Even when she was terrified, as she was at the moment, there was a peace she could not explain.

Not so when she visited Bryon in the park. That peace dissipated, and a niggling uncertainty would scratch its way into her conscience. They should be forthright about their intentions, not sneaking around. As much as she loved their time together, something felt off.

"Don't take the skin off," Nurse Bridgett said.

Amelia jumped.

"A little nervous I see." She patted Amelia's shoulder. "I fainted the first time I attended a surgery. I keeled over when the doctor took the saw to his leg." She laughed.

"Oh dear, I'm not sure if that makes me feel better or worse." Amelia finished up at the basin.

Nurse Bridgette laughed all the harder as she scrubbed up. "You'll do just fine. I'll be watching for the faint, but at the very least keep a bucket near. You may feel the need to use it."

~

"*J*'ll talk to my parents soon, I promise." Bryon brushed his hand down the side of her face, and Amelia could barely think straight.

"All my conversations about how nice your grandparents are must be working. Mother is allowing Rose to attend the functions hosted by your grandmother."

"But you've been saying you'll talk to them for a while now about choosing your own bride." Amelia made a deliberate pout. He dropped a kiss on her lips.

"Stop that. You're too good at distracting me." She pulled back and waved a finger in his face. "Honestly, Bryon, Grandmother is driving me crazy with all her shenanigans to ensure our paths intersect. I feel dishonest knowing we're together almost every day."

"But hasn't it been a wonderful summer—our private place in the world where no worries exist, where we can concentrate on getting to know each other." He spread his hands out to the James River in front of them, and up to the sugar maple with its low hanging branches, carefully hiding their special bench from the public eye.

"Yes, it has been nice—"

"Then trust me. I'll make *us* happen. I no longer care about anything—my job at the bank, the family, the money, my parents' ridiculous pretentiousness. I'd be willing to leave it all and work the land with your pa if it meant being by your side."

"But *I* care. Family is important. I couldn't imagine giving up my sisters, or Ma and Pa, and I don't want you to do that either. Your mother and father's approval matters, and you're no farmer—"

His kiss silenced further protest, and a ripple of delight ran up her spine.

She pulled away. "That's not playing fair."

"I have to run, sweet one. Same time tomorrow?"

She nodded, and he gave her one more lingering kiss.

They parted ways before reaching the busy street, and she waited from a distance, as she always did. Soon, he would reach the solid bank doors and turn in her direction with a smile. She imagined the day she could walk freely by his side through those great doors, kiss him on the cheek farewell after a leisurely lunch, and tell him she would see him at home. She loved that dream.

His firm steps, stately stature, and handsome physique approached the door. Just before he would've turned one last time, a loud cry above the din snapped Amelia to attention. The clip-clop of horse's hoofs, the shrill of a whistle, the cry of a boy hawking newspapers, faded. The bustle of activity slowed in motion.

"Bryon...Bryon." A beautiful woman with long flowing blonde hair ran toward him, her face filled with joy. "Oh Bryon, I've missed you so much."

Amelia's legs wobbled and her hand flew to her throat as Shelby flung herself into Bryon's arms and kissed him full on the mouth. It took everything Amelia had not to crumble to the ground as she witnessed the exchange. Bryon pulled away, but the striking beauty draped her arm around him in a way that spoke of genuine possession. Amelia turned and fled.

She stifled a cry with a hand to her mouth and walked back to the hospital. She pressed the tears down long enough to tell nurse Bridgette she was feeling very ill and had to get home.

A fiery thorn of fury stabbed deep. What a fool she'd been.

Bryon had spent the summer with her, but obviously had not broken off with Shelby. The way she kissed him and wrapped her arms around him, there was no mistaking that she believed a lot more than friendship was going on. Amelia had made it so easy for Bryon to live a double life with both women on his arm.

On her way back to her grandparents a little while later, sorrow and anger contended for position. Hot tears burnt a path down her cheek.

The door swung wide on its hinges and crashed into the wall behind her. Oh goodness, she had not meant to let her anger get the best of her. Amelia hurried up the stairs and down the hall to her bedroom. She heard her grandmother call out her name but couldn't answer. She fell on the bed in a heap and gave way to heaving sobs.

"Amelia. Whatever is the matter?" Warm arms circled her body and hugged tight. "There, there, everything will be all right."

A numbing chill spread from tip to toe as she lifted her head from her wet pillow and sat up.

"No, it will never be all right. I never should've..." She choked out a cry. "I should have told you. This never would've happened had I..." She covered her face with both hands. "I'm so sorry."

"Take your time, dear. Gain your composure and come downstairs when you're ready. I'll get the cook to put on the tea." She patted Amelia's shoulder. "I have nothing but time. And no matter what happened, you know that I love you. We'll sort this out together."

The soft swish of her dress and the click of the bedroom door, and Amelia was alone. What had she been thinking? She would never fit into the Preston family. Bryon must've realized the truth. But why play with her emotions and string her along?

The Bryon she knew and loved was too kind to be so cruel. Why would he say he loved her with such sincerity?

There was only one conclusion. She obviously didn't know him, and it was time to accept the obvious. She wiped the tears from her face with an angry swipe and rose from the bed. She had some apologizing to do.

CHAPTER 17

"*I*'m so sorry, Grandmother." Amelia couldn't hold her grandmother's gaze.

"I know you are, my dear. I understand the confusion and headiness of love, though I do think you took that suggestion of one kiss a little far. That's why there are strict courting rules, so that you have others to help you along the way."

"Can you forgive me?"

"Fiddlesticks, that's already been done." She batted her napkin into the air. "What I want to know is why he would do such a thing? Something doesn't add up."

"It doesn't matter. I'm done with him. And if he comes calling, promise me you'll send him away."

She nodded. "I understand. But as sure as I'm old and gray, there is more to this story than meets the eye." Grandmother reached across the table, bumping her teacup in the process. Brew splashed all over her white linen tablecloth, but she held onto Amelia's hand. "Are you going to go home? I'd understand if you want to, but your grandfather and I would miss you something terrible. Life has been so wonderful having you around."

Amelia's decision came easily. "If you'll forgive my stupidity, I'd like to stay. I love nursing and know it's what I was born to do. And truthfully, city life is in my blood. Why should the likes of the Preston family send me running when Richmond feels like home?" Her words sounded tough and strong, but on the inside, she was dying. She had trusted Bryon. She had trusted Edmund. What was wrong with her that men would treat her this way? She was done with them.

Grandmother stood and threw a hug around Amelia's shoulders. "But that boy needs a good tongue lashing. How dare he trifle with your emotions." She clucked her tongue. "I'll indeed take care of him if he comes calling." She squeezed Amelia's shoulders. "I know I'm being selfish, but I'm thrilled you're staying. Your work is a fine and respectable endeavor no matter what the upper echelons may think. What would we do when we got sick without hard-working trained professionals like you?"

Amelia's stomach gurgled and complained. That endless drip, drip, drip of not feeling worthy was back in the form of a flowing stream, and Grandmother didn't even realize her words had just added to the current.

~

*B*ryon had a real mess to clean up...a mess of his own making. His first need was to explain to Amelia. He had seen enough of her face after Shelby kissed him to know she'd seen them together and assumed the worst. And then she was gone.

He stood outside the hospital until she came out at lunch. "Amelia."

Without a word, she turned and went directly back in.

The next day the same thing happened. By the third day, he

had almost lost hope she would ever speak a word to him again. "Please, Amelia. Hear me out. It's not what you think."

She stood at the top of the hospital stairs looking down at him. "I know full well what my eyes saw, and after confiding in you what Edmund did to me, you have the nerve to do the same. How shameful."

"But I can explain. It's not at all like Edmund."

"Bryon, all I ask is that you respect me enough to leave me alone. Nursing is all I have left, and I'm darn good at it. If you keep calling, it will jeopardize my future. My superiors will think my goals are divided, and I can assure you that is no longer the case."

She moved down the steps and swept by him. When he tried to follow her, she turned with fire in her eyes. "Don't follow me, and don't ever come here again. Do I make myself clear?"

Bryon stopped dead. He watched her walk out of his life. He deserved her anger. He was angry at himself. He should've been forthright all along. Even if it meant waiting a summer to have her, he should've waited. Now, he couldn't have her at all.

He swallowed back a knot in his throat and cursed under his breath. He deserved the agony, but she did not.

~

SEPTEMBER 1869
SHENANDOAH VALLEY

*J*osiah spent more and more time in bed.

Seth was his constant companion. His red curls bounced as he jumped up and down. A spattering of freckles spread across his tiny nose. He giggled as Josiah tickled his tummy. Josiah's heart wept at the thought of not seeing him grow up.

Often at night, he'd hear Katherine's muffled cries and soft sniffles, though she made a valiant attempt at bravery during the day. That pain was harder than living with his diminishing strength and shortness of breath.

And so, he prayed. He prayed for healing but grew sicker. He prayed for strength but grew weaker.

He prayed almost constantly. One troubled prayer toppled upon another. "Please God. Hasn't my Katherine suffered enough? Why now when we're so happy? Who will teach my son the ways of a man? Who will love him with a father's heart?"

Day after day, these same questions battered the doors of heaven without any answers. Despair was edging in.

"God, please hear my cry...I long to surrender and leave this in your trusty hands. So why do I feel there is something I'm missing?"

In the stillness of surrender, God birthed a plan. As natural as a spring rain, it fell into his soul. Peace immediately followed.

Only one prayer remained. "Lord, please grant me the time."

~

*K*atherine tossed upon her bed. She had barely slept. Though she was trying to be brave for Josiah's sake, as his strength waned, her sorrow increased. She vowed never to love again. The pain was unbearable.

Fear banged on the door of her heart, and darkness descended. Her life has been one tragedy after another. Trouble found her and everyone she loved. Her brothers, her friend Charles, now Josiah. Her chest felt tight, ready to explode. What if Seth was next? Despair pulled her down like a spiraling current in the Shenandoah River. Though she tried to fight its angry force, her sadness held no borders. Weak. Worried. Weary. The darkness beckoned her, and she jumped. Swirling. Spinning. Sucked into the deep.

She flipped the covers aside and slid out of bed with care so as not to wake Josiah. She shut the door to the adjoining bedroom with a gentle click and flung her body across her bed. Both fists pounded the bed beneath her as she muffled her screams into the dusty pillows.

"Why God? Why would you teach me to love and then snatch that love from me? I'll do anything for you, just please don't take Josiah. Please don't take him." She slid to her knees. That was what she would do, she would pray with enough faith to move a mountain. And this mountain of sickness would be cast into the sea. She would claim that Bible verse as her own.

~

The train jostled on the track shivering down the long steel rails. Colby shifted in his seat, removed his hat, and ran his hand through his sun-streaked hair. He was on his way to a town he thought he would never set foot in again—Lacey Spring. How could Josiah be dying? And how could God expect him to return? He plunked his hat back on his head with more force then needed.

Colby had come to peace with granting a dying man his wish that he visit. But that was then, and this was now. Each mile he chugged closer, the knot in his gut grew. Doubt slipped through the back door of his mind.

The argument he had with God replayed over and over.

From a distance, he was free from all feelings for her. He kept busy. He gave of his money and time. He had achieved success in most everything he touched. But to go back... *Why, God, are you demanding something so difficult?* His silent prayer echoed in his head.

I will give you strength.

But you told me to leave and flee temptation.

That was a long time ago. You are no longer a babe in Christ, you are a man of God.

154

"Mind if I sit here?"

Colby turned from the window as an attractive young woman slid from one side of the aisle to the empty seat beside him. She leaned close, and the assault of too much perfume bit at his nostrils.

"The man over there"—she nodded toward her former seatmate—"has terrible garlic breath. I do declare, I cannot abide another moment in such close proximity." She waved her hand in front of her dainty nose.

Colby had paid for two seats in order to prevent having to converse with anyone. He was also aware of every trick in the book. He was constantly bombarded with female attention, none of which he needed today.

"If you can remain quiet, no problem."

"But of course."

Her batting eyelashes and practiced pout irritated him. He turned toward the window.

"Where are you headed, cowboy?" Her silence lasted all of a minute.

"Look Ma'am, I don't mean to be rude. But I'm on my way to visit a dying friend. No offense, but my mind is on little else. Why don't you take this window seat farthest away from"—he nodded his head toward the man across the aisle—"and I'll take the one you vacated."

He rose and squeezed past her, dropping into her warm seat. The older gentleman sitting next to him did not bear a trace of garlic. Colby slid down, stretched his long legs in front of him, and lowered his hat over his eyes. Hopefully, she'd get the message.

He had not lied. Thoughts of Josiah and Katherine consumed him.

He was thankful Josiah had remained his friend and his partner, despite his obvious infatuation with Katherine. It was a testament to Josiah's forgiveness and character. Even though

Colby knew that God had forgiven him, it had been a battle to let go of the damage he had done. The full weight of guilt finally slid from Colby's shoulders the day he received a letter from Josiah telling him of the happiness in their marriage and the birth of their son. He had no desire to resurrect any of those feelings and threaten his hard-earned peace, and so he prayed.

Since leaving the Shenandoah Valley, Colby had asked God to provide him with love, with a wife, with a family. He had come close with Charlotte, yet not close enough. He pulled his legs up and removed his hat, fingering the felt around the rim as he remembered his battle to forget Katherine. He had done well until Charlotte pressed for marriage, and then things unraveled.

The rattle of the train jarred him back to the present. His hat dropped from his fingertips, and he crushed his head against the seat in front of him trying to retrieve it.

That memory stirred his gut and was the reason he would never get married or have a family. He would live alone. He would love—but never be loved.

And pray like never before.

CHAPTER 18

*A*melia waited until the end of her shift before approaching. "Nurse Bridgett, may I have a word with you?" She clasped her trembling hands together. The older nurse may see her request as evidence that Amelia was not fully committed to her nursing, but God kept nudging her spirit and wouldn't let go. She had to obey.

"Yes." The stern gray-haired lady sitting at her desk behind a mountain of paper looked over her glasses.

"I have a request, but I want you to know I am most dedicated to becoming the best nurse possible." Amelia took a deep breath and plunged ahead. "My brother-in-law is dying, and I feel I must go help my sister. I was hoping I could take any lessons and books you would recommend for further reading, and you would consider this as part of my practicum?"

Nurse Bridgett's face softened, and she removed her glasses. "I would not think about giving this privilege to anyone else who started their training when you did, but you are the most advanced student by far. I'll have to run this by Dr. Meade, but when my husband passed away, I would've so appreciated the help."

Amelia let out the breath she had been holding.

"May I ask what he is dying from?"

"My sister said it is damage done to his heart from a severe case of diphtheria he had in the war."

"I'm so sorry to hear that. I'll get you all the information I can find so that you'll know how to make him as comfortable as possible."

"Thank you so much."

"But don't go counting on this until I speak to Dr. Meade—"

"Did I hear my name?" The gray-haired stocky man steered into the room from the hallway.

"Seems Miss Williams is needing a month or so off to go help a dying member of her family. It'll be good experience for her, as she will put her nursing into practice."

A stern look came over Dr. Meade. "And lose the best student we have?"

"You won't be losing me, sir. I love nursing, and I'll keep up with my reading—"

"Then go. If you can handle nursing a family member, you'll have conquered one of the hardest challenges nursing has to offer. But you must return. You are a very talented nurse with advancement in your future. We'd hate to lose you."

Amelia worked hard not to break out into a wide smile. That was high praise. "I will. I promise."

Nurse Bridgette nodded her head. "Report to me tomorrow, and I'll have your reading and the information you'll need to best care for your brother-in-law. Go with God."

Praise flowed out of Amelia's heart. God had taken care of every detail, even the austere Dr. Meade. The peace of obedience washed like a healing balm covering the broken bits of her heart.

≈

LATE SEPTEMBER 1869
SHENANDOAH VALLEY

*J*osiah loved watching her.

Katherine helped him sit and fluffed the pillows behind his head for the umpteenth time. "I personally scrubbed every inch of this dust-ridden room before moving you down here." She tucked and folded the blankets at the foot of the bed yet again. Her long dark hair caught in a sloppy knot at the nape of her neck made him long to set it free...waving down her back in a curtain of silk. To bury his head and get lost in her loveliness—that loss was one of his deepest sorrows. To admit he no longer had the strength to climb the steps to *their* bedroom left a deep ache.

"Are you comfortable? Doc Phillips said you can take as much laudanum as you need for the pain."

"Come here, my love." He patted the bed beside him. "None of that stuff today. I want to be clear-headed."

She came to the edge of the bed but looked straight through him.

"I have something to tell you about Colby."

"Colby?" Her gaze snapped to his, confusion clouding it.

"I know you feel uncomfortable about the past, but we have to discuss him in order to address the future. He's still my partner."

"And he'd be at your side helping you right now if I had not ruined everything."

He squeezed her hand. "You did not ruin our friendship." He pulled her closer. "Lie beside me."

She eased slowly to his side as if he were a piece of fine china.

"I won't break."

She nuzzled closer and relaxed against him. He smoothed a hand down her back. "Ahh, this is nice."

Her head moved up and down against his chest, and he kissed the crown of hair he so loved. He enjoyed a few still minutes of bliss.

"We're having a visitor today," he said. "You may want to change for supper this evening."

Her head snapped up, and she twisted in his arms to look at him. "You're in no condition to receive guests. Who on earth did you invite?"

He took a deep breath in. "Colby should be here by four this afternoon if the train is on time."

"What?" Her eyes flashed with more fire than he had seen in months. "You invited him without talking to me first? Do my feelings count for nothing?"

"Of course, they count—"

"It'll be so...so awkward. Don't you understand, I've wrecked everything between you two?" She rolled away, but he sat up and caught her arm before she escaped. He kneaded her shoulders and worked out the knots as he used to do. Her spine curved against him as she relaxed into the bed.

"Things are fine between Colby and me. We all made mistakes back then. You don't get to carry that load alone. Besides, that's the wonder of forgiveness. We remained partners and friends. And I need my friend."

He leaned forward and dropped a kiss on the back of her neck as his hands moved up and down her spine. He was in terrible pain, but he would never let her know.

"You have enough to do with Seth and looking after me. I don't want you worrying about the ranch as well."

"What about Hank?" Her voice wavered.

"He's a great foreman, but he's not capable of taking over the whole operation when I'm gone."

Her shoulders stiffened.

"Kat. We need to talk about this. Every time I bring up the future, you shut me down. But I'm dying, and time is running short."

She pulled free and leapt to her feet. His weakness prevented him from keeping her close.

She stomped back and forth. "Don't you think I know you're dying? There I said it. Does it make you feel better to hear me say those words? You're dying. You're dying." She paused and massaged both sides of her temples. "Oh, dear God in heaven, you're dying, Josiah, and we have no future." Her lips trembled, and her face turned as white as a starched veil.

"*We*, no. But you have a future, and we need to talk about the ranch, about—"

"No. No. No." She covered her face with her hands. "I don't want to talk. I want to scream. I want this nightmare to end. I've been praying in faith, and yet where is God?"

"I've yelled into the heavens myself, and then I found peace."

"Peace?" She stepped forward, towering over him, a storm flashing in her eyes. "I don't want peace, I want healing."

It took all he had to rise from the bed and wrap his arms around her. His legs wobbled beneath his thin frame whittled to half the man he used to be, but somehow God gave him the strength to hold her.

"How am I going to live without you? I love you more than life itself."

"God will make a way."

She rocked in his arms, a moan twisting from deep within. "He's not making a way. He's taking you from me."

"I know—"

"I hurt so much I think my heart is going to burst right out of my chest." She placed a hand over her heart. "And what about Seth? He needs his daddy."

He kissed the top of her head. "I love the both of you more

than words can say, but I know God loves you more." He ran a knuckle lightly down her tear-stained cheek.

Her eyes, dark with pain, met his. "How did you find peace?"

"There is only one way—I prayed and I surrendered." He wrapped his once strong arms around her. "Sit with me. We'll pray together."

"Goodness, I wasn't thinking." She pulled him to the side of the bed. "You must've been in such pain standing there holding me while I..."

He dropped a light kiss on her cheek, and her words trailed.

When they were settled, she said, "I don't think I can pray. I have no words left." She leaned into the curve of his arm stretched around her. "I'm so angry."

The bands of his heart tightened. Colby better get here soon. He had only one plan left and, if that failed... No, he could not go down that road. In faith he would believe what he heard from the Lord.

❧

How awkward his arrival would be for Katherine, for him, but then how could Colby say no to the request of his dying friend. He felt the tug of their worlds colliding like the reins pulling in his hands. Why was Josiah so insistent he come? As uncomfortable as it may be, Josiah's wishes trumped all else, but had he made it in time?

Colby feared the worst as he approached the ranch. He turned onto the pebbled drive, shifting uneasily upon his mount as he spurred the flanks of the old nag. A far cry from the horse flesh he normally rode, but he was grateful to Tom at the local livery for so generous an offer and the fastest way to the ranch. He swung from the saddle and tied the reins to the hitching post in a rush. He would see to the horse after. Right now, he needed to know, had his prayer been answered? Would he get to hug his dear friend one more time?

A sigh of relief pressed through his lips as he approached the front door not covered in black crepe signifying death. Nor was the customary wreath of amaranth leaves tied with ribbon hanging there. His knocking knees subsided as fear drained from his body.

"Thank you, Lord." He whispered into the heavens.

Colby raised a shaky hand and knocked.

CHAPTER 19

*B*ryon walked up and down the street in front of Amelia's house a dozen times before he found the nerve to knock on her door. He had to try one last time, if for no other reason than to say he was sorry. Those should've been the first words out of his mouth instead of his excuses.

Standing outside her grandmother and grandfather's home, he couldn't help but think how they must hate him. But the need to voice his sincerest apology outweighed all discomfort.

No one knew, but his foolish heart could not let her go. For the first week after they'd broken up, he'd used his lunch hour to watch her come and go from the hospital while respecting the distance she desired. He finally stopped that craziness and hoped his apology would help him say good-bye for good. He had left a note at her house requesting a meeting and received no response. The past few days he had waited outside the hospital to no avail. Had she left Richmond again? Was his behavior responsible for quashing her dream of becoming a nurse?

He prayed it was not so. A barb of guilt pierced his heart. He had rarely prayed in the past, but of late had taken up the practice. The more he prayed, the more sorrow he felt at the way he had handled the situation. It was what propelled him to her door.

Lydia, the maid, opened the door.

"Is Amelia in?" His eyes darted down the hall, hoping to catch a glimpse of her.

"One moment, please." She slammed the door in his face.

Everything within him wanted to run, but he stood his ground. Even if Amelia never spoke to him beyond today, she deserved an apology and hopefully an explanation.

The door swung wide. Amelia's grandmother stood tall and erect with a look on her face that told him in no uncertain terms she was a force to be reckoned with.

"I can't believe you have the nerve to darken our door." She looked down her nose at him. The landing was a step lower, putting them eye to eye.

"You're quite right. Nevertheless, I need to I speak to—"

"You may not. You lost that privilege when you played her like a fiddle all summer and then started back up with Shelby as soon as she arrived back from Europe."

He couldn't hold her beady gaze. His eyes flicked down.

"May I please talk to her? At the very least I need to apologize." His words tumbled out. "And maybe if she understood—"

"You've done enough damage. She is not here, and even if she were, I wouldn't let you talk to her. She gave strict instructions to send you packing, and that's exactly what I intend to do."

"Can you tell her I'm sorry?"

The door slammed in his face.

He stood without moving for a long moment. Every bone in

his body wanted to break that door down and beg an audience, but her grandmother was right, he didn't deserve Amelia. He lowered his head and turned toward the street.

There was nothing left to fight for. Amelia was gone from him forever, and he deserved what he got. His heart felt like a candle had blown out within the depth of a deep black cavern. No grief. No sorrow. No self-pity. Nothing.

And that was scarier.

Shelby still wanted to marry him, even after he'd told her how he'd spent his summer. Even after he told her that he didn't love her. She viewed their relationship as well-suited and pleasant.

How could that be enough?

The one thing he could do right after making such a mess would be to respect his parents' wishes and bring happiness to them and to Shelby by agreeing to marriage. Maybe that would somehow redeem his soul.

~

LATE SEPTEMBER 1869
SHENANDOAH VALLEY

*T*he door knocker hammered. Katherine's stomach twisted and knotted. Colby was there.

She stood, but Abe waved her away.

"I'll get the door." He ambled slowly out of the parlor.

Katherine moved across the room and lifted Seth from Delilah's arms. She would present a united family unit with a clear message. Her legs quivered beneath her skirt. She ruffled Seth's hair, and he buried his head in her shoulder. His thumb went in his mouth as he snuggled in. Her hands moved up and down Seth's tiny back.

Though she had railed at Josiah for not giving her fair warning, she was actually thankful there hadn't been much time to fret about meeting Colby again. But oh, how she wished Josiah were strong enough to stand beside her now.

∽

Colby entered and extended his hand for a hearty handshake. Abe drew him into a hug.

"Good to see you, Abe."

"The same, my boy. The same." Abe slapped him on the shoulder before he pulled away.

Colby lifted his head as Katherine and Delilah entered the hall. He stepped forward, relieved to see welcome in her eyes and a child in her arms. The presence of the Spirit cloaked him in peace, so it didn't hurt to look at her the way it used to.

Delilah opened her arms. "Land sakes boy, don't just stand there. Come give us a hug." She gathered Katherine and Seth close, beckoning Colby into the warmth of a family hug.

Colby wanted to kiss Delilah for her intuitiveness. She'd broken an awkward moment and brought them all together.

"Well, who do we have here?" Colby said, pulling back, as the bright haired child took the opportunity to playfully swat at him.

"This is Seth," Katherine said. "He's our pride and joy, aren't you, little scamp? Be nice now and don't hit the guests." She grabbed his chubby hand in hers. He arched in her arms squirming to be put down. She bent forward to release him. "Since he started walking, there's no keeping this boy in one place for too long."

To Colby's amazement he ran straight into his legs and held his hands out to be picked up. Colby didn't hesitate.

Delilah and Katherine looked at each other with raised eyebrows.

"Well, if that don't beat all." Delilah planted her hands on her generous hips.

Katherine nodded, and they both laughed.

"What?"

"He doesn't go to many and especially not strangers. But for some reason, he likes you. Well not that you're odd. What I mean is..." Katherine turned bright red.

"I've been called worse." Colby laughed and Seth giggled. The group joined in, and Seth giggled all the more. Colby raised him high above his head and back down, and Seth clapped his chubby hands in delight.

"He's a lively one."

"Yes, and you don't know what you've started if he takes a shining to you. You may very well have a shadow." Katherine reached out to take Seth, but he turned away. "You little peanut. All right, a few more minutes with your new friend." She smiled, but the smile didn't reach her eyes.

"Josiah's been looking forward to your visit." At the mention of his name, a mixture of sadness, confusion, and fear, painted her face. "Follow me." She waved him forward to a nearby room, stopping at the door. "Prepare yourself," she whispered.

He stepped inside. The drapes were pulled, and the bed seemed too empty and the man too small to be the friend he knew. "Colby, my friend, come here and give me a hug." Josiah's voice was weak, but he pushed himself to a sitting position. "I'm way past the point of worrying about being a tough man." Josiah's smile disappeared behind sunken cheeks.

Colby worked hard to hide the shock from his face. The once huge man was nearly a skeleton.

"I'll get this little man out of your way." Katherine took a none-too-pleased Seth from Colby's arms. "You two need some time alone."

"I've missed you." Colby moved toward the bed as Katherine closed the door behind her. Unbidden tears stung behind his eyelids. "Wish this reunion were under better circumstances." His voice caught, and he swallowed hard against the knot in his throat.

"You and me both."

$\sim$

Seth twisted in Katherine's arms, grunting out his need for release until he noticed the tears rolling down her face. Mesmerized by the flow, his dimpled hands reached out to rub them.

Katherine hurried up the stairs to the nursery and clicked the door behind her. Her tears flowed in earnest.

Seth quieted and laid his cheek against hers. His little arm came around her shoulder and his hand rested on the back of her neck. She inhaled the sweet scent of baby skin and relished the warmth of his silken curls pressed against her cheek. A little touch of heaven seeped through in that hug, and the presence of Someone much bigger filled the room. Many moons ago she had agonized over her arranged and loveless marriage to Josiah and had wondered if God cared about her plight. He had not only met her, He had saved her and their marriage, bringing more love than she'd dreamed possible. Somehow, she had to find the faith that God still held her, even if He didn't do things her way.

She sank into the rocker by the window and gazed at the gathering darkness. In the quiet, prayer filled her being, and peace replaced the angst. Seth fell asleep in her arms, sucking his thumb. His curly red mop and cherub cheeks stirred her heart until it was bursting with love. He was the reason she had to find a way through the sorrow. She kissed his forehead tenderly.

His relaxed body curved against hers gave credence to the passing of time. She stood from the rocker and laid Seth carefully in his crib. Turning, she tiptoed out. With the soft click of the nursery door she took a deep breath. He was asleep.

The day had been filled with too much emotion. A hot cup of tea was just what she needed as she headed down the stairs into the kitchen. In a matter of minutes, she was settled at the table. She had missed supper but was not hungry.

"Katherine."

She jumped at the sound of his voice, and a spot of tea splashed onto the old wooden table. She rubbed it away.

"Sorry about that. I didn't mean to startle you. Do you mind if I join you for a moment?" Colby's eyes dropped to the floor. "I think it's best we talk. Clear the air—"

"I think that's a wise idea." She didn't want to go on feeling uncomfortable in his presence.

His eyes shot up at her answer.

"With Josiah so ill..." She looked aside and shut her eyes to press back the tears behind her eyelids. "Grab a mug and sit. I have some extra tea in the pot."

He filled his cup and slid into a chair across from her. "How are you doing?"

Her heart squeezed tight and her throat grew thick. How could she even put into words her pain? "The truth?"

"You always did have a way of getting to the point."

She looked past him to the pots hanging from the hooks, the kettle steaming on the wood stove, the same wooden table where they had shared many meals. The crackle of the wood in the stove snapped and popped.

"Honestly. I'm surviving one day at a time." She wouldn't tell him she'd been fighting with God and not winning. Those words to the Lord's prayer, *Thy will be done*, were not slipping off her lips.

"I've been there." He averted his eyes.

"I'm not sure I'll ever understand—I've prayed for healing but..." She held up her hands. She was still pleading for a miracle and wrestling with God's sovereignty all at the same time. There were no words.

"You believe in God." His eyes opened, and he smiled.

"I guess you wouldn't know. After you left. I figured I'd lost my last friend."

"I'm so sorry—"

"You did the right thing. Your leaving prompted my journey toward faith. I want to thank you for going and say how sorry I am for my part in encouraging a relationship that was wrong." Heat swallowed her face despite her best efforts to stop the blush.

"I'm sorry too."

"I know." She lifted her head and found the courage to look into his eyes. "And so does Josiah. It took time, but God brought us together and blessed us with Seth. I've been so happy, until —" Her voice broke and she dropped her head into her hands. Her elbows shook and collapsed beneath the weight. With arms folded around her head and slumped on the table, she gave way to the racking sobs. Slowly the pain oozed out, and silence and sniffles remained.

Had Colby slipped out to leave her to grieve alone? She looked up to find him with his head bowed, eyes closed and lips silently moving. He was praying. That simple act of faith brought far more comfort than any spoken words.

"Thank you."

He lifted his head. "You're welcome, my friend."

CHAPTER 20

*A*melia grabbed her coat and headed out of the farmhouse. The squeak of the screen door followed by the familiar bang brought a smile to her lips. She was halfway down the porch steps when she reversed her direction and deliberately opened the screen door once again to hear that simple country sound.

The crisp autumn air bit into her cheeks as she headed down the well-worn path to Katherine's house. The crunch of orchard leaves beneath her feet and the pungent smell of apples rotting on the ground filled her senses and signified the turning of the seasons. Soon old man winter would be bearing down.

She pulled her cloak up around her ears and bent her head into the wind. What would today bring? The pending doom of death knocked loudly, and she shivered more from that thought than from the cold.

"Katherine." She yelled as she let herself in. "I'm here."

The sweep of a dress rounded the corner before her graceful sister with child in arm appeared. It never ceased to amaze Amelia how beautiful Katherine was. Even with dark circles under her eyes and her hair swept up in a sloppy bun, elegance radiated.

"How would I have managed without you these past few weeks?" She gave a quick hug and kissed Amelia's cheek. "You truly are an angel."

"Hardly. If you knew how much I wanted to get away from Ma's relentless quest for information, you'd know I'm no angel."

Katherine laughed. "She is good at information gathering."

"Where can I be of most help today?"

"Well, I'm not sure. Seth is teething and grumpier than a bear. Josiah is in need of almost constant supervision. His breathing is labored, and I hate leaving his side." She wiggled her messy bun and scratched her scalp. "And I can't go another day without washing my hair."

"I'll take Seth," Colby offered as he rounded the corner from the kitchen. "Sorry, but I couldn't help but overhear the conversation. And Amelia, since Josiah says you have the knack for making him comfortable, it makes sense you go in that direction."

"Don't you need to get outside to the men?"

"I've got Hank and the boys squared away for the morning."

"I want to check on Josiah anyway," Amelia said. "Go have a bath, and I'll sit with him. Get your hair washed and enjoy a few minutes to yourself. Don't rush, we'll all be fine without you."

Katherine gave a shaky smile. "Thank you both."

Seth started to scream as Katherine held him out to Colby. He grabbed him quickly and whirled him in a circle above his head. "Come, little man. I may not be as good as your mama, but I do know that all little boys like cookies."

"Colby, it's ten in the morning," Katherine said.

"Let it be," Amelia said. "Whatever it takes, and today it takes something sweet to combat the sour. Now go." She flung her hand in the direction of Katherine's bedroom. "I'll send Annie to help with the water."

Colby headed for the kitchen with the screaming child. Amelia followed. She grabbed the cookie jar where Delilah kept the sweet biscuits and gave one to Seth to gnaw on.

He instantly quieted.

"Katherine told me you came from Richmond to help," Colby said. "You're a good sister."

"I guess I could say the same about you being a good friend."

"Well, I'm a partner too. It stands to reason that I should help."

"Well, I'm family—even more reason."

He laughed. "'Tis true. But it doesn't go unnoticed. I was getting worried about Katherine's crazy schedule until you came on the scene. Even though we've spelled each other sitting with Josiah day and night, she was not about to trust him with the hired help. And with running ragged trying to juggle Seth and this household, it was too much for her. Delilah and Abe do the best they can to help, but they're getting up there."

"I'm glad God laid it on my heart to come."

She moved forward and bent to tickle Seth's rosy cheeks. "You be good for Colby now, you hear." Seth lifted his freckled face to Colby and held out his gooey cookie to share. Colby pretended to take a big bite and ruffled his mop of curly red hair. "Wow, this kid gets you right here." He pounded his chest.

"He sure does. You know where to find me if you need anything." She headed down the hall toward Josiah's room.

When Amelia had first arrived, she'd braced herself for a different Josiah, but nothing could have prepared her for the huge man shrunk to half his body mass with skin hanging on his lanky frame. Her training had helped steel her reaction, but still every time she entered his room she steadied herself. It was much harder watching someone you loved waste away than seeing the same happen to a stranger.

"How are you doing with the pain?" she asked as she walked

in. "And no trying to be brave with me. Remember, I'm the one person you need to be frank with."

"I'm thankful you're here, Amelia. Every time I had to ask for laudanum, Katherine would come undone. It hurt her so much to think of me in pain."

"That's why I check in regularly. You don't have to concern her with the medical end of things. And it's why you need to be honest with me. We can keep you comfortable."

"Breathing is tough."

"Let's get your head up a bit." She helped lift his body and stuffed some pillows beneath him.

"Doc Phillips said it won't be long now."

"Yes." She held his gaze. "With all the reading I've been doing, your symptoms are final stage." She steeled the catch in her throat and turned so he couldn't see the mist in her eyes. "Making you comfortable is of utmost importance, and that, I know how to do."

"Thank you—for coming, for caring."

Amelia turned back to him. "I could do no less for the man who has helped our family so much and loved my sister so well." She didn't hold back her tears, instead let them flow freely. There was no point in trying to hide how much she cared.

"We'll be there for Katherine and Seth too," she promised.

~

*K*atherine lay slumped in the chair next to Josiah, fighting off the weariness that had seeped into every bone. She didn't want to miss a moment. The rattle in his throat and his labored breath had kept her vigilant most of the night.

She shook the haze out of her head and pulled the chair close enough to gather his hand in the warmth of hers. His cold sent a shiver scuttling up her spine.

"Katherine." A strangled whisper slipped from his lips, and she rose to lean over him.

"I'm right here."

"Love you...so much." His words were drawn out and soaked in love.

She placed her hands on either side of his face. "I love you, Josiah Richardson, more than words can say."

His lips moved, and she leaned her ear close.

"Promise me."

A shudder worked through her slim body. "Anything."

"Love again."

Tears silently streamed. She wanted to ask him how she was supposed to live without him and beg him not to leave her. Instead, she hugged him close. She would let him go in peace, though everything inside her was screaming, *"Oh God, please don't take him. Please. Please. Please."* A ragged breath ripped across the room, but it was her own.

The love of her life was gone.

～

*K*atherine rose from her bed. She shuffled across the floor like an old lady with barely enough energy to lift her feet. She looked at the adjoining door into what had been their bedroom. Would she ever gain the courage to walk back in there?

She peeked out of her lacy curtains. What kind of weather would be fitting for the day she buried her husband? Certainly not what she saw. The late October morning burst with sunlight and color. Leaves sifted down from the trees that lined the drive, touching the landscape with gold and yellow. Crisp. Clear. Cheery. She snatched the curtains closed.

How would she find the strength to stand before the crowd that was sure to gather and watch her husband lowered into the cold, dark earth? She had cried so many tears these past five days, she now felt numb.

She did what was expected of her as the day passed. Every step was measured, every detail accomplished by rote. Before she knew it, the yard was cluttered with wagons, and people milled all over her property. She slipped back up to her bedroom. All she wanted was for Josiah to shake her shoulders and wake her from the nightmare. She closed her eyes and imagined him healthy and strong, gathering her close whispering how much he loved her. Tears streamed down her face.

A slight rap on her bedroom door, and Amelia's head popped in. "Delilah told me to bring up your gown. Clarisse just arrived with it. She said to tell you that it was her gift—a thank-you for Josiah's patronage at her dress shop."

Katherine let out a sob.

Amelia's arms instantly folded around her. "If I could take some of this pain for you, I surely would."

Katherine nodded into her shoulder. "I don't wish this kind of pain on anyone."

Amelia pulled back and offered a handkerchief. "I have a pocket full of these today. Come, I'll help you get dressed. The service is in less than an hour."

Katherine looked at the black dress that held not a stitch of color. She swiped at the tears that continued to fall. She finally knew why people wore black at funerals, it mirrored a world devoid of joy, much like hers was now.

Another knock on the door, and Jeanette and Ma piled in. "Is it too much if we're here?" Ma asked tentatively. Katherine didn't have the heart to tell her yes, so she nodded. Everyone was trying so hard to help, when there was nothing to be done. The ache flowed from a bottomless pit of sorrow.

She did what her sister said, donned the black dress and sat still while Amelia brushed her hair.

"There you go." Amelia placed a black hat with a black

feather on her head, keeping her hair cascading down her black dress. Her pale white face contrasted drastically with the ensemble, making her look almost as dead as she felt on the inside.

They ushered her down the steps, out to the formal gardens where rows of chairs faced the solarium. Reverend Jude stood behind a makeshift pulpit. She longed to slip into a chair at the back but instead had to hold her head up and make her way to the front, enduring the stares of pity. Sniffles and sobs filled the air. She slid in beside Pa, who held Seth. Lucinda, Gracie, and Colby completed the row to the left, with Ma, Amelia, and Jeanette to the right.

Seth immediately lunged her way. She pulled him close, and silent tears fell into his curly red locks as small warm arms circled her neck. Here was her one reason to find a way through. She knew only God could give her strength.

Dear God, please help me. Her simple silent prayer lifted into the heavens. A warming fanned out straight through to her core. She knew she was not alone. A strength she had not possessed a moment earlier spread supernaturally through her. She rose with the congregation to sing Josiah's favorite hymn —*Amazing Grace*. His coffin lay in front of her, but he was no longer present. He was free. He was home. His suffering was over.

Hers had just begun.

CHAPTER 21

CHRISTMAS 1869
RICHMOND

*W*ith a slight rap on Amelia's bedroom door, her grandmother swept in.

"Do you need any extra help getting ready?"

"All good, Grandmother. I'll call Lydia when it's time to do my hair, but it has to dry first."

"I love Richmond's Annual Christmas Fundraising Ball. My highlight of the year."

Grandmother's voice sounded an octave higher than usual and grated on Amelia's already frazzled nerves. She wished she could find a good excuse to miss the occasion like she had the year before when she'd not been feeling well. If only she could tell her grandmother the truth—she was attending the dance to make her happy. Amelia was through with the social scene and men in general.

"Good heavens, forgive my rattling on, but I do so look forward to this evening. It's my one night to shine." She sat on the edge of Amelia's bed.

"Shine?"

"All the donations for the fundraiser go to the local orphanage, but the fun part is that no one knows what the next person gives until the end of the evening when the top three donations are revealed. Just so happens that your grandfather and I typically come in as the biggest donors." Her eyes sparkled, and she rubbed her hands together.

"Some good old-fashioned rivalry, all for a good cause."

"Oh my, yes. And to prance up there in front of the likes of Melinda Preston. Maybe I shouldn't take such pleasure, but I do." She giggled like a child and raised her finger to her lips. "But you mustn't tell a soul of my true confessions."

Amelia smiled. "Your secret is safe with me, but I do believe the Lord loves a cheerful giver who does so—privately."

"Well, the good Lord can enjoy my private giving all year long, but tonight, if the only pleasure I get is to see their faces drop when I'm honored and they're not, that's all the joy I need." She laughed.

"Grandmother." Amelia turned from the mirror where she combed her long hair. "You're a bit of a rebel."

She waved her hand, dismissing the remark. "When you're as old as I am, fun comes in different forms. However, your enjoyment will be in making Bryon Preston regret he ever played with your emotions."

"I intend to ignore him." She turned her gaze back to the mirror as if practicing. Though she spoke the words, she knew how hard it would be to see him waltzing around the ballroom floor with his fiancée. The news had become official shortly after she'd returned from the valley in the beginning of November.

"Ignore him if you please, but I want to be sure he sees you." She swung open the door of Amelia's armoire. "This dress is not simply any dress." She pulled the gown free and held it in both hands. "Imported from Paris in the latest fashion, made with the finest silk... Put your cheek to this material, pure heaven." She pulled the fabric up to touch her face.

Amelia moved closer and held the folds. "I can't understand why you spoil me so. I don't need all this finery."

"Balderdash. Nothing is too good for my granddaughter.

She held up the gown and twirled it around. "You'll have the young men lining up."

"But Grandmother, I don't—"

"No buts. You shall dance your way right out of this heartache. Do you hear me?"

Grandmother sat on the edge of the bed and then stood suddenly in a spry fashion that bespoke more spunk than Amelia could muster. "Oh yes, I almost forgot. I shall be right back."

Amelia let out a big breath. The thought of seeing Bryon again made her stomach coil in knots. Her fingers twisted and untwisted in the folds of her dress. She no longer wanted to get ready.

The bedroom door creaked on its hinges as Grandmother returned. "I have just the added touch you need for that dress." She held out a glittering necklace. "Sapphires." She held them up to the light of the window. "Come, take a look at this beauty."

Amelia rose from her perch on the bed and stood beside her grandmother. The necklace was stunning.

"Heavens, no. Wearing that would frighten me half to death. What if I lose it?"

"Never you mind that worry. What is a piece of jewelry if not to be worn? You wear this with all the grace and confidence you can muster. It only adds to your natural beauty."

"I'm not a beauty. Wait until you meet Katherine."

Firm hands grabbed her shoulders and marched her over to the mirror. "Tell me what you see. Every time you come back from the valley you go on about Katherine's beauty. Being around her seems to diminish the view you have of yourself. So, tell me."

"Well, I guess—"

"No guessing. Look at yourself. Really look, my dear."

Amelia stared into the mirror.

"Can't you see those large hazel eyes of yours that sparkle with flecks of gold. And those fringed sooty eyelashes that most women would die for."

"What about these?" Amelia pointed to the freckles she had always hated.

"What's wrong with cinnamon-toned freckles that kiss your nose, not to mention this fine-grained alabaster skin. Oh, how I miss the beauty of youth." She ran a finger down Amelia's cheek. "And this hair." She lifted some in her wrinkled hands and let it slide through her fingers. "Look at this silkiness cascading down to your waist."

"But it's boring brown, not glossy black like—"

"Oh, no you don't." She waved her finger in Amelia's face and turned her sideways before the mirror so that the late afternoon sun streaming through the window could catch the strands. "This is not boring brown. Look at the copper highlights."

Amelia swung her hair in the sunlight and had to admit there was merit to what Grandmother said.

"And what about the rest of you?"

Amelia gazed into the mirror. Sculptured cheeks had replaced the chubby, and her figure, previously lost in the folds of extra weight, curved with elegance.

"In case you haven't noticed, you're not only beautiful on the inside but on the outside as well." Grandmother leaned in and hugged her. "I'll send up Lydia. It's time for the beauty to prepare for the ball."

"*T*ake a look," Lydia said. "You're very beautiful."

Amelia turned toward the full-length mirror and sucked in a sharp breath. The cool periwinkle dress with a molded bodice accented her womanly curves to perfection. The latest style plunged a little too deep at the neckline for her modest taste, but she had to admit she did look good. She swiveled from side to side. The folds of silk danced upon the bustle.

"Do you mind if I go get Bethany?" Lydia asked. "She wanted to see you all dressed up."

"That's fine."

After Lydia hurried out, Amelia touched the filigreed tortoise-shell Spanish comb in her upswept hair one last time and caught the twinkle of the sapphire necklace in her reflection. It seemed to mock the princess and the pauper all wrapped up in one. She knew who she was—a country girl born and raised wrapped in a beautiful gown bought and paid for by her wealthy grandparents. Obviously, the likes of Melinda Preston knew that too. Silk could not erase the farm.

Her heart dropped. A thought of the handsome prince who would never be hers brought a rush of unwanted tears. Try as she might, she couldn't eradicate Bryon all together. "Stop with the tears." She spoke into the mirror. "You'll become the best nurse ever and leave this social world far behind."

She lifted her chin in a show of confidence that did not touch her heart. She no longer had a penchant for the fake world of putting on airs. Everything she had learned at finishing school seemed to present that which was not. She had tried to fit in and had failed. The sooner she could get her grandmother to understand, the sooner she could leave the social world forever. She was a nurse now, someone who could take care of herself.

Men and marriage were off her list.

~

*G*randmother squeezed Amelia's arm as they stepped from the carriage. "Look around. 'Tis the evening you'll see the most beautiful horses pulled by the most stylish carriages." Excitement sparkled in her eyes. "To your left"—she nodded politely in that direction—"a Barouche carriage, with upholstery, carved wood, and brass fittings imported all the way from Italy."

Amelia could not muster up the excitement her Grandmother had. It was lovely, but just a carriage, after all.

"Don't look now"—Grandmother nodded in the other direction as they climbed the steps—"but there's Mr. Preston showing off his latest Phaeton. And Melinda, in what I have to admit, is a stunning dress."

Just the mention of the Preston name twisted Amelia's stomach into a knot. She kept her gaze ahead. All she had strength for was to whisper a prayer. *Dear God, please help me through this evening.*

From her entrance into the grand ballroom in the senator's home while the full orchestra played strains of what her grandmother whispered was Mozart, opulence filled the air. Her eyes swept from floor-to-ceiling. A beautifully decorated Christmas tree with hand-painted glass balls that sparkled in the shimmering light of an overhead chandelier stood in all its splendor. How many hungry mouths would the cost of this decorating alone feed? Not to mention the food, the drinks, the clothing…

"Smile, my dear." Grandmother leaned in. "You're wearing the most troubling frown. It does not do justice to your dress."

Amelia worked hard to change her expression. She had promised to make the best of the evening, and her grandmother had spent an enormous amount of money so she could dress the part. She would do her utmost to comply, but this would be the last of its kind if she had anything to say about it. If only she could have made a good excuse and stay home like Grandfather did.

She pasted her smile in place as she made the rounds and bobbed and curtseyed like a puppet on a string. Her dance card immediately filled, except for planned breaks, so Melinda Preston must've been keeping her end of the bargain to not reveal the truth of Amelia's humble background. Not that she cared. She had no intention of marrying into this world. Part of her actually craved that the truth be known. Both Edmund and Bryon were prime examples of what living a double life cost her.

She popped an hors d'oeuvre into her mouth rather than place it neatly onto a napkin before doing so. She was not sure what it was, but it crackled with a savory flavor. She repeated the most unladylike behavior and smiled at her rebellion. Eating was going to be the best part of her evening. A whole table of decadent sweets in perfect bite-sized pieces winked at her from across the room, but she had her first dance commitment with Thomas Ratcliffe to attend to.

Ever since the spring ball, Thomas had singled her out at most every function. Tonight was no different. He had beelined her way to claim her first spot on the dance card only minutes after she had walked in. Etiquette demanded she accept but, when he asked for two more spots, she declined. Best not to encourage something that was never going to be.

She smiled up at him politely as he led her onto the ballroom floor, and they began a slow waltz.

He leaned as close as propriety would allow. "How long are you going to keep me at arms' length?"

She smiled up at him. "If I told you I was a farm girl born into near poverty, would you still be interested?"

He laughed. "With a dress like that, there is no doubt you come from wealth, breeding, and all that matters."

All that matters. As if any of that mattered. Her stomach knotted, and it took all she had to finish the dance.

He whirled her around and squeezed her waist inappropriately. "Are you sure you don't have room on that card for at least one more?"

"No." Her answer was swift. He was like all the other shallow men to whom beauty, wealth, and standing meant everything.

She had barely rested between dances all night and had successfully managed to avoid Bryon. But one sideways glance, and there he was. Immaculately groomed, expensively tailored, and possessing all the confidence that affluence and status gave a man, he danced with his beautiful blonde fiancée an arms' breadth away. Her heart hammered, and her mouth went dry. Their eyes met as the happy couple twirled by.

She wanted to hate him or, at the least, keep the fire of anger stoked, but sadness oozed from his eyes as if he were trying to convey a message. She looked away, but her foolish heart had her gazing his way again. He kept his eyes fixed on her. His head bobbed from one side of Shelby to the other as he kept her in view.

In the midst of the crowd, a sudden loneliness hit her. She spoke to her dance partner. "I'm sorry, Clarence, but these new shoes are really hurting. I need to take a break, if you don't mind." He nodded graciously and escorted her off the dance floor.

In a whirl of rustling starched bustles and swishing silk, she escaped. She had no idea where she was going but had to get away from the pressing crowd and Bryon's expressive eyes. Her lungs wheezed as the walls of her chest tightened. Her heart thumped as if it were beating in molasses. Why did he still stir unwanted emotion in her?

With a look to the left and to the right, she passed by rooms until finally she found the library at the end of the hall. To her delight, a door onto a small balcony provided a much-needed oasis. She slipped out and took a deep breath as relief swept over her. Alone at last. Her eyes closed, and she sucked the cold winter air into her lungs until the feeling that she had been held under water abated.

"Amelia."

Bryon's soft voice carried on the wisp of the wind and sent a tremble tripping up her spine. She willed the dream away. When she heard the rich timbre of his voice the second time, her eyes popped open, and a gasp slipped from her lips.

He stood right in front of her, scant inches away. She stepped back, bumping against the wall. Bryon moved closer.

"Amelia, I'm so sorry for what happened last summer, but it's not what you think." He touched her arm.

She yanked it away. "I saw with my own two eyes the way she fell into your arms and kissed your lips as if she had every right to be there. And if I harbored any doubt, the ring she wears on her finger proves I was right."

"I should've told you from the start. She left for Europe after proposing we marry. I said no, but she begged me to wait until she got back to give her my final answer. That suited me fine because it kept my parents from throwing other women my way. But I swear, I never intended to marry her. And the minute you and I met up in the park, I knew that you were the only woman for me." His words spilled out fast.

What was he saying? She could barely think straight.

"Will you forgive me? I was selfish. I was wrong. I knew you wouldn't want anything to do with me until I sorted things out with Shelby, but I wanted to be with you."

He reached out to touch her. A searing sensation of desire shot up her arms where his warm hands lay. She pulled them back.

"You didn't want to be with me, and I'm clearly not the *only* woman for you, or you wouldn't be engaged to her right now." Though the air was cold enough to see their breath, she did not feel the chill. Anger burned hot. She hated the fact she still felt that quickening of her heart and the pull of desire.

"I thought you had gone back to the valley for good and that you'd never forgive me. But seeing you here tonight—"

"You should not have followed me out here, and you know it."

"I've wanted to apologize for months."

"Do you love her?"

He didn't answer. Sadness filled his eyes.

"As an engaged man, the first thing out of your mouth to that question should be yes. I shouldn't feel sorry for you, Bryon, but I do. You're so trapped in a world of expectation and family duty that you can't recognize the truth when it's staring you in the face."

"Please—"

"Please what?" She could not handle the agony. She had to make sure the temptation of Bryon was forever gone. "Besides, I've met someone at the hospital who I work with, and I really like him. He's in my social class and we have far more in common than you and I ever had."

She turned from his crestfallen face and left him standing like a statue in the cold. She had not lied. She did like Gilbert— as a friend—and they did have a lot in common.

CHAPTER 22

*H*eat seared through Bryon's veins. Amelia's very presence made his temperature soar.

What had he done? Amelia was right. To agree to his parents badgering and become engaged to Shelby had been wrong. When Amelia had returned to the Shenandoah Valley something had died inside him. Nothing had mattered. He had not cared a wit who he married or if he married at all.

He cared now.

It was time to stand up. Coming face to face with Amelia gave him the courage. She was the only one who could make his heart come alive. Tonight, he would become his own man. If Amelia still wouldn't have him, then so be it. He wouldn't marry a woman to please his parents or to make society happy.

He returned to the ballroom. One quick look toward the door revealed Amelia leaving. She caught his eye and looked away, and his heart twisted.

Shelby. Where was she? He scanned the room to find her smiling into the eyes of the senator's son. He moved swiftly across the dance floor, dodging the happy couples until he stood beside his fiancée. He had to touch her arm before she noticed him. Startled, she turned his way.

"Oh Bryon, meet Henry—"

"We've met." Bryon nodded in his direction with a quick smile. "I need to talk to you for a moment. It's urgent."

Her brows lifted. She turned to Henry and smiled. "I'll talk to you later. We must finish this most stimulating conversation." She gave a demure grin.

"Indeed." The arch of the man's eyebrow and the smile he gave welcomed her return.

"Was it necessary to interrupt my conversation so rudely? Do you know who Henry's father is? That's Senator John Johnstone's son."

"I'm aware. This won't take long, and then you can get back to your *stimulating conversation.*" He drew out the last two words.

"It's not like you to be jealous, Bryon."

"That's part of our problem. I should be when the two of you are flirting right in front of me, but I feel nothing." He pulled her into an alcove at the end of the hall. "I'm breaking off our engagement."

"You're what?" She stepped back, eyes wide.

"You were just making eyes at the senator's son. Surely this is not a shock."

"You're breaking off the engagement because I smiled at—"

"It's more than that."

"It's that Amelia, isn't it? I saw her here tonight."

"Yes." He watched her reaction, worried he might see some sign of sadness or hurt. Instead, she seemed...relieved.

"I understand." Her sigh was long. "I've so enjoyed our friendship, but it's nothing compared to the way I feel about Henry. To be honest, you've saved me from what I imagined would be an awkward conversation. No offense."

He was so relieved, he nearly laughed. "None taken. I've

enjoyed our friendship as well, but that's not enough for marriage."

"I agree. I'm so glad I met Henry before we—"

He held up his hand. "No need to explain."

"When we were dancing earlier, I noticed the way I disappeared the moment you noticed her. She really is lovely. I hope your mother—"

"It doesn't matter what my mother thinks. I'd marry her in a heartbeat despite what the esteemed Mrs. Preston thinks, but I've ruined everything with Amelia. She'll never have me now. But that doesn't mean I'm prepared to ruin everything for you. You deserve to be happy."

"I feel genuinely sorry for you, Bryon. My new choice will more than satisfy my parents, but yours..." She shook her head. "I shall always treasure our friendship." She slid off her engagement ring and pressed it into his hand.

"So, you're all right? I haven't crushed you for life?"

She laughed. "Of course not. Let's just tell the world this is a mutual agreement. That way no one needs to feel the sting of rejection in the public eye."

The thought of what Bryon did to Amelia smarted. She would see that as rejection when in truth all he wanted was to be with her every day. What a fool he had been.

"Run along then, Shelby, and find enough happiness for the both of us."

She kissed his cheeks. "We tried to satisfy our parents, did we not?"

"We did. But no more."

She returned to the ballroom. His shoulders lifted, and he held his head high, following Shelby and feeling as if a heavy weight had been lifted from his shoulders. With renewed confidence, he walked through the crowd, stopped at the door to pick up his coat, and stepped into the cold night.

Tomorrow would be soon enough to take on his mother.

And what he had planned was far more than breaking off an engagement.

~

*A*melia tossed on her bed. With the new year about to unfold, she had two New Year's resolutions. She would become the best nurse possible, and she would get over Bryon Preston once and for all.

Their meeting the other night at the ball had unraveled her. She had thought she was way farther along than she obviously was. One look into his baby blue eyes, and her sorry heart did not cooperate with her head.

Had he really told Shelby that he didn't want to marry her before she left for Europe? Then why the passionate kiss when she returned, as if she belonged in his arms? And what kind of man went along with such shenanigans for the sake of keeping his parents at bay?

No, even if it were true, that did not excuse him for not sharing that information with her. He should have told her everything and let her make her own decision. He was right when he deducted that she would've waited until after Shelby returned. And then for him to agree to marry Shelby after the summer they shared... there was no excuse good enough for that one, even if he had thought she was gone forever. After all, she hadn't agreed to marry Thomas, or Clarence, or any of the others who came knocking feeling the way she did about Bryon. How could he?

Thoughts bounced back and forth. Why did she even bother trying to sort out the jumble in her head? She had to forget him, plain and simple. She flipped her pillow over and punched it down.

She was done with men. She was done with the social scene. She was done. All she craved was for the hurt to be over.

Please God, heal my broken heart. I know I didn't exactly ask you whether I should allow Bryon to court me in the first place, but in the future, I'll steer clear of all men.

The answer was swift and surprising. *Seek first the kingdom of God.*

The words were from the sermon on Sunday. The only things in the past year she had felt God's peace about was becoming a nurse and going to help Katherine with Josiah. The rest of the year, she wanted to bury and forget.

Don't bury, learn from your mistakes. Seek Me first.

It was as if God were speaking into her soul. Was that where she had gone wrong—not seeking Him first?

$\sim$

"You will not break off your engagement to Shelby and embarrass our family name."

"Mother, this is my life. My decision, and it's already been done." Bryon turned from the library window to look at his parents.

"You have our reputation to uphold."

"I have my good conscience to uphold. I will not marry one woman while in love with another. Seeing Amelia again—"

"Oh, please." She waved her hand in the air. "That backwards country girl cannot hold a candle to Shelby. How do you really think she'll fair hosting a Charity Gala or a dinner party with your colleagues? How could your children possibly be raised with the etiquette necessary to survive in our world? You'll soon tire of the lack of sophistication and culture, and then what?"

Fury rippled down his spine. "You will not speak of Amelia in that demeaning way. She is far too good for the likes of me."

"Whatever do you mean by that?"

"She didn't spend a whole summer lying to me like I did to

her." Bryon sank into the soft cushions of a nearby chair but folded his arms across his chest.

"Well, she shouldn't have been sneaking around meeting you in the park. Surely she knew something wasn't right about that."

"She was scared of you, Mother. She was waiting for me to step up and be a man. I waited too long."

"Just as well. Let bygones, be bygones, and be a man of your word concerning Shelby. You'll grow to love her."

"I can't just manufacture feelings for Shelby, and at this point she has her eyes set on another."

"There is more to life than chasing your desires. As the eldest, you have a God-given duty to carry on the family name and do your parents proud. This home has been in the Preston family for over a hundred years, and your ancestors helped build this city. Do you really want to be the one to throw it all away? Shelby's inheritance and your legacy will bring two great historical families together and strengthen them both. Surely, you can go to her and beg her forgiveness for taking so long to make up your mind."

"I do not love Shelby. I love Amelia."

"Amelia. Amelia. That's all I hear."

"And that's all you're going to hear. Her beauty and goodness radiate on the inside as well as the outside. She has no airs about her, like most of our family and friends, including Shelby—"

Mother whipped around to his father, who sat in a chair looking like he wished to be anywhere but in the room. "Alex, can you believe such disrespect? Whatever are we going to do with the boy?"

"I'm not a boy." Bryon kept his voice steady and sure. "I'm a twenty-four-year-old man who is finally going to act like one."

She stomped across the room to Bryon's chair and wagged her finger in his face. "Is this what we get after all the years of raising you to carry on our family name?"

"Mother, did you get to pick your husband, or was he chosen for you?"

She whirled away. Bryon knew their love story. They had both fought their parents' choice in order to be together.

She paced the hardwood floor. "Alex, say something. Set your son straight."

"He does have a point. Our parents weren't happy, but they let us choose each other, and it's not turned out so badly."

"That was different. At least we were from the same social standing."

Bryon stood and looked down at her. "Do you hear yourself?"

"I hear myself just fine. Can you blame a mother for wanting what is best for her son? If our friends were to catch wind that Amelia grew up milking cows, for heaven's sake, what do you think your life would be like? Is it so terrible not to want you to suffer the hardship of social disgrace?"

"You just don't get it." He ran his fingers through his hair, tempted to pull it out. How could she be so certain and yet so wrong? "There is no disgrace in milking cows, nor is anyone really a friend if they have such shallow expectations. I'm sorry, Mother. I'm sorry that I refuse to conform to your idea of what is right and wrong. My mind is made up."

She lifted her chin in a stubborn stance and whirled to face Father. "The wedding is only weeks away, and we've invited the whole community. Surely you can talk some sense into him."

"For the first time in months," Bryon said, "I understand what having good sense means."

She turned back to face him and stepped closer. "Think of poor Shelby. Do you really want to break her heart like this?"

"Shelby was relieved. As I've said, she already has her eye on the senator's son. We enjoyed each other, but we did not love each other."

His mother pulled her handkerchief from her sleeve and

waved it in front of her face. "I dare say, I will not be able to bear the shame. And if you marry that—"

"Amelia is far too good for the likes of me, besides she's seeing someone else. I won't be getting married at all. I'm leaving for England."

His father snapped to his feet. "What about us, Bryon? Don't you care how we'll enter our later years with barely enough to get by? I took care of my parents at this stage in life and it's your duty to do the same."

"Howard has come a long way. The extra responsibility and work has done wonders for tempering his wild side. He's ready to take over, and he wants to."

"Howard wants all the responsibility?" His father ran his hand around the back of his neck.

"Yes, he does, and he's stayed clear of the gambling. I think this will be good for him." Bryon squared his shoulders in a show of confidence.

"But...but your investing contacts at the bank. They love you there. Don't throw your future away."

"I've already been offered and accepted a position at the Bank of England."

"You what?" They both closed in.

"If you go, you can say good-bye to your inheritance," Mother said, with steel in her voice. "You'll be on your own."

"Melinda—"

"Don't Melinda me, Alex." Fire flashed in her eyes. "He says he's a man, so he has a choice to make. Stay here, beg Shelby's forgiveness for breaking the engagement, and take his rightful place as the heir, or leave and make his own way in the world."

A taste of bitter acid rose in the back of Bryon's throat. She spoke as if to punish him when she was offering exactly what he'd requested the prior year. His only regret was the rift this would cause between them. If only they could remain on good terms.

He would continue to send money home but had already talked to Howard and secured his promise to never speak of it. "I will leave and make my own way," he said, with sadness in his voice. Bryon fingered his pocket watch and glanced down. "I must go. Good-bye, Mother. Good-bye, Father."

CHAPTER 23

Spring 1870

A steady drizzle fell from steel gray clouds. Amelia opened her umbrella as she stepped out of the hospital.

"Amelia. Wait up."

She turned to see Gilbert running after her.

"How about sharing that umbrella up the street to my boarding house?"

She nodded, and he took over the job of holding it. Silence filled the space between them. Gilbert was never silent. He twirled the umbrella around and around, splashing droplets of water over both of them.

She stilled his hand. "I think the idea is that the umbrella is meant to keep us dry." She kept her voice light and teasing.

"Uh, sorry. I…uh…have really loved getting to know you over the past few months. I hope you've enjoyed our time together as much as I have?"

Amelia didn't answer. He was nice looking. Pleasant. Even made her laugh, but she could not get Bryon out of her head.

"I'm wondering if we could officially court—"

"Oh, Gilbert…" She turned toward him, gathered under the protection of the umbrella, and looked up into his expectant eyes. With all her heart she wished she could carry on with the relationship, but she felt nothing.

"I can see it in your eyes." His mouth formed a grim smile. "This is about the time you tell me you've enjoyed our time together but…there's always a but. Not sure when I'll find the girl of my dreams."

"You will Gilbert. It's just not me. You're charming and funny, and I had so hoped and prayed I would feel more, it wasn't fair of me to use our relationship to try and forget—"

"Bryon Preston?"

"Yes. Bryon."

He held up his one hand and handed the umbrella to her with the other. "I'm going to leave before hearing the *let's be friends* speech. Besides, what average guy like me has a chance with the likes of Bryon waiting in the wings?"

"He's not waiting—"

"I'll always remain your friend, and if you do get over the man…" He lifted her gloved hand to his lips and kissed lightly. "…keep me in mind."

She watched him walk away before purposefully taking the longer route home, the one that did not include a walk past Bryon's house. The thought of him still clogged her mind with sorrow. She worked hard at managing her broken heart but, try as she might, unlike the physical wounds she treated, which steadily improved, this one was a slow heal.

She had not run into him since the Christmas Ball and was determined to forget him, hoping that Gilbert's easy-going company would help—all to no avail. Though concentrating on her nursing, achieving top grades and accolades from her peers, she could not eradicate the memories.

"Grandmother, I'm home," Amelia yelled as she shook off her umbrella and hung it on the peg beside the door.

"Land sakes, girl. Why are you walking in the rain?" Grandmother rounded the corner into the entryway hall, wagging her finger. "I told you William is available in this kind of weather. All you had to do this morning is let him know your schedule."

Amelia flashed her brightest smile. "I won't melt in the rain. Besides, it's spring. And warm. And refreshing—"

"And wet. Now go get changed. Meet me in the parlor, I have some news for you, and the fact that you're wet makes the wait longer."

Amelia laughed. "You do have a hard time keeping the latest under wraps, don't you?"

"This news you'll want to hear. Now hurry it up."

Amelia scurried to her bedroom. Her uniform came off, her day dress on, in record time. What in the world was Grandmother in such a dither about? Amelia was back down the hall before the tea was served.

"Do tell." She plunked her weary body into a chair and waved Grandmother on.

"I ran into Sophia Trundell. She's one of Melinda Preston's best friends, but oddly enough, she still likes me. That's good, otherwise I would've never been privy to this most delicious piece of information." She straightened her back, rubbed her hands together, and laughed in delight. "And to think, I still wouldn't know, had I not run into her today."

"Grandmother, please. Get to the point."

"Oh my, yes. All is not well at the Preston manor, namely concerning Bryon."

Amelia's heart skittered at the mention of his name. "Whatever do you mean?"

"Sophia told me Bryon called off the wedding, but Melinda is keeping it all hush-hush, embarrassed that her son hasn't done her bidding. That's why we haven't heard a snippet of news regarding their nuptials. And trust me, I've had my ear tuned to the rumor mill."

"It's...it's off?" She swallowed hard against the lump that formed in her throat. She didn't want to care, but she did.

"Shelby isn't wasting any time either. Rumor has it she's been seen with the senator's son already, and of course, her spin is that she broke off the engagement. But the juiciest tidbit..." Grandmother took a long sip of her tea.

"What?" Amelia fought the urge to entertain any thoughts about Bryon or why he may have broken off the engagement.

"Bryon left for a trip overseas. The word is Europe. This can mean only one thing. He's taken his mother on in the best way possible—and won. He's no longer engaged. He's becoming his own man, and he's removed himself from the oppressive influence of his parents. I think he'll be a better man for it. I just wish he'd done it a whole lot sooner for your sake."

"Grandmother, I'd rather not talk—"

"Of course, my dear. I do understand. How insensitive of me. I wasn't thinking... Truth is, I shouldn't be so delighted, but Melinda Preston is getting a taste of her own medicine. She's seeing what it's like to have her children do something she doesn't agree with. And after running me into the ground as a parent, well, it feels a tad like justice."

Amelia stood on shaky legs, working hard to not show her emotion. "Thanks for the update, but I must go now and see to my studies." She walked down the hall with her spine as straight as an arrow. She opened and closed her bedroom door quietly behind her. Then, she allowed the tears to fall.

Bryon had finally gotten the courage to stand up to his parents when it was far too late for them. She was angry that she cared.

Oh God, when will this heartache end?

∿

Spring 1870
Shenandoah Valley

*T*he chatter of early morning birds chirped outside her window as the slow light of dawn crept into her bedroom. When had winter turned into spring and brought the birdsong back? The past months for Katherine had unfolded in a blur. She tossed about on her rumpled sheets. She had always loved spring, especially when the barren trees burst forth with new foliage. But this year Katherine felt trapped in a place where the cold, harsh, and desolate remained—a world with no color, muddied with pain. That worst stage of winter, when the sparkling white melts into gray, resembled her dreary life.

Seth whimpered in the nursery next door. Somehow, she had to find the strength to rise from her bed and attend to her son, but not quite yet. She rolled over on the bed to Josiah's empty side and placed his pillow over her head, longing to smell his essence.

"Please God, let there be a scent. A trace. I miss him so much."

She took in a deep breath. Nothing. Her tears had long since washed him away. If not for Seth she wouldn't have the will to carry on. He was her only joy, that bundle of energy, demanding her attention, demanding her love. He ensured a small corner of her heart lived on.

She went through the motions with Seth because she had to and filled her days with monotonous work, but the cold, lonely nights were her undoing. Fitful sleeps and hours staring at the ceiling made the hours between dusk and dawn her worst enemy. In the dark, grief swallowed her up with a pain that reached higher in her chest every day. She punched her pillow down and flipped onto her back. Brushing the wet from her cheeks, she worried the tears would never stop.

One blessing she thanked God for daily was Colby. It wasn't

fair to lean on him the way she did, but she couldn't have managed the ranch in her state of mind. Even doing the book-keeping, which she loved, took too much concentration.

Colby had stepped in to help. Without words he took the lead. Katherine hadn't considered the social ramifications of being a widow and living in the same house as a very eligible bachelor but thankfully Colby had been thinking for her. He deemed it inappropriate to sleep under the same roof, no matter how many bedrooms and wings lay empty in her rambling stone mansion. He'd bunked with the hired help until he'd finished building a small log cabin to move into.

Why had she given little thought to what it must be like for him to be saddled with a grieving woman, a busy ranch, and a two-year-old who adored him. Seth shadowed him every moment he was around. Somehow, she'd have to find a way to free Colby from this obligation.

Fear bit at her mind. Who would take over the financial and operational decisions of the ranch? Though she understood a lot, her first responsibility was to Seth and the household. She didn't have the time, nor the inclination with grief still heavy upon her, to learn to run the ranch. Who would she talk to, weep with, and share her memories of Josiah with, if not her friend Colby?

She slid from her bed, irritated at where her mind had wandered. Why should she contemplate losing Colby? Hadn't she lost enough? Yet the truth pressed in.

He was a handsome man who deserved a wife and a family of his own, not to be burdened with the care of someone else's.

She would talk with him tonight.

～

*C*olby pushed back from the table and stretched out a yawn. It'd been a long day, and he was tired.

"You two scat. Don't be needing any help." Delilah waved her hand. "Annie and Ruby are around if I need 'em."

"Thanks, Delilah," Katherine said.

Colby's eyes followed Katherine as she planted a kiss on the top of Delilah's head.

"Glad you could join us for supper, Colby," Katherine said. "I'll get Seth to bed, and we'll meet in the library." She gathered Seth in her arms and made him giggle with a tickle to his tummy as she walked away.

They were so beautiful.

The past half a year had been torture, watching her go through the motions, consumed with pain. The only one who could make her smile was Seth. When she looked at her little boy, her blue eyes would brighten, and occasionally her lips would soften into a smile. The rest of the time, her beautiful eyes were soaked in sadness.

Colby drew a deep breath. Evening was both the best and worst time of his day. He headed to the library and picked a comfortable chair to await her return. She had no idea how he felt, and he prayed she wouldn't read the truth in his eyes.

Josiah's worn leather desk chair brought back the memories of him lying sick in his bed.

"Will you promise me?"

"I'll do my best, Josiah."

"I need a promise. I need to know she'll be taken care of and loved—" His raspy cough cut into their conversation.

The clearing of Katherine's throat startled Colby back into the present. His eyes flew open.

"If you're too tired, we can do this tomorrow."

"No, no. I was merely resting, taking advantage of a few

relaxing moments." He pulled in his extended legs and sat higher in the chair.

"Well good. I have something I need to discuss with you." She fidgeted with the folds in her dress.

"Sounds ominous."

"Not ominous, but necessary."

"All right, shoot."

"It's been six months since Josiah passed away." Her eyes darkened.

"Yes."

"It's time I release you of this burden and let you move on."

He worked the knot in his throat down with a swallow.

"What I mean is, I've been leaning on you too much."

Colby rose and crossed the room to where she stood. "What's this all about, Katherine?" His voice sounded harsh even to his ears, but he had to sidetrack the beat of his errant heart. He softened the tone. "I own a good chunk of this ranch. It's my duty to care."

"It's not fair to you. You're a wonderful man who should have his own home and family, not be saddled with—"

"If I wanted a wife and family, don't you think I'd have one by now?" He had to make his words sound convincing. It was too soon to tell her what Josiah had asked of him.

Her brows knit together. "So, you're good with the way things are?"

How could he answer that question honestly? "I'll always be invested in this ranch. It's my livelihood as much as yours. Besides, if and when I'm interested, there are many lovely ladies at church and plenty of land to build my own home." Not that he'd ever do that.

She nudged his arm. "That's true. There's been no shortage of eligible women since the war, from young ones to ones who come with ready-made families like mine. And it hasn't escaped my notice how much attention you get either."

The dream of only one ready-made family swept through his mind and clamped down on his heart. He turned away and walked to the window. "I'm right where I should be, doing exactly what I want to be doing." He faced her with what he hoped would be a convincing smile. "Now, let's go over these numbers, I think you'll be pleasantly surprised." He lifted the ledger book from the desk.

❧

LATE SUMMER 1870
ENGLAND

*B*ryon walked along the bank of the Thames River in the cool of the early morning, as was his habit. Wisps of silvery mist floated above the water, and sunlight spanned across the eastern horizon. He couldn't believe how fast 1870 was rushing by. Summer was winding down with fall right around the corner.

So much had happened in the span of the past year that he could barely grasp the difference in his life. He wanted the simple life, and he'd gotten it. A small flat, work as an investor at the Bank of England, and his God. He smiled into the heavens. He had never felt more at peace.

A squawk of a seagull overhead brought the memory of meeting his new friend Harry on the ship crossing the Atlantic. He'd never felt so low, nor so ready for change in every area of his life. Sorrow at what his selfishness had done to Amelia and their chance at love, weighed heavily. His apology to her had fallen so short. How could he expect her to forgive him when he couldn't forgive himself?

A brute of a man in plain working clothes had yelled from the deck below as Bryon leaned over the rail. "What's it like up there so close to heaven." His voice boomed over the water. To this day, Bryon couldn't explain what drew him to this stocky fellow with his crop of shocking red hair. Must have been God's divine timing.

"What's it like down there?" Bryon had asked the shipmate.

"Come on down, Mate, and see for yourself. They'll never stop you from coming down, but they'll surely stop me from coming up." He laughed as if it didn't bother him at all.

On the ship with nothing else to do, Bryon had thought, why not? He'd climbed down to meet the man, and a friendship was born. During the long journey across the Atlantic, Harry had taught Bryon what it meant to live the Christian life. It wasn't the occasional Sunday service to meet your girlfriend, as he'd practiced with Amelia, but a heart-changing transformation. He could not believe the difference not only in his ideology but in the way that his new faith compelled him to care, love and want to help people. Once they'd landed in London, Bryon had joined Harry in his work at the church. They went out every Saturday and Sunday to deliver food to women and children living on the street in the heart of London's most impoverished neighborhoods. What an eye opener. The squalor, the suffering, the sorrow. What he did felt like a tiny drop in an ocean of need.

A couple more seagulls dipped and swooped. He kept his eye on those mangy birds, as they had a habit of finding his hat and letting loose. He was on his way to meet Harry for their early morning coffee and Bible reading in the square before they headed in different directions for the day—Harry to the shipyard and him to the bank. The last thing Bryon wanted was to arrive with yet another splotch on his hat. Harry had a fondness for howling every time that happened.

"Over here." Harry waved from a corner table outside their favorite shop. Two mugs steaming with hot brew waited. "Ha! I see you made it without incident. Now, where am I going to get my morning laugh?" His booming voice carried across the square as Bryon slipped into the chair.

"You keep going on like that, and I'm going to pray you're equally blessed."

His laughter grew louder. "Ah, but I wouldn't care as much as you. That happens all day long at the shipyard. It's only funny because I think God is trying to teach you a lesson in not having to look so dapper all the time."

"That could be. Seems He's teaching me new things every day. But I'm struggling with something."

Harry took a swig of his coffee. "Lay it on me, brother. That's what this time is all about. We grow in the Lord together."

"If I'm forgiven, and grace covers all my sins, why do I still feel so badly about what I did to Amelia?"

"No *if* about it. You are forgiven. But accepting God's forgiveness, really accepting it, is a hard one. Satan will keep trying to bring up the past, to distract you from the good God wants to do in your future. I have a verse for you. Just let me find it." He pulled his very worn Bible from his inside coat pocket and flipped the pages.

"Here it is. Ephesians chapter one, verses seven and eight. 'In whom we have redemption through His blood, the forgiveness of sins, according to the riches of His grace. Having made known unto us the mystery of His will, according to His good pleasure.' This means God takes pleasure in extending His grace, though He knows we're all sinners. Memorize this verse, my friend, so that, when Satan reminds you of your past selfishness, you can say this verse out loud and send him running. How about we pray about this right now?"

Bryon looked around the square where people were milling in increasing number. "Can we do that here, with everyone looking on?"

"We can pray anywhere, and we don't have to make a show of it. God doesn't need us to bow our heads and close our eyes to hear us. We'll just talk to him like we're talking to each other."

Bryon raised his brows. "Really? Isn't that sacrilegious or something?"

Again, Harry's laughter filled the square. "You can talk to God anytime, anywhere. I do it all day long while I'm hauling lumber or hammering nails or drinking a good cup of coffee." He lifted his mug.

CHAPTER 24

December 1870

Shenandoah Valley

*C*olby looked up as Katherine and Seth entered the room. He straightened his tall frame from his bent over position and stood back from the Christmas tree he had just put into the stand.

"Mommy, Mommy. Come." Seth pulled at Katherine's hands, bouncing up and down. "Tree. Tree."

Colby put on a happy grin. He didn't care that she was frowning. He had to do something to get her out of the doldrums. "Good. Seth found you. Does the tree look straight? Is it where you want it to be?"

The pucker in her brow deepened.

"Where do you want to start?" He pulled the lid off a box of decorations. His insides flipped. He was taking a necessary risk in pushing her, but someone had to. Everyone else let her fade into the background.

"I don't feel much like doing this."

He ignored her. "This room looks great." His hand swept out

as he pointed to the boughs on the fireplace mantlepiece with red bows tied to each end, numerous decorations, special candles, and holly berries interspersed throughout the area. "Did you do all this?"

"No. Lucinda, Jeanette and Gracie came over yesterday."

Of course, she hadn't done it. She was far too lethargic and withdrawn these days. "They did an excellent job. If this doesn't get a person into a festive mood, I don't know what will."

She remained quiet, as was her way the past few months. She had stopped talking about Josiah, and then she had stopped talking at all. It scared him.

"Delilah brought us these strings of popcorn," he said. "Do we start with them?"

Her gaze dropped, and she hung her head.

"Come on Seth. You want to help mommy decorate the tree?"

He jumped up and down. "Yes. Yes."

Colby swung the little boy into his arms and moved really close to Katherine. "How can you say no to this face?"

"I'm not...maybe we could call the girls back tomorrow. I don't much care about decorating these days." She turned to leave.

"You need to care." He said the words softly, gently, but his tone made no difference.

She whirled around, her eyes wide. "What did you say?"

He set Seth down. "You need to care. You have a son to look after."

"Don't you dare accuse me of not looking after my son."

"I didn't mean it that way. It's just that—"

"Why don't you try losing all that I've lost in one lifetime and then come back and criticize me. I'm doing the best I can." Her voice trembled as she turned away. Seth pulled at her skirt, and she picked him up.

Sharp shoulder blades protruded from the back of her black

dress, which hung on her like rags on a scarecrow. Her body trembled, racked by sobs, and his gut twisted. He'd not meant to make her cry.

He silently prayed for help, for wisdom.

Go to her.

Seemed a risky move, all things considered, but he moved closer and did the one thing that he had not allowed himself to do the past year. He turned her around and pulled her close, locking her in a warm embrace. Her chin wobbled as tears flowed. He held her in a circle of three.

"Mommy?" Seth's dimpled hand traced the tears down her cheek. He turned with a scowl toward Colby and batted him on the head.

"My mommy." His frown deepened.

Katherine grabbed his little arm. "Seth, no." She looked up at Colby as he backed out of reach, and they both laughed.

Seth squirmed to be put down and was off running around the tree.

"You deserved that, Colby Braddock." A smile flickered and kicked up the edges of her lips. "If Seth hadn't done that, I was about to. You're not supposed to make a girl cry." For a split second, a spark of mischief lit her eyes.

Colby would have paid a much higher price than a two-year-old's smack for what he had gained. He'd made her frown, scowl, cry, laugh, and smile. He'd made her *feel.*

~

Christmas morning dawned bright and beautiful in a blanket of purest white. Katherine gazed out her bedroom window, awed by it. The snow had started the day before with large twirling flakes that melted as they hit the ground. Slowly, the earth transformed from dreary to sparkling white. Today, the early morning sun shone on its ethereal beauty.

All too soon Seth would be calling out, and, after Colby's brave attempt to pull her out of her grief, she was determined to make the day special, even if it killed her. Which, it might. Depression continually nipped at the ragged edges of her mind, trying to pull her down.

If her own backyard could change before her eyes from bleak to beautiful, perhaps there was hope for the cold, lifeless place her heart had resided for months. A flicker of Christmas spirit rose within her. Feeble. Flimsy. Fragile.

If she were honest, the warmth from Colby's hug had melted a small chunk of ice inside her soul. His inept words and bumbling attempt to communicate had struck a chord. She didn't like the sullen, unhappy person she had become, and he was right. She had a son who deserved more.

Dear God, help me, I cannot do this without Your strength.

~

*K*atherine looked around the decorated parlor. She loved how the families had become enmeshed. Her ma, pa, and sisters, Abe and Delilah, and a smattering of helping hands who had nowhere else to go at Christmas. And there was Colby with Seth on his knee. Katherine wasn't sure how, but the group worked. What would Josiah think if he were looking down? The memory of him brought sadness, but she shook it off. He'd want her to fight through, and she had not been very successful this past year. Tears pressed behind her lids, but she stifled the flow.

"Jeanette, how about you play the piano for us, and we'll sing some carols?" It took all Katherine had to suggest such a thing, but she was rewarded with smiles from everyone in the room.

"Wonderful idea." Pa clapped his work-worn hands. "Best I just listen though with the voice I have."

Katherine laughed. "Yes, that would go for me too."

The rest of the family chuckled and nodded in agreement.

"Hey, that's not very charitable," said Colby. "If a person wants to sing, they should sing."

"Have you heard them sing?" Doris asked.

"No, but—"

"Exactly." They all laughed.

That evening, Katherine reflected on the day. It had been wonderful. She had joined in the festivities, not only in body, but in spirit. They'd exchanged gifts, had a feast fit for kings, and spent the rest of the evening singing and playing games. After she waved goodnight to the last of them, she shut the door with a sense of accomplishment. She had more than survived Christmas. She had lived it. She climbed the steps to the nursery with a lightness in her step that she hadn't experienced in a long time. Hopefully, Colby had succeeded in settling Seth. He seemed to have a knack that no one else had.

A peek in the room mesmerized her. Together, Colby and Seth slept on the rocking chair embodying a picture of peace and love. Tears filled her eyes. Seth slept soundly in Colby's arms, wrapped in his favorite blanket, sucking his thumb.

Colby had his eyes closed. The look of innocence made her chest tighten. She crept closer but couldn't bring herself to disturb them. They looked as if they belonged together. The realization both comforted and terrified her.

How had she let them get so close to each other? What if Colby decided to leave? How would they manage without him? Her heart picked up speed and pounded in her ears. What would it do to Seth to have him say good-bye?

Colby was a handsome man. Why had she ignored how many young women in the community were interested in him? At church, the hired help, the ladies in town—a prick of emotion she was not yet ready to dissect stabbed through—he got attention wherever he went. Why did that bother her?

She reached for Seth and gently pulled him free. Colby's eyes opened slowly, and Katherine witnessed an unguarded look of desire.

Desire?

He hid it immediately behind a stretch and yawn. His muscles, taut and hard, filled out his shirt across his chest.

For over a year, she'd gotten accustomed to Colby the rancher and Colby the friend. Suddenly, she was aware of Colby the man.

She turned and gathered Seth closer. He stirred in her arms, and she kissed his curly mop. Before she could lay him down, Colby was there, lifting the covers and, once she deposited Seth, tucking them securely around the boy. He bent to kiss the sleeping child. Love for Seth oozed from him.

How could she have been so blind? How had she not noticed what was happening right in front of her? Seth was as attached to Colby as Colby was to him. Where grief had blinded her, a light now came on inside her dead soul. Truth be told, she and Seth had both become attached, counting on Colby far too heavily. The urge to flee rose up, and she turned and hurried from the room.

Colby followed and reached out to stall her escape to her bedroom. A shot of awareness spiked up her arm, and she snatched her hand free.

He stepped back. "Will you come into the library? I have a gift for you." Excitement lit up his eyes, much like Seth being told to sit and wait for another present. "Please." He offered her his arm.

His enthusiasm and infectious smile drew her in. Where seconds earlier she had panicked, needing distance, now her hand curled around the crook of his warm arm. How weak her resolve when he smiled at her like that.

They glided down the steps in silence. Awareness exploded as he slid his hand into hers and pulled her into the room. "I've been looking forward to this all day. Sit." He waved her to the closest chair, and she settled herself in it. "Now, close your eyes —and no peeking."

She did as he said, hearing some rustling.

"Are you peeking, cause if you are, you're in big trouble."

She couldn't help but smile and squeezed her eyes even tighter. "You think so little of me? Of course, I'm not peeking, but hurry up already." A bubble of laughter she hadn't heard in a long time slipped from her lips.

"All right, open your eyes."

One look, and she blinked back a rush of tears. Her legs trembled as she attempted to stand.

"I figured this would be emotional. That's why I left it until you'd have some privacy. Do you like it?"

"Colby, how? It's…it's amazing." She stepped toward the easel propped on the fireplace mantel. Her fingertips traced their way down Josiah's face. He looked as if he could step out of the painting. She closed her eyes and remembered. Her tears flowed freely.

Colby's voice broke into the moment as he stepped closer. "Josiah had this daguerreotype taken after he realized he was sick. He asked me to find someone to paint it so that Seth would always be able to look at his daddy and you would always remember his smile."

Colby touched her arm when a sob slipped from her lips. She turned and flung herself into his embrace. He wrapped his arms around her, and she sank into the warmth, soaking up the pleasure of human touch. They stood in silence for a long comforting moment before he stepped back enough to put space between their bodies. His hand gently patted her back.

A choke pulled from his throat. "I miss him too, Katherine." He stepped out of the hug with his hands steadying her shoulders. "I'll leave you now. You need some time alone. Merry Christmas, my friend." Before she could respond, he was gone. The library door closed firmly behind him.

~

*F*riend…what an understatement.

Colby yanked his coat from the hook at the front door. He had to get out. The solid wood door creaked on its hinges, laughing at him. He heaved it shut and cringed at the slam that echoed in his wake.

A cold blast of winter air hit him as he marched toward his cabin, a welcome balm to his overheated state. The pleasure and pain all tangled together had smashed into his soul as she'd processed the gift. Obviously, the past year had done little to heal her grief.

What had he expected? Of course she would cry. Of course that picture would conjure up loss. Obviously, it was too much to hope that enough healing had transpired for the picture to bring more joy than pain.

And what a fool he had been to touch her. He had started the agony when he curled his hand around hers on the way to the library. Though surprised by the way she threw herself against him, he could've put space between them way sooner than he did. Instead, he soaked up her embrace like rain to drought-ridden earth.

With her warm arms wrapped around him, memories long buried exploded back to life. For a split second, his fingers had smoothed their way through her long wavy hair, and he had almost lost reason. That one half-step backwards had saved him from taking more—much more. The closeness had been both heaven and hell, all wrapped together. He hadn't wanted to feel the pleasure but couldn't deny what she did to him. Instead of running, he stayed long enough to inhale deeply, breathe in her scent, and enjoy the smell of spring-washed lilacs. It wasn't until his breathing became jagged and he strained against the desire of lowering his lips to her mouth that he pulled away and beelined for the door.

How was he going to go on, loving her as he did, when they were so close and yet so far apart?

CHAPTER 25

*T*hrilled with the gift, Katherine was embarrassed by her behavior. She'd let Colby slip away without properly thanking him and sharing how much the gift meant. Instead, she'd wept like a baby, obviously making him feel uncomfortable, or worse yet, feeling as if he had done something wrong. She wouldn't rest without setting things right.

The picture of him cradling her son in his arms flashed again and reinforced her need for conversation. She bundled up to face the outdoors. Another half a year had gone by since she'd encouraged Colby to move on, and still she held him captive. It was time to release him. He had been more than kind, but she couldn't continue to expect him to put his life on hold. More than that, she couldn't allow her son—or herself—to become more attached to him than they already had.

The snow crunched beneath her boots and she pulled her cloak up around her ears to guard against the biting wind. The moon winked from behind a wispy cloud, giving enough light to make her way. *Oh God, let me have the right words.* As she neared the cabin, she sighed in relief. Light poured through his window. Good, he had not yet gone to sleep.

She raised her hand to knock, then lowered it. What was she doing? With a half turn she stepped away.

No. If she left things, tomorrow would bring a hundred reasons not to address the situation. She must follow through.

She rapped on his door before she could change her mind. "It's me, Katherine."

The door swung open. Colby's brows lifted. "What are you doing here?"

She stepped past him into the warmth of the room. "Don't just stand there, shut the door. It's freezing out there."

The creak of the hinges and a click filled the silence, but he stood with his hand on the knob. "I don't think you should be here." He brushed one hand behind his neck and wouldn't make eye contact.

"I won't stay long but I felt so badly, I needed to apologize. You gave me that wonderful gift, and I was so wrapped up in the emotion that I neglected to thank you."

"This could've waited until tomorrow." His voice sounded gruff.

She stepped forward. "Have I offended you?"

"No. It was clear you loved the painting, but I'm really tired. Do you think we could talk about this tomorrow?" He opened the door.

Her hand pushed the door shut. "I know you better than that." She waved to the chair. "Please. Can we sit for a minute? I have something I need to ask you."

He complied but perched his body on the edge of the kitchen chair. He looked as if he would rather eat a bucket of mud than have a discussion with her. A stern frown scrunched his forehead into worry lines.

"What is it?" Katherine asked.

"It's just that you...that we shouldn't be here...together."

"I've been here many times before. What does it matter?"

"Always with Seth or Delilah or a ranch hand. Not alone, and certainly not at this hour."

"Oh that, pshaw." She waved her hand. "Everyone knows that we're only friends."

She didn't miss the flash of disappointment that flicked across his face before he schooled his expression. He stared straight through her as if she weren't there.

"Colby?"

"Like you said, friends, but we can't be too careful." His voice sounded wooden.

"I get it." What could she say to lighten his concern? She added a teasing tone to her voice. "You don't want your reputation in question in case it hurts your chances with the eligible young ladies."

He snapped up and stepped to within inches, towering over her. "I don't find this amusing. I don't care a wit for the eligible ladies out there, but I do care about my Christian example." His voice thundered.

"Sorry. Truly I am. I was only teasing." She stood and touched his arms.

He jumped back as if a flame had scorched him.

She swallowed the hurt his reaction caused. "I just wanted to say thank you for such a thoughtful gift, and you're right I should go. But can you answer one question?" It took every bit of strength to boldly meet his gaze. "Why have you stayed at the ranch?"

A troubled light stole into his brown eyes, and the golden flecks darkened. He said nothing.

"What will we do when you decide to go on with your life, get married, and leave Seth and me behind...as it should be?"

They stood silent for a long, brooding moment. He let out a deep sigh before his expression opened, and the guarded look disappeared. A mixture of desire, love, and invitation beckoned her.

She sucked in a sharp breath. The revelation was like a candle had been lit in a very dark room of her mind. Dare she enter in?

The air prickled with tension, and his stare grew hot enough to melt snow drifts in a blizzard. "There is only one reason you should not be here right now, which is the same reason I will not leave you or Seth unless it is your wish."

His words, drenched in longing, slammed into her heart. Her throat constricted, and she swallowed hard against the knot of emotion gathering there.

His hands gently framed her face. One thumb rubbed slowly across her lower lip, which trembled involuntarily. A warm tingle spread through her limbs.

He bent toward her slowly, giving ample time to retreat. "Katherine?" he whispered. A question, a yearning, a hunger wrapped the way he said her name around her heart. When she did not pull away, he closed the distance between them.

His lips brushed hers with aching tenderness, and she was shocked at the bolt of fire that ripped up her spine. What started as a gentle kiss suddenly blazed with intensity, and she responded without reservation.

Terrified by the onslaught of emotions coursing through her being, she pulled away and bolted for the door. In the span of a few moments, she had felt way too much. Connection without words. Physical attraction and desire. A deep stirring within a soul she had sworn would never love again. She ran into the biting cold. Her feet slipped on the icy terrain, but she pushed through the snow. He called her name, but she did not turn back.

With a burst through the front door, she discarded her evening cloak in a heap on the floor and stumbled up the stairs. She didn't care that the bottom of her dress was wet and covered in snow. She collapsed on her bed and let the tears flow. She laughed, and then cried, and then laughed some more. She felt more alive than she had in a long, long time.

And she was terrified.

~

*C*olby slammed his fist onto the table and folded in a heap on the kitchen chair. His elbows hit the table with a thump, and his head fell into his hands. How could he have made such a mistake? For over a year, he had held a tight rein on his emotions and an even tighter rein on his will. In a single moment—gone. Good intentions reduced to sawdust.

Why had the battle suddenly become so difficult? The simplest things would send him reeling—the way she tilted her head, a smile for her son, or her singsong voice bantering with Delilah. But when she'd cried in his arms, what little resolve he had left crumbled. The desire to share everything—from work to joy to pain—grew unbearable. He had run for his cabin for fear he would do the very thing he had done…kiss her with years of pent up passion.

Why, God? He lifted his eyes upward. *Why, when she's so far from ready and I'm at my weakest, did you allow her to come? Did I not do the honorable thing and leave her moments earlier? Did I not stifle every urge and run? Yet You sent her back to me.*

He pushed up so quickly, his chair shot backwards. The back smashed to the hardwood floor and broke into pieces.

He ripped his hands through his hair.

She needs you.

But she'd fled from him. He paced, kicking the remains of the chair that lay scattered about.

She fled, because you made her feel.

The words gave him pause. He'd made her feel, and the feelings frightened her. But what were they? Did she care for him at all? Could she ever?

And even if she did, how could he remain so close to her after that kiss? How could he trust himself to do the right thing with the aching need inside of him sparked into flame? How could he distinguish between his desire and God's will?

I placed that love inside of you. I made sure it never left for this very season.

But...could that be right?

Do you love her?

Did he love her? With all his heart he loved her.

I will make a way, but be prepared to wait.

Prepared to wait? He'd been prepared to wait for Katherine forever.

But maybe that's not what God was asking. Maybe there was hope.

Peace settled over Colby unlike any he had experienced before. With a guide to light his path, the turmoil quieted. He was no longer lost. Wisdom had come. Wisdom had spoken.

~

Katherine moved restlessly on her bed. How could she sleep after what just happened? Tangled in her covers, she wrestled free and flipped onto her stomach. She punched her pillow and flopped her head back down. Unable to drift off, she pulled her weary body out of bed, wrapped a blanket around her shoulders, and stood at the window. The moon-washed landscape with silver beams flickering off black shadows was like a window into her soul. The flow of disturbing revelations held previously in the dark now had a shaft of light illuminating their truth. Dare she peer as steadily as that full moon into the depths of her feelings?

She still missed Josiah with passion, but she'd let Colby slip into their lives and fill the empty spaces. She had used his kindness. This truth filled her with deep regret and guilt.

Determined never to feel again, preferring to remain numb, she hadn't questioned his attentive care. She'd just soaked it up. She'd been more than content to join in the teasing of finding him a wife, as if he wanted someone other than her. His eyes had spoken truth, but she'd found it more comfortable to deny the obvious.

The moon disappeared behind a large cloud, casting the room into pitch black. She reached for the side of the bed and sat.

The complicated emotions of long ago, when she had needed Colby instead of Josiah, muddied the waters. After removing those forbidden desires years earlier, she didn't want to sully Josiah's memory by allowing them to resurface. But why did her heart feel so alive, so open? Why had she responded to Colby's kiss with equal desire?

The truth was too revealing, too thorny. She had to gain control of the runaway train inside her head. This ride made her feel, made her heart palpitate, made her come face to face with living, not just existing.

A jolt of hope filled her being. Could she be happy again?

No. The trip was too dangerous, too daring. She wanted off this locomotive of madness. Yet the questions persisted. Like the endless cadence of wheels on rail, her train of thoughts steamed ahead.

How could she set Colby free? She needed his help with the ranch. She enjoyed his conversation, his comfort, his advice, his companionship. She loved the way he loved Seth. She couldn't ask for a better father for her child.

A stab of pain split through her heart as a trail of tears broke free. How could she tell Seth that another daddy was gone? For Colby had become a father to Seth, and she had willingly let it happen.

Oh, God. What have I done? Tears dropped from her weighty lids.

At that moment, a shaft of milky white illuminated the room. She stood and walked to the window. The dark cloud parted, and the moon's light broke through a wedge of uncluttered sky. The ominous black shifted in the heavenlies until the moon bore brightly down.

Had God parted the darkness and asked her to step into the light, to consider living again? All she had to do was step away from fear. But the memories of Josiah's death, the raw ache of grief, the months of pain, were too close. No, she could never do that again. There had been good reason to shut herself down.

The two sides warred as she waffled between light and darkness. She couldn't manage the battle and flung herself on her bed, begging God to give her the strength to say good-bye to Colby while she still could.

The moon's light disappeared. The room went black.

CHAPTER 26

"*A*melia, can I see you in my office?" Dr. Meade called across the long open room filled with beds and patients.

Amelia's head lifted from her current patient. "Be right there, Doctor Meade." She tucked the blankets in and smiled down at the old man with bushy eyebrows, which bobbed above sad eyes.

"Must you go so soon?"

"I'll be back. I promise." She patted his arm. "Can I help you take another sip of water before I go?"

When he nodded, she propped his head up with pillows and grabbed the cup. He choked down a few sips.

"There, there, that's a wonderful effort."

He smiled. "You bring out the best in a grouchy old man."

She laughed. "Grouchy my eye. You're nothing but sweetness through and through, and you can't hide that from me."

She heard his chuckle as she walked away.

A quiver turned into a quake as she headed down the hall to Dr. Meade's office. He was cold and demanding at his best. He frightened her most days.

Had she done something to displease him?

Amelia took a deep breath, squared her shoulders, and lifted her head like Mrs. Felicia had taught her. She would present confidence whether she felt it or not.

Seek ye first the kingdom of God.

There it was again. That still small voice. Every time she fell back into presenting something that wasn't, God would remind her to seek Him. *Forgive me, Father. Give me strength.*

She knocked on Dr. Meade's closed door.

"Come in." His voice always sounded terse as if he were perpetually barking out orders. "Sit." He waved to the chair across from his desk.

She sat on the edge of her seat with her back straight and her hands folded to still the tremble in her fingers.

"Do you like your work?"

Her stomach twisted like a dishrag. Here it came. He would threaten to let her go, as he had with so many others, unless she stepped things up in the area he deemed she was lacking.

"I love being a nurse."

"Well, it shows. I want you to train alongside me. You have great potential."

Amelia couldn't contain her smile. "Really?"

"Now, don't let this go to your head. You have much to learn."

"Yes, sir."

"I particularly like the fact you aren't distracted by handsome male patients like so many of the others, twittering and dallying about, giving far too much attention to some and not enough to others. You attend professionally to the old and young, men and women alike, and that has not escaped my notice."

Amelia breathed easy. Little did he know she had eyes for only one man, and he'd broken her heart.

"If you're agreeable, we shall change your shift schedule to mirror mine. Be prepared to work long hours, learn a lot, and become the best nurse in the district. I will expect no less."

"Yes, Dr. Meade. Thank you."

He waved her off. "Go now. Get your last decent sleep. If there are circumstances in which I need you in the middle of the night, you'll be summoned. My driver will pick you up on a moment's notice, and I expect strict adherence."

Amelia nodded.

"Off you go. I have reports to finish." He waved her away like a pesky fly.

She had to force herself not to skip with joy out of the room. This opportunity was a gift—heaven sent. She hated the social scene. With no shortage of attention, she found it exhausting to put off the constant invitations from men. The whole idea of presenting someone she was not no longer held any appeal. She didn't trust a one of them not to go running if they found out her background, and she didn't have the energy to play the game. She was finally getting to the point that she didn't think of Bryon every free moment. That kind of heartache she never wanted to repeat. Grandmother would most certainly balk, but now she had good reason to avoid the social scene all together.

Dr. Meade had solved two problems with one brilliant stroke—she'd be too tired when she laid her head down to sleep for distant memories of what might have been, and she'd be too busy to attend the constant drudgery of social gatherings that did no more than emphasize her loneliness. She would have a good excuse to thwart her Grandmother's continual pestering on how she should accept the many social invitations sent her way.

∼

*B*ryon accepted his boss's invitation. He was not involved in the social scene in London, but some activities were impossible to refuse without offending. This was one of them.

The door to the bank manager's home opened before he knocked, and he was ushered in, his coat taken. He pressed down a yawn and pasted on a smile. The hired hand waved him forward, and all he had to do was follow the music, the raucous laughter, and the noise he had not missed one whit.

He pulled at the tie around his neck to get a bit more air, squared his shoulders, and walked into the ballroom as if he had the world by the tail. His breeding served him well in these moments. He could skillfully project the opposite of what he was feeling.

"Bryon, my star employee." His boss, Mr. Allen, hurried in his direction and shook his hand. "So glad you made it."

A few of his colleagues looked his way and lifted their heads in disgust. Why did his boss keep saying things that clearly showed his favoritism? Didn't he know others were murmuring about the accounts Bryon was given? He'd heard them refer to him as Golden Boy Bryon.

Bryon would distance himself as quickly as possible. "I'll get myself a drink," he said with the hopes of slipping away.

Mr. Allen snapped his finger, and a waiter with a tray of beverages slid into view. With no other choice, Bryon took one. One sip and the sting of alcohol burned its way down his throat.

"What you need to do is get yourself out there dancing and having some fun, old chap," Mr. Allen said. "You work too hard, but tonight is the time to play hard." His too-loud laugh had more heads turning. "Look at all the pretty girls." He pointed to one who was giving Bryon a saucy grin. An inappropriate amount of bosom spilled from her dress.

Bryon looked away. She was beautiful all right, but no one could rival the way he felt about Amelia.

"She has eyes for you. And from what I've heard about Sally"—he bent in to whisper—"she'll give way more than just a dance, if you know what I mean." He slapped Bryon on the back and winked.

Bryon cringed. The thought of using a woman for nothing more than the physical grieved his spirit.

"To be honest, Mr. Allen, there's a woman back home—"

"England is your home now, old boy, and she's not here. Nothing cures the ailments of the heart better than a little fun. And fun is what you're going to have tonight."

He waved at Sally, and she sauntered their way. "Sally, darling, I want you to meet one of my prize employees. He seems to have a broken heart that requires mending, and I think you're the very distraction he needs."

Bryon could feel heat rise from his neck to his hairline. That's what he gets for confiding. He should know better.

Sally pulled at his arm. "Let's dance?" She looked back and winked at Mr. Allen.

How in the world could he get out of this mess? He did the only thing that worked for him these days. He prayed. The whole time they whirled about the dance floor, he looked above her head and talked to God. When the dance finished, the woman grabbed his hand and pulled him off the floor and down a hall. She knew exactly where she was going. He could've stopped her, but he might as well get this over with sooner than later.

They slid into a nearby den, and she boldly closed the door behind them. The practiced jiggle of her well-endowed bosom and the look of victory on her face said it all. She cozied up, but he stepped out of her embrace.

"Sally, is it?"

"You can call me anything you like." Her eyes took on a sultry look. "Even your old girlfriend's name if it helps."

"Sit." Bryon motioned to a nearby chair.

"How about you join me on that settee over there?" She pointed across the room invitingly.

"Did Mr. Allen set this up?"

Her eyes widened. "Why ever would you think that?" She batted her eyelashes at him. "You're an attractive man. You don't need anyone to set anything up for you."

"Please sit," he said. "I'd like to get to know you. Is your name really Sally?"

Her brows lifted. "Well, I'll be. No one has ever stopped long enough to ask me that question. Actually, it's Sarah, but Sally sounds more fun, don't you think?" She slid onto the chair.

Bryon sat across from her. "Sarah is a beautiful name."

"Not in my line of work." Her hand went to her mouth. "I didn't mean for that to spill out, but you caught me off guard with all this talking."

"Your secret is safe with me, Sarah. There was never going to be more than talk anyway."

"Why not? Am I not your type? Most men don't have a type once they catch a glimpse of these." She pointed to her bosom. "And I won't get paid—"

"Mr. Allen hired you to make me happy. Correct?"

"Yes, but—"

"What makes me happy is talking to you. Though you are indeed lovely. I'm not interested in using you or any woman to satisfy my carnal need." There, he said it plain. Leaving no room for temptation, for she was a beautiful woman and he was very much a man.

"Carnal need? Ha. I haven't heard words like that since my ma was alive. From the Bible, right?"

He nodded. "Your mother was a believer?"

"Yes, but she up and died and left me alone on the streets. Seems her God didn't care much about me."

Bryon took in a sharp breath with a silent prayer tumbling through his brain. *Dear God, help me here. Give me the words.*

"God loves you very much."

"As if." She burst to her feet. "He took my mama away when I was only fourteen, and I was left alone on the streets. Do you have any idea what it's like to be dirt poor and look like this?" Her hands swept over her body. "After being raped a couple times, I got smart and used my body to my advantage. If men were gonna take it anyway, might as well make them pay."

Bryon sucked in a breath. "I'm so sorry, Sarah."

"And stop calling me that. I was named after Sarah in the Bible, and she was a godly woman. I am not."

"You can be."

"And what, live off a faith that will have me starve to death?" Her eyes flashed stormy. "I can tell you come from privilege and would never understand."

"I'll help you. I make way too much money for a single man, plus everything I invest in, God turns to gold. Maybe He does that so I will have plenty to help others. I'll pay for an apartment. I'll help you find meaningful work. I'll introduce you to my friends at church, and you can leave this world behind."

She settled back into the chair, eyes narrowed. "Why would you do that for a complete stranger? What's in it for you?"

"A chance to live out my faith."

"I don't understand."

"Do you want a fresh start?"

She covered her face with both hands and sobbed. He let her cry and prayed for her. The Spirit of God was palpable.

She lifted her head. "I never wanted this life."

Bryon scooted his chair closer. "Do you mind if I take your hands? I could pray with you?"

She laughed. "You ask to hold my hands?"

"You're God's creation and deserve to be treated like one."

She nodded, and he took her hands in his and bowed his head. He had never led anyone to Christ before, but the Scriptures he'd been reading came to mind, and the words flowed freely.

"The Bible says we have all sinned and fallen short of the glory of God. The wages for our sin is death, but the gift of God is eternal life through Christ Jesus, who died for us. And whoever calls on His name will be saved. All I did was ask him to forgive my sin. Do you think you could do that?"

She nodded and prayed a halted, broken prayer, so beautiful Bryon had to wipe tears from his eyes.

"I memorized Romans ten, verse nine because it seemed too good to be true," Bryon said. "I wanted to keep reminding myself when my sins would come back to haunt me. It says, 'If you confess with your mouth the Lord Jesus and believe in your heart that God has raised Him from the dead, you will be saved.' I've been living a different life ever since I committed those words to memory. When I remember that I lied to the love of my life and did a host of other things, I meditate on God's promise that He has forgiven me. It never ceases to amaze me."

"I believe," she said. "For the first time in my life, a man wants to help me, not harm me."

He lifted his head and she lifted hers. "Your ma is so proud of you right now."

Sarah swiped the tears from her face and stood. "I feel so amazing, and so...what's the word I'm looking for? So clean." Her smile radiated with joy.

"That's a sure sign of the Holy Spirit. You're now my sister in Christ."

She beamed. "Sister. I like that. Is it all right to hug you in a completely sisterly way?" She giggled. "Imagine me being careful with a man. That's what I call instant change."

After they hugged, he said, "How about we go say good-bye to Mr. Allen and get out of this place?"

Her eyes widened. "I don't want to go back to the brothel."

"Of course not. I'll take you to my friend Harry's place. I know his wife and he will take you in until we get you settled in your own place."

"What will you say to Mr. Allen?" A tremble took to her voice.

"He didn't force you to come here tonight, did he?"

"No. But Madame Decloutte might not be happy with me leaving. We're hired at a handsome fee to make our clients happy."

Bryon laughed. "Well then, nobody should complain, for you have made me happy."

They barely got out of the den and into the ballroom before Mr. Allen came running with a grin on his face.

Before the older man could speak, Bryon said, "Thanks for introducing me to Sarah. That's her real name, by the way."

His bushy brows hit the ceiling.

"She won't be available again for the type of services she was hired for tonight. She's become a Christian, like me, and I intend to help her find a line of work more fitting for a woman of God."

"Bryon, I'm sorry. I didn't know you were a...one of those. I thought I would be giving you what most men—"

Bryon held up his hand. "No offense taken."

He turned his attention to Sarah. "You do look different." His brows knit together in confusion.

She smiled. "For the first time in a long time, I feel genuine peace."

He shook his head and raised both hands. "This is not quite how I anticipated this going but—"

"See you on Monday, Mr. Allen." Bryon offered Sarah his arm and they headed for the door.

⁓

"Did you hear, Golden Boy here left with a lady of the street the other evening?" Marcus said the words loudly enough for the whole office to hear. "Yet he acts like he's so much better than us."

"Most of us don't mind a dally with Sally, but we don't have to take the wench home."

Bryon's heart sank. He had been worried about his reputation being seen with her, but God had other ideas and Bryon was not disappointed that he had obeyed. But if his coworkers thought he took her home, he would have to set them straight. When he was done, they'd have more to mock him about.

He walked over to the group of men, who were itching for a reaction. He would give them one. "I thought it best she not return to a brothel after I led her to Jesus, so yes, I did leave with her, but I took her somewhere safe and it wasn't my place."

"Jesus?" They all howled. Marcus stepped forward and leaned in. "So, you're one of those do-gooders who think you're better than the rest of us."

"I've been the worst of sinners, and still make my fair share of mistakes. However, getting Sarah off the streets was not one of them." Bryon walked back to his desk.

"I knew there was something strange about him," one said. "Who still believes in that God stuff except for little old ladies and the weak who need a crutch to lean on?"

"Yeah, he's all work and no play," another said. "Always trying to show us up."

"The worst thing is what a bootlicker he is," Marcus said. "He's got the boss wrapped around his baby finger so he gets all the best accounts."

Bryon held his tongue. He could defend the fact that he worked for every account he received rather than stand around wasting time, as they were currently doing. Instead, he silently prayed.

"Golden Boy who follows the golden rule. How pathetic."

Bryon ignored them, but it hurt to be hated.

God help me love them.

CHAPTER 27

*K*atherine could not abide the tension between her and Colby one more day. The past two weeks had been way too long. The New Year had arrived, and she still hadn't talked to him. She trudged across the yard from the icehouse to the main house. The silence would end today. She stomped the snow from her boots and yelled down the hall.

"Delilah, I got your preserves and milk and I need—"

"Land sakes," Delilah said as she rounded the corner from the kitchen. "Why you talking to me from out here? You know my ears don't work from one room to the next."

"Sorry." Katherine wrapped her arm around Delilah's fleshy shoulders. "I need someone to keep Seth out of trouble when he wakes up from his nap while I talk to Colby."

"Well, that's good. You two moping around not talking to each other has me in a dither. I'll get Annie to help out with Seth." She pointed out the window. "He's a-comin'."

238

Katherine's stomach lurched. If Delilah was upset now, she would be most unhappy with what was to follow.

She met Colby at the door. They looked at each other without casting their gazes away from each other.

"We need to—"

"Talk." He finished the sentence for her.

"Yes."

He followed her into the library and shut the door. The walls closed in. Why did she wrestle with running into his arms and out the door at the same time?

He turned toward her, and golden specks flashed in his eyes, much like a man with hope. She looked away, willing her mind to stay on task. She couldn't get sidetracked with his rugged build or the sun-streaked blond in his hair. And she certainly had to guard against the thought of his kiss.

She mustered the strength to meet his gaze. She didn't like the confidence that oozed from him, nor the way her heart tumbled over itself as he met her stare.

As much as this would hurt her and Seth, it was imperative she got the conversation done. Not another day could pass. She had used Colby long enough. Twisting the folds of her skirt in her hands, she stepped forward.

"I've been remiss. In fact, I've been very wrong to allow all this time to pass without considering you...or your feelings." She peeked up at him, but he remained stoic. "I'm truly sorry. We should've had this conversation long ago."

"Meaning?" He stepped closer. Close enough for her to smell his woodsy scent and pull in the faint aroma of leather and horses and... She was losing focus. She stepped back. How could she kindly suggest he leave after all he had done?

"You know what I'm trying to say." She waved her hand between them. "What happened at Christmas was a mistake and—"

"No, I don't know what you're trying to say." He stepped closer.

"I realize you feel more for me than I do for you. And I'm sorry." She turned away.

He gently spun her around to face him. His strong arms encircled her waist. She shuddered at the power of his proximity. "Are you sure about that?"

She couldn't think straight. Between the mind-bending sensation of having him close enough to feel his breath on her face and the relentless tick of the grandfather clock that emphasized how effectively he had silenced her protest, time froze.

Powerless against the pull of emotion, she stood paralyzed while his hands slid slowly up to cup her face in their strength and warmth. Her pulse skipped erratically, and she gulped back a knot in her throat.

"I'm going to kiss you now."

She shook her head, but her body swayed toward him, not away.

"Yes, I am."

She was shocked at his comfort, his boldness. She wrestled with fleeing and relaxing all in one crazy moment. Her eyes closed against his magnetic stare. The touch of his mouth on hers was like fire to kindling. There was no mistaking his message. He knew exactly what he was doing, and she couldn't hide her response. Rhythmically, like a well-rehearsed concerto, he played a song, his mouth dancing upon hers. She gave in to the melodic flow.

He lifted his head from her responsive lips in an agonizing exodus and gently ran a work-roughened knuckle down the side of her face. She closed her parted lips when he ran a thumb along the bottom. The room grew cold when he stepped away.

She smoothed her hair and fidgeted with the filigreed comb that had come loose.

He wore a look of such confidence that her anger flared. "How dare you?"

"I dare because I care, and so do you, more than you're willing to admit."

She gasped at his stark truth, her fingers covering her mouth.

His voice gentled. "I know the speech you had prepared for me today. The good-bye, the thanks-for-everything. But I own half this ranch, and I'm not going anywhere. And by design, Josiah has the other half in Seth's name, so I don't think you'll be going anywhere either."

"What?" Her heart dropped to her shoes.

"I was hoping not to have to tell you. Josiah had me promise I would only use this information if I had to."

"What are you talking about?" Her voice warbled.

"You never asked to see the will, and Josiah counted on that."

"But I did see the will."

"Before I arrived. Before Josiah and I talked. And before he amended it."

There had to be a mistake. Josiah would never do this to her. "Why would he cut me out?"

"There's a perfectly good reason, and it's time you know it. Please sit." He pointed to the nearby settee.

She glared up at him, unwilling to believe the words he'd said.

Colby kept his arm aimed at the chair. "You need to understand how Josiah prepared for your future. Please."

Katherine walked on weak legs and practically collapsed into the cushions.

Colby pulled a leather-bound copy of Sir Walter Scott's *Collection of Works* from the top bookshelf behind the desk. He blew a layer of dust off the binding and opened it. A thin parched envelope fell free. He crossed to where she sat and handed her the envelope. Josiah's handwriting was sprawled across the front. *To my beloved Katherine.*

With shaky hands, she reached out.

The seat sank beneath Colby as he sat down beside her. He placed a hand over hers to still the opening.

"I'm going to leave you to read this in private. But I need to tell you one more thing. Within the first five minutes alone in Josiah's company, he asked me if I still loved you. I was shocked and embarrassed, but I couldn't lie to him. When I admitted I had tried and failed to forget you, even after being engaged to another woman, he smiled."

"He smiled?" Her head swam. Colby loved her. Josiah knew.

"He said it confirmed what God had told him to do. So, if you're confused right now, trust me when I tell you that I know what you're going through."

She gazed at the crisp paper in her hand. Josiah's words, to her.

"Read his letter, and then we'll talk." Colby kissed her lightly on the cheek and left the room.

Katherine stared at the familiar handwriting for a long time before she gathered the courage to lift the flap and pull the yellowed paper from the envelope. A blob of ink spread across the corner. A smile pulled at her lips, and her eyes filled with tears. Josiah had always had a habit of putting his pen down in the middle of his work. The ink would leak and leave a mess on most every page. She had nagged him about this quirk, but now the memory was sweet and personal, as if he were reaching from the page.

Dearest Katherine,

If you are reading this, I have undoubtedly been gone for some time now. Colby was decidedly uncomfortable with this decision and balked at what I suggested, but I made him under-

stand. I hope he has not taken too long. Life is too precious to
be wasted. You and I know that better than most, don't we?

You must trust that what I'm about to suggest is not done
without a lot of prayer. Though I'm sure some of this will come
as a surprise, I trust you will search your heart and call on
God. He will make the truth as clear to you as He has to me.

The last number of months, I have agonized over two things.
One, that Seth will grow up without the love of a father. The
other, my guilt for having forced you to marry me. I know we
found love, and I'm blessed beyond measure, but I cannot get it
out of my head that, had I not forced the issue, you would be
married to a fine young man and not be a widow today.
Thankfully, I rest in the truth that God has forgiven my selfish
ways, but I want to ask your forgiveness.

Katherine wiped away the tears that had fallen on the fragile
paper. She wanted to hug him, hold him, and tell him that he
had made her happier than anything she could have imagined.

She relaxed into the seat and raised the paper in front of her
so her tears wouldn't mar his message.

What grieves me the most is that I overheard you telling
Delilah you would never marry again and open yourself to
another heartache. I know you were watching me decline, but I
also know how stubborn you can be when you make your mind
up about something...like when you decided to love me back
into your life. (That was a good thing, by the way.)

She smiled, missing his silly humor.

However, if you're reading this letter, I know that sufficient
time has passed, and you have not changed your mind on the

matter. Therefore, I cannot leave this unsaid. You know how much I loved Georgina, and you know how much I loved you, so you know it's possible to love again. I'm begging you to consider what I'm suggesting. In fact, you may well think I'm playing God, but you'll have to trust that I'm at peace.

This letter is written to say unequivocally that Colby is the man I entrust with my family. He still loves you, though he has tried hard not to. Now, knowing I will leave you, his undying devotion makes sense to me. I believe he is the Lord's provision for such a time as this.

I want you to consider opening your heart to him. You had strong feelings for him at one time, and because of this you may feel guilty, or you may feel that you're not honoring my memory. I don't want you to feel this way.

This all came clear to me one night when I was praying for Seth and you. God told me he kept love alive in Colby's heart so that I could rest knowing you two will be loved and cherished. At first, I wasn't sure I was hearing right, so I requested that Colby come. When he couldn't deny his love for you, I knew that all was as it should be.

Then, when Seth went to him at first glance when he's timid with strangers, that was further confirmation. This hope has given me peace to let go and look forward to seeing my Jesus.

A sob ripped from her throat, and tears splashed down her cheeks.

Colby is more than my friend. He's like the brother I never had. I love him as much as I love the two of you. He is a good man, but more than that, he is a godly man. I would feel honored to have him love and care for my family. I trust him with the greatest treasure life has given me...you and our son.

As far as the business side of things, Colby was already my partner, so a lot of this is made easy. Rather than sell off his portion immediately, I asked him to honor my request of staying at the ranch for the next four years. He said that he could spend a lifetime and it would not change the way he felt about you. I pray you have found his presence comforting.

The will states that Seth and Colby have equal ownership of the ranch, for the next four years. The reason you are not mentioned, dear Katherine, is so you stay put, and allow time to heal and allow love to grow.

I remember after Georgina died how I wanted to sell everything and get as far away from the memories as possible. Had it not been for Delilah and Abe, I know I would've done something rash. I don't want you selling in the midst of your pain, nor do I want you struggling alone.

If I'm wrong about all of this and in four years you have decided against marrying Colby, then he has agreed to sell his half of the ranch to you. At that time, all will be in your hands to do with as you please.

My prayer, of course, is that Seth will have a father and you, a wonderful husband long before the four years are up. It would thrill me to know that Seth has brothers and sisters to play with, something I never had and desperately want for him.

Forgive me if you find this disagreeable, but unlike our arranged marriage, you do have an out...albeit a number of years from now when the grief has subsided and your thinking will be clear.

I will always love you, my dearest Kat...with an everlasting love. Tell Seth all about his daddy in heaven, and please promise me you will try to love again. Every moment with you was a pleasure.

Trust again. Love again. Be happy, my love.

Yours forever,

Josiah.

The letter dropped from her fingers and floated to the floor. Katherine's head dropped into her hands and she wept.

CHAPTER 28

*K*atherine wanted to talk to Colby the next day and yet could not settle the jumble in her brain. Everything had changed, and she was reeling. Her emotions vacillated. One minute she was up and the next down. She couldn't deny that Colby had awakened feelings she thought long buried, but they were new and frightening.

Dear God, help me. I need wisdom. I need words. I need a little time to sort my thoughts. Please help Colby understand.

Each day as January slipped into February, she prayed the same prayer. She wrestled with God, begging Him for wisdom, and finally came to peace with what she needed to say. But every time Colby came into the room, she got tongue-tied.

It was the day before Seth's third birthday, and she wanted the air cleared between her and Colby before they were thrust together in a group, but she had still not found the courage. *Please help me find the words.* She whispered the prayer as she stirred the cake batter.

"Seth, no. Do not touch." Katherine moved quickly to grab his hand as he reached for the shiny silver handles on the wood stove. "Hot." She picked him up and carried him across the room. "Don't you touch that stove. You hear?" She set him down and picked up the bowl of cake batter, looking back to double-check.

Seth had toddled halfway across the room. Katherine slammed down the bowl and moved toward him. He took a step closer to the pot-bellied stove.

"Seth. No" Katherine was firm, but he took off running. She reached him just before he touched the hot surface and swung him into her arms. "Mama said no." He squirmed, screamed at a high pitch, and reached up, batting at her. She grabbed his flailing chubby arms and held them tight.

"What's going on in here? Are you being a bad boy for your mama?"

Seth twisted in Katherine's arms, thrashing to be set free. Colby hurried forward and steadied them both.

"He was going for the hot stove and wouldn't listen."

Colby's kind eyes bore into hers. His hand stayed firm on her arm, and awareness tickled down her spine.

"Daddy." Tears ran down Seth's chubby cheeks as he threw his body toward Colby.

Katherine's heart lurched. *Daddy?*

"No Seth," Colby said, "You've been a bad boy, and you must tell Mama sorry and give her a kiss first."

Fat tears rolled free as Seth kept reaching for Colby.

Colby repeated his command. "Give your mama a kiss sorry, and then I'll take you."

The tension drained out of her son's body as he relented and collapsed against her chest.

Colby smiled and whispered, "We won." Pleasure crinkled the corners of his eyes in a most endearing way. She had to look away to concentrate.

Seth lifted his head, his thumb in his mouth. He pulled it free long enough to pucker his lips. Katherine kissed her son's pudgy cheek, and he cuddled against her, no longer feeling the need to be out of her arms.

She looked up at Colby. "Thank you."

"My pleasure." He headed to the stove. With one hand, he grabbed the blue enameled coffee pot and with the other a thick stoneware mug from the counter. He poured himself the brew and took a long swig.

She put Seth down, and he ran and pulled on Colby's legs. "I go get my train. You play."

"Okay. Go get it, and we'll build a big track in the next room and let your mama finish her cake."

His chubby little legs took off in a run.

"Did you hear what he called you?"

"That started about a week ago. I wasn't sure how you would feel about it, so I didn't say anything. You have enough to sort through." His eyes darkened and grew dangerously soft. "I want to be his daddy."

She looked away and was thankful when Seth reappeared with his train. She turned back to her batter. "Give me a few minutes to get this in the oven, and I'll ask Delilah to watch the cake and Seth. We need to talk."

"I'll take Seth to the library and play with him. Send Delilah in to get him when you're ready." He lightly touched the back of her shoulder, and her heart instantly picked up speed.

But fear ripped through her. She wanted to spend the rest of the day getting that cake in the oven, but she had spent too long procrastinating as it was.

An hour later and she was ready. Delilah had collected Seth and was reading him his favorite picture book.

She lightly rapped on the library door, entered, and closed the door behind her. She stood for a moment, looking at the man who had become her best friend.

He stretched back in the chair and smiled. "Should I be smiling?"

Katherine sat on the settee. She folded and unfolded her

hands in her lap. "I've wrestled with not what to say, but how to say it. But having Seth call you daddy finally snapped me out of my stupor. I'm at peace with my decision and pray you will be too."

His brows rose in question. He stood and walked around to the front of the desk and leaned against it. One long leg folded over the other, and his strong arms tightened as he crossed them in front. "I'm listening."

"First, I have to apologize. I haven't been thinking of anyone but myself this past year, and for that I'm sorry. Truly sorry. To be completely honest, I had a good inkling you cared for me, and I certainly knew my son loves you as much as you loved him."

His eyebrows lifted.

"I needed you, but not in the way you needed me."

He moved closer, and she put up her hand.

"Don't worry," he said. "I'll never again initiate anything between us. If anything happens...well, that will be up to you. But I kissed you that last time for a very specific reason, and, by the way, you did respond. I hope your answer will reflect that truth."

"I'm not explaining this very well. I'm so thankful that you care for Seth and me—"

"No, Katherine, I don't care for you. I love you. Both of you. Let's at least be honest about that much." He turned his back to her and walked to the fireplace, staring blankly into the flames.

Fire stirred in her gut. "I am being honest." She stood and joined him at the fireplace, and he turned to face her. "I've been grieving. I'm still grieving. You covered up your love for me. Then, you unloaded it all at one time, including a letter from my husband. You've given me little time to catch up to where your head has been. Now, you expect what?" Her hands flew up in the air. "Please, tell me, Colby. What do you expect?"

His eyes, so full of hope a moment before, filled with sadness.

"Years ago, while you still loved me, I had to squelch every feeling I had for you and learn to love the man God gave me. While you and Josiah concocted a plan, putting my future into one neat little package, I was saying good-bye to the man that I barely had time to love before God took him from me. This past year, while you allowed the hope of love to grow inside you, I've been grieving, sadder than I've ever been in my life. So, don't... don't expect me to turn my feelings on and off at will." She couldn't stop the sob that worked its way from her heart to her lips.

Suddenly, she was in his arms.

"I'm so sorry," he said. "Please forgive me." He smoothed his hands down her back and whispered the words over and over until she quieted.

He gently eased away. "I can leave. I know I made a promise to Josiah, but—"

"Please, don't go. I know it's selfish to ask that things carry on as they have been, but if you could please give more time?" She bit at her lower lip. "Obviously, I find you attractive and I have...feelings. But I'm so confused...afraid to love again. Everywhere I go, sorrow and sadness follow me."

He wrapped an errant curl behind her ear. "Time I can give. As much time as you need. There's nowhere I can go to outrun this love. But you'll have to let me know...if and when."

She nodded.

"And Seth?"

"He loves you." She stepped away, finding it difficult to think at such close proximity. "I can't take him from you no matter what happens between us. Even if *we* never work out, I hope you build yourself a big home on the property, marry a beautiful woman, and always remain Seth's father. You deserve at least that much after all you've invested in his life. And he needs you."

"Thank you." A breath whistled through his teeth, and he ran a hand through his hair. The blond curls bounced back into place.

"Friends?" He smiled down at her.

"Always and forever friends."

CHAPTER 29

May 1872
RICHMOND

A robin swooped low from an overhead branch, trying hard to distract Amelia from disturbing her nest. Amelia ducked and laughed. "It's all right, birdie, I'm only passing under." The robin flitted out of sight.

Amelia loved her walk to the hospital this time of year. Lilacs perfumed the air, and the world came alive with vibrant greens, flowers painted in every hue, and sunshine cast from a canopy of blue. She took a deep breath and quickened her pace. She best not dally, or she'd be late for her shift.

She loved her work, loved her patients, and laughed at how she had even grown to love Dr. Meade. His stoic and often brusque manner with the staff was contradictory to his gentle care for his patients. His reputation for being the best doctor in Richmond was well-earned. Amelia had learned fast that, if she kept her focus on her patients, she couldn't have a better mentor, teacher, and friend than Dr. Meade.

Her life in Richmond had settled into a safe routine. On the days she wasn't working, her only social outing was church on Sunday. Life was good but for one niggling problem. Amelia had little patience for the Richmond social scene, and Grandmother wanted her to return, retry, revive, her love life. She, on the other hand, was content to give her life to nursing. Hard work brought the freedom of being able to take care of herself. There were no men wreaking havoc and breaking promises. Life was steady. Sure. Stable. Just the way she liked it.

Once in a long while she thought of Bryon. What had become of him? Had he married a nice English girl? His ex-fiancée, Shelby, had not wasted any time. The papers had delighted in telling of her whirlwind romance and subsequent marriage to Henry Johnstone, the senator's son. A pang of sorrow occasionally sliced through Amelia, like it did in that moment, but she had learned to discipline her mind to go elsewhere. As she swung through the front doors of the hospital, she was happy that, for the next ten hours, she would be far too busy for what-ifs and what-might-have-beens.

Emily scurried forward, her nurse's cap bouncing on her head. "Everyone is in a dither. Rumor has it that a very prominent patient is arriving shortly. Apparently, she's donated hundreds of dollars in charity to our hospital, and Dr. Meade's been asking for you. My guess—you'll be summoned to work alongside him again." She smirked. "If he weren't twenty-five years your senior, I'd swear he has a thing for you."

"Oh fiddlesticks. He has a thing for a willing servant." Amelia said it with a laugh and removed her cloak and hung it on her peg.

"Something I'm clearly not." Emily laughed. "Can't wait to get married and get on with my life. You on the other hand, think this is your life."

Amelia ignored Emily's disparaging remark. Had she gone through the heartache Amelia had, getting married would not be a top priority. "Who is our mystery patient?"

"No one has been told, but Helen was sent to prepare a private room. You know how that goes—only the best for the rich." She lifted her nose and shook her head. "And the rest get"—she pointed to the large open room with beds lined side-by-side. "It's rather annoying."

Amelia threw her arm around her friend. "Let's give the benefit of the doubt. Maybe this woman has something infectious."

"One can hope."

"Emily." Amelia tried to look stern, but laughed despite herself.

"Amelia." Dr Meade entered the main room and waved her over.

Emily snickered. "Told you."

Amelia laughed. "Want to trade places?"

"Not on your life."

Amelia put on her smile and headed toward him. "Good morning, Dr. Meade."

"Top priority. We have a patient who will need the utmost of care." His usual calm voice sounded flustered. "And good morning."

The corners of Amelia's lips lifted. It had taken over a year of consistently saying good morning with no reply before Dr. Meade had paused long enough to reciprocate.

She walked swiftly to match his long strides. Her long dress whooshed around her ankles as they headed toward the private wing of the hospital.

"She's arrived through the back, and Helen has settled her in. I don't want her in contact with anyone else. Her pneumonia is acute. She's bringing up rust-colored mucus, which indicates how advanced the problem is. Her lungs are severely compromised." He shook his head, a look of frustration pulling his mouth taut. "She should've been hospitalized long before now."

"Why wasn't she?"

255

"They had a doctor coming in daily and thought they could manage with homecare. Her husband said she was quite resistant to leaving her house. Now, it's up to you and me to try to save her. But without the help of the good Lord..." His words trailed, and they walked a few paces in silence before he continued. "You've witnessed firsthand how pneumonia goes. We lose at least one third of our patients, and the numbers are worse when they're this far gone."

"I'll do my very best."

"Expect to work long hours."

"Of course."

They turned the corner of the long hall and stopped outside a door. Dr. Meade rested one hand on the knob and the other on her arm. "It's time to give back to a wonderful lady who has given our hospital so much. I can think of no one I trust more than you."

Amelia took his praise with a smile as they entered. One look at the pale face nearly lost against the stark white sheets, and she stopped short. Her smile vanished. Somehow, Melinda Preston managed to look intimidating even in her weakened state. Amelia sucked in a deep breath.

"Dr. Meade," she whispered in a low voice. "I...I don't think that I'm the right person for this job."

He whipped around. "Why not? You've done a remarkable job looking after pneumonia patients in the past."

"We have history. I don't think she would like me taking care of her."

"What I think, Amelia, is that Mrs. Preston wants to live. And right now, we are her best chance. You're as much a part of this effort as I am. Can you remain professional?"

"Absolutely."

He nodded. "Very well then, you are the right person for this job."

Amelia looked down at the sleeping Melinda. Part of her

ached to see her so helpless, and part of her struggled to even think of forgiving her. She would give excellent care—until Melinda got strong enough to demand otherwise.

Suddenly, she realized that she may well see the whole Preston family, including Bryon. The thought set her mind spinning. Her neatly ordered world, the one where she had control, was being shaken by the very hands of God.

∾

MAY 1872
SHENANDOAH VALLEY

*K*atherine flipped from one side of her bed to the other. Why was she awake again? For the last three nights she had awoken suddenly from a dead sleep for no apparent reason. The same question immediately echoed in her spirit.

Do you trust me?

Her answer remained the same. *Of course, I trust you, Lord.*

Unlike the last two nights, she did not fall back to sleep but kept mulling over the words. Did she trust? Colby had been waiting for over a year since their last talk, giving her the time she requested, and yet she was content to keep things friendly, warm even, but at a safe distance.

Can trust and fear live side by side? the voice asked.

Her heart rate picked up pace. *Not really.*

Pick up that dusty Bible of yours.

Katherine flipped over under her warm covers and placed the pillow over her head.

Get up and read what I have for you.

Katherine lay for a few more minutes and then tossed the covers aside. She felt around in the dark for her lamp and lit one lone candle before padding over to the dresser top. Sure enough, her Bible had a good layer of dust on top. With a hard blow and a swipe of her hand, she removed the sign of neglect. She returned to the side of the bed and sank down, wrapping the warm coverlet around her. *Lord, I'm here.*

Her hands randomly opened to the center of the book, and her gaze fell on the fifty-sixth Psalm. *Whenever I am afraid, I will trust in You... In God I have put my trust; I will not fear.*

The book trembled in Katherine's hands. God was speaking.

She carried fear everywhere she went. She did not fully trust.

"God, I've been so disappointed since losing Josiah. That experience devastated me. I prayed for his healing, but You took him anyway."

Tears blurred her vision, and she swiped a hand across her face to keep them from falling on the thin pages. She read the next passage.

You number my wanderings; Put my tears into Your bottle; Are they not in Your book? When I cry out to You, this I know, because God is for me ... In God I have put my trust; I will not be afraid.

Katherine slid to her knees beside the bed. Great sobs wrenched forth, racking her frame. "God, you're for me. You've counted and placed each tear I've cried in a bottle and kept record of them in your book. You've not left me nor forsaken me, yet I've wandered from you. Please forgive me."

She bowed her head to the floor. "You brought Colby into our lives to be a daddy to Seth and an enormous help to me. You've surrounded me with loving people, and I thank you for Abe and Delilah, the support of Ma and Pa, the love of my sisters. I am blessed. I don't need to be afraid to love."

Then give me your fear.

Her hands lifted into the air as she raised her body from the floor. "Lord, I surrender my fears to you. Take them...take every one. They've kept me captive for far too long now."

She slid back beneath the covers with the distinct feeling

that this moment of surrender had the power to change her future.

$$\sim$$

May 1872
England

ryon stood on the deck of the SS Adriatic. Its bragging rights included crossing the Atlantic in two to three weeks instead of the six weeks it had taken Bryon to sail to England. He prayed this would be the case on this journey.

He turned his face into the wind and hung onto the rail. His knuckles whitened at the thought of arriving too late. All the telegraph had said was,

Please return home quickly. Stop.

Your mother is deathly ill. Stop.

For the past year, he had felt the persistent urge of the Spirit to return home, but he hadn't heeded it. Instead, he'd wrestled with God.

He'd explained all the wonderful work he was part of in helping the less fortunate. As if God didn't know.

He'd reminded God of how well he was doing at the bank and how much he was able to give because of that success. Surely God didn't want him to give that up.

He'd promised to write a letter to his parents and ask for their forgiveness, but every time he sat down to write, not a word would land on the page.

God kept whispering. *You need to make amends in person, and not only to your parents.*

No matter what he did or where he went, the truth kept drip, drip, dripping. One big obstacle kept him back, kept him making excuses, kept him stagnant—Amelia.

He still loved her. She was probably married to a nice man after all this time. Safe in England, with an ocean between them, he could manage the pain, but if he were to see her, his world would be turned upside down.

A splash of sea spray carried on the wind whipped across his face. He looked up into the heavens and prayed for the first time with utmost surrender. *Thy will be done.*

CHAPTER 30

*N*ow that the spring showers had turned into the warmth of May, Katherine loved their Sunday afternoon walks to the creek. She smiled at the constant barrage of questions that Seth had for Colby and his incredible patience. Seth's chatter continued all the way to their favorite spot, where a sleepy stretch opened to a natural beach, perfect for Seth's safety. Once this year's spring showers were done, they made their way most Sundays after church for a picnic. Skipping stones, swimming, and lying on a blanket in the shade of a large oak took up a good portion of the Sabbath.

The still air magnified the humming wings of busy bees that went about their work. Katherine spread the blanket in the cool shade of the sprawling branches and plunked her body down. She kicked off her shoes and stretched her toes in the sun. A surge of joy bubbled in her heart as she looked around. Wild pink azaleas and yellow daisies graced the landscape with color. A soft breeze ruffled the grass. Behind them, acres of their pastoral fields and bordering meadows rolled in lush green. The neighing of a few playful horses in the far pasture added to the muted song of the babbling water. Steep rock-strewn slopes rose in the distance, skirting the forbidding and craggy Massanutten. She took a slow breath, enjoying the fresh air. Enjoying life.

Colby and Seth were happily making a commotion. Rufus, their mangy pup, frolicked in a game of keep-away. His incessant growl and bark brought squeals of delight from Seth as he and Colby threw the stick back and forth. Rufus didn't catch on and ran like a wild one between the two, jumping up in an effort to intercept it.

Ever since that prayer of surrender the past week, Katherine had realized a simple truth. She was happy. Memories of Josiah no longer brought tears. Cheerful memories flowed. She smiled and laughed freely and was now able to keep the fear of something happening to Seth at bay. Her grief had healed, gradually and thoroughly, and Colby had been a big part of the process.

Since her plea for more time a year ago, he acted the perfect gentleman. He would offer his arm when they walked but had not reached out for more.

Where had time flown? Josiah had been gone for two and half years, and Colby had been patiently at her side ever since. A shiver of awareness raced up her spine as she lifted her eyes and stared at him. His broad shoulders, trim physique, and tanned arms stole her attention. Her heart palpitated, and her palms sweated, but she was conflicted. Everything was comfortable and uncomplicated the way it was. Did she dare upset that balance?

She could no longer deny the longing she read in his eyes when she caught him gazing. Before he slid on his mask, the raw ache of yearning shone through.

He looked in her direction. An easy grin curled the corners of his mouth, deepening the grooves that edged his attractive smile. She sucked in a sharp breath at the handsome picture he made and smiled back. Her mind wandered into that guarded, forbidden territory of her heart. What would it be like to allow love in? To sate the loneliness? Feel the warmth of his embrace? Enjoy the intimate touch of a lover's caress? A searing warmth burnt across her cheeks as she let the thoughts tumble in.

The whole package drew her—and every available young woman in the area. How could she blame them? His godly spirit, infectious personality, and lean rugged build were hard to miss. And that soft drawl of his voice, the golden flecks dancing in the depths of warm, kind eyes—what was she waiting for?

She openly stared, loving the way he removed his hat to ruffle his flattened hair. Streaks of blonde, bleached by the sun, sprang free of his fingers before he plopped the Homburg back on. She closed her eyes and brought the daydream to life. His laughing eyes ignited with a blaze of passion as she drew his head down to meet her lips...

"Mama, Mama, I'm hungry. Can we eat now?"

She started at the sound of Seth's voice so close, and her eyes flashed open. She found herself staring directly at Colby. His eyebrows lifted, but she was unable to break away.

"Mama," Seth whined. "I'm hungry."

She dropped her gaze and bustled into action, happy to have something other than Colby occupy her mind.

A quick glance in his direction revealed he was seated on the blanket with a grin on his face. He winked, and she looked away.

She could hardly blame him for flirting after eyeing him like a piece of candy at The General Mercantile.

All this time, feelings had simmered below the surface. Now, finally, she had the courage to not squelch the need. She was seeing, feeling, and shaking on the inside like a teenager on her first social outing.

Katherine spread out the fixings and filled a plate with food for Seth. Her hands trembled as she tried to ignore the man beside her. She piled up his favorites, as she always did, while he poured the drinks. They had a routine as if they were an old married couple.

Guilt settled in her stomach. In Colby, she had a business partner, a lead ranch hand, a good friend, and a father for her son, but what did he have? The one thing he had made all too clear, the reason he rebuffed the obvious attention of many women, was the one thing he still did not have—her love.

Their hands touched as they exchanged the food and drink. Katherine's heart raced. In her haste to pull away from him, a splash of apple juice hit the front of her muslin gown. The blotch grew bigger as she rubbed at it.

"What is with you today?" He laughed. "You're like those young fillies out yonder." His head nodded toward the pasture. "Skittish as they come."

She joined in the laughter. "Clumsy, I guess."

Silence fell between them while Seth chatted up a storm. "I'm gonna find the best skipping stone."

Katherine did her best to concentrate.

"Daddy says the real flat ones are the best."

The way Seth said Daddy only emphasized what she had been avoiding for far too long.

"We're gonna have a contest. But I'm going to find the rocks myself." He shoved a large piece of bread into his mouth. "I'm gonna—"

"Seth, finish what's in your mouth before you rattle on to your mother." Colby ruffled Seth's head of shocking red hair. "How do you expect her to understand what you're saying?"

In every way, Colby was her boy's father.

Their eyes locked, and his lips twitched with humor. Laughter bubbled from his voice. "I'm not sure what's gotten into you, Katherine, but you're looking at me like—"

"I'm just happy."

He lifted a lop-sided grin. "Happy is good."

"Can I go now?" Seth pulled at Katherine's hand. She was still lost in Colby's smile.

"Go." Colby waved Seth on. "But take the rest of your carrot and finish it on the way."

Seth was up and running.

Colby's warning rang out. "Stay within sight, and only pick up the really flat ones. Then, we're on."

Seth looked over his shoulder. "I'm gonna beat you this time."

"You can try." Colby laughed.

"He's a smart one," Colby said. "The last few times I've sent him out to get our skipping stones, he's brought back thicker ones for me. He's getting really good at throwing them too. Pretty soon I'll have to find my own, or he'll whoop me for sure." He fell back on the blanket with his arms under his head and stared into the blue. "My turn for some shut eye."

Katherine busied herself packing up the picnic basket, then sat beside him. Acutely aware of the man, she watched him sleep. An intense urge to run her fingers through his hair and down his cheek—and kiss those waiting lips—filled her being. She didn't dare, but she did move closer and studied his profile. A network of fine lines etched the corners of his eyes, and she reflected on the passage of time. Soon she would be twenty-eight and Colby would be thirty-two.

Josiah hadn't wanted them to waste precious time. He'd wanted Seth to have brothers and sisters. The thought brought heat to her cheeks. Like a gentle breeze bringing life to dying embers, desire stirred. She loved everything about Colby, it would not be a far reach to...

Unable to still her wandering hand, she touched his cheek with her knuckle. She remembered their kiss too well and, even in her confused state back then, she hadn't been confused about her response. She closed her eyes against the pull and ran her fingertips close to his lips.

Suddenly he was sitting, and her straying hand was caught around the wrist. Her eyes flew open. Awareness trembled between them. The air pounded with tension, vibrating with consciousness.

"What are you doing?" he asked.

A knot the size of a fist stuck in her throat, and she swallowed against it. "I...I—"

"I'm not complaining. I just need to know. What do you want from me?" His breathing sounded shallow and irregular. He gently stroked the inside of her wrist with one hand and lifted the other to caress the side of her face.

She could take the sweet agony no longer and leaned into him. Only inches from his mouth she paused, willing him to close the gap.

"May I kiss you?" His breath fanned her cheeks as he waited.

"Yes," she whispered.

His head bent toward hers.

"Daddy, Daddy, I found some good ones. Can we throw them now?"

Like a cloud burst on a sunny day, Katherine awakened to the world around her. She leapt from the blanket.

Colby's expression, filled with love and desire a moment before, now looked hurt and confused, and she felt horrible.

"Later, Katherine." He headed off with Seth.

Katherine knew he meant it. Her blood ran hot, and then cold. What had she started?

CHAPTER 31

*Q*uestions and possibilities roiled in Katherine's mind as
she watched Colby and Seth skip stones. Like life
returning to frostbitten limbs, the prickling sensation
of living again spread through her being. Wonderful. Terrifying.

*Dear God, can I really let go of my fear and widen that circle of
love to allow Colby in.*

You've already let him in.

She sat up straighter. Colby was in her heart whether she
wanted to acknowledge the truth or not.

All that's left is to open up so Colby can see your love.

*I want to Lord. I beg You to help me. Even though I've surrendered,
I'm frightened and unsure and need your strength moment by
moment.*

A soft breeze washed over her, and peace flowed into her
soul. She watched Colby and Seth—her family—and joy over-
flowed. She called, "Come on, you two!"

A moment later, they were walking toward her, Seth's little
face awash in happiness. "I won. I won. Daddy said we'd play
until you called, and I'm ahead, so I won."

She looked up at Colby with an arch to her brow. "Really?"

"He won. I had other things on my mind." He snatched the picnic basket. "Let's get back. I need to feed the animals."

She looped her arm in his as she always did. "And I want to make a nice meal for the two of us tonight."

Rather than answer, he handed her the basket and swung Seth up onto his broad shoulders. Seth's chatter covered the silence between them as they walked back.

Colby was understandably confused and angry. Katherine didn't blame him. The way she had encouraged his advances in one moment and leapt away in the next was crazy. Yet she could barely understand the onslaught of feelings herself. Like a Chinook wind, what had been cold and dormant below the surface had melted from winter to spring in a matter of minutes.

What a difference trusting God and surrender made to the soul. Why had it taken so long to realize that she loved everything about Colby? His smile, his warmth, the way he loved Seth, the way he loved her? Why did the possibility of being with him, which had scared her for so long, now feel as natural as a rain shower in April?

He was in for the surprise of his life, and it took everything she had not to laugh as he glowered at her before heading to the barn. "Later." His warning was clear. "Come on, Seth, you need to feed Rufus." He held out his hand to the boy.

"Later." She answered sweetly to his retreating back.

She couldn't contain the skip in her step as she burst into the kitchen. "Delilah, I need your help."

"Land sakes alive, girl. You just about scared me plum off this stool," Delilah said. "What are you fussing about?" Her heavy frame shifted, but her weathered hands never paused in their peeling of a potato.

Katherine hugged her tight.

"Now, don't you be thinking a little hug is going to still my poor old racing heart." A smile tugged at her plump cheeks.

"Could I impose at this late hour to have as many of Colby's favorites for supper that you can rustle up? And I'll help with whatever."

Delilah harrumphed. "That won't be hard, I'm fixing Colby's favorite potato and chicken pie. Abe's gonna love it, too."

"I'd like the two of us to eat alone tonight."

Katherine picked up a knife to help peel, but Delilah shifted on her chair to stare Katherine down.

"Well, I do declare. 'Tis about time, girl. You've been slow... real slow. I was thinking you done never gonna see the light."

Katherine's cheeks burnt hot.

"If you want a special supper for Colby, then you're surely going to get one." Lumbering across the kitchen, she yelled down the hall. "Delores, Ruby. Need some extra hands in here."

~

The distant clatter of dishes and the chatter of the women, filtered down the hall and into the library. A medley of tantalizing aromas filled his nostrils and made Colby's stomach grumble in anticipation. But if Katherine thought a good meal of his favorite food was a way to soften the blow for playing with his emotions, she could think again. His insides jumped with nervous tension. He could do or say nothing while Seth was underfoot, but she would have some real explaining to do come evening.

He looked at the grandfather clock, willing the minutes to speed up. He had promised God he would never again make the first move. She would have to. After all this time, he had shut down and shut off the possibility of that ever happening. She had been more than content with their relationship, part business, part friendship, and zero romance, and he loved her too much to risk the good thing they had.

He would never love another, so it was inconceivable to be anywhere but right where he was. At least he got to be a father to Seth, whom he loved with all his heart, and a friend to her. It was enough. At least it had been, until today, until she'd started looking at him the way a woman looks at a man. Then, her touch on his skin and the way she'd practically swooned in his presence, everything about those lips begging for a kiss.

He leaned back in his chair. His eyes closed. Against his will, the image of her beautiful lips coming toward him filled his mind. He popped his eyes open, rose from the chair in an angry burst of energy, and shook his head. His hands raked through his hair.

Why had she opened the door to that dust-ridden room, disturbed the peace, and then jumped away like a scared rabbit? At the very least he deserved an explanation, and with her being well past the point of frailty, he aimed to get it. His heart stuttered at the mere thought of more than friendship, but he had gone there too many times before and suffered such brutal disappointment. No, he would not allow his heart to get battered again and would tell her in no uncertain terms that she was not to flirt with him again unless she was prepared to get serious about a ring on her finger.

~

*A*ll of his determination to stay aloof crumbled at her enchanting presence and engaging conversation. She'd taken care to sweep her hair up from the sides into a becoming knot but leave a thick glossy section hanging free and glorious down her back. Her gown was one he had not seen before, and the blue silk accented her eyes and her trim figure to distraction.

For certain she was trying to make up for her mistake. She had arranged his favorite meal, dessert, and after-dinner port. Not one pleasant detail was overlooked. She was overtly friendly, catering to his every whim. It hurt to have her try so hard to make up for what she clearly regretted. He wanted to put her out of her misery, but not until he reminded her to keep her distance or he would not be responsible for the consequences.

Seated upon the settee, he stretched his long legs in front of him and closed his eyes for a moment. He wasn't sure how to broach the subject, yet it had to be done. Startled by her presence as she eased down beside him, he pretended not to pay her any mind. But she was far too close to ignore. Where was the careful distance she always kept? He drew in the faint smell of summer roses and willed his mind to go elsewhere. All he longed to do was take her in his arms and never let go.

At the touch of her hand on his arm, he pulled away. "What happened today cannot happen again—"

"Colby, I'm sorry."

How he longed to hear anything but the words *I'm sorry.* "I'm not looking for an apology. I need you to understand." He leapt up and paced the room.

Such disappointment flooded his being that he worked to stifle a groan. Her apology had cut him off before he could finish his thought. *Unless you want more in the relationship.* If only she understood how he had finally got his sorry heart not to kick madly every time she came into view and accepted that friendship is all there would be. Why did she stir everything up only to second guess her lack of good judgement earlier? He couldn't take it. He had to get out of there.

"Thanks for the nice meal." He turned and headed for the door.

"Colby."

He stopped at the sound of her strangled whisper but didn't turn around.

"Before you go, I have to ask…"

The soft pads of her feet moved toward him, and the tug of her hand on his arm was more than he could resist. He turned to look down into her beautiful eyes filled with a sheen of tears.

"Are you happy?" she asked.

The sound of their breathing filled the room as the silence thickened. He wanted to assure her that all was as it should be, but he couldn't find the words. He lifted both hands and slowly cupped her face within the warmth. He forced a slight smile. "Don't worry about me. I'm fine." He lightly kissed her forehead and turned abruptly. He had to get away. Far away.

～

Katherine rubbed her eyes and slid out of bed. She slipped to the window and flung open the curtains. A faint blush of dawn draped the valley in a mysterious glow, not a cloud in view. She smiled. A new day. A new hope.

She turned with a bounce in her step. She had a plan. If she could remember how to flirt, she would put it into action. Surely if Colby wanted to be with someone else, he would've been long gone by now. A surge of confidence filled her being.

A white note that had been slipped under the door caught her eye, and she stooped to retrieve it. Maybe Colby was putting into words what they both had found so hard to say the night before.

Dear Katherine,

I'm leaving for a bit. I stopped in and kissed Seth good-bye. He was somewhat coherent, enough to hug me anyway. Sorry this

*is on such short notice, but I've been meaning to do this for
some time now. I have some business in Richmond I must
attend to. Not sure how long I'll be gone. The weather is great
this time of year, and the timing is perfect.*

*Don't worry about the ranch. Between your dad and Hank, I'm
confident all will run smoothly. Very quickly you'll realize how
little you need me around.*

*Don't forget to give Seth a hug from me every day. Love
that kid.*

Your friend,

Colby.

A mad sorrow gripped her heart. She sank onto the edge of
the bed.

Finally, her grief and numbness were gone, but had she
waited too long? She should've anticipated the change all this
waiting could make in a relationship. She could hardly fault
God. She'd wasted a perfect opportunity to love and be loved,
and she only had herself to blame.

His letter was succinct and to the point, with a semblance of
friendliness, but had she made him so uncomfortable the day
before that he couldn't face her with an honest good-bye?

She got it. Her waffling deserved the response she was
getting. Had she just kissed him plain and simple without
worrying that it was in front of Seth, he would've known her
heart. But instead, her insecurities had gotten the best of her.
The way she had jumped away would have felt like rejection.
Especially considering he hadn't exactly turned down her invitation. Or, if she'd found the courage to openly declare her love
after supper and let him see into her heart instead of asking him

if he was happy, everything would be different. Her way of doing things had left her in limbo, loving him without the freedom to show it—like it had been for him for much too long. The coward in her deserved every bit of loneliness she now felt.

She'd give him some space and pray he would return quickly. She wouldn't let him go without a fight. That much she knew.

CHAPTER 32

*A*melia worked long hours through the first few weeks while Melinda Preston slept between bouts of coughing, acute fever, and delirium. She battled to keep Mrs. Preston's fever under control spending hours cooling her limbs, alternating between sponge baths and cool compresses on her brow. When awake, the opium administered to keep the pain down made Mrs. Preston anything but lucid. At Doctor Meade's instruction she administered blistering agents to her chest to draw the pneumonia out of the lungs. Mercury was given to clear the bowels and Antimony to induce vomiting. Every way of cleaning out the body was administered in hopes of ridding the body of the disease, yet death was ever so close.

Amelia lifted the frail woman as another coughing bout racked her slim frame. "Try to breathe between the coughing Mrs. Preston," Amelia reminded her. Her short ragged breaths and serrated pulse concerned Amelia deeply. They were in grave danger of losing her.

Mrs. Preston groaned and pulled at her side. Amelia recognized the common symptom of piercing pain that stabbed into the side of her pneumonia patients. "I know it hurts, but you're a fighter," she whispered into Mrs. Preston's ear. "Your family needs you." The best she could do was make Mrs. Preston comfortable. She filled the hypodermic needle and administered another dose of morphine.

With every act of kindness, a softening happened within Amelia's heart. She remembered the feisty lady with a sharp tongue, but oh how different this Mrs. Preston was. Weak. Worn. Wavering between life and death.

How angry and hurt Amelia had been at being so easily cast aside. Mrs. Preston had not even tried to get to know her. But now, all this time later the Holy Spirit was nudging at some unfinished business. Amelia had never forgiven the lady. She had successfully stuffed the pain of rejection, and the lost love of Bryon, but she had never faced it, nor dealt with the bitter memories long since buried in the past.

As she smoothed a cool cloth over a sweaty brow the pain surfaced, and large tears leaked from her lower lids drawing scribbled lines down her cheek.

Dear God, Help me. I need your power. Nothing about forgiveness feels natural. I want to forgive, but if I'm honest, after all this time I still feel the ache of loss and the sting of rejection.

Memories of a sunset and a curly haired man with shocking blue eyes came to mind. His smile cut both dimples in place. Strong arms enveloped her as she rested her head against his thumping heart.

A sob slipped from her lips as she looked down at the woman who had been instrumental in taking that love away from her. Why did she have to remember Bryon? Why couldn't she just forgive, but leave him buried back there?

To forgive you must acknowledge the loss, the pain, the sorrow, and give it all to me.

But God, I'm a nurse now. I have a fulfilling life. I've accepted what is.

But you have not forgiven?

No. I have not forgiven. I hate everything about the prejudices cast upon those of us not born into privilege.

To be free, you must forgive Mrs. Preston and the likes of those who erroneously join her.

Amelia lifted her head into the heavens. *Thy will be done, Lord. I want to be free of this nagging, niggling, unrest that keeps welling up.*

She looked down at Mrs. Preston, and for the first time since she had been thrust into the role of looking after her, she felt nothing but peace. She smiled and lifted the tepid cloth from Mrs. Preston's scorching brow. It was time to give her another sponge bath and cool that body down.

~

It was the end of May, and Mrs. Preston had missed the splendor of spring with weeks in bed, first at home and then in the hospital. Dr. Meade had restricted visitors to Alex Preston only. As she entered the room at the beginning of her shift, he rose from the tiny cot.

"Another night on that uncomfortable cot?" she asked.

He nodded. Rumpled and ragged, he slid in a chair beside his wife and picked up her listless hand.

Amelia was grateful she went unrecognized and could concentrate on her job. But then she shouldn't be surprised that Mr. Preston didn't recognize her. They had only met once, and she looked nothing like she had that day. Most likely, all nurses looked alike to him. Dressed in her uniform, with her cap and a severe bun twisted tight at the nape of her neck, she bore little resemblance to the high-fashion pretender who'd come for Christmas tea.

But what would it be like when the others came? Highly unlikely they would not recognize her. A knot of apprehension twisted in her stomach at the thought. And what about Bryon? Had they called him home? She shook her head. She could not go there in her mind and concentrate on her job.

"Can I get you anything, Mr. Preston? Water, tea, a blanket?" He shook his head.

"How about some food?"

"Not too hungry these days."

Amelia tucked Mrs. Preston's covers in and moved around the bed to where Mr. Preston sat. She pulled up a chair adjacent to him.

"Can I talk to you for a minute?" She placed her hand on his arm, and his worried gaze turned her way.

"You have to eat, Mr. Preston, or you could risk getting sick yourself. Pneumonia is no respecter of persons, especially when you're around the germs all day long."

"I suppose that does make sense."

"You've been here almost around the clock. I know that the cot we set up for you is far from comfortable, so I rather doubt you're sleeping much."

"Dr. Meade said no one else can visit, and I don't want to leave her without family."

"There's hope." She tried to infuse the words with enthusiasm. "The coughing has decreased, which lessens the risk of spreading the pneumonia, and her fever has broken. How about I talk to Dr. Meade and see if some other members of the family can spell you?"

His eyes widened. "Would you? That would mean the world to me, and to the others."

"No promises, but I'll try. But you have to eat. Deal?" He nodded.

"And from now on, I'm bringing you a meal each time we serve them."

"Thank you."

He returned his gaze to his wife, and he was once again, lost in grief where only the two of them existed. "Come back to us." His eyes pooled with tears, and his weathered hand stroked hers.

As Amelia looked on, thoughts of Bryon folded in. Would he take after his father and love as deeply? She reined in the thought immediately, angry at where her mind had wandered. These wayward thoughts were becoming more frequent and less controllable with Mr. Preston in the room. Bryon looked so like his father.

She marched out of the room and down the hall, in search of a plate of food. Tears blinked free. She brushed a hand across her cheek, irritated by the surprise emotion. The polished, professional Amelia did not cry. This was indeed a problem.

~

*A*melia entered Mrs. Preston's room after a day off and came face to face with Rose sitting at her mother's bedside. A tremble took to her hands, and she stuffed them in her uniform pockets.

Rose cocked her head. She stood slowly and moved toward her. A frown puckered her brow. "Amelia, is that you?"

Amelia had hoped that no one from the Preston family would recognize her. "It's me."

Rose's dark brows lifted. "You just disappeared off the social scene. Now I know what you've been doing the past couple years. Dr. Meade couldn't say enough good things about you. I had no idea he was talking about the same Amelia." Admiration shone in Rose's eyes. "Bryon was right about you. You are someone special, taking such good care of our mother after what she did—"

"That was a long time ago." Amelia forced a smile.

"Bryon never got—"

"Let's not discuss Bryon. And promise me you won't tell the others who I am. It would only lead to discomfort and awkwardness, and I want to keep things professional."

Rose squinted her dark eyes. "Are you sure? The wonderful way you've taken care of Mother—"

"I want no setbacks in her recovery, and if she remembers down the line, we'll face it then. For now, her healing is my only focus."

"Daddy obviously did not recognize you."

"No, and I want nothing to get in the way of the help your mother needs."

"You're so kind. I think we'd have been great friends, given the chance. But I do have something I've wanted to thank you for." Her voice gentled and hushed. "Please, may I say this one thing, and then I'll say no more regarding Bryon?" Her eyes flitted back and forth between her mother and Amelia.

Amelia nodded.

"I'm sure Bryon broke off his engagement and left town because of his feelings for you."

So, Bryon had been the one to break off the engagement? Amelia's head didn't want to entertain any information, but her heart disobediently kicked up speed.

"Mother changed after Bryon left. She no longer meddled in affairs of the heart. She has even allowed my engagement to the man I love, though he wasn't her choice." She squeezed Amelia's arm warmly.

The door opened, and Mr. Preston walked in.

"Daddy." Rose spun and gave her father a hug.

He turned toward Amelia. "Thank you for talking to Dr. Meade. I finally relaxed enough to go home and get some rest now that the family can help."

"No need to thank me, Mr. Preston. It's my joy to serve."

"Please, call me Alex. After all you've done, I feel like you're next thing to family."

"Daddy's right. We cannot thank you enough."

Mr. Preston sank into the chair next to Melinda and raised her hand to his lips. "Hello, my dear."

She lay still, and he did not wake her, knowing that she would battle coughing fits if he did.

Rose stepped away and waved Amelia close. She whispered, "Daddy's not doing too well. None of us have ever seen her anything but strong. It's so scary."

Amelia had seen her share of strong men break at their loved one's bedside.

Rose moved close to kiss her father on the cheek. "I'll go now. Dr. Meade said there can only be one of us in the room at a time."

After she left, Amelia prayed Mr. Preston would not be angry if he figured out who she was, for she'd grown close to him.

"Amelia, thank you. You've made this horror so much more bearable."

She busied herself with checking Melinda's temperature. "I should be thanking you too. I've so enjoyed our visits."

"So have I." He remained silent for a moment, his eyes blank and distant. "Did you know she didn't only donate money, she started to volunteer at the orphanage?"

Amelia shook her head.

"Melinda loves children. We only had the three, but she always wanted more. It was not to be."

Amelia kept silent. He needed a listening ear.

"That's how she got sick." His voice hitched. "She was there when the flu epidemic hit. First, she got the flu, then it turned into pneumonia." He choked back a sob.

"Mr. Preston, I'm so sorry," Amelia came around the bed and squeezed his shoulder.

"I can't go on without her." His frame shook as sobs racked his body.

Amelia crouched down and took his bony hands into hers. "She's improving. The fever has broken, her cough is less pronounced, her breathing is less raspy. And she's strung a few words together. Besides, Dr. Meade would never let the others visit if things weren't substantially better. There is hope."

His tear-filled eyes lifted and brightened.

"And I pray for her," Amelia offered.

"Why would God do this? I can't make sense of it." A tremor of anger filled his voice.

"Not that I've learned everything there is to know about being a Christian, but I think it's about trusting God even when we don't understand." She wasn't sure where those words came from. They were speaking straight into her own heart.

The lines around his eyes crinkled into a tired smile. "When you're on shift, I feel more peaceful."

Ever since Amelia had said yes to God and forgiven Mrs. Preston it had been a gift to serve the very one who had made her feel less. Miraculously, God had filled her heart with love and each act of service had somehow strengthened her. The last few weeks had been difficult but good in letting the past go. Forgiveness had not happened all in one moment, but she could now allow the memories and they didn't hold the power of pain and anger like they had before. Something wonderful had happened within her soul and she knew where that source of peace that Mr. Preston felt came from.

CHAPTER 33

*T*he carriage wheels crunched on the gravel up to the old rambling mansion. Bryon slipped out and paid the driver who had jumped down to unload his trunk. He was surprised how much he had missed his childhood home, the rich Virginia soil, the bustle of Richmond, his family, and, as always, her. He pushed the thought of Amelia aside and swung the door open. One bellow from the entry hall, and Howard and Rose rushed to greet him.

"How is Mother?" Bryon avoided all pleasantries and cut to the point.

"She's finally improving." Rose assured him. "Things are looking positive."

He let himself breathe as she reported what had happened in the last few weeks. He had made it in time.

"Glad to see you arrived safe and sound." Howard slapped him on the back. "Didn't think I would miss you so much, but wow, life was a lot easier when you were carrying the load." His laughter bellowed out.

Their long-time butler stood in the wings. "May I see to your trunk, Mister Bryon?

"Yes, thank you, Robert."

"So glad you're not going to miss my wedding," Rose said. "It's scheduled for this fall. Without your influence, I would've never been given permission to marry Davis."

"He's as poor as a church mouse," Howard said. "And certainly not able to help our financial situation. Looks like it'll be left up to me to marry for money."

Rose rolled her eyes. "Like that will be a hardship."

He laughed. "You're right about that. I have my eye on one right now that may set me up for life, and she doesn't look half bad either."

"You're incorrigible—"

"Please forgive me." Bryon kissed his sister and patted his brother's back. "I'll catch up with you two later, but I'm going to head to the hospital as soon as I change out of these travelling clothes."

An odd expression flitted across Rose's face. "I should probably tell you something before you visit Mother." She looped her hand in his arm as Bryon headed down the hall.

"Hey where are you going?" Howard yelled. "Whatever you're going to tell him, I want to know."

Rose spoke over her shoulder. "This is something I've promised to hold in strict confidence."

"Then why does he get to know," Howard asked.

"This concerns him, not you."

"I can see you're glad to have your favorite brother home."

She ignored the remark as they climbed the steps to his bedroom.

He glanced around the room and discovered that not a stitch had been changed. The room smelled fresh.

"It's like I never left."

"Mother's instructions were that this room would be cleaned weekly, linens replaced, and a fire set in the hearth in case you ever decided to come home."

Bryon gulped back a knot in his throat. "What do you need to tell me?"

"Amelia is mother's private nurse."

Bryon's hands turned clammy, and his heart raced. *Really, God? I'm not home two minutes and I have to face meeting up with the girl I've never stopped loving?*

"She's an amazing nurse. Practically nursed mother back from impending death."

What was God saying? Bryon had prayed all the way home that he wouldn't see her unless... God had a plan for their life.

"So, Amelia's not married with a passel of kids?" he clarified.

Rose's knowing smile should've irritated him, but he didn't care what she thought. Only how she answered. "Not married at all. She's the head doctor's assistant and a very respected nurse."

"How did father and mother receive her?"

"Daddy doesn't recognize her, and mother is still too sick and too heavily sedated to have made any connection."

"Wow." Bryon ran a hand through his curly mop. "I didn't expect this."

"You still love her, don't you? That's why you've never married or come home?"

Bryon hated his sister's perceptiveness. He could say yes to all three questions, but he wasn't ready to share that truth with himself let alone anyone else. "I'd better get changed."

"All right." She patted his arm. "I'll leave you to prepare to see Mother."

And Amelia, though Rose was kind enough not to say it.

~

*B*ryon was escorted to Dr. Meade's office where introductions were made. He stood extending his hand for a hearty handshake. "Follow me." He waved Bryon on. "I'll personally take you to your mother's room. Your family was so relieved to hear you received the telegram and were on your way home. And you should've seen your mother's face when your father told her that he had sent for you. I swear from that day forward, she has steadily improved."

"How is she, really? Rose said she thinks she's improving, but..."

"We almost lost her." Dr. Meade shook his head and patted Bryon on the back as he stopped outside her room. "But the Lord was gracious. You'll be the best medicine yet...though that nurse there is hard to beat." He pointed through the glass window. "She's worked tirelessly, beyond the call of duty. She's one in a million, that one." He gestured to the door. "Go on in. I'll leave you some privacy." He turned on his heels. The echo of his sturdy work shoes on the polished floors faded.

Bryon stared through the glass. First, at his mother who he had never seen in bed in the middle of the day, especially looking so weak and fragile, and his father sitting close, holding her hand. He was thankful God had given him more time with both his parents.

Then his eyes gravitated to *her*. Rose had warned him, but nothing prepared him for the sight of Amelia bending over his mother. He hesitated to soak in the moment. His heart bucked wildly as he wrestled to rein in his emotions. He'd longed to forget her. In fact, he'd spent the better part of the last two years drowning himself in work and volunteering for that very reason.

One look proved the futility of that discipline. He didn't deserve her, but Amelia lived in his head, his heart, and those haunting memories.

He gripped the doorknob. How would she feel? Would their meeting be as shocking to her as it was to him? He would give her time to process his return by concentrating on his mother. He entered the room. "Father, I'm here."

"Bryon, you made it." Father shot from his chair and enveloped Bryon in a fierce hug. "So glad to see you, son."

Bryon looked over his father's shoulder at his mother, shocked to see her once-regal stature reduced to a bony shell. "How is she?"

"Thankfully, she's finally coming along." His father patted him on the back, and they moved closer.

Amelia bent over and whispered something to his mother. Then, she straightened. Her wide hazel eyes locked with Bryon's for one brief second, and he nodded. She looked away and left the room.

"Bryon, my dear son." A weak voice whispered his name.

"Yes, Mother, it's me. I'm here." He bent down and folded her thin frame gingerly in his arms, with a kiss to her sunken, hollowed cheeks. Her cold hands lifted to his cheeks.

"I'm so sorry. After I came down ill, I was so afraid that I'd never get to see you again and tell you how sorry I am in person." Tears filled her eyes. She blinked, and they rolled down her waxen cheeks.

"All is forgiven, Mother." He smoothed a lock of silvered hair from her brow. She had gone considerably grayer. "I'm sorry too. I never should've left without talking things through." Bryon hugged her again. "Please forgive me."

"And you, me." Her hands flopped back weakly onto the sheets.

$\sim$

*A*melia stood shaking in the hallway. With one hand over her mouth and her body leaning against the wall for support, she muffled her cry.

She had done everything right—stifled all feelings for Bryon, poured her energy into her education, and worked hard. She'd left the social scene and thwarted every man's attempt at courting her, giving her life to nursing. She'd honored God by attending church. She'd built a protective shell that fiercely protected her heart from bad decisions. And everything had been going well, until a moment ago. What was God doing in allowing their lives to collide?

One look into Bryon's expressive blue eyes, and her head no longer felt in charge. Crazy butterflies she had not experienced for years did somersaults in her stomach. The mere power of being in the same room brought a tingle to her hands and a tug on the very heart she had thought successfully shut down.

Rose had warned her that they'd sent for him, and she'd mentally prepared, believing she was over him. She opened her balled fists and glanced down at her trembling hands. Obviously, her head hadn't told her heart. She would never be good enough for the Preston family, and she was never going back to needing a man—any man. That ship had sailed when Bryon left for England. And he could just go back there, hopefully sooner than later.

She lifted her chin. She could do this. She was a trained professional. But she wouldn't arrive back in the room empty handed. Some fresh water and another pillow would make it look as if she hadn't fled like a scared rabbit. Even if she knew the truth, Bryon didn't have to. She dallied in the supply room, taking her time. *Dear God, have mercy on me. I've obeyed your every command.*

Did you?

That one question stalled her hand, and she stood in the storage room. Hadn't she? Why did she think the Spirit was trying to tell her something?

Seek first the kingdom of God.

But she had.

Have you?

In the stillness of the storage room, a truth busted in. She'd poured her life into nursing with the purpose of taking care of herself, making sure she didn't have to rely on anyone. *Even God.*

She picked up a clean pillow, grabbed a bottle of cough medicine, and poured a fresh glass of water. She would have to dissect her thoughts at a more opportune time.

Amelia peeked through the window on the door and let out the breath she had been holding. Bryon was gone.

"She's fallen back to sleep," Mr. Preston said when she entered. "All the excitement of seeing our son has her tuckered out, but you should've seen the smiles. Why did you leave? I wanted you to meet my son."

"Thought I'd give you a little time alone." Amelia's stomach twisted in a knot. She bit down on her lip, forcing herself to remain calm. "There'll be plenty of time for that."

"Bryon recognized you. He said he knew you from the past."

"Oh, that." Amelia waved her hand in the air. "I used to frequent some of the social events with my grandparents before I decided to give my life to nursing." Amelia snugged both trembling hands into the folds of her uniform. Why would Bryon say anything? What was he thinking? Surely Rose had told him that his parents didn't recognize her.

"It made me realize how you've let this old man ramble on, rarely saying anything about yourself. I know so little... but Bryon will be right back, and he asked that I don't let you run off again. He wants to thank you in person for all you've done."

Heat worked its way from her neck to her hairline. She straightened her back and lifted her shoulders and went about her work as if nothing were out of the ordinary. She prayed for calm, dreading his return. *Dear God, could You have made this anymore impossible?*

Bryon's tall frame filled the doorway, and he stopped short. He held a plate of food in one hand and a cup in the other. His Adam's apple bobbed as he stared at her.

She couldn't tear her eyes from his face. Her hands dropped

to her sides and twisted in the folds of her uniform apron. A weighted silence hung between them as their gazes locked.

Mr. Preston cleared his throat with a hearty cough. "Bryon, are you going to bring that food in or just stand there?"

Amelia snapped into action. She scurried to Melinda's bedside in a show of responsibility.

Bryon finally moved from the doorway into the room. "I wanted to thank you—"

"Since you two already know each other," Mr. Preston said, "why don't you take Amelia for lunch as a proper thank-you from the family? I always spell her during her break, and your mother's sleeping anyway."

Bryon met Amelia's eyes. "I'd love to take you for lunch, if you'd like." Uncertainty wavered in his voice.

She might as well get this over with. No better way than having the opportunity for a frank discussion. She turned to Alex with a smile. "Who turns down a free lunch? Not me. But I'll have Helen peek in on you while I'm gone."

"I can call someone if need be."

Amelia headed toward the door, and Bryon followed. Safely in the hall and out of earshot, she said, "I'll have lunch with you, Bryon, as long as there's no fiancée or little wife in England I need to know about."

"I know I deserve that, Amelia, but I assure you there's been no one, not since Shelby and I parted ways."

That declaration did strange things to her resolve. "Well then, let's catch up and get rid of this awkwardness between us. I want to be able to look after your mother without complications." What an understatement. He was far more than a complication.

CHAPTER 34

*A*melia settled into her chair at the outside café table. She'd insisted they go to a very public place. Never again would she make the mistake of sneaking off to a quaint little hide-away with Bryon or any other man.

"I'm so proud of you, Amelia. Rose tells me you are one of the finest nurses in the city." He moved his arm across the table and opened his hand.

"Hard work and dedication pay off." She ignored his invitation, keeping her hands tightly folded together on her lap.

"By the sound of it, it's more than both those things. You're gifted."

"Bryon, can we cut through the pleasantries and get to the heart of the matter. The only reason I agreed to this lunch is to make an awkward situation liveable. I don't need your compliments..."

He removed his hand from the table, but looked across into her eyes with such intensity she stopped talking and had to look away.

"I know I've said sorry before, Amelia, but something has happened inside my soul that makes me truly sorry. Not sorry for the pain I caused myself, but more for the pain I caused you. I should have been completely honest with you, and I'm truly sorry. Will you forgive me?"

She couldn't believe the gentleness in his voice, as if he meant every word from somewhere deep inside. But then he had always been good at sounding sincere, hadn't he? Funny how his apology made her realize there was a part of her that had held onto that pain, that hurt, that transgression and let it affect how she shaped her future and felt about men.

She glanced at him long enough to catch the glint of tears in his eyes and then looked quickly away. The city around her held her focus and helped her remain aloof.

"Can I tell you how I met God, really met him, on my way to England, and how that's changed me?" When she didn't answer, he launched into the story about his friend Harry, the church he attended in England, and his ministry to the broken living in the slums of London.

She couldn't believe her ears, for if she did, she'd be drawn to this changed man and his life. But no, she was not going down that road again. "Sounds like you've made a life for yourself there." She purposely kept her profile turned toward the street.

"I told my boss and friends I wouldn't be back. I've felt God's leading to come home, make peace with my family, and live true to my new convictions, and maybe we—"

Her head snapped back to look at him. "There is no *we*, Bryon, I've long since gone on with my life. I love nursing and won't be giving that up for any man." Was his faith genuine or was he using Jesus as a convenient way to lure her in? "What do you really want from me?" Her voice sounded sharp even to her own ears.

"Your forgiveness, though I don't profess to deserve it, and if at all possible, your friendship—" He leaned forward, daring her to hold his gaze.

"It's far too late for friendship. Friends need to trust each other, and I do not trust you." She lifted her chin.

"I expected as much. But if you'll give me a chance, I'd like to prove that I'm a transformed man. And I'll be completely honest up front. I want to earn your trust, for I've never stopped loving you."

She threw down her napkin. "To what end? Nothing has changed. In the hospital, I'm a respected nurse, but in your world—Richmond society—I'm still the lowly working class, uncultured and unworthy of the Preston bloodline. It's cruel of you..." She choked down a sob, stood quickly, and took off down the street.

His feet pounded behind her. "Amelia, please."

She spun around. "I came between your mother and you once, and I'll never do that again. Your parents haven't recognized me yet. But when they do, you'll find that little has changed. Many people of your standing accept and appreciate me when they're sick, only to turn the other way when I meet them on the street once they're well." She fought back the tears that pooled in her eyes and turned her head.

He placed a hand on her arm, and she wrenched free. "Please don't make me fall in love with you again. I just can't bear it."

"But, Amelia," he reached out, and she stepped back. His hands fell. "I don't care about those things. I'm a different man. Money and status have never meant much, but now they mean even less."

"What about your family? They need you. I noticed the way your mother looked when you came in the room, and I will not stand between you." She straightened her uniform and pushed her shoulders back. "Now, I must get back to work."

She turned and hurried down the street toward the hospital. The feelings of inferiority and insecurity she had worked so hard to bury welled up. All the accolades she'd achieved came back hollow, empty. She blinked back a rush of stinging tears.

My precious child, why do you still believe that lie? All are precious in My sight.

She balled her fists and marched on. Those still small words from the Spirit cut deep. Convicted her. She slowed her pace and wiped the tears from her eyes. *Well then, why don't You tell the privileged and pampered this message, not me.* She threw the words into the heavens. *Then maybe, I'll believe them too.*

The truth will set you free.

She scurried up the steps into the hospital and slammed the door behind her. The upper windows on the floor rattled, and all eyes turned in her direction.

"Sorry," she called out. "The wind..."

Rather than finish the lie, she hurried to Melinda's wing.

~

*B*ryon watched her retreating back. Everything within him wanted to chase her down and beg her to give them a chance, but the Spirit whispered. *In My time, not yours.*

Can't we even be friends, or am I wanting my way and my desires once again?

The fact you care to look inward and ask those tough questions shows growth.

Was it possible to win her trust once again?

With Me, all things are possible.

But she's right, God. Nothing has changed. My mother, my father, the prejudices and the pride of life—

Leave your family to Me and pray.

And Amelia?

Live the life and trust Me.

A calm flooded into his soul. He didn't have to figure out his next step. He only had to trust.

One look at her had sent him reeling. One word in her soft lilting voice had confirmed. One gaze into her wide autumn eyes and he knew. Nothing had changed. He was as madly in love with her as he had been from the first moment she paused in front of his house, and he caught sight of her from his bedroom window. Even more so now. Her maturity, strength of character, and gift of nurturing and caring for the sick only heightened the ache, the longing, the need. She was more woman than he deserved, and so he prayed.

~

Summer 1872
Shenandoah Valley

*K*atherine sat on the portico shelling peas. She stopped for a moment to lift her thick hair and let the soft breeze tickle her neck with coolness. The ache in her shoulders from being hunched over could be stretched out, but the ache in her heart had settled in for good.

Delilah looked up from a bowl of peas and sat back in her rocker. The weathered oak chair squeaked as she rocked.

"Girl, you're moping 'round here like the sun is falling from the sky. Ever since that boy left, your happiness has up and gone too."

Katherine's hands stilled over the basin of peas. She wanted to deny the truth, but those kindly black eyes had not missed a detail.

"I never thought I'd miss him so much, and Seth is driving me crazy asking when he'll return."

Delilah rocked. "Yes'm, 'tis hard missing the ones we love."

Was Katherine so transparent? She'd barely conceded the fact that she loved Colby herself, and Delilah already assumed as much.

"That boy has loved you for years, since long before it was

right to do so. And you love him. What I don't understand is why, after all this time, you two pretend it isn't so?"

Katherine gulped back the lump in her throat. "It's my fault. I left it too long. I've confused the situation—"

"Fiddlesticks. He's been a-loving you from the moment he laid eyes on you." She wagged her finger. "Nothing has changed. I understand why he left the first time, but why now?"

"That's just it, I don't understand his hasty departure. We were down at the river, and while I was watching him with Seth…" She raised her hand to her burning cheeks, not sure she could voice her feelings.

"Don't stop now. This is getting good." Delilah's cheeks jiggled as she laughed.

"It hit me how much I loved him. One thing led to another, and he asked if he could kiss me, but Seth interrupted us. Later, after thinking about things, he said that it couldn't happen again."

"One thing old Delilah knows. He needs you, and you need him. Seth needs the both of you. It's not that hard to figure. Some plain talk between the two of you is what is needed, not this dancing around the mulberry bush."

"I agree." Katherine put her bowl of peas aside and stood, brushing the stray shells from her apron. "The minute he gets back, I'm going to speak the truth."

Delilah clapped her weathered hands together. "Now that's the spirit. When did that letter say he would return back?"

"It didn't really, but I'm assuming soon. How long does it take to do a little business?" Katherine bent forward and planted a kiss on her ebony cheek. "I love you. You're the best friend any girl could have."

"I'll be reminding you of that the next time I need a favor."

Her toothy grin brought a smile to Katherine's face. She straightened with her hands on her hips. "All I can hope is that

Colby gets home soon." She picked up her bowl of peas and moved across the porch. "This waiting is killing me."

"I do say, you deserve a little waiting after all you've done put him through." Delilah wagged her finger.

"Why do you always have to be right?" Katherine said, as she headed into the house.

Delilah's laughter echoed after her.

CHAPTER 35

*W*ith Bryon's experience and letter of recommendation, he was able to pick up clients at the bank and resume working, but life lacked purpose. Just the thought of returning to the social scene, as Howard had encouraged, turned his stomach.

He walked through the doors of the church. *Dear God, I need to find a group of young people active in their faith like I had back in England. I need something meaningful to do with the time I'm not working.*

He almost slid into the pew a few back from where he knew Amelia would sit but decided against it. He best keep his mind focused on God. He slid into a pew near the front. She may see him if she showed up today, but he would not see her. For the past few weeks, she'd worked on Sundays, and he had worked all week, and their paths had not crossed at church or at the hospital. Part of him hoped it would be the same today, but the other part, like a sorry traitor, quickened at the thought of a single glance.

God heard the cry of his heart. It was no coincidence the founder of the local orphanage spoke that morning.

"The streets are full of lost and hungry children far too young to be on their own. The need is great. The opportunities to serve are endless. You can come and serve meals, help clean, play with the young people, rock babies to sleep, cook in the kitchen, befriend kids on the street, and bring them to safety. Don't let it be said there's nothing for you to do."

A warm sense of the Spirit quickened in Bryon's heart.

"Jesus said, 'feed my sheep,'" the man continued, "and we have many little lambs to tend. Will you answer the call? If you've been blessed financially, then give of your money, but don't let that be enough. It's your time these children need the most. If you're interested, join me up at the front, and I'll answer your questions."

Bryon stood without hesitation. This was just what he needed.

~

*A*melia slid into the pew in her usual spot and lifted her head. Was that the back of Bryon's head? She couldn't miss his curly hair and wide shoulders. It was bad enough she ran into him at the hospital, though it had not been as often lately. Bands of tension tightened across her chest.

Dear God, help me. I have to get over him. The silent plea lifted to the rafters but seemed to bounce right back down.

Interesting place for Bryon to sit, considering he knew exactly where she'd be. He couldn't see her unless he tried. For that she was thankful. But couldn't he attend one of the other churches?

The passionate plea for help with the orphaned children got her mind off of him and had her on her feet before she knew they were moving toward the front. Maybe she could offer some free medical help. She wasn't alone. People of all ages were gathered at the front. It was too late to turn and run when she registered that Bryon was in the group.

He caught her gaze and smiled. She refused to give an answering smile, but her heart raced. It made her angry how it instantly kicked up speed.

~

*V*isit after visit, Amelia was subjected to the same agony. Could life get any crueler?

"Bryon, my dear, how I love your visits," Mrs. Preston said as he walked into the room. She pointed to the chair nearest to her bed.

"Does my heart good to see you improving, Mother." He kissed her cheeks before sitting and glancing in Amelia's direction.

She looked down at the chart she was filling out on Mrs. Preston's progress. Her pen stalled as she could not think straight.

"Good morning, Amelia."

She responded without lifting her head. "Good morning."

With Melinda's steady improvement, she would be going home within the month. For Amelia, that meant the pain of seeing Bryon daily would cease. But that wouldn't end seeing him. They now shared work at the orphanage. When she arrived to check the kids' medical needs, he would often be serving up a meal or playing with the boys. From scraped knees to rashes to picking lice out of the hair, Bryon worked alongside her, never crossing the boundary of friendship. But it was his eyes, his smile, the way he said her name like a soft caress, that spoke what words could not.

"Amelia."

Mrs. Preston's voice brought her back to her task of filling out the chart. "Yes, Mrs. Preston?"

"How many times have I asked you to call me Melinda? After all we've been through together, surely the necessity for such formalities can be relaxed, can they not?"

Amelia smiled and made her way to the bed. "Yes." The sick Melinda was not hard to love.

"I've raved about you to anyone who will listen. I shall never be able to repay your kindness. Dr. Meade swears you almost single-handedly saved my life." She took Amelia's hand. "And the effort you continue to put into making me comfortable… you truly are a blessing."

"Thank you, Mrs., er, Melinda."

Mrs. Preston turned to Bryon. "Bryon, darling, you've met Amelia, have you not?"

"Many times."

"But of course. My brain still gets befuddled, and I forget the simplest things. You just said hello to her, didn't you?"

"I did."

"Dr. Meade assures me my memory will improve as I get stronger and off all this mind-numbing medication. Isn't that right?" She turned toward Amelia with hopeful eyes.

"You're improving daily. The fogginess will clear." How it would upset Melinda to remember their first meeting that cold winter's day all those years ago. Amelia prayed it would never happen or, if it did, it would be long after her hospital stay. The dear soul she had come to know and love was the one she wanted to remember.

Melinda turned to Bryon. "No finer woman to be found than this kind nurse."

Bryon looked at Amelia, a slight smile playing on his lips. "That is true, Mother. I don't doubt it for a minute." His eyes spoke a thousand words, and he opened his heart for her to see inside.

A jolt of heat shot through her body. Her face burned hot. Every nerve tingled with awareness. She turned away. Why would he look at her that way? Did he not get it? Things were over between them. She had a wonderful career without the complication of men, and she had every intention of keeping it that way.

"I used to think so differently than I do now." Melinda's voice went soft and quiet. She obviously didn't pick up on the tension in the room. "I used to place value on the wrong things and the wrong people."

Amelia had seen this before with patients. Once Melinda returned to full health and her normal routine, things would revert back to the way they had always been. The vulnerability of illness temporarily broke down barriers, but they would be rebuilt, of that she was sure.

"Would you like to sit up while you visit with your son?"

"That would be lovely. Could you add an extra pillow behind my back?"

While Amelia retrieved a pillow, Bryon said, "Did I tell you that Amelia and I joined the same group at the church that helps out with the local orphanage?"

"Oh, I love the children," Melinda said. "I so miss them."

"You know the children at the orphanage?" Bryon's eyes popped wide. "I knew you gave money, but—"

"I guess you wouldn't know. It was after you left that I started visiting. There's this little girl named Daisy—"

"I know Daisy," Amelia said. "She's such a sweetie. Her hair is almost bigger than her head."

"That's the one. She just stole my heart. Can you be sure and give her a hug from me and tell her I'll be there to read her a story as soon as I can?"

"I'll do that." Amelia lifted the pillow.

Bryon sprang to her aid, and they both gently pulled Melinda into a seated position. He held onto his mother's frail body while Amelia placed the pillow behind her.

Their hands touched, and Amelia pulled back so fast she

almost hit the wall behind her. The pulse in her throat hammered. She worked hard to hide it. She didn't want him to know how much his simple touch cost her.

Sadness filled his eyes. Her adverse reaction hurt him, but what did he expect?

"I'll give you time to visit," she said to Melinda with her most professional voice back in place. "I have others to check on." She patted her arm affectionately and hurried from the room.

The only thing she could think of was getting as far away from Bryon as she could. Why did he have to look at her that way? Why did he have to keep showing up at church, at the hospital, at the orphanage?

Dear God, what are You doing? I told You, I'm done with men, and I love my work. Nursing is my life, and I won't give that up for anyone.

Not even for me?

A chill ran over her skin, giving her goosebumps. Surely, she wasn't walking in disobedience being responsible and taking care of herself. She'd been a fool to give her heart away so frivolously in the past. God should be proud of how much she'd grown.

Yet, you still do not ask Me.

She didn't have time for that right now. She had work to do.

CHAPTER 36

*K*atherine slipped from bed and dressed for another day without Colby. Summer was fading, and there'd only been one letter from Colby saying he was staying in Richmond for a while. Katherine became desperate. She could feel him slipping away. Uneasiness grew inside her, nibbling at the corners of her mind. There were so many things she wanted to say and she had tried to write, but the words would not come. She needed to speak with him face to face.

Like weeds popping up after a spring rain, tormenting questions surfaced. Had he met someone else? Now that the ranch ran smoothly, would he ever return? Did he miss Seth? Did he miss her?

She slammed her bedroom door shut behind her. She was going to lose her mind if she didn't do something, anything, to get him back. Deep in thought, she took the steps at a good clip and rounded the corner into the hall, bumping into Abe.

"Whoa, Nellie. Where you headed so fast?" He rocked on his feet.

"I'm sorry." She reached out to steady him. "I'm so preoccupied these days."

"That's no secret. You've been pert nigh riding them clouds up yonder, with your feet nowhere near the ground. I want to ask you something, but my old bones need a chair."

Katherine followed him into the parlor, where Delilah was already seated. His bent spine hunched over his cane, and the shuffled steps gave credence to the long hours spent slaving over his work for far too many years. He eased into a chair.

Katherine slid into one adjacent to him and waited.

Delilah just smiled but said nothing. That was not like her. What were these two cooking up?

Abe leaned back and lifted soulful eyes in her direction. "I have a little something I'd like you to do."

"Anything."

He fished in his pocket for a piece of paper and held it out. A name and a Richmond address filled the page. "If Colby had told me he was leaving for Richmond, I could've gotten him to do this, but he ran off like a wounded puppy, and now I need your help."

"Do you want me to write a letter for you?"

"Already sent two, and I've heard nothing back. I'm fearing the worst. I need you to go to Richmond and check in on him."

"While you're there, you could go visit Colby too," Delilah piped in.

Heat rushed to Katherine's cheeks. "Are you two suggesting I go to Richmond and find Colby?"

"For a smart girl," Abe said, "you've let this go on way too long."

"You gonna let a good man like that just walk right out of your life?" Delilah added.

"And what about your boy? He needs his father," Abe said.

"All right. All right." Katherine held up her hands. "I get what you're suggesting, I should go find Colby and bring him back."

Both heads bobbed up and down.

"Is there really a friend in Richmond you want me to check on, or is this a ruse to get me headed in that direction?"

"Well now, that depends on how stubborn you gonna be."

Katherine let out a laugh and stood. "Abe, you crafty one, you." She planted a kiss on his weathered brow. "But I do like the sound of your plan." She paced, a finger pressed to her lips. "Yes. I can do that. I'll visit Amelia and take Seth to meet his great-grandparents, and if I can track down Colby..." A smile pulled at her lips.

"You can thank Delilah too. We were cooking up this side dish for a bit now. Can't bear the way you're moping about."

Katherine wagged her finger in Delilah's direction. "That sounds like you." She flounced across the room and kissed her chubby cheek, then threw her arms around Abe, hugging tight.

"Whoa, girl. Don't be crackin' these old bones with all that excitement. Now get. Be ready for that next train out."

～

The jerk of movement and a rumble of wheels rippled through the compartments. Katherine let out a sigh of relief. They were finally in motion and could wave good-bye to the last stop along the way. The train picked up speed, scuttling down the rail toward Richmond on the final leg of the trip. Seth's constant chatter and endless questions had her frazzled mind on edge.

"Mama, how does the train stay on the track? How did they make the track?"

"Seth darling, I don't have all the answers."

"If daddy was here, he would know. I miss him."

A kind set of eyes caught hers as the conductor inched his

way down the aisle. He leaned forward with a smile, his curved mustache and trimmed beard softening his angular face. "How would your boy like to meet the engineer? He's been cooped up on that seat for much too long now."

"Mama, can I please?" Seth's red curls sprang up and down as he bounced in the seat. "Can I? Can I?"

Katherine smiled at the conductor. "You have no idea how much that would mean to him. He's been driving me crazy with questions I can't answer."

"I heard." He winked and held out his hand.

Seth bounded out of the seat, needing no further invitation.

"Be good, Seth. Remember your pleases and thank yous."

"You get some rest, madam." He tipped his cap as he carried on down the aisle with Seth in tow.

Exhausted from travel and the nervous tension caused by every mile the train chugged closer to Colby, she drifted off.

"You have a smart one here."

Startled by the sound of the conductor's voice, her eyes flew open. Seth slid into the seat beside her.

"I'm sure we have a budding engineer in our midst."

Seth beamed.

"Thank you for the reprieve."

"My pleasure, Ma'am. We're almost there." He tipped his hat and wandered up the aisle.

"Mama, I could do it. I could wear that big hat, and..." His hands moved up and down as if he had control of the throttle.

Katherine barely listened as he launched into detail about everything he had learned. She nodded every few minutes, but all she could think about was her reunion with Colby.

Seth grabbed her chin with his tiny hand and pulled her head in his direction. "Don't say yes, Mama."

She laughed and kissed the top of his head, pulling him close. He knew she wasn't listening.

Seth didn't let her hold him long before he squirmed free.

Seated proudly, he was so much like a little man that it brought tears to her eyes.

The acrid smell of soot, coal dust, and stale air was getting to Katherine. She was overjoyed to hear the conductor announce their impending arrival. "We're almost there, darling," she whispered to Seth. "And you're going to meet your great-grandparents and visit with Aunt Amelia very soon." She squeezed his little hand in excitement. A patchwork of thoughts crisscrossed one over the other—meeting her grandparents for the first time, seeing her sister, and finding Colby...always Colby.

She hadn't told Seth about the possibility of seeing him in case things didn't turn out as she hoped. She didn't want to disappoint him. She wished she could dispel the nagging worry, but after a summer of absence, she couldn't be sure what his response would be.

One glance around as she stood on the platform told her Richmond was a city of sophistication and beautiful women. She could hardly keep from staring at the clothes the women were wearing and pressed her hands to smooth the wrinkles from her four-year old traveling dress. With a hand tented over her eyes against the glare of the sun, she scanned the crowd for her sister, praying her telegraph had reached them.

"Katherine, Katherine." Arms waved above the crowd.

The voice was familiar, but Katherine barely recognized the vision in front of her. The tailored suit with matching jacket and skirt hugged Amelia's figure to perfection. Everything from her matching long gloves and hat to her upswept hair proved her sister had become a cultured city woman.

"Amelia. You're stunning."

Katherine was pulled into a tight hug. "Don't be fooled. I'm the same country bumpkin down deep." She bent down and swept Seth into her arms. "You're not too big to give your auntie a hug, are you?" Seth melted into her embrace, his chubby arms circling her neck.

"Come." She waved Katherine on. "Grandmother and Grandfather are so excited to meet you. They can't handle the crowds these days, but they're waiting by the carriage." She pushed through the pressing people with an air of confidence Katherine had never witnessed before.

Tears glistened in Grandmother's eyes, and one trickled down Grandfather's weathered cheek as he bent to talk to Seth. In looking at them both, she could see the family resemblance. She clearly had her grandfather's eyes, and her grandmother's beautiful head of hair. Another piece of the missing puzzle fit into place. A part of her felt like it was coming home.

"I never thought the day would come when I'd meet my great-grandson." He patted Seth's head with one hand and pulled his handkerchief from his back pocket with the other. As he stood, he dabbed at the corner of his eyes, turning to Katherine. He reached out to touch her cheek. "You look so much like Emma—"

Grandmother gasped.

Katherine caught the raised eyebrows and bulging eyes that both Grandmother and Amelia directed Grandfather's way.

Katherine laughed. "No need to hide the fact I look like Emmaline on the outside, as long as you don't make the mistake of thinking we're the same on the inside."

He relaxed, and so did she. Seemed they were trying just as hard as she was to make a good first impression.

"This is a day for celebration indeed," Grandfather said. "We have a grand meal prepared for you, the best room in the house, and lots and lots of fun planned for Seth."

"Why George," said Grandmother, "give the girl a chance to catch her breath before you smother her with affection and all your plans." She patted his shoulder. "We don't want to scare her off, now do we?" Humor bubbled in her voice.

Katherine felt at ease. Everything was going to be all right. They were not at all like her birth mother Emmaline, and neither was she. Seemed they all had fears and insecurities that could be put to rest.

"And what's this about the best room in the house? I thought I had that," Amelia said with a laugh as they loaded into the carriage.

~

*A*melia did a soft knock and poked her head into Katherine's bedroom. She tilted her head in Seth's direction. "Is he asleep?"

Katherine nodded as she rose.

Amelia waved her over.

"Girls. Is that you up there?"

Amelia put a finger to her lips. "Shh."

"Do come down if you're not too tired." Grandmother's shrill voice called up the stairs.

Amelia waved Katherine down the hall into her room. They giggled like schoolgirls in hushed tones and quietly clicked the door closed.

"I'm laying claim to you before Grandmother snags you for another evening." Amelia rolled her eyes and laughed. "I love her, but she has monopolized your every waking moment these past few days. I've been dying to get you alone. Now, out with it, Katie. How are you really doing?"

"I'll tell you my secrets if you tell me yours."

A flicker of alarm scuttled up Amelia's spine. She did not want to be the one talking.

"So, you do have secrets," Katherine said. "I can see it in your eyes."

Amelia nodded. "A few. But you first."

Katherine shared her story of the past few years. From grief, to guilt, to accepting the gift God had given her in Colby.

"Colby will be so shocked to see you standing at his door. He's in for a lovely surprise."

"I sure hope I'm not too late. I've been allowing fear to have the last word for far too long."

"Fear?" Even thinking that word brought it alive. If anyone was afraid, it was her, and she didn't want to talk about it.

Katherine continued. "I've been afraid to love or be loved in case something else bad happens. But I'm done with fear. It's way too lonely a world."

Amelia pulled at a piece of fluff on the patchwork quilt. Lonely was something she understood all too well.

"Your turn." Katherine took Amelia's hands in hers. "It feels good to unload. Talk to me."

Amelia opened her mouth, and the story poured forth. She finished with, "I thought I was over him but..."

"But what?"

"He apologized. Said he met Jesus and is a different man... and he is. There's a depth about him. A kindness I can't refute. A strength of character he never had before. He keeps a respectful distance, yet I catch him looking at me with such...love in his eyes. It scares me." Tears pooled in her eyes, and she blinked them free. They rolled down her cheeks.

"Ha, don't I know what that feels like. Colby did the same." Katherine handed Amelia her handkerchief. "Why are you so afraid?"

"I love being a nurse. I find such pleasure in helping people. I work hard, and quite frankly, I don't let *me* down." She laughed to cover the pain. "I like taking care of myself—"

"Then you don't have to trust anyone, not even God."

"No. That's not what I was saying."

"Yes, it is. If you let yourself fall back in love with the changed Bryon, you would have to trust both him and God. That's what's scaring you. Have you prayed about this?"

Amelia studied her lap. The last thing she wanted was for

her sister to look inside her soul and see the truth. It was much more comfortable *not* to pray.

"Ahh, you're even afraid to pray for fear God will ask you to give up your security blanket. Do you know how I know this?"

"Hmm." Amelia didn't look up.

"I did the exact same thing. To love again takes trust. Trust in God to help us through whatever life brings, be it the good or the difficult."

Amelia stood and stalked across the room before spinning to face her sister. "What would be the point? Nothing's changed with his parents or that hoity toity high-society life."

"The point would be if you love him. Do you?"

"I don't want to."

"That's not what I asked."

"All I know is that I'm being wise and not rushing into anything."

"Are you brave enough to pray for God's wisdom with an open heart?" Katherine arched her brows when Amelia didn't answer.

"I'll be honest. If God told me to give Bryon a second chance that would mean giving up my nursing—"

"It could also mean to love and be loved."

Why did that sound so wonderful too? No, she couldn't... wouldn't open herself up for more heartache. Amelia lifted her fingers to her temples. "I'm so confused. I thought you said talking would help?"

"Just promise me you'll pray. I think you'll be surprised what you find out when you're not telling God what to do."

Amelia smacked her arm. "You're the bossy one in the family, not me." Humor always worked to take conversation in a different direction, and Katherine was hitting way too close to the truth to continue.

Katherine laughed. "Seems you picked up a few of my bad habits then." She slid from the bed and threw her arms around

Amelia. "If talking doesn't help, then food is a close second. Do you think we could sneak down to the kitchen at this late hour? What time do you think it is?"

"It's got to be past midnight, but like always you seem to read my mind." She looped her arm into Katherine's. "I happen to know where to find a large piece of apple cobbler and some fresh cream. How does that sound."

"Absolutely divine."

~

*W*hat was Amelia doing standing right beside him. Bryon could barely breathe. She had gone out of her way to stay as far away from him as possible, but today she had offered to help him serve the soup. A nervous chatter took over. "Had a craving for a fresh apple yesterday, so I headed to the market on my lunch," he said. "That craving turned out to be a divine appointment."

"How so?" She looked at him. Really looked at him, not just a sideways glance and away, but one that held his gaze.

"There was this street kid trying to steal an apple, and the market owner had him by the scruff of the neck screaming for the police. I don't know what came over me, but I begged the stand owner to let him go and offered to pay for anything he stole plus buy the kid a bag of apples. I told the owner how much farther ahead he would be, seeing that I had only planned on buying one apple. He let the kid go, and of course he ran."

"So, you didn't get to meet him then?" She stacked the bowls in preparation for the meal.

"Patience, my friend. The best part of the story is yet to come."

She flashed him a genuine smile, and he almost forgot the rest of the story.

"I paid the vendor what he thought would be fair for

the stolen goods and bought the bag of apples I had promised. I was walking out of the market when the kid appeared out of nowhere, clearly hungry enough to risk being fingered as a thief. He had the gumption to ask for the bag of apples. I gave them to him, but not before telling him about the free suppers we do each night here. I sure hope he comes."

"What's the success rate?" she asked.

Even the sound of her voice did him in. "Sometimes, the kids come, but most times they don't. They're afraid of being held against their will."

"How old do you think he was?"

These were more words than she had spoken to him in a month. *Dear God, have mercy. Give me wisdom.* "Maybe ten. It's hard to tell when they're so underweight and small for their age."

They began serving the soup. Amelia passed him the bowl, he filled and handed it to her. She placed the soup and a bun on a plate and handed one to each child who took it and made their way over to a long run of tables. Soon the room was full of little people with grubby fingers and skinny bodies.

Bryon watched as she smiled at each child and said a kind word. Their fingers touched over and over, and not once did she yank back as she had at the hospital. There was a rhythm, a camaraderie, a peace.

"There he is," he whispered in her ear. "Four down the line." His smile split free.

She looked at the child and looked at him with the oddest expression on her face.

"What?"

"This actually makes you happy."

"Of course. Even a small victory is a victory indeed."

She continued to stare at him. He didn't mind, but the lineup halted. "What?"

"Nothing." She handed him an empty bowl. Man, he wanted to know what *nothing* meant.

The child hadn't given his name the day before, and Bryon hoped to gain enough trust to get at least that.

"Told you we give out a free supper every evening."

"What's the catch?" The kid's gaze darted around the room as if he were sure someone was about to clamp chains on him.

"There isn't one. Ask any of these kids."

Amelia held out the bowl and gave him the biggest bun in the basket. "Trade you the meal for your first name," she said. Somehow, she'd read Bryon's mind. She smiled that wonderful smile that could move a mountain, her voice so tender and soft.

"I'm Sam, ma'am."

"And you're a poet and didn't know it."

The kid laughed and took the food. He looked at Bryon. "Thanks again for the apples yesterday. Filled my stomach, but sure have a gut ache today."

Amelia said, "And I just happen to be a nurse, and I know what to do about that. Come see me after you eat your soup. But eat it as slowly as you can and keep the bun for tomorrow morning. All right?"

Sam nodded. "Sure will, ma'am."

When he walked away, Amelia said, "So polite. Doesn't that just tug at the old heart strings?"

"That's why I love this so much. I don't care that I don't get home until late and often eat a cold meal. It's worth it."

"By the way you know each kid by name and how they respond to you, I can see it's rewarding to you."

"It is."

"Is this work similar to what you did in London?"

He was thrilled she was conversing with him. He could barely contain the erratic beat of his sorry heart. "I worked more with teens and adults. Quite different in the approach, but the need is the same."

"I can imagine."

They worked side by side until the food was served and the dishes cleared. There was another crew in the kitchen to wash the dishes.

When she was finished, she walked toward him. "Have a good evening, Bryon."

He couldn't believe his ears. She'd made the effort to personally say good-bye. What was happening? It took all he had not to grin like a fool. "Same to you, Amelia."

She turned to go.

"Can I ask you one thing?"

She turned back with raised eyebrows. "Well, now, that all depends on the question."

"I was just wondering what the *nothing* was earlier. When I—"

"Oh, that." She waved her hand. "I was just thinking about how handsome... I mean happy you looked." She turned that lovely shade of red that she always did when truth spilled out unfiltered. "Something so small and beautiful like seeing a child you helped on the street show up for the soup line brought you such joy. It was heartwarming." With that she turned and walked away.

The blood in his veins ripped and rumbled like a swift running creek. What had just happened? Had God finally answered his incessant prayers and opened the door of her heart a tiny crack?

~

"Seth," Katherine called across the courtyard. "Mama's going out for a bit. You be a good boy playing with Bethany. You hear?"

"Yes, Mama." He looked up from the mud pies they were

making in the dirt and waved a grubby hand. She dared not get close enough for a kiss or she would be covered.

"Lydia, you're sure it's not too much that Seth joins you for the afternoon?"

"Not at all. These two are having so much fun together. And you don't have to worry. I'll have him all bathed and clean by the time you return."

"Thanks so much." Katherine waved good-bye, but Seth was too busy to notice.

Grandmother's carriage driver sat waiting and ready on the street. She slipped into the carriage, and they were off. The view around her blurred as she took the time to pray. She had one purpose only. Today was the day she would talk to Colby. *Please God, help me. You know how scared I am. And you know me. I'd rather not know if the answer is not favorable. That's why I've procrastinated as long as I have. Please give me courage.*

Amelia had been her accomplice, her helpmate, her spy. She had scouted out the return address on the one letter she had received from Colby and found that it was a boarding house. Upon inquiry, Amelia confirmed that Colby Braddock indeed resided there.

Now, all was set. The time was at hand. It would have been easier to write a letter and beg Colby to come home, but each time she had tried to put words to page, she felt a check in her spirit, as if she was to make more effort and really show Colby she cared. If he was not in today, she would leave the letter she penned. At least he would know she cared enough about him to follow him to Richmond.

It was a fine September morning. The sun shone bright. Birds darted and dipped. A slight breeze rustled the leaves in the trees overhead. With the recent cooling in temperature, autumn-gold edges warned of change to come. Her heart echoed the same. She lifted her soul in praise. God had this, no matter which way the colors turned.

CHAPTER 37

Katherine stepped from the carriage and informed the driver to head back, as she planned to hire a hack for the way home, optimistic that Colby would be with her. She stood on the sidewalk until the clip-clop of the horse's hooves could no longer be heard. The two-story boarding house with clapboard siding, lacy curtains in the windows, and a large front porch invited her closer. The house exuded welcome, but her feet stayed put. A sign hung over the porch entrance, slightly swinging in the breeze. Bordered in charming painted flowers, it read "Welcome to Anna's Place."

She inhaled deeply and tried to still the tremble that shook her hands. *I have to do this. I will never be able to live with myself if I don't follow through.*

Come on, you can do this, just put one step in front of the other.

She straightened her shoulders, lifted her head, and marched to the entrance. Before giving heed to any more fear, she rapped on the door loudly.

The door opened to a graceful young woman. "How can I help you?"

"May I speak to the proprietor?" Katherine's voice wavered,

and she cleared her throat. Everything within her wanted to run.

"You're speaking to her." Her voice carried a lilt that sounded like the music of wind chimes. She held out her hand in welcome. "I'm Anna Harris."

This was not what Katherine expected. She had envisioned the proprietor to be a kindly gray-haired soul, not a vision of youth and loveliness. She sure hoped there was a Mr. Harris around.

"You look surprised."

"I...I was expecting someone a bit older."

She waved her hand and laughed. "Everyone makes that mistake. But you'll have to trust me when I say, I run the best boarding house in the city. I rarely have availability, as is the case right now. But my kitchen is always open for a cup of tea. Do come join me."

Katherine followed her into the kitchen where everything was both feminine and orderly.

"My husband was killed in the war, and I had to do something to make a living. This is it." Her hands opened to the room. "The house was far too lonely and rambling for me to live in by myself. I guess God knew exactly how to take care of me, despite the loss." She pulled a lacy handkerchief from her pocket and dabbed at the corner of her eye.

Katherine's heart dropped into her shoes. This lovely, lonely widow was a Christian too. She was everything Colby needed in one beautiful package.

"I'm sorry I can't offer you a room, but I do make a wonderful cup of tea and I have some fresh cinnamon buns hot from the oven."

Katherine hadn't eaten for all the nerves dancing in her tummy, and the smell of cinnamon was surely tempting, but she had interest in only one thing—finding Colby. She stood in the doorway of the kitchen without moving.

"I apologize. I didn't make myself clear. I'm not here for a room. I'm actually looking for one of your tenants, a Mr. Colby Braddock." Katherine's hands broke out in a sweat at the mention of his name.

Anna's hand stilled over the kettle of water she was filling. She turned toward Katherine. Her eyes narrowed ever so slightly, and a flicker of disappointment flashed across her face.

"He's not in at the moment." The kettle rattled as she placed it on the wood stove. "I could pass along a message." The welcome in her voice disappeared and she went from friendly to business-like. "Whom may I say stopped by?"

"My name is Katherine Richardson."

Anna's face whitened, and her expression hardened. Her gaze went up and down Katherine. "So, you're the woman Colby has mentioned." Her words had a pinched clip to the tone of her voice.

Why was she using Colby's first name so intimately? Had they become friends, or possibly more? Her heart raced in a random fit of stops and starts.

Anna moved forward swiftly. With a firm hand under Katherine's elbow, Anna propelled her to the front door, which she yanked open with a gust of energy. "I'll be sure and tell him you called." She nudged Katherine through the frame. A moment later, the door shut firmly behind her.

Katherine stood on the front porch in a stupor. What had just happened? She hadn't even left the letter she'd written the night before in the chance Colby wouldn't be home.

She knocked on the door. She had come too far to depart without making every effort. When Anna didn't return, Katherine knocked more firmly.

The solid wooden door swung open. Anna stood there, her lips pinched tight.

"Colby is a paying guest, correct?"

"Yes."

"Then I'd like to leave him a letter." She pulled the envelope from her reticule. "If you could direct me to his room, I will not bother you any longer. I would like to slip this under his door, then I'll be on my way."

Anna held out her hand. "I'll be sure he gets it." Her cheeks went from white to red.

"Will you?" Katherine raised her eyebrows.

"Don't you think you've done enough damage?" Anna spit out her words. "It's time to let him go and quit playing with his emotions."

"I see." Katherine folded the envelope in her hand. Colby had confided in this beautiful widow. A stab of jealousy and determination hit her. "This is for the two of us to discuss, and none of your business."

"No, you don't see." Anna's hands flew into the air. "When Colby arrived, he was the saddest man I'd ever met. Over these past few months, he's changed...for the better, I might add. He smiles. He laughs. He's living again. It's because he's finally free of you."

Katherine gasped. Anna's words rubbed like salt in a wound.

"If you care about him at all, Katherine, you'll leave and never come back. He...we ...have a chance for happiness. From what he's told me, one visit from you would steal the peace he has worked so hard to obtain. I beg of you, let him be happy."

The letter trembled in Katherine's hand as she dropped her arm to her side. She had never been more confused in her life. Obviously, Colby still had feelings for her when he left, or was his sadness due to leaving Seth? Questions whirled in her head while the gorgeous Anna waited.

Oh Lord, help me.

Slip the letter under his door and wait on Me.

"More than anything I want him to be happy," Katherine said. "But what happens next will be his decision. I insist on slipping this letter under his door myself. And if you have a master key, which I'm sure you do, don't even think about destroying it, because if I haven't heard from him in a few days, I'll be back, and back again, until I talk to him face to face."

Anna opened the door wider. "Fine then. Up the stairs, second door on the right."

"Thank you." Katherine lifted her head and crossed the room. She climbed the steps and delivered her mail. Without saying a word, she swept back down and out the door.

Now, all she had to do was wait on the Lord, but oh the agony.

∽

*C*olby climbed the steps of the boarding house porch in the cool of the evening. He entered with a heaviness in his heart. He had walked for miles, wrestling with God, before finally accepting His words obediently. God was right. It was time to get back to the Valley, to his son. How he missed that little boy. His absence was not fair to Seth. He could be a father, and a father he would be.

But Katherine...? Bands of tension squeezed at every thought of her. The same wrestle with God had ensued for a couple of months now—God telling him to return, and him needing time to shore up his broken heart and find the strength to accept that he would never be her husband.

"Colby, my friend." Anna came around the corner, her dark eyes swimming with friendliness. "I'm kidnapping you for an evening out, and I won't take no for an answer."

She spun in front of him. "Do you like it?"

She'd made quite an effort to ready herself. Donned in a gown of muted pink, the tight bodice and sharp cut in accented her tiny waist. She radiated elegance and invitation, and his heart sank.

Not again.

"I haven't been out for an evening of fine dining since my dear Will passed on, and you are the perfect gentleman to impose upon." She smiled wide. "You're far too kind to say no to a woman who has spent the best part of the day preparing, now aren't you?"

A lone candle cast wavering shadows across the room as he entered further into her dimly lit parlor.

She grabbed his hand and pulled him close.

He pulled away instantly. "Anna, I'm sorry if I've given you the wrong impression. I enjoy your companionship, your friendship, but I cannot give you more. I thought you understood what I feel for Katherine." Nerves pulsated in his jaw. "Nothing has changed." His voice broke as he raked his hands through his hair.

Torment clouded her dark brown eyes, and she stepped away. "Colby, it is I who must apologize." She turned and paced away before spinning to face him again. "Katherine came by today, and I thought maybe, just maybe, I could make you forget her."

Her words took a moment to register. "Katherine. Here?"

"She slipped a letter under your bedroom door."

He turned and climbed the steps to his bedroom two at a time. There it was. Her handwriting. He wasn't dreaming. She really was in Richmond. He flopped on his bed and tore open the envelope.

Dearest Colby,

I had sincerely hoped to catch you in. However, I must leave this letter in my stead. Words are ever so inadequate when trying to express matters of the heart. Nevertheless, I will endeavor to bare my soul as if you were standing before me.

Colby, you've been sorely missed by all. Abe and Delilah send their love, as well as Ma and Pa and the many ranch hands. Everyone is continually asking about you. Seth is absolutely driving me crazy, wondering when his daddy will return, and his mother is wondering the same. I have missed you more than words can say. I will be completely truthful. That way, if you don't feel the same as I do, you can choose to move on with your life.

Colby, I love you. I've been a fool to leave you hanging so long without acknowledging my feelings. I beg your forgiveness for allowing my fear to keep us apart. I know God has wanted to heal my broken heart and have me trust Him with both you and Seth, but I've been paralyzed with fear, choosing to believe all the terrible images my mind can conjure. Slow. Stubborn. Selfish. Call it what you will, I took so much for granted without opening my heart in the way you needed—in the way I now need. I'm dreadfully sorry.

I wanted to tell you how I felt that evening before you left, but it seemed you were most uncomfortable in my presence. After a night of soul searching, I realized the truth may get uncomfortable, but you were worth the risk. However, I awoke to find you gone.

After all these months of missing you, I am far past the worry of propriety. I have followed you to Richmond in hopes of begging for your love. I would follow you to the ends of the earth, if need be.

Colby, I love you more than words can say, and Seth loves and needs you, too. You are his daddy in the truest sense of the word. He asks about you incessantly and misses you as desperately as I do.

If you think you can open your heart to me, then come to me. I am staying with my grandparents here in Richmond.

Please come to me, my dearest Colby. I promise I will make up for the lost time.

All my Love,

Katherine

My grandparents live at...

Colby wanted to rush to the address handwritten so delicately on the bottom of floral embossed writing paper, and yet it was far too late to make a respectable appearance. Had Katherine really followed him all the way to Richmond to tell him that she loved him? As a whiff of lilacs wafted up as he folded the letter, a jolt of joy clamped down on his heart. It was going to be a long night.

He slid to his knees in gratitude, scarcely able to believe God had finally granted him the desires of his sorry heart. How could it be that, on the day Colby surrendered his will to the Lord and decided to return to the ranch, Katherine would come looking for him. If only he had surrendered earlier, for God had known she was waiting for him. He would not forget this lesson anytime soon. When he slipped into bed, he couldn't contain his excitement, and he most definitely couldn't sleep, so he prayed the night away through fits and starts of sleep. He was up and dressed as the fingers of dawn threw its first traces of light across an inky sky.

*T*he hired hack could not move quickly enough. Colby wished he had one of his fine stallions to get there. The letter scrunched in his hands at the tension screaming through. He couldn't wait to fold Katherine in his arms and give her the kiss he had been longing to give her for way too long now.

The hack lurched to a stop, and he was out. His heart beat a frenzied pace as he took the steps with an added bounce. His bang on the door rattled the windows. An older lady answered with Seth at her side.

"Daddy!" Seth hurled himself into Colby's legs. He bent down and swept him into his arms.

"I've missed you so much, little man." A sting of tears filled his eyes as he pulled back to look at the boy clinging so tightly to him. Suddenly he was home. On a stranger's doorstep, in a strange city, with a little boy's arms around his neck he was more at home than he had been in months.

"Where have you been, Daddy? I've missed you so much. I'm really good at skippin' stones now. I'll whoop you for sure and for good."

A stab of guilt pierced Colby's heart. He should've listened to the nudging of the Spirit sooner.

Seth's tiny arms curled around Colby's neck and hugged tight. "You're coming home with Mama and me, aren't you?" A quiver filled his tiny voice.

"I sure am, Son. I sure am."

The old woman beamed at him from below a crown of gray hair. She started to speak but was interrupted by someone deeper in the house.

"Grandmother. Seth. Who's at the door?"

Colby heard Katherine's singsong voice before she rounded the corner.

She stopped short. He held up the crumpled letter, and she

squealed in delight. Before he could speak, she launched herself at him. The three of them were hugging and kissing and laughing in delight. Somewhere the tears started flowing, he wasn't too sure which ones were his and which were hers. They were mingled together with quick kisses and Seth's giggle.

"Mama and Daddy are kissing. Look, Great-Grandma, Mama and Daddy are kissing."

"Seth, darling, how about we give Mama and Daddy a bit of time alone and you come with me to the kitchen for some sweet sticks." The older woman held out her hand to Seth as Colby put him down.

"Sweet sticks. I love sweet sticks." He bounced up and down.

"Thank you." Katherine and Colby said simultaneously, and then laughed.

"We'll make introductions after you two love-birds get reacquainted." She took Seth by the hand.

Colby put his arm around Katherine as they watched him chatter down the hall. "Great-Grandma did you know that I have two Daddies? Mama says I'm the luckiest boy alive."

"Let's find some privacy." Katherine pulled him closer, an arm around his waist.

A jolt of awareness coursed through his body. They had better marry soon.

As the library door closed behind them, she turned in his arms to face him. "Colby, I'm so sorry—"

His lips crushed down on hers, silencing all need for words. What started out slow and sweet quickly turned delicious and dangerous. Her touch was like a brush fire in August—all consuming. A sigh shuddered from the soles of his feet, and he was lost. He dug his fingers into her hair and kissed her as he had imagined a thousand times. Her hair, her cheeks, her neck, and then back to her beautiful mouth. With her warm pliant lips moving so hungrily over his, that ripple of pleasure steaming up his spine erupted into an inferno. She pressed closer and his senses ran sharp. Her touch, the sweet aroma of lilac-washed hair, the taste of her lips—a potion concocted to squeeze his heart right out of his chest.

It took every bit of Colby's strength to pull from her warm embrace and step aside.

"Colby?" She touched his arm, and he moved out of reach.

"Give me a moment." He waited for his breathing to slow and the heat racing through his veins to simmer and cool.

"I hope a quick wedding suits you," he said, "because I've waited too long, doing everything right, to spoil it now."

She nodded. "We not only need to get married quickly, but a chaperone would be a great idea as well."

His laughter mingled with hers.

CHAPTER 38

*A*melia could barely sleep these days. She tossed around in bed for the third night in a row. Ever since Katherine and Colby announced their engagement, somehow her nursing, as much as she loved it, did not look as wonderful as the love they shared. Watching them together brought back old dreams and old wounds.

She had done as Katherine suggested and asked God what He wanted for her life rather than tell Him what she wanted. He led her to the soup kitchen to work alongside Bryon every free day she had. Not to be surly and distant, but as a friend. From that vantage point, she was able to see firsthand the man Bryon had become through the eyes of the children who loved and trusted him.

At church she watched as he intermingled with every class of people. There was no distinction. Sometimes he sat with his old friends from the upper class, the ones who frequented church occasionally. Other times he had a couple kids from the orphanage with him or was sitting in what was considered the poor section, where maids and hired help sat. Always he was chatting up a storm with someone.

And then, with his mother, his father, and his siblings in the hospital, there was always a tenderness, a kindness, a respect. Even when Howard rolled his eyes and mocked what he called Bryon's "do-gooder work," Bryon never retaliated. He just smiled with a knowing smile and said. "I'm right where I'm supposed to be, doing exactly what I'm supposed to be doing." There was such a confidence about him.

Amelia did not have that confidence. She still resented the social classes, and abhorred the fake world of the upper echelons.

Ask yourself why?

She could hear the whisper of the Spirit.

Because they make me feel less than.

Your self-worth is not based on the family you were born into, what you look like, or what you portray. You will not have confidence until you understand this.

But God, I left that world behind.

No, you traded one lie for another. Your confidence and self-worth cannot be tied to your hard work as a nurse or how smart you are either. It should be based on how I see you. And I love you just the way you are. You have nothing to prove. Bryon has figured this out.

Did this mean Bryon would stand up for himself? Every day his mother grew stronger. Would he fight for his freedom?

As much as Amelia did not want to admit what was happening within her heart, there was an awakening of attraction she had thought she'd successfully buried. Bryon would touch her arm in passing, and her whole body would tingle. He would flash those dimples, and she couldn't help but smile back. He would chatter about all the happenings on the street, at the orphanage, at his work as if she were his very best friend, and she couldn't help but enjoy it. Truth was, she wanted to be his best friend and a whole lot more. She was falling madly, crazily, hopelessly in love with the new Bryon. She had clearly been attracted to him before, but this was deeper, scarier. Still, they had tried to meld their two worlds once before, and it had been disastrous.

Why, God, would you bring him back into my life? I did just fine—

Were you fine? Self-sufficient is not fine. It's pride.

Amelia sat up in bed. She felt for a match and fumbled with the candlestick holder. She pulled the wick straight and the flame took hold, allowing golden light to fight back the darkness.

Why would God say that? Was she truly filled with pride? Weren't working hard and taking care of herself honorable traits?

But do you trust? Anything short of trust is fear or pride, and both are bondage.

Like lighting a candle that peered into her soul, she could finally see. She had experienced her fair share of fear and pride. First, she had placed her trust in men and marriage, which led her to trusting her appearance—looking just right, saying the right thing, living the façade Richmond society expected. Then, her trust had shifted to her skills, her brains, her nursing, and the ability to take care of herself. God had been conveniently placed on the sidelines through every decision—unless she needed Him. *Oh God, I'm sorry. I was so blind. Please forgive me. I don't know what You have planned for me, but I know I want to hear Your voice and listen.*

Then choose to trust Me.

Could she trust and let nursing go? Could she trust God enough to love again? One thing she knew for sure. There was no going forward without trust, and she was tired of forging ahead on her own.

She blew out the candle. Snuggled back beneath the blankets, drowsiness covered her in warmth. She drifted off in a state of peace never experienced before.

❧

*E*ver since Amelia had decided to trust God, she found herself drawn to that old bench beside the sugar maple tree overlooking the James River. The summer she and Bryon had met there every day to share kisses had been her best and her worst. She had basked in the joy of being loved, and then it had gone so awry. Now, she could go back, relive the thrill of young love, grieve the sadness, but also sift through the rubble. God had needed to change them both. They had both been selfish in their quest for each other. They both had withheld information from the ones they loved. For the first time ever, Amelia could see that she had been no better than Bryon.

The soft breeze of September whipped a few tendrils of hair free from her neat bun. She removed the pins and shook her hair so it fell unrestricted down her back. She would have to redo it when she returned to work, but for the moment it felt good to rub the pin grooves from her scalp.

"I always did love your hair down."

Startled at the voice she instantly recognized, she twisted around. "Bryon." Her hand flew to her heart. "Goodness, what are you doing here." She stood slowly.

"I guess I could ask you the same."

"How did you know I would be here?"

"I didn't, but I've come here almost every day on my lunch since I've been back and prayed for you, for me. For us."

Why did he have to say the most wonderful things?

"I remember how you used to unwind that coil at the nape of your neck and shake it free." He moved closer, and she was spellbound. His hand slowly lifted to the side of her face, and he brushed a tendril back. He lifted a lock of hair in his hand and let it sift through his fingers.

Her feet were glued to the spot. She turned toward the warmth of his hand that gently cupped her cheek.

He stepped closer. The other hand came up and cupped the other side.

Why wasn't she running? She should be objecting. She should...

He leaned so close that his breath fanned her cheek. "Do you have any idea how much I've longed to go back and redo that summer?"

She held her breath.

"First of all, I would've been honest from the get-go." He smoothed his thumbs in a circular motion just under her chin. His eyes seemed to drink her in. "Then, when you told me we could not see each other, which you would have, I would've begged that we meet as friends, in public places, at your grandparents or wherever, and use the time to deepen our friendship." One hand lifted, and his knuckles gently slid down her cheek before cupping her face again.

His touch was intoxicating. She wanted to speak, but a knot clogged her throat.

"Then when Shelby returned, I would've made it clear to her that I'd meant what I said when we first started attending functions together, that I did not want to marry her. And I would've taken on my parents and demanded my right as a man to choose the bride I love." One thumb moved up and gently grazed her lower lip.

She sucked in a breath. What was happening? Every cell in her body was responding to his touch, to his words, to his slow torture.

"Then, and only then, would I have met you underneath this sugar maple tree, knowing full well I had every right to not only court you but to marry you...like I do at the moment."

What was he saying? Had he talked to his parents?

"Then I would ask you Amelia, if I could kiss you with the deepest love in my heart. A love that is willing to extend self-sacrifice, protection, and utmost loyalty. A love that will forge streams, climb mountains, fight back the dragons of social injustice. A love that will never fail because it has the power and strength of God as its driving force." His hands stilled, and his gaze bore into hers. "May I kiss you, Amelia, with that kind of love?"

She couldn't hold back the tears. "Yes."

He leaned close and kissed the tears that dropped on her cheeks.

She closed her eyes, and her arms instinctively found their way around his neck. Like a gift from the past, the years melted away, and she breathed in the wonder of holding him close once again.

His lips descended upon hers. The kiss, a mere whisper on her lips, waited for her response. A tender agony played as they both soaked in a long, savoring kiss. The tender agony blazed into flame. His arms crushed her close, and she was lost in his embrace, matching kiss for kiss.

He dragged his lips free. "Sit with me a moment. I have much to explain." He held out his hand, and she placed hers in it. They sat on the bench, shoulders touching.

"I talked to my mother and father a few days ago. I told them that the nurse Amelia they so love is the same Amelia they once kicked out of their home. Mother started to cry. She wants to talk to you herself, so I'll say no more. But I asked her to wait until I had a chance to talk to you. I thought it would be later this week when we help at the orphanage, but here you are..."

The deep rumble of his voice filled an ache, a longing so deep it could not be denied. "Your parents know?"

"Yes, I also told them that I've never stopped loving you and intended to wait for you for the rest of my days if that was what it took to prove my love."

Her heart skittered at his admission.

"Then I made a promise to God, I would respect whatever

time you needed and wouldn't initiate anything unless you did first, or I found you under the sugar maple."

Love swept through her being and clamped down on her heart. Now, what was she going to do with it? His gentle hand, his woodsy scent, and his warm arm against hers as they sat side by side brought back tender memories, ones she had worked very hard to bury.

"The best moments of my life were spent right here. You, me, and the James River. Can I show you something?"

At her nod, he pulled her up and swiveled her around. "Look up."

Amelia gazed at a heart carved into the tree. *BP Loves AW for always and forever.*

She gasped. The carving was clearly weathered. "But we never carved anything into this tree."

"I did, before I left for England, in hopes you would visit someday and notice it. Since you weren't talking to me, it was my only hope of sending you a message from my heart."

"It's been here the whole time?"

"Yes."

"Bryon, I don't know what to say."

He placed a finger on her lips. "I don't need you to say anything. You can take all the time in the world to pray, to process, to talk to your grandparents and my parents, to consider your nursing career, because I know how much that means to you. Whatever you need. Let's just sit for a few minutes and enjoy the view before we have to go back to work." He placed his arm around her shoulder, and they slid back down to the bench.

She felt the danger, the pull, like being swept down the James River during the spring melt. Emotions moved in currents beneath the surface. Attraction the undertow. Desire the whirlpool. She didn't want to feel so out of control, but there was no denying the power.

~

*A*melia stood outside Melinda's room with her hand on the door. After what Bryon had told her over lunch under the sugar maple tree, she wasn't sure how to remain professional.

Dear God, help me. An instant peace came over her, and she sighed in relief. She may not know, but God did. Didn't matter if her prayers were long or short, God seemed closer than He had been in years. Ever since she stopped telling Him what to do and decided to trust Him, He showed up. She swung the door open with confidence. The old Amelia was gone. Never again did she have to pay homage to insecurities or uncomfortable social demands. She could just be herself.

Amelia walked into the room. Melinda's eyes followed hers. There was a sadness Amelia had not noticed before. "I met Bryon at lunch...he told me he talked to you—"

"Amelia." Melinda held out her hand. "There are no words. I'm... I'm so sorry." Tears blinked free of her lashes.

Amelia took the outstretched hand. "No need to find any more words. Your apology has said it all."

"But, Amelia, let me assure you, the old Melinda is gone. After I lost my son because of my haughtiness, I got down on my knees and begged God to change me from the inside out. My first real big test came when Rose wanted to court a penniless man. But God helped me open my eyes to what a wonderful person he is and how well suited he is for my Rose. I gave my blessing with peace in my heart, as I now want to give you and Bryon as a couple."

"I'm not sure what will happen. My life is nursing and I love it...we come from different worlds." Her words sounded like the old her, the untrusting woman she no longer wanted to be.

"Don't you feel anything for him anymore? Have I destroyed everything? I thought I noticed a spark—"

"There's always been a spark. That has never been the problem, but a lot of other things have."

"Like me."

"Yes, Melinda, like you." Amelia could not sugar-coat the truth. "I forgive you, but to think of courting Bryon, knowing I'm way below your dreams and aspirations—"

"But I no longer feel that way. I know I don't deserve your trust, but can you believe me when I say I've grown to love you like a daughter?"

Was Amelia hearing correctly? Were all the walls she had so carefully erected collapsing before her eyes?

"What about my grandparents? I love them, and my life will always include them. They're getting older, and I intend to care for them in the future. With you two feuding, how do you think that will work come Christmas, or sharing grandchildren, or a host of other occasions?"

"Another area in which I was wrong. My judgements were harsh concerning your grandparents. It wasn't until Bryon left, Rose wanted to marry someone outside our social status, and all Howard wanted to do was have a good time that I understood. Knocked down a few pegs, my pride got a beating, and I realized I'd lose all my children if I didn't learn how to love unconditionally."

"So, you'd be cordial if you found yourself in the same room as my grandparents."

"If they could find it in their hearts to forgive me." Melinda said the words without hesitation, and Amelia knew she spoke the truth.

"And I've been thinking about your nursing," Melinda said. "You don't have to give it up entirely. I serve on the board at the orphanage, and we've been saying for a long time that we need a nurse on staff. It's just one of those things we haven't gotten to. I know a few women personally, myself included, who would be more than happy to make sure the funds are there for that worthy cause, and who better than the most gifted nurse in the city?"

Amelia couldn't contain the beating of her heart thrashing on the walls of her chest. Every excuse she had made was crumbling into dust.

Do you trust me enough to love again?

There in that hospital room, with Melinda looking on, those same words from the Holy Spirit came back to her again. Was trusting Bryon more about trusting that God would always be with her, no matter what?

"I...I need some fresh air." She ran from the room, straight into Dr. Meade.

"Amelia, are you all right."

"Honestly, no." She rubbed her temples. "Could I be spelled off for the afternoon. My head is splitting and—"

"Say no more. Go. I'll make sure your shift is covered."

Amelia grabbed her cloak and headed home. Laid flat across her bed, she wrestled with every excuse she had for not giving Bryon a second chance. She prayed, asking God for His wisdom. The afternoon sun inched across her bedroom floor and the shadows lengthened.

At peace, she rose from her bed and headed to Bryon's home. A maid opened the door, and she handed her a note. "Please be sure Bryon gets this as soon as he gets in."

"He's upstairs changing. Would you like to come in and wait?" She opened the door wider.

"No, thank you. Just please deliver this promptly."

"Yes, ma'am."

With a quick turn and the sweep of her dress, Amelia was off, up the hill past her grandparents' house and beyond. She didn't stop until she came out of the copse of trees to the outcropping where she found the same rock she had once shared with Bryon. She sat and waited.

The September air held an evening crisp with only a

sprinkle of fall color touching the edges of a few trees below. The sun dipped lower, and the horizon glowed with hues of red, pink, and violet burnished against the deepening blue-gray sky.

"Amelia."

She turned to the sound of Bryon's voice and stood on shaky legs as he moved closer. "I love you, Bryon Curtis Preston the Third."

He crushed her close and kissed her lips. Her body tingled with awareness as her arms circled the muscled column of his neck. Her fingers errantly played in the soft curls at the nape of his neck as their bodies melted together. He groaned and, with tearing slowness, his mouth left hers. "I love you more, Amelia Florence Williams."

He slid down on one knee. Behind him, the sun, in a blaze of glory, winked good-night on the western horizon. There could be no more beautiful setting in the world to hear the words she had long thought she would never hear."

"Will you marry me?"

"Yes," she whispered. "Most definitely, yes."

CHAPTER 39

"Katherine, what are you doing in Grandmother's kitchen?" Amelia asked. "You're supposed to be having a break from household chores."

"I can't sit around, so I found out what Grandfather's favorite pie is, and I'm making it for our last night here. We head home tomorrow."

"Tomorrow. Really? I was hoping to propose an idea. But we'll need a few days to work out the details."

"An idea that takes days to work out? Now I'm intrigued. Pull up a chair and talk while I finish this pie crust."

"Before I sit down..." Amelia held out her hand, where a large sparkling diamond had taken up residence.

Katherine squealed and dropped the rolling pin. Though her hands were covered with flour, she threw a hug around Amelia's shoulders. "Congratulations." She held up her hand next to Amelia's so the diamonds sparkled side by side. They looked at each other and giggled like they were ten again.

"Bryon and I want to get married straight away," Amelia said.

"Us, too." Katherine admitted. "Ma is going to have a crow

when she realizes that not one wedding is in the immediate future, but two."

Amelia snagged a tiny piece of dough.

"Scat." Katherine smacked her hand. "What's this idea of yours?"

"Where do I begin?" She pressed a finger against her lip as she slid into a kitchen chair. "Bryon and I have been talking. His mother is almost ready to come home from the hospital but still isn't well enough to attend a social function. I'd like to get married back home and invite the town of Lacey Spring. After all, my lifetime friends are there, and some of my few new friends from here would love an excuse to travel."

"So far, I'm not seeing a problem." Katherine brushed a lock of hair from her cheek, leaving a trail of flour.

"I don't want to conflict with your wedding plans, and we both want to get married as soon as possible. Before winter hits, right?"

"That's why we're heading home. I want to get on with the plans. We want to be married before the nasty weather hits. By the end of October at the latest."

"Me too." Amelia lifted her eyebrows. "Now, do you see what the problem is?"

"Not if we have a double wedding."

Amelia jumped from her chair and clapped her hands. She threw her arm around Katherine's shoulder. "My plan exactly. I knew I could count on you to think the same way I do. Most of the time, we're in each other's heads anyway. Do you think Colby will mind?"

"Colby already told me he doesn't care about the cost, the number of guests, the 'hoopla,' as he calls it. All he cares about is the timing—the sooner the better."

"Bryon talked to his family about getting married in the valley, and all of them want to attend, excluding Melinda for obvious reasons. But she's given her blessing and is excited to be left in charge of planning a wedding reception in Richmond for all their friends. She's already working on the details and says it gives her such joy to have something to do from her hospital bed." Amelia still couldn't believe this new Melinda. She really was a changed woman.

"Which brings me to my next question," Amelia continued. "Do you think you can open up some of those empty wings of that grand home of yours for our guests from Richmond? And of course, we'll need your ballroom for the event. And I was thinking—"

"Whoa." Katherine held up her hand, her laugh bubbling free. "I'm going to have to take notes, and my hands are deep into pie dough at the moment."

"That's why you and Colby can't leave tomorrow. We need a couple more days to formulate plans, and I'll write a letter for you to give to Ma and Pa. How I wish I could be there to see their faces when they find out we're both getting married."

"Why can't you? If we're going to pull this off in a few weeks, I'll need your help."

An excellent point. Amelia paced the kitchen floor. "To be honest, I hate the thought of leaving Bryon behind so soon after finding him again."

A bubble of laughter slipped free. "I get that," Katherine said. "If you asked me to leave Colby behind right now, I'd scratch your eyes out."

Amelia chuckled. "You do get it."

"I have the perfect idea to surprise Ma." She pointed her rolling pin into the air. "Sit and listen. I'll stay a couple more days, and we'll make all the plans with Grandmother's help. She'll love to be a part of this."

∼

OCTOBER 1872
SHENANDOAH VALLEY

*A*melia's eyes swept the parlor of the farmhouse home. Thankfulness for the gift of a loving family after seeing the plight of the orphaned children almost overwhelmed her.

Colby held Seth on his lap on one side of the room, and Pa lounged in his favorite chair on the other side. He winked when she caught his eye.

Fifteen-year-old Lucinda, with her sassy grin, was perched on the arm of Pa's chair, as pretty as a spring bouquet.

Jeanette, now a nineteen-year-old lady, stood against the far wall, quiet, and introspective, as was her way. She peered around the room through her horn-rimmed glasses with a half-smile.

Eleven-year-old Gracie bounced on her heels with one hand over her mouth to hold back a laugh. She could barely contain her excitement.

Amelia's heart nearly burst with joy. What a rare occasion to have all her sisters present in one room with a surprise that everyone was in on—except Ma. Katherine's idea had gone off without a hitch.

Amelia stifled a giggle as Ma shuffled in with a tea towel tied around her face, hiding her eyes.

"Land sakes alive, Katherine, I'm too old for such nonsense. Not to mention I have a pile of cookin' to do for your wedding, girl."

"A wonderful surprise is never nonsense, Ma." Katherine steered her to the center of the room and stopped.

"Well then. Get on with it. These eyes don't much like being shut down and not in control."

Gracie let out a snicker.

"All right, Ma." Katherine untied the tea towel. "Open your eyes."

Ma's eyes blinked open, and then blinked again. "Amelia!" She rushed forward and threw her arms around her in a bear hug. "They told me you couldn't make the wedding, that you had to work. I was most disappointed."

Everyone laughed.

"Fiddlesticks and flumadiddle, you've surprised the socks right off me." She stepped back. "Let me look at you. I plum cannot believe my eyes."

"And that's not all," Amelia teased.

"I'm not shutting my eyes again."

"For this you'll need your eyes wide open." She held her left hand with her engagement ring in front of Ma's nose.

"Mercy sake, girl. Is that what I think it is?"

The room exploded in laughter and cheers as Bryon came around the corner from the room off the parlor. Amelia held out her arm and gathered him close.

"Ma, meet Bryon Preston, the love of my life."

Ma gasped, and her eyes filled with tears.

Bryon held out his hand, but Ma grabbed him close. "Any man that loves my daughter, is loved by me." She pulled away blinking back tears.

Both the sisters looked at each other and nodded. Katherine put her arm around Amelia and waved the men close. Colby, with Seth bouncing in excitement, moved into the grouping.

Amelia nodded, and they spoke simultaneously, "We're having a double wedding."

"And we've brought some surprise guests from Richmond," Amelia added.

"Surprise, more surprises," Ma said. "I do declare, you're going to make my heart stop dead." She held a hand over her chest.

Amelia waved in Grandmother and Grandfather from

around the corner. They entered the room with question in their eyes.

"We hope we're not overstepping, Doris," Grandmother said, "but we so wanted to be part of the excitement and see where you live."

Tears poured down Ma's face.

"I do hope those are happy tears," Amelia said.

Ma raced across the room and engulfed her parents in a hug.

Amelia stepped back and leaned against Bryon as pandemonium broke out, everyone crowding in for hugs and welcome.

"I love your family already," Bryon whispered into her ear.

"And I love you." She planted a quick kiss on his cheek.

$\sim$

*A*melia was thrilled that so many of her friends had come. She peeked out the front window, where carriages and buggies made a continuous train up the gravel drive. The whole town of Lacey Spring, not to mention the surrounding area, had been invited to celebrate.

She sneaked into the kitchen before putting on her dress to find that the church ladies had insisted on each bringing their own specialty. Extra tables had been brought in, and they groaned under the weight of succulent turkey, pork, beef, every type of vegetable, and a host of flaky pies and decadent desserts, all awaiting the banquet to follow the ceremony.

"Look at this." Delilah's hands flew wide. "This will be the feast of the century."

"I'm so excited," Amelia said. "And so many guests."

"But of course. This is the most excitement this valley has seen in years. No one is missing this event. Now you go and pretty yourself up."

Amelia headed down the hall to the large room Katherine

had prepared for the two of them to get ready. She had arranged for a team of lady's maids to attend to their needs.

Amelia slipped into the gown her grandmother and Katherine had helped her choose. Flowing with layer upon layer of lace, silk, and crinoline, there were hundreds of beads hand-sewn into a fitted bodice. Amelia felt every bit the princess. The veil cascaded far beyond the length of the dress, adding to the elegance.

After she helped Katherine dress, they stood before the mirror. Amelia threw an arm around her sister.

"Your hair looks amazing swept up like that," Katherine said. "It's perfect with that stunning headdress."

"You don't think it's too much?"

"You don't think it's too simple?"

They spoke at the same time, then laughed. "You're in my head again."

Katherine ran her hand down the off-white moiré-silk gown with simple lines, which accented her tiny waist and beautiful dark hair. "It's my second wedding but Colby's first, so I was trying to find something in between."

"You're both classy and elegant. But I'll look a tad overdone next to you," Amelia said, gazing at their reflections.

Katherine turned toward her. "We'll be unique in our own way. As it should be. Besides Pa will be between us, and you know him. Farmer through and through." They giggled.

"But how are you wearing your hair?" Amelia asked. "Do you have a veil?"

"No veil."

Katherine's hair was pulled from her face and coiled at the top, but a good portion was left long and flowing down her back.

"Oh goodness, I have a veil with a train as long as a country mile, and you have nothing? We sure didn't arrange this very well."

"I love that we're distinctively different." Katherine turned from the mirror. "I do however, have something for my hair." She picked up a small wreath of flowers from the dresser. "This is my crowning touch." She pushed the band of color on her head.

"You look amazing, Katherine."

"And you, even more so, dear sister.

Violin music drifted on the wings of the breeze through the open window.

"I think they're trying to tell us all is ready. Shall we?"

Amelia nodded. "We shall."

CHAPTER 40

*A*melia's heart fluttered and skipped a beat as she remembered a Christmas years prior. She gathered her courage and her skirt in her hands and climbed the steps into the Preston manor. She shouldn't feel nervous with Bryon at her side, but still she had to shake that memory from her mind and remind herself that things were not as they had been back then. He held the door open as she swept inside.

Their honeymoon had been all that dreams were made of, and they had purchased a small home which Amelia absolutely loved. They were both more than all right with the newly-engaged Howard taking over the manor when he married.

But now it was time to face reality—a Christmas Eve reception at the Prestons' to honor their wedding for all the who's who of Richmond upper class. Little would they know, that sprinkled between the layers of pomp and circumstance, a few of Amelia and Bryon's humble friends would attend. Amelia had made sure that her fellow nurses had the right attire for the occasion, and Bryon had done the same for some of the orphanage workers and everyday people he'd invited.

The hoopla was a tad overwhelming, but Melinda Preston had gone out of her way to ask Amelia's advice and include them in all preparations. Her eyebrows had lifted at some of the names on the guest list, but she'd kept quiet and respectful of their choices.

Bryon squeezed her arm in comfort.

"I don't know why I'm so nervous. I was her nurse for months attending to very personal needs."

"I know, my dear, but Father confided that Mother was in a dither trying to make this evening perfect for us. Seems she's as nervous as you are."

"Wish me luck." She smiled up at him.

"You don't need luck, my darling. You've won their hearts, as you did mine all those years ago." He kissed her cheek one more time for reassurance and turned the door handle.

"Bryon, Amelia, do come in." Melinda swept through the parlor doors with regal elegance. Her upswept hair, the waft of expensive perfume, and her gorgeous navy-blue dress with a dangling gem around her neck looked much like the old Melinda. Amelia's heart picked up speed.

She took Amelia's hands. "Your grandparents are already here, and we've had the pleasure of getting reacquainted."

Drat, she had told Grandmother not to arrive early, as she'd wanted to be sure she was present. But Grandmother and Grandfather were more than able to take care of themselves.

"Alex and I invited them for late afternoon tea, and don't look so worried. We've been having a lovely visit." She gave Amelia's arm a gentle squeeze.

"Did I look worried?"

"Downright terrified." Melinda laughed. "I had a few apologies to make and didn't think your reception would be appropriate timing."

Bryon gave a wink. Amelia let the breath she had been holding slowly out.

"I do hope the decorations will be to your liking," Melinda said. "Your grandmother loved them. Very festive with no expense spared. Nothing is too good for the celebration of my son and his beautiful bride."

Bryon and she had cringed at the waste of money needed to create such a splash but had decided that it was important to allow Melinda to share in the joy. This was her way.

"The guests will arrive soon, but do take a peek." Melinda led the way to the ballroom. "Here you are." A sparkle filled her eyes as her hands fanned out to the room.

Amelia stepped into the ballroom, and she couldn't stop her jaw from dropping. "Oh my." She could not take in all the splendor at a glance and turned, slowly, in a circle. Far above the dance floor, sweeping swaths of sheer fabric were strung from the crystal chandelier in the center to each corner of the room. Bright red holly berries were twisted into the fabric for color, and hundreds of flickering candles in individual holders hung from a line above the fabric making it appear as if the candles were floating in clouds of swirling tulle. The light cast a flickering romantic glow across the dance floor. A magnificent floor-to-ceiling Christmas tree with a hundred shimmering gold bows graced one end of the room. Side rooms were open, and tantalizing smells filled the air. Tucked in the corner was the symphony warming up for the gala.

"Mother, you've outdone yourself." Bryon dropped a kiss on her beaming cheek.

Amelia took Melinda's hands in hers. "Thank you for all your hard work. Especially considering how taxing this last year has been on your health."

"My pleasure."

"Truly, what a gift." Amelia kissed her other cheek. "I feel loved."

Melinda drew her into a hug. "I was hoping you would." She pulled back. "But what I'm most excited about is meeting all your new friends, Bryon, and seeing some of the nurses from the hospital."

"Really?" he asked.

"Yes, really. It's more than time for the hard-working people of this community to be honored and shown the respect they deserve. This won't be easy for some to accept, and we won't change our world in one evening, but we have to start somewhere, do we not?"

"Indeed, we do," said Bryon. "Indeed, we do."

"I'd better get back to the foyer to greet my guests." She slipped from the room.

Bryon turned to Amelia. "Don't move." He raced across the empty ballroom to the orchestra and spoke to the conductor, who nodded his head.

Bryon returned, his arms held out. "May I have the first dance and the last, and every one in between? Never again let it be said that I waited until your dance card was too full."

Amelia laughed as she slid into his open arms. "Yes. Yes. And yes." She kissed him between each word.

The instruments began, and Amelia relaxed in the arms of the man she loved more than life itself. Her feet glided, barely touching the floor, as their bodies moved in sync, creating a music all their own. This is what it felt like to be one—one body, one mind, embodied by one Spirit. On every level, their lives collided and intertwined. She whirled and twirled, laughing as the slow waltz picked up speed into the Viennese Waltz. Sheer joy bubbled out.

"Happy?" he asked.

"Very happy." In his arms, whether working side-by-side at the soup kitchen or whirling beneath the splendor of a thousand Christmas candles, she was home.

~

CHRISTMAS DAY 1872
SHENANDOAH VALLEY

*K*atherine was bursting with pent-up excitement. She'd been the perfect lady all day. A doting mother to Seth, a wonderful daughter and sister hosting her family for the Christmas festivities. She had overseen dinner, gift giving to employees, and family alike. The evening entertainment included a carol sing-along, and now all she wanted was for everyone to disappear...everyone except Colby. She couldn't wait to get him to herself.

All day he had sent longing looks her way, slipping a warm arm around her shoulder between running about for this or that, or squeezing her hand to let her know he was thinking of her. They communicated without words. Emotion flowed between them as if a well had been dug and hit an underground spring. Intensity surged and melted from one into the other, a knowing, an understanding, an intuitive connection. Marriage had not been an adjustment, it had been a fulfillment of depth she could've never dreamed possible.

"Now that everyone is finally gone, I have something special for you." She nuzzled close and caused her eyebrows to dance. His eyes darkened with pleasure. In his eyes, flecks of gold melted into pools of liquid heat. She pulled at his hand, leading him to the newly renovated north wing, which they had made their own.

Katherine giggled when Colby swept her into his strong arms and carried her as if she weighed next to nothing. She kissed the cleft of his strong chin and smoothed the soft bristles of his mustache with her fingertips. His steps quickened as he neared their bedroom.

"Well, Mrs. Braddock," he asked as he laid her on the bed. "I'm most interested in that gift you said I had to unwrap."

His eyes widened when she leapt from the bed and crossed the room to the top drawer of the bureau.

"Well, Mr. Braddock, as it happens, I really do have a gift." She sauntered back with a sway to her hips and handed him a small package with a pink and blue ribbon tied in a bow.

A frown furrowed his brow when he took the gift. He shook it next to his ear.

"Open it. I've been going crazy all day at the excitement of giving you this."

He shook the package one more time for good measure.

"Hurry up already." She swatted his arm.

He removed the ribbon with care and pulled the brown paper packaging off the small oblong box slowly, donning a lazy, charming smile.

She lunged at the package, but he kept it well out of her reach. A mischievous grin tugged at his cheeks.

"Colby Braddock. You are incorrigible."

"All right. All right." He lifted the box lid, and his jaw dropped. Nestled in a bed of velvet lay a tiny sterling-silver baby spoon.

The look on his face was an expression Katherine wanted to hold in her heart forever.

"A baby spoon? Does…does this mean you're going to have our baby?"

"Yes, silly. And here you were, tormenting a poor pregnant lady."

He lifted her up and fell on the bed, taking her with him, laughing and kissing, and then laughing again. As he rolled beside her, she swept a hand through his curly blond hair.

He whispered into the heavens, "Best Christmas ever."

Did you enjoy this book? We hope so!
Would you take a quick minute to leave a review where you purchased the book?
It doesn't have to be long. Just a sentence or two telling what you liked about the story!

Receive a FREE ebook and get updates when new Wild Heart books release: https://wildheartbooks.org/newsletter

Don't miss the next book in Shenandoah Brides Series!

Lucinda's Defender

JULY, 1874
SHENANDOAH VALLEY

Joseph Manning watched Nat slide into the pew like he had every right to sit at Lucinda's side. The bent whisper and Nat's familiarity irked him something fierce. Not even a sacred place like church was honored by that reprobate.

The only consolation was the fact Lucinda moved closer to her Ma. Maybe she was finally rebuffing Nat's advancements, and was over the infatuation she had with him. Maybe there would still be hope for a hard-working farmer like him to win her heart.

He had loved her for so long now, the ache inside his lonely heart felt as much a part of him as his skin and bone. Why did she seem oblivious to the obvious?

When the sermon began, Nat, the poser, fell instantly asleep. His head nodded up and down throughout the service. He said something to Lucinda and got up and left before the last song was even done.

An instant desire to slip out his cowboy boot and send the man sprawling came over Joseph as Nat smugly sauntered by. Not too Christian, he knew, but after doing a little investigation on his own, the rumors were true about that man. Currently, Nat had three girls on the go and was still chasing Lucinda.

A tightening pulled across Joseph's chest as Lucinda hurried out after Nat. He swallowed hard against the bile rising in his throat. As he came out the church doors, his fists clenched tight at the sight of them together. There was Nat leaning against the tree with confidence and swagger. There was no way a boring farmer like Joseph could compete with that kind of dashing dark debonair. He pulled off his cowboy hat and ran a hand to the back of his neck before slamming it back on his head.

He moved down the steps and stood in the shadows across the church yard. He was not about to leave until that man was out of sight. Lucinda's Ma and Pa watched from a distance, as well. Jeanette had her glasses pinned on Nat.

At least Lucinda was not alone. She had people around her who cared. As a long-time friend, he should have that talk with her soon. Warn her of Nat's lack of character before it was too late.

Joseph couldn't see Lucinda's face, but he could tell by the way she shifted her feet and pulled her hands free of Nat's that she wasn't comfortable as the man closed in. The sneer on his face erased his good looks. Man, Joseph wished he could hear what was being said.

He breathed out a long breath when Nat turned away and Jeanette closed in. All was safe for another day, but he'd have to find the right time for that conversation soon.

Get LUCINDA'S DEFENDER at your favorite retailer!

ABOUT THE AUTHOR

*I write because I can't **not** write. Stories have danced in my imagination since childhood. Having done the responsible thing—a former businesswoman, personal trainer, and mother of two grown children—I am finally pursuing my lifelong dream of writing full-time. Who knew work could be so fun?*

A hopeless romantic at heart, I believe all stories should give the reader significant entertainment value but also infuse relatable life struggle with hope sprinkled throughout. My desire is to leave the reader with a yearning to live for Christ on a deeper level, or at the very least, create a hunger to seek for more.

Blossom Turner is a freelance writer published in Chicken Soup and Kernels of Hope anthologies, former newspaper columnist on health and fitness, avid blogger, and novelist. She lives in a four-season playground in beautiful British Columbia, Canada, with gardening at the top of her enjoyment list.

She has a passion for women's ministry teaching Bible studies and public speaking, but having coffee and sharing God's hope with a hurting soul trumps all. She lives with her husband, David, of thirty-eight years and their dog, Lacey. Blossom loves to hear from her readers. Visit her at blossom-turner.com and subscribe to her quarterly newsletter.

Don't miss Blossom's other book, *Anna's Secret*, a contemporary romance and Word Guild semi-finalist.

BOOKS IN THE

SHENANDOAH BRIDES SERIES

Katherine's Arrangement (Shenandoah Brides, book 1)

Amelia's Heartsong (Shenandoah Brides, book 2)

ACKNOWLEDGMENTS

I sincerely thank my support team, my big picture editor Erin Taylor Young who dutifully analyzed each scene with the scrutiny of a detective, Robin Patchen who fine-tuned like a wedding cake decorator putting on that touch of beautiful, and Misty M. Beller, an attentive publisher and incredible author/businesswoman. My book has been elevated way beyond its original first draft because of your expertise and thank you does not say enough.

To my critique partner Laura Thomas, I thank you for the hours you put in championing my work and making it better. To my street team and writers' group, your encouragement has inspired me onward and I thank God for you.

And last but not least, I thank God for my health, the opportunity to write, my imagination and the tenacity to place word after word upon page until the story is completed. I feel honored to write a genre that lifts Him up and gives Him the glory.

If you love historical romance, check out the other Wild Heart books!

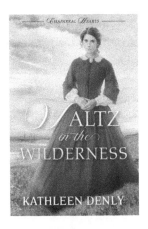

Waltz in the Wilderness by Kathleen Denly

She's desperate to find her missing father. His conscience demands he risk all to help.

Eliza Brooks is haunted by her role in her mother's death, so she'll do anything to find her missing pa—even if it means sneaking aboard a southbound ship. When those meant to protect her abandon and betray her instead, a family friend's unexpected assistance is a blessing she can't refuse.

Daniel Clarke came to California to make his fortune, and a stable job as a San Francisco carpenter has earned him more than most have scraped from the local goldfields. But it's been four years since he left Massachusetts and his fiancé is impatient for his return. Bound for home at last, Daniel Clarke finds his heart and plans challenged by a tenacious young woman with haunted eyes. Though every word he utters seems to offend her, he is determined to see her safely returned to her father. Even if that means risking his fragile engagement.

When disaster befalls them in the remote wilderness of the Southern California mountains, true feelings are revealed, and both must face heart-rending decisions. But how to decide when every choice before them leads to someone getting hurt?

∾

Marisol ~ Spanish Rose by Elva Cobb Martin

Escaping to the New World is her only option...Rescuing her will wrap the chains of the Inquisition around his neck.

Marisol Valentin flees Spain after murdering the nobleman who molested her. She ends up for sale on the indentured servants' block at Charles Town harbor—dirty, angry, and with child. Her hopes are shattered, but she must find a refuge for herself and the child she carries. Can this new land offer her the grace, love, and security she craves? Or must she escape again to her only living relative in Cartagena?

Captain Ethan Becket, once a Charles Town minister, now sails the seas as a privateer, grieving his deceased wife. But when he takes captive a ship full of indentured servants, he's intrigued by the woman whose manners seem much more refined than the average Spanish serving girl. Perfect to become governess for his young son. But when he sets out on a quest to find his captured sister, said to be in Cartagena, little does he expect his new Spanish governess to stow away on his ship with her six-month-old son. Yet her offer of help to free his sister is too tempting to pass up. And her beauty, both inside and out, is too attractive for his heart to protect itself against—until he learns she is a wanted murderess.

As their paths intertwine on a journey filled with danger, intrigue, and romance, only love and the grace of God can overcome the past and ignite a new beginning for Marisol and Ethan.

∼

Lone Star Ranger by Renae Brumbaugh Green

Elizabeth Covington will get her man.

And she has just a week to prove her brother isn't the murderer Texas Ranger Rett Smith accuses him of being. She'll show the good-looking lawman he's wrong, even if it means setting out on a risky race across Texas to catch the real killer.

Rett doesn't want to convict an innocent man. But he can't let the Boston beauty sway his senses to set a guilty man free. When Elizabeth follows him on a dangerous trek, the Ranger vows to keep her safe. But who will protect him from the woman whose conviction and courage leave him doubting everything—even his heart?

CPSIA information can be obtained
at www.ICGtesting.com
Printed in the USA
BVHW040109090221
599482BV00004B/10